A
KILLING
AMONGST
THE DEAD

A
KILLING
AMONGST
THE DEAD

AN EVERETT CARR MYSTERY

Matthew Booth

LEVEL
BEST BOOKS

Historia
ESTABLISHED 2017

To Alodie and Asa Rose,
With love and hopes for the future

Praise for the Everett Carr Mysteries

"Everett Carr is … a marvellous protagonist. This is a descriptive, well-paced mystery…a very well-written first in series and a recommended read for mystery lovers."—Fiona Alison, The Historical Novel Society

"a slightly macabre but satisfyingly cosy crime. Booth handles the introduction of his quite significant cast with grace and ease. … the opening scenes flow so beautifully together and the murder itself does not disappoint."—Mairi Chong, author of the Dr Cathy Moreland Mysteries, Amazon

"…an engrossing mystery, with a despised murder victim and a group of suspects, each of whom has a strong motive to kill the victim. The description of each character is finely drawn, the setting atmospheric and the conclusion to the mystery eminently satisfying."—Laraine Stephens, Goodreads

"An Everett Carr Mystery is not to be missed. The sense of time and place is there on every page, and author Matthew Booth knows how to spin a tangled web of people, murder and blackmail in a fashion reminiscent of the best 'Golden Age' mysteries."—Helen (helenfrominyocounty), Goodreads

"Booth's work is about as good as it gets. We see the master craftsman at work. His characters not only behave in a believable fashion, they speak in a believable fashion. Echoes of Christie and Sayers here and the plot, characters, and dialogue are all of the best and all fit together perfectly."—John Hall, author of Death of a Collector: A Freddie Darnborough

Mystery

"a classic locked room mystery in the finest tradition which will delight old and new readers alike"—Dr M Jones, Amazon

"A classic page-turner and must-read for all fans of Christie, Sayers, James and the country house murder mystery genre"—Ms M Powell, Amazon

"Enter the marvellous and enigmatic Everett Carr, who sees beyond the seemingly impossible...a wonderful homage to the Golden Age of crime"—intheamazone, Amazon reviewer

I

PART ONE: SUICIDE

Chapter One

William Lorrimer died by his own hand.

There had been little doubt about it, either for those directly concerned with him or for the village of Little Marsham as a whole, so that the official verdict of the coroner's court came as no surprise. The official finding only served to lay the matter of Lorrimer's death to rest, just as finally as he had laid himself to rest.

Died by his own hand...

The words echoed now in Harriet Delaney's head. Hearing them said out loud in the court had chilled her, as if the air in her lungs had been turned to ice, and they now reverberated in her memory like a final knell of death. They were an end to it all: to the wickedness, to the malice, to his life. But Harriet knew that it would not be the end of the furtive, accusing glances to which she had been, and would continue to be, subjected. Nor was it the end to the pursed, unforgiving lips of the Little Marsham gossips, for whom the verdict of suicide should have been one of murder. Those who found other people's lives more interesting than their own would consider that the finding of suicide was incomplete. William Lorrimer may well have taken his own life, they would say, but it was on account of Harriet Delaney. She had all but murdered the man, they would think, as they stared at her in disgust. Even now, eyes were on her. Some tried to hide their fascination; others purposefully, and maliciously, did not.

Harriet had not wanted to come for a drink after the inquest. She had wanted to go back to her cottage, to close the door and never open it again, to lie in darkness and pretend none of it had ever happened, and to forget about Lorrimer and what he had done. It was self-indulgent, she had no doubt of that, but it was an overwhelming desire and one which had begun to consume her almost as soon as the coroner had begun to speak. But Edgar had insisted that a drink would benefit both of them and, somehow, when she looked into his imperfect eyes, one an oceanic blue and the other a luxuriant shade of brown, she had been unable to refuse. Harriet never cared when Edgar's eyes were on her, not like she did when other men stared at her. With Edgar, it was different.

And what, she wondered, did they all see when they looked at her? Was it her own paranoia or did they really think of her as a murderess? If they thought she had caused William Lorrimer to end his life, what else could they call her? She was aware suddenly of her vulnerability. Sitting in the corner of the pub, her legs crossed at the ankles and her hands clasped in her lap, she might otherwise have seemed to possess a beautiful fragility. Her blonde hair and the paleness of her skin might have seemed as delicate as the finest porcelain, the blue of her eyes soft like a marine haze, and the red of her lips as vibrant as a summer rose. But the spectre of Lorrimer's death would surely twist those impressions into malignant reflections of themselves. The porcelain skin would become the paleness of death, the blue of the eyes cold, and the red of the lips nothing more than a smear of blood. People's perceptions so often were twisted by their perceptions.

Edgar had arrived with the drinks. He placed the glasses onto the wooden table and sat down beside her. "I thought a brandy and soda would be just the thing to take off the edge."

Harriet looked down at the drink and found she was unable to think of anything worse. But she was not immune to the childish benevolence of the generosity behind it. Edgar had only meant well, and he would have been incapable of thinking that this particular public appearance, at this particular time, might be torture for her. It was not that he was unsympathetic, only that he was naïve. Life was simple for Edgar, and he accepted it for what it was. For Harriet, he could be a breath of invigorating air through the fogs of her own gloom. Similarly, on occasions such as this, he could be as suffocating as the thickest of mists.

"People are staring at me, Edgar," she said.

He looked around. "Nobody's staring at you."

Harriet sipped at the brandy. "You know what they'll be thinking. *She's the girl who drove a man to death.*"

"They won't be thinking anything of the sort," insisted Edgar, "because it's not true."

Harriet glanced across at him. "And do you know what they'll think of you? *Poor old Corrigan, putting himself in danger by falling in love with her. Look what she did to the last one.*"

Edgar's easy optimism clouded over. His jaw clenched, and his brows creased, as if she had physically wounded him, and he was biting back the pain. "I wish you wouldn't talk like that."

"It's true, Edgar."

He twisted in his seat to face her. "If it's true, then let them think it. What they think has no impact on me, and it shouldn't on you. We did nothing wrong. What William Lorrimer did, he did to himself. We knew it, the law now knows it, and anyone in here can know it too."

Despite herself, Harriet smiled at him, placing a hand gently into his. "How I wish the world was as straightforward to me as it is to you."

He leaned forward and kissed her cheek. "There we are. That shows them that whatever they think means as much to me as a tinker's curse."

Her smile widened, and she tightened the grip on his hand in a gesture of grateful solidarity. "All the same, that is what people will think about us. Some of them, anyway."

Edgar shrugged. "Only the ones who have never truly fallen in love. It's none of anybody's business, Harriet, and don't let them persuade you otherwise. There was never any doubt about the verdict, of course."

The change in subject, however slight, was obviously deliberate, and Harriet was not imprudent enough to ignore it. "I never thought he could be capable of it. And I had no idea he owned a gun. Why did he have a gun?"

Edgar, unable to answer definitively and desperate not to upset, chose his words cautiously. "Perhaps none of us really knew him well enough at all."

If Harriet was offended, she did not show it. "We knew he was spiteful and malicious."

"Only after the event," argued Edgar. "You didn't think he was either of those things when you first met him. I doubt you would have fallen in love with him if you did."

She looked at him, her eyes fixing on his, as if to assure him of the truth of her words. "I don't think I did love him. Not really. I certainly didn't feel the way I do with you. Perhaps nobody knows what love is until it announces itself once and for all and leaves you in no doubt."

"Perhaps that's what he came to realise, too." Edgar spoke gently. "Maybe he saw that you were different with me. Maybe he realised that what he had with you was something else, something weaker."

"And that's what drove him to do what he did, you mean?"

Edgar shrugged. "That's how I understood his letter."

The letter.

Harriet thought back to when it was read out in court, recalling now only snippets from it, but remembering only too well its overall impression: *"...your betrayal of everything we felt for each other..."*; *"...you knew that my life could never be the same without you..."*; *"...I will never forgive you and, be sure, I will never forget...".* She had known Lorrimer could be spiteful, but the malice in the written words had surprised and terrified her in equal measure. She could not doubt that the people who heard the letter being read aloud would also detect the malice behind it, but she knew that they would also realise how much Harriet had hurt the dead man when she had walked away from him and into the arms of Edgar Corrigan. The letter was a condemnation of both her and her actions, and Harriet doubted the jury, the coroner, or any of those seated in the public galleries could have thought anything else.

"I wish he hadn't addressed it directly to me," she said.

"Yes, it was the most personal of suicide notes."

She ignored Edgar's tactlessness. "It left nobody in any doubt about me, did it?"

Edgar kissed her hand softly. "It left nobody in any doubt about *him.* People fall out of love. Relationships fail. It's cruel, but it's true. Not everyone does what William Lorrimer did, though. That was down to him entirely. It wasn't anything to do with you. Or me, for that matter."

She removed her hand from his and sipped more of the brandy and soda. "Perhaps you're right."

"Besides, what do you think these people you're so worried about would say if they knew what Lorrimer was doing to us? What if we told them all about how he would follow us around, turn up at restaurants just so he could sit and watch us eat? Or about how he would call you and hiss profanities down the line to you? Perhaps we should tell them about all that. About how he stopped me in the street and threatened my life."

Harriet had closed her eyes against the tirade. "Please, Edgar..."

"I'm just trying to get you to see the whole picture, Harry."

The diminutive again, the one she hated so much but for which she could never bring herself to admonish him. It would have been like punishing a loyal dog for scratching at a table leg. "I can see the whole picture, Edgar. Please, can we go? I think I just need to be on my own for a while, really. Do you mind?"

He smiled at her, showing the slightest glimpse of the teeth, which were as flawless as his eyes were not. Harriet found herself realising again, as if for the first time, how handsome he was. Not in a masculine way, though, she thought; it was almost as if he was beautiful rather than handsome. His hair, a shade too dark to be entirely blond, was swept back across his high, intelligent forehead, as if to prevent itself from obscuring the face. His long nose sloped away from the contrasting eyes, coming to rest over the wide, optimistic smile. His features were even, so much so that the faded childhood scar across one of the angled cheekbones became alluring rather than intrusive. It was strange, she thought, that these serious imperfections of nature could make a man all the more attractive to her.

"Of course, I don't mind," he was saying, although she barely heard him. "Drink up, and let's march."

She obliged, and he rose from the table in order to assist her. They made their way to the front of the pub, and he pulled the door open for her. As he stepped out, he looked back over his shoulder and offered those eyes which had followed them a cheery good morning. It had the same effect as if he had offered them what he had always believed to be an Agincourt bowman's salute.

By the time they had reached Harriet's cottage, a chill wind had risen, and a dampness in the air suggested that rain was inevitable. Harriet felt all the more relieved that she would be at home when it did come, and the allure of a warm fire, a hot cup of tea, and her own, silent company was impossible to resist.

"Do you mind me wanting to be alone for a few hours?" she asked. It was not an obligatory question, but a genuine enquiry, and her hope that the answer would be a negative one was equally sincere.

"Of course not." He leaned forward and kissed her. It was not passionate, and nor did she expect or want it to be, but it was the kiss of a man whose world had Harriet Delaney at its centre.

As soon as he ended it, she kissed him again. "I do love you, Edgar."

He knew it, but to say so would have been unconscionable arrogance. Instead, he gently stroked her cheek and smiled. "I love you, too. And remember, Lorrimer can't hurt us or bother us anymore."

He had meant it as an assurance, which she acknowledged with a nod of the head, but his words had not entirely had their desired effect. Instead, they had reaffirmed in her conscience the fact that William Lorrimer, a man she had deserted, was dead. Perhaps only now, standing on her doorstep, did she realise how final it was. She would never again see Lorrimer walking through the village, never hear his voice in the street or on the telephone, and never again would she have to endure his bitter malevolence. Only one thing connected to William Lorrimer would remain with her for the rest of her life: her regret and guilt over his death.

She watched Edgar walk down the path of her small garden, blew him a kiss when he looked back at her as he closed the gate and finally closed the door. Now, she was alone with the silence which she had craved and, as she sank to her knees against the locked door of the cottage, that coveted silence seemed so oppressive that she felt as if she were being crushed under the weight of it.

Chapter Two

Gerald Bowers knelt on the marble steps, carpeted in crimson velvet, and looked up at the painting which had been hung above the altar. He gazed at it with a sense not only of a duty fulfilled, but of pride. If it were sinful to do so, Bowers felt God would forgive him his sense of admiration at the image which now looked down over the pews of the Church of St Bartholomew. It was not only that the painting was of such fine quality, but that it was hoped that its presence in the chapel would serve to attract new members to the congregation. Bowers, who had been the vicar of the parish of Little Marsham for the last five years, had actively sought a wider church community, and the donation of the painting had been a welcome tactic to achieve it, both for Bowers himself and for his bishop.

The painting, titled simply *The Trial Before Pilate*, depicted precisely that. Christ, his wrists tied behind his back, clothed only in a simple garment of white, stood with head bowed, as the Roman governor, depicted as a man with a sneering, dismissive expression of face and a dominant, pointed an accusing, extended finger towards him. Roman guards were shown closing in on the submissive figure of the Nazarene, their faces contorted in a thirst for the blood of the imminent scourging and its later, more terrible sequel. In the background, Pilate's wife, Procla, pleaded with her husband for clemency, her face clearly showing her apprehension of the meaning of those dreams in which she had suffered on account of the condemned man. To Bowers, it was a striking depiction of a moment of immense importance, and the impulse to weep at it was almost impossible to resist.

He stood now in the chapel, looking up at the scene, his mind recalling the moment when it had been donated to the church. At the time, and even now, Bowers had not expected such generosity from Arthur Corrigan, a man Bowers would not have said was known for his generosity or kindness of spirit. And yet, according to Laurence Fisher, the idea had been Corrigan's alone.

"I think perhaps he wants people to see him a little differently," Fisher had said. Bowers, unable to agree, had simply smiled benevolently and bowed his head. A suggested agreement was easier on his conscience than a verbal one.

"It is a remarkable painting," Bowers had commented instead. "I confess that I am not aware of the artist's other work."

Fisher had not been surprised. "He isn't well known at all. Criminally underrated, which is sad. The name Meryk Van Jansen should be on the lips of everyone with even a passing interest in art. You can see for yourself," he had added, pointing up at *The Trial Before Pilate*, "that he was an artist of exceptional skill and with a distinctive flavour of his own."

Bowers, whose own knowledge of art was rudimentary without being ignorant, had been able only to agree. "There is a definite sadness about the image. The submissive attitude of Christ, in particular."

Fisher had nodded. "Which, I think, is emphasised by the obvious cruelty in the Roman soldier's faces."

A silence had fallen between them as they stared up at the painting, as if in deference to the ignominious suffering and the saving sacrifice which would have followed the image shown. It was Bowers who broke it. "Was the painter a religious man himself?"

Fisher had shaken his head. "I'm afraid he was a doubter. But an optimistic one, I think. I don't think he believed God had gifted him with his talent."

"And yet you say he painted other religious scenes?"

"*The Baptism in Bethany* is the most well-known of them. And *The Stoning of the Adulteress* is a shocking, almost sadistic treatment of Christ's intervention in Mary Magdalene's punishment. But," he added, his voice carrying in it a note of caution, "we must not read any religious belief into

Van Jansen's choice of subjects. He just as readily painted images from mythology. As a matter of fact, our excavation of his work discovered *Theseus in the Labyrinth*, which shows in some bloody detail the battle with the Minotaur. Mr Corrigan is in negotiations to sell it to an American collector."

"Very impressive," Bowers had felt compelled to say.

The church had not been expected to buy the painting. It had been a donation and whatever cynical views Bowers or any of his flock might have had about Corrigan's intentions, there had been something in Fisher's youthful excitement about his rediscovery of Meryk Van Jansen's work, which had been infectious. In its own way, it had diluted any suspicion of Arthur Corrigan.

"How do you know so much about this man, Van Jansen, Fisher?" Bowers had asked.

Fisher had shrugged and had run a hand through his mop of unwieldy, ginger hair. His nose, mottled with faint freckles, had wrinkled at the memory, and his intense eyes had glittered with emotion. "I became fascinated with him when I was studying in Copenhagen. I saw one of his paintings reproduced in a textbook, but I could find nothing about him in any other books I found. I became fascinated by the lack of awareness of his work, because I couldn't understand why he wasn't more well known. His work was so impressive to me that it seemed inexplicable."

"But you managed to trace something of his life?"

"Eventually. I'm afraid it affected my own work for a time. I didn't perform as well in my own studies as I might have done. In that respect, at least, I have something in common with Van Jansen."

"In what way?"

"He had an obsession which destroyed his career, too." Fisher's voice had lowered, as if the spectre of the destructive force on this forgotten artist's life had somehow come to blight his own.

"What obsession was that?" Bowers had asked.

"Alcohol and paranoia," Fisher had replied.

For a moment, Bowers had felt it improper to speak any more. Fisher's

11

regret, as if on behalf of Meryk Van Jansen himself, seemed so intense in that moment that speech would have belittled it. Bowers, a man of compassion, had allowed the memory of the confession to fade before he said any more.

"We all of us have our ghosts which we cannot exorcise," he had said.

This small discussion had taken place only a few days before William Lorrimer had taken his own life. On the night when he had heard the news, Bowers had prayed hard for forgiveness. God, he knew, was aware of his sins, and He knew of his feelings towards Lorrimer. Only once, in a moment of extreme despair, had Bowers wished Lorrimer dead, and the words had almost choked him, as if hearing them aloud, even in the lonely privacy of the vicarage parlour, had revealed the depth of wickedness inside him. Now that the man was dead, it was impossible not to see the tragedy as some perverse kind of wish fulfilment and Bowers was adamant that God should know that it was no such thing. He had prayed with conviction, almost pathological in its intensity, and he had punished himself for his treachery against his fellow man. Punished himself more severely than ever before and in the only way he knew.

Perhaps it had been this guilt which had prompted him to request an audience with his bishop, in order to request permission to bury Lorrimer in consecrated ground. The bishop had been typically supportive.

"You are a little behind our times, Gerald," he had said.

"No doubt, my Lord, but I would rather have your blessing to do it."

"We don't bury such unfortunates in the north side of our churches anymore, Gerald. No more do we relegate them to unconsecrated ground or deny them the proper burial rites."

"Suicide is still a crime, my Lord."

"Let the law take care of that. We are concerned only with God's law. And His doctrine, His demand on us, is that we forgive those for their sins. We are Christ's messengers, Gerald, and His message was one of forgiveness and tolerance. Why should a man who is so unhappy that life is a burden rather than a gift be denied that forgiveness and tolerance?"

"Thank you, my Lord." Bowers had resisted the urge to weep.

"Besides," the bishop had continued amiably, "the law has moved with the times just as surely as we have done. It has been permissible to do as you wish for this poor man for over fifty years."

"I am grateful to you, my Lord."

And now, Lorrimer was in the churchyard, buried amongst the other dead, ancient and recent. If Bowers had hoped to bury his guilt with the body of the man whom he had despised, he was to be disappointed. As if it were the ghost of Lorrimer himself, the guilt only intensified after the dead man had been laid to his rest. Bowers, tormented by his hate and the underlying cause of it, had dealt with it once more, again in the only method he felt appropriate to apologise to God.

He moved away from the Van Jansen painting now and walked down the aisle, out of the church, and back to the vicarage. In doing so, he passed where Lorrimer lay, but he refused to look down at the simple stone marker of death. He slowly closed the door of the vicarage behind him and, for a long moment, he savoured the silence of the hallway, as if it was a glimpse of the kind of peace which he could enjoy if his conscience was not blighted by his sins.

He walked slowly up the narrow staircase to the upper landing and towards the door of his bedroom. His intentions were clear to him, as were their consequences, but these moments of uncontrollable weakness were common and, as God knew, Bowers' ability to resist them was as weak as the flesh itself. And Gerald Bowers was aware only too painfully of how weak the flesh could be.

He stepped into his bedroom and gave in to his impulses. He pulled open the drawer of the small cabinet beside his bed and, from the depths of it, he took out the framed photograph of the woman who had set him on his path of iniquity. How could someone so beautiful have been created by anything other than God? Only He could have had the goodness to sculpt such perfection in a human face. And yet, that same God had created the sinner who now sat on the single, uncomfortable bed and wept silently. It was impossible to reconcile the two facts with each other, and Bowers knew that to attempt to do so would be to try to understand God absolutely. And that was something no man could ever hope to achieve.

Bowers knew that the woman had been a test. And he knew that he had failed it, letting down not only her, but himself, and God. Looking at her image now, just as he had gazed at the Van Jansen depiction of Christ prior to his scourging, Bowers could understand once again what goodness had been and what the world meant when it talked about purity. She had been all of those things, before he had torn them down with his betrayals and his selfishness. But had it not been a misunderstanding? Had her husband not failed to grasp the intentions which Bowers had, allowing them to be manipulated by gossip and innuendo? Certainly, William Lorrimer had been incapable of comprehending those complex emotions which had existed between Gerald Bowers and Mary Jerrold. Bowers had attempted to explain, of course, but the words had meant nothing. In the end, Henry Jerrold had been left with no option. He had taken Mary away, far from Little Marsham, and she had never contacted Bowers since. But the truth of it was harder to bear. It had not been Henry Jerrold who had forced her away. Nor had it been William Lorrimer, or any of the other malicious and scandal-hungry minds of the village. It had been Gerald Bowers himself.

Admitting the truth had not made him dislike William Lorrimer any less. He had played his own destructive part in the business, of that Bowers was in no doubt. He doubted that the memory of what had happened between Bowers and Mary Jerrold had been part of the reason that Lorrimer had done what he had. His death was surely a consequence of something much more personal, but, nevertheless, Bowers hoped that Lorrimer had given some thought to Mary Jerrold when he placed the cold, cruel muzzle of the gun to his temple and allowed it to perform its devastating duty.

Bowers, conscious now of his own duty to his conscience and to God, rose from the bed and replaced Mary's photograph in his drawer. Slowly, purposefully, he straightened to his full height and removed his dog collar. Almost automatically, he began to unbutton his shirt, peeling it from his back like the skin of the serpent in Eden. He walked to the closed door and raised his hand to the small hook screwed into the back of it. From it, he took the lash in his hands and ran his fingers slowly, almost reverently, along the leather thongs which hung loosely from the handle. Bowers walked to the wardrobe and pulled open the door. He glared at himself in the long mirror fixed to the inside, his face twisted in loathing and repugnance. He twisted his spine as far as he could, so that the red streaks of retribution in the flesh of his back could be seen. They were painful expressions of his penance, of his remorse, and of his devotion to God.

Straightening his spine, his teeth clenching in anticipation, Gerald Bowers brought the leather thongs fiercely across his back. He grunted at the pain which he both deserved and welcomed. This was the burning fire of punishment and his blood on the leather, seeping also down his spine, was the price of absolution of his sin. His was a far less noble sacrifice than that of Christ, whose suffering had not been for his own wickedness, but for those of others. Bowers' blood was offered only in retribution for his own transgressions.

Only after half an hour of this punishment did he stop, sinking back onto his bed, his back on fire, his eyes weeping with shame as much as agony, and the leather whip hanging loosely from his weakened fingers.

Chapter Three

Elsa Corrigan watched her husband pour himself a large measure of malt whisky. She considered it too early in the day for such a powerful stimulant, but she knew that any attempt to protest against it would be met with customary derision, if not ignored completely. There was no reason why that afternoon should be any different to countless others over the years. An inquest into a violent death in the village had been something which Arthur had greeted with equanimity, so that it was hardly something which would demand a calming drink afterwards. No, Elsa knew that the whisky was an indulgence and nothing more. Whether or not it was designed to irritate or offend her purposefully was something she was not prepared to consider and too tired to contemplate in any event.

For herself, Elsa had found the inquest both shocking and exhausting in equal measure. From the moment she had heard of the death of William Lorrimer, she had felt a keen, personal affinity with it. It was not that she had liked Lorrimer, or even known him particularly well, but she was acutely aware that her son's love affair had forged an undeniable connection between her family, Lorrimer, and, ultimately, his death. If she had moments of wishing that Edgar had never met Harriet Delaney, Elsa had kept them to herself. She knew only too well how difficult it was when a relationship was interrupted, without warning, by the arrival into one's life of an unforeseen complication, just as she knew how destructive those interruptions could be, whether they ended a previous relationship or not. Her own experiences could not, she knew, influence Edgar's choices; to allow them to do so would have been to suffocate and alienate him. But, without any personal hostility towards Harriet herself, Elsa had wished that Edgar had never met her, let alone fallen for her.

"Let's hope that's an end to it all," she said now. Her voice was so gentle that she might have been alone in the room, talking only to herself.

Corrigan looked across at her. "Course, it's the end of it. What else could be said about the man's death?"

Elsa felt her skin prickle, as if she had forgotten that he was in the room, and being reminded of it chilled her. "I don't just mean William Lorrimer's death, Arthur. I mean the troubles between Edgar and Harriet. Let's hope they've been put to bed once and for all."

Corrigan sniffed and drank a mouthful of whisky. The gesture of raising the glass to his lips, the swift swallow of the drink, and the baring of his teeth afterward were all soured by a suggestion of contempt. "Given it was Lorrimer who was causing all that trouble, I'd say a bullet in his brain was exactly what was needed to put a stop to it."

"Do you have to be so brutal about it?"

"I'm just being frank, Elsa," he argued. "If that means being brutal, it's because the truth is brutal."

"If you say so." She ran a hand across her forehead, shielding her eyes from his glare. "What are you doing for the rest of the day?"

He drained his glass and refilled it. "I have to see Fisher. Finalise the donation of the painting to the church. I may have dinner with him, too. We have a lot to discuss."

Elsa made no further comment. The business relationship between her husband and Laurence Fisher was one which neither interested nor concerned her. Her knowledge of art was, at best, rudimentary, and she made no pretence to the contrary. If she had shown any obligatory interest in it, she was under no illusion that Corrigan would have dismissed it or belittled her attempts to ingratiate herself. The project was his and Fisher's, and, as far as Corrigan was concerned, Elsa had no part to play in it. She had tried to be dispassionate about the isolation, telling herself that she wanted nothing to do with this venture to resurrect the reputation of a minor Danish painter from three hundred years before any of them were born. She had overheard various conversations between her husband and Fisher, both in person and over the telephone, but always behind closed doors, which had suggested that the scheme had been lucrative, but Elsa had seen no physical evidence of it, and she doubted that Corrigan would have shared it with her in any event.

And, she thought, now that he had left her alone, what did any of it matter? If it hadn't been these paintings, it would have been something else. The pertinent fact was that any distraction for Arthur Corrigan was for him alone, and involving Elsa in any of it would be to taint the enterprise with her presence. Even a walk in the woods which surrounded Little Marsham would have been a chore, rather than a pleasure, if he had undertaken it with her by his side. And yet, she could not say honestly that she felt any differently towards him. Beyond meals and any acceptance of mutual invitations to social engagements, their lives were almost entirely independent of each other. If she had walked out of the house, fled to some northern spa hotel, and given no clue as to her whereabouts for a week or so, Elsa doubted Corrigan would suffer any interference in his routine. He would notice her absence; she could not deny that. He might even wonder about it. But she doubted he would be troubled by it. Elsa was not naïve, about herself or her marriage. Her condemnation of Corrigan was not exclusive; she was honest enough with herself to admit that any criticism of her husband could easily apply to her if their roles were reversed.

Had it always been like this? No, it had not. To say as much would be as churlish as it was inaccurate. In the early days of their relationship, prior to their marriage, they had lived very much as Elsa had assumed love would be. Corrigan had been charming, ambitious, always polite without being sycophantic, loving without being overbearing, but never once leaving her in doubt that he desired her. What she saw now as cold arrogance had seemed, in those youthful days of long-passed sun and laughter, like a fierce, determined energy. Even now, sitting alone in the drawing room of their extensive property, her stare glazed over by memories and regrets, Elsa could remember how seized she had been by Corrigan's zeal, intoxicated by his proud dominance, as if it had been the most expensive and superior champagne.

The marriage had been inevitable, so much so that the engagement had been nothing less than perfunctory. It had been as if neither of them had wanted to delay the formality of their union. The ceremony had not been extravagant, a small gathering of family and close friends, but she had not wanted more than it had provided for her. All that had mattered was that her life was being joined with that of Arthur Corrigan, and no man was capable of putting it asunder. She recalled now how the marriage had been consummated with a fierce but meaningful passion, which had both thrilled and frightened her. It had been beyond her experience, of course, and she had wondered immediately afterwards whether it would always be the same. Time would deprive her of the thrill of the fantasy, but that first experience of it would never leave her. Perhaps now, tainted with a bitter familiarity, she might question the ferocity of Corrigan's lovemaking, its motives, and its intentions, but, in the moment, all those years previously, she had been consumed by it. Looking at Corrigan now, that intensity of feeling seemed to her to have turned to something approaching cruelty, as if his capacity for passion had darkened, having been poisoned by time and regret, so that the man she had been in thrall to as a young woman now seemed to be something entirely different. It served only to emphasise the length of time which had passed since that first night of marriage and his present disregard for her.

The thoughts were neither helpful nor productive, and Elsa was irritated by them and annoyed with herself for having them. They were as pointless as they were self-indulgent, and she refused to allow them to overwhelm her. Such recriminations were common with her, since the thoughts of which she disapproved were themselves recurring ones. Elsa knew that the real problem was one which she could not yet bring herself to admit, even if it was something of which she was painfully aware. It was possible, she supposed, to know a fear existed without having to confront it. And Elsa's darkest dread, the tumour on her soul which refused to subside, was the knowledge that her love, her attraction, and her obsession with Arthur Corrigan had been so intense that it had burned out in a flickering moment of time, so that the years which had passed since its last embers faded had been without any emotional depth or meaning, evaporating even before she knew they were hers to enjoy.

Elsa rose from her seat and walked out of the room, as if by doing so, she could distance herself from her anxieties and her thoughts. She climbed the curving staircase which stretched out from the centre of the hallway, familiar both in its appearance and its loneliness, and she made her way across the landing. Her bedroom, a haven of privacy for her, was at the end of the passageway, as far away from Corrigan's as possible. If he had ever wondered about her choice of room, once the decision to sleep apart had been made, he had never said as much. She wondered now, strangely enough for the first time, whether that was because he had no interest in her selection or whether he was grateful for it and, by extension, was reluctant to be seen to suggest that she should change her mind about it. Either option seemed to be equally dismissive of her. She was surprised, if only slightly, to find that she was not unduly offended by it. Taking offence would have surely meant that some feeling or emotion, however bitter, still existed between them.

Sitting down at her dressing table, she pulled open one of the drawers and took the photograph from its hiding place inside. She could have no certainty that Corrigan hadn't found it at some point, buried beneath her personal items of clothing at the back of the drawer, but she doubted it. Surely, even his apathy towards her would have been shaken into some form of reaction if he had. Despite its pristine condition, the photograph was old, its subject a little over twenty years of age. Now, like Elsa and Corrigan, he would be in the middle stages of his existence. Nevertheless, she found it impossible to think of him as being old. There had been something so vibrant about his nature that to imagine that such vitality could wither with age and illness was almost impossible, just as it had been impossible to believe that he and Corrigan had ever been friends.

And yet, they had been. It had been Corrigan who had introduced her to Edmund Draper, an irony of life which would have been comical if it had not been so tragic, and Elsa assumed that her husband had never entertained the possibility that anyone would, even could, have found her attractive. But she had enjoyed three months of illicit love, the furtiveness bringing with it its own sense of excitement, and Elsa had been invigorated by it, as if she were living in a world in which nothing else mattered, and nobody else existed. Three months, perhaps, but time had meant nothing to her; days were marked only by the expectation of seeing him and the reluctant but fond farewell when he had to depart. The rising of the sun and the ebbing of the tides meant nothing when she was by his side or in his arms. She recalled now the sensuality of it, so far removed from Corrigan's urgent, panting advances, a cohesion of body and spirit, expressed in sensual, breathless rhythms. Elsa had felt alive, complete, and she had no regard for the more intense wilderness which must surely come once the affair was over. She had been in no doubt that it could only be temporary and so she had made sure that she experienced it as if its duration was the definition of forever. By the time he had been called back overseas, and Elsa was forced to contemplate a return to the reality of the life which had chosen her, the affair was already becoming a memory. And yet, she had assured herself, it was a memory which would be treasured, as priceless as any historical artefact buried in the endless sands of the desert.

She could not say how long she had been crying. She seemed to become aware of the tears almost without warning, as if they had been slowly forming in her eyes and rolling down her cheeks long before she noticed them. Quickly, almost haphazardly, she wiped them away and stuffed the photograph back into the drawer, as if she had already been discovered in the surreptitious act of gazing at it. Her conscience, seemingly guilty despite herself, had made an audience of accusers in her own mind, all of whom condemned her for her betrayal of her vows and for daring to love a man with whom she was far more compatible than with her husband. There was no excuse in the caprice of time which had dictated that she had met the man she knew she had been waiting for too late for it to be legitimate. She had her life, and she must bear with it. *Till death...*

Death. Her mind now was back with William Lorrimer. Harriet Delaney had done what she, Elsa, had been unable to do. For that, perhaps, she should be admired and not derided. Harriet had looked romantic failure in the eyes and defied it, turning her back on Lorrimer in favour of Edgar Corrigan. The village might hate her for it, but she had been true to herself. Elsa wondered whether Harriet's love for Edgar was worth the stigma of being the woman who had driven a man to take his own life. Whether it was or not, Harriet had made her choice, and she had pursued happiness, refusing to compromise her happiness for respectability. Elsa, for her part, could not testify to the same courage or conviction. Her choice had been to allow her happiness to sail across the ocean away from her, so that it was obliged to remain confined to a small piece of photographic card, hidden away in a drawer, only to be remembered in tearful moments of self-indulgent regret.

Chapter Four

Everett Carr sat silently in the church.

He had always found the tranquillity of the houses of God to be soothing in their own right, even without the formality of actual prayer. It was a special kind of peace, one which could not be found in any other institution where silence was taken for granted. It was as if the stone and masonry of a church, its very structure, and architecture, could themselves offer salvation to those who were willing to open themselves to it. It might be too much to say that the atmosphere of a church was infused with the spirit of God, and Carr's faith was not sufficiently keen to admit such an idea, but he could not deny the sense of placid calm which soothed him whenever he entered a place of worship, as if stepping over the threshold of any such place brought its own immediate and particular sense of veneration. In his more religious moments, Carr might have considered the feeling to be the closest he might ever come in life to being in the presence of God.

A week had passed since the inquest's finding that William Lorrimer had killed himself, an event of which Carr was unaware. His interest in Little Marsham was connected with theological art rather than sudden death. It was not that Carr was a connoisseur of art, quite the opposite. He was a man who could admire talent, certainly, and one who knew well enough which paintings and sculptures appealed to him and which did not, but his interest did not extend beyond such personal preferences. It was not a field which he had studied, nor one in which he frequently indulged. He preferred the images and language of literature and poetry to those manifested in works of oil and marble. And yet, there were certain subjects that fascinated him and, on occasion, those subjects were immortalised in those same materials. When Carr had read of the recent acquisition by St Bartholomew's church in Little Marsham of a religious painting by a forgotten Danish artist, the interest piqued had seemed to justify the visit.

Carr had found both the village and the church without difficulty. He had been restless of late, his rooms in the Albany seeming to him to be more claustrophobic than comforting, and London itself had threatened to overwhelm him. The capital had seemed to Carr to be a barely simmering melting pot of debate and emotion. Discussions within the walls of the Icarus Club, his usual haven for relaxation and escape, were tainted by the machinations of politicians over the globe. Those same discussions seemed to be reflected in almost every newspaper which Carr had the misfortune to read. There was growing unrest in Europe, not least in Italy's war with Ethiopia and Germany's removal of itself from the League of Nations finally coming to pass. Even the British parliament had begun to consider dissolution and a general election. Carr had unspoken fears about the future, but whether they would come to pass was impossible for him to say, still less for him to influence; but their collective effect on him was to long for escape. He had reached this untypically despondent conclusion when, almost simultaneously, he had read of the discovery of *The Trial Before Pilate* and its gifting to St Bartholomew's. It had seemed to provide him with the ideal opportunity: he had never visited Little Marsham before, but he suspected that he knew exactly the sort of place it would be, and it would offer the perfect retreat from the gloom and infectious pessimism of London.

The church of St Bartholomew was as impressive as it was comforting. The tower was immense, stretching up into the heavens, and the stonework and design of the place, so obviously placed in a cruciform shape, suggested an origin dating back to the late 18th century. Inside, the stained-glass windows, depicting various Biblical scenes of importance, indicated some form of restoration after the Catholic revival in the early 19th century. Its interior, impressing on Carr his usual sense of reverence, was solemn without being austere, so that it demanded awe but offered sanctuary in equal measure. The arched shape of the narthex continued throughout the overall shape of the structure, so that the nave and chancels were overseen by the same overreaching arc, as if God's reach was extending over the whole community. A large marble statue of Bartholomew himself, his flayed skin held in one hand and the curved knife of his torture held in the other, stood in one corner, while a raised pulpit dominated the other. The altar, above which the Van Jansen was displayed, was impressive without being ornate. The marble was plain, so that the elaborately carved crucifix which was placed in the centre of it seemed to be all the more imposing.

The painting above the altar was everything Carr had hoped it would be. The solemnity of the depiction of Christ, His stillness and His stoicism, was remarkably well captured and, as Laurence Fisher had said to Gerald Bowers, the cruelty and sadism etched onto the faces of those surrounding the holy prisoner only emphasised His placidly willing acceptance of His mission. Carr was no expert, nor did he pretend to be, but the brushwork, the composition, and the execution of the piece seemed to him to be deceptively simple, and he wondered whether this was a possible reason for Van Jansen's descent into obscurity. Had this illusory simplicity of style, which Carr suspected was paradoxically intricate and complex, been too subtle for his contemporaries and those who followed? Whatever the reason, Carr could not help but think that the rejection of the artist had been both unforgivable and unwarranted.

His thoughts were interrupted by the sound of footsteps behind him. Carr turned round and found that he was looking at a woman standing in the recesses of the nave, having just entered the church. He had the impression that she had stopped herself when she saw that the church was not empty, and, for a brief moment, Carr felt as if he had intruded on her own meditations rather than the reverse. He could not see her clearly, as she was too far away, but he had a distinct sense of grief about her. She wore black, a veil over her eyes, contrasting with the paleness of her skin, which was obvious even from a distance. The hair was dark, so much so that the hat and veil seemed to be part of her rather than sartorial expressions of sadness. Carr sensed that she was attractive, but he could not see enough of her features to be sure. Certainly, there was a nobility about the erectness of her spine and the clasped hands suggested a knowing elegance. Her age was impossible to tell, but Carr doubted she was any more than forty and, he confessed to himself, that might have been doing her a disservice.

She gazed at him for a long moment, and Carr rose to his feet with difficulty. He had been sitting long enough for his damaged leg to seize up, and, as he leaned on his silver-handled cane for support, an involuntary grunt of effort exploded from beneath the heavy white moustache and Imperial beard. The movement seemed to startle the woman in the distance, and she turned away from him and left the church, as if any proximity to Carr might somehow betray a secret.

He had not quite reached the heavy oak doors of the church when Gerald Bowers appeared before him. A glance over the vicar's shoulder showed that the woman, whoever she had been, had gone, but Carr could not doubt that Bowers himself had seen her.

"Forgive me, but was that lady one of your parishioners?" he asked.

Bowers looked over his shoulder instinctively but, when he turned back to face Carr, he was shaking his head. "No, I've never seen her before. Many people who are not regular members of the congregation do come to visit our church, however. Especially since we acquired the Van Jansen."

Carr smiled. "I am one of those curious few myself."

"I thought you must be. I presume you are Mr Carr."

"Indeed." Carr offered his hand, and the vicar took it gently. "I hope you didn't mind me writing to you in advance. I wouldn't have liked to turn up here unannounced."

"Not at all."

"And thank you for the swift response," added Carr. "It is pleasant to be away from London."

Bowers smiled in appreciation. He was younger than Carr had expected, not yet forty if Carr was any judge, so that the dog collar and the spectacles were the only items of his appearance which Carr had anticipated. The hair, the colour of the ripest chestnut, had a healthy shine to it, like the pelt of an animal, which was matched by the dark brown of his eyes, whose depth of colour seemed to give an assurance of dependability. Carr would have expected the benign but handsome face to come with a perpetual smile, but there was a solemnity rather than a warmness to the lips, which suggested to him that there was the possibility of a profound sadness behind the external benevolence of Gerald Bowers.

"You have brought a valise, I see," said the vicar, pointing to the small travelling bag which Carr had placed beside the pew he had occupied. "I assume it is yours, at least."

"Yes, indeed," said Carr. "I thought I might stay in the area for a few days. Get some clean, country air. I suppose you could recommend an inn where I might stay."

Bowers was quick to oblige. "You must stay at the vicarage."

But Carr was equally swift not to be a hindrance. "Thank you, no. It is very kind, but I should hate to impose. And, if I may say so without offence, I have been alone for so long that I am better suited to my own company these days."

Bowers conceded the point. To have insisted would have been rude, and he had no wish to appear so, even if the request, to his own conscience at least, had been a perfunctory one. "I am sure you will find room at *The Marsham Tuns*, our local inn."

Carr nodded his thanks. "I came principally, of course, to see the painting."

Slowly, they walked together back down the aisle of the nave towards the altar. The painting seemed to loom over them the nearer they came to it, so that both of them were silent in its presence for a long moment.

"Is it as impressive as you imagined, Mr Carr?" asked Bowers at last.

"It is remarkable. So simple on the face of it that it must be a complex piece of work. I hope you understand the paradox, Mr Bowers."

"Just so. You should speak to Mr Fisher, our resident artist, on the subject. He is the expert, not me. But he assures me that the picture is, as you say, a work of high talent. We are lucky to have it here at St Bartholomew's."

"It was gifted to you, I understand?"

Bowers' spine visibly stiffened. "By Mr Corrigan, yes."

"Is there something wrong?"

Bowers shook his head. "Mr Corrigan is a difficult man to understand. You may think I am speaking out of turn, Mr Carr, but I am not able to say with certainty that his generosity was entirely selfless."

"Dear me," muttered Carr. "Mr Corrigan does not perform acts of kindness without expecting something in return, is that it?"

"Perhaps I have been unkind," said Bowers.

Carr smiled and waved his hand dismissively. "In the house of God, Mr Bowers, we must all speak the truth, no matter how distasteful or ungrateful it may sound."

Bowers turned to look at the diminutive man who stood beside him. He found himself wondering about him: about the lameness, the extravagant moustache and eccentric beard, the suit of black contrasting with the lurid necktie and handkerchief, and about the lapel pin in the form of a human skull with rubies for eyes. "Are you a religious man, Mr Carr?"

The reply was some time in coming, the silence consumed by careful thought on how to respond. "I think God understands me."

Bowers found the reply intriguing. It was evasive, but not blatantly so, which suggested perhaps a belief which was capable of being shaken with ease. Carr's God might understand him, Bowers thought, but Carr himself might not have been able to reciprocate. There seemed, perhaps, more conflict than comprehension on Carr's part, and Bowers found himself wondering about the cause of that struggle.

"Does God understand you well enough to appreciate the skull you wear on your breast?" asked Bowers.

Carr looked down at the pin, his moustache and beard bristling as his lips stretched beneath them into a smile. "That is a gentle reminder, Mr Bowers, nothing more."

"Of what?"

Carr's dark, almost black eyes raised up to meet Bowers' stare. "That death is always with us."

Bowers was not sure what response he had expected, but he had not been prepared for the one he received. "You're a very interesting man, Mr Carr."

Carr did not reply. He returned his attention to the Van Jansen painting and spent a few long moments looking at it. It was one of those works which seemed to change with each viewing, so that every time an admirer examined it, a new facet of its creation, which had not previously been evident, seemed to appear. For Carr, it was the sudden realisation that the artist had depicted a serpent, coiled around the foot and calf of Pilate, seemingly unnoticed by the governor. The inference demanded by the snake was clear: here was Satan, insidious and hidden in plain sight, revelling in the humiliation of the prisoner, which was to follow Pilate's judgement, perhaps even manipulating events to his own purpose.

"It is truly remarkable," he said, so softly that Bowers had no doubt that he was talking to himself rather than to the vicar. Accordingly, he gave no reply. Carr, breaking the spell of the painting with a sharp intake of breath, turned to his companion. "I wonder if I might visit the church again tomorrow, to see the painting once more?"

"By all means, Mr Carr. You must feel free to come and go as you please. Our church is always open."

Carr bowed in gratitude, the gesture both elegant and polite. He bent down to pick up the valise which he had left by the pews. "I think I shall enquire at the inn you mentioned. Is the food there adequate, would you know?"

Bowers nodded. "Simple, but well prepared. Our nearest town, though, is Hillington, which is only a few miles out of the village."

Carr demurred. "Local hospitality will do me very well, Mr Bowers. I am obliged."

They walked out together. The early afternoon sun was bright, but there was a chill breeze accompanying it, so that there was an autumnal freshness to the air. Carr breathed it deeply, filling his lungs with the clarity of it, the ghosts of the fumes and stenches of London dissipating with the cleansing chill of the country atmosphere. He stopped walking suddenly, surprising Bowers, and closed his eyes.

"Listen to it," he said. "The silence, the calmness. You may not be as taken with it as me, of course, since you have the good fortune to live here permanently. For me, though, it is such a soothing contrast to London."

Bowers said nothing, as if to do so would have been to ruin Carr's enjoyment of the peace. It was a different stillness and soothing silence to that of the church. This was a natural silence, rather than a spiritual one. For Carr, there was a distinction, even if it transpired that the elements of nature had been formed by a spiritual force.

He opened his eyes and breathed deeply once more. His smile was both wide and genuine, but, as he looked across at Bowers, it faded, and a crease formed between his brows. "I say, there's that lady."

Bowers followed his gaze and saw her at once. The woman, dressed in black, her hands still clasped together in her tragic sophistication. She was standing at a grave, her head bowed, but her body rigid with respect for the dead. She was motionless for a long while, until, finally, she raised her head and looked up at the sky. The movement, even at a distance, told Carr that she was weeping, and the gentle rocking of her shoulders, now only too evident, proved it. She brought her gaze back to the headstone and laid her fingers on the top of it, a futile yet understandable attempt to connect with the soul of whoever it was she mourned.

Bowers turned to Carr. "You must excuse me, sir. She is clearly in distress, and my place is with her, stranger or not."

"Of course, my boy," said Carr, placing an encouraging hand on the young vicar's arm. "You must go to her. I shall return tomorrow."

Bowers nodded in appreciation and turned on his heel. Carr watched him walk towards the woman, his pace slow enough to show respect and cautious enough not to disturb her or force her to flee. Carr, for his part, walked away from the church and the weeping woman at the grave. The chill of the air seized upon his broken knee, and his limp became more acute, forcing him to stop when he reached the gates of the churchyard. He leaned against the stone wall which surrounded the cemetery and caught his breath. Looking back across the cemetery, he could see that Bowers had approached the woman and had begun to engage her in conversation. The woman, however, gave a shake of her head and began to walk away. Bowers' attempts to prevent her went unheeded, and, as she walked past him, Carr made no effort to stop the woman in her tracks.

He looked back and saw Bowers staring after the woman. He saw Bowers give a shrug of his shoulders and walk solemnly back into the church. It was then that Carr noticed the silhouetted figure of another woman standing in the distance, some way off amongst the graves and shaded by the trees. The woman in the shadows stared across the headstones of the cemetery, her eyes fixed on Bowers and the young woman. There was something disturbing about the way her hands had clenched into fists, about the way her eyes were glaring with intent on the vicar and this stranger to the village, and about the rapid explosions of air from her nostrils, like small and angry pistol shots. At no time did she look across at Carr. She was too engrossed in her own thoughts to have noticed him at all. Instead, her attention had been fixated on Bowers and the woman by the graves. As they parted company, this other woman turned on her heel and vanished into the trees.

Carr remained in motionless silence, before deciding that there was nothing he could do. He winced in pain as he pushed himself off the churchyard wall and placed his weight back onto his feet. The ache in his knee intensified, and a thousand spiders seemed to crawl across his spine, and yet, somehow, he was sure that none of it was anything to do with the coldness of the breeze.

Chapter Five

The memory of seeing the mysterious woman in black and Gerald Bowers in the churchyard was still in Dorothy Parrish's mind when the ring of her doorbell chimed. From the moment she had seen this funereal stranger, standing amongst the dead of Little Marsham, Dorothy had felt a dark premonition of disaster shroud her in dread, and the persistent recollection of the woman seemed to torture her. It was not something she could explain, only something which she felt she must endure. At least the ringing of the doorbell was a distraction from it, although these fears of personal catastrophe were never far from Dorothy's mind, even as she now poured out the tea.

She didn't want any. Her mouth was dry, but she doubted that she would be able to taste the tea or that it would go to any lengths to quench whatever thirst she had. She had made it because when Thomas Lewton had suggested it, as soon as she had answered his ringing of the bell, he had seemed to expect it, as if tea were some sort of requirement to any social interview. But perhaps Dorothy was being unkind. The suggestion had not been made out of anything other than kindness, and her churlish dismissal of it, whilst private, was unfair. Lewton had not been intrusive by suggesting tea and nor, she was certain, had he any hidden motive behind the idea. He would have found it an outrageous accusation, and it would have embarrassed him as much as it would have offended him. Dorothy was ashamed of herself for her petty irritations, dismissing her disdain with a bitter curse. And so, the tea was poured without any further debate.

Accepting the cup, Lewton said, "How have you been, Dorothy? Since the inquest, I mean."

Dorothy looked across at him. His thin lips were pursed as he blew cold air onto the hot surface of the tea, his eyes narrowed slightly behind the lenses of the circular, tortoiseshell spectacles. He was not necessarily a handsome man, which made her attraction to him all the more inexplicable. His hair was thinning, but he was far from bald, and it was neatly combed over the dome of his head. His eyes were a subtle shade of green, and they might have been fascinating were they not dimmed by an incessant impression of melancholy, as if some trauma had occurred which had blighted their colour forever. The same sense of sadness was reciprocated in the sloping of the mouth, so that his natural expression was one of gentle sadness, as if grief was something with which he had learned to live. There were flashes of crimson across the otherwise pale cheeks, where veins had broken under the skin, suggesting that he had indulged in an excess of alcohol at some point in his life, although Dorothy had never seen him take anything more extravagant than a glass of wine with an evening meal. Any such indulgence must have been in the past, she thought, long before she had met him. And yet, for all his faults, Dorothy Parrish knew that if she did not already love Thomas Lewton unconditionally, she was not far from it.

She wondered what he made of her. Without any pretensions to arrogance, she suspected that he felt similar emotions towards her as she did for him, and, in her own mind, they were equally incomprehensible. She had never considered herself a beautiful woman, although there had been brief, spasmodic love affairs in the past, but she had never fooled herself into thinking that they were anything other than shallow, opportunistic moments of pleasure. She had never truly understood what love was, although she was sure that she had not experienced it, not in the ways demonstrated by the romantic novels which she had devoured during her adolescence and early adulthood. Until, perhaps, she had met Thomas Lewton. She had never questioned why these feelings should only come to her when she was of an age when she should surely begin to think that her life was turning into its final phase. She had simply accepted the feelings for what she assumed they were, a love which she felt she could understand

and in which she could believe. Perhaps Lewton did not care that her hair, now lined with the grey tracks of time, was no longer the luxuriant black of her youth. Maybe the fact that her mouth was a little too large for the slimness of her face wasn't a concern for him. And, she supposed, it was possible that what she saw as a debilitating shyness meant nothing to him other than an endearing coyness.

She would remind herself that such analysis of the situation was futile. They had never expressed their feelings, after all, so she could not be certain that he had experienced anything of what she had felt about him. She would allow herself these self-indulgent assurances, but there was only the flimsiest of evidence in support of them: his kindness, his gentle insistence that she accompany him to lunch, dinner, or even afternoon tea, his general interest in her life, and his apparently genuine happiness in her company. Did such things equate to love? If they did not, then what she felt was more complicated than she had imagined. And yet, such doubts as these never seemed to persist, often being dispelled by a smile from him, or a touch of his hand, or a glance which said more to her than any romantic literature had ever been able to achieve.

"As well as can be expected, I suppose," said Dorothy, in answer to Lewton's questions. "The thought of what he did still makes my skin crawl."

Lewton could hardly disagree. "Almost impossible to imagine, isn't it? Although, medically speaking, he would have felt nothing. Small comfort, of course."

"Even talking about it is like walking over one's own grave." Dorothy wrapped her arms around herself, as if the coldness of death had already descended onto her.

Lewton seemed not to have heard her. "You can't help but feel sorry for the poor Delaney girl."

"She drove him to it," said Dorothy, rather more venomously than she might have intended. "How can you feel sorry for her?"

Lewton's expression was not condemning, but there was something of a sense of reproach about his tone of voice. "All she did was fall in love with someone else. And none of us can help who we love."

The words were heavy with implication. She wondered whether he was trying to tell her something, using Harriet Delaney as some sort of emotional metaphor for his own feelings towards Dorothy Parrish herself. She waited for him to say more, but nothing came, and the inference she had drawn from his words shattered into pieces in her mind.

"I don't suppose Lorrimer was an easy man to love," she said. "Perhaps falling for Edgar Corrigan was a far simpler thing to do. Is love that fickle?"

Lewton sighed heavily. "I'm hardly qualified to answer a question of that depth. But I agree that Lorrimer would have been difficult to love. I'm sorry to say that I never really liked the man at all."

"He's dead, Thomas." Dorothy's words were spoken without recrimination, being merely a statement of fact.

"I have no qualms about speaking ill of the dead," Lewton replied. "Especially about William Lorrimer."

She found his attitude confusing. "Did you dislike him so much? Why?"

"I have my reasons." He did not meet her eyes when he spoke. "And I doubt I'm alone in my dislike."

"What do you mean by that?"

Now, his eyes did lift to meet hers. They were not accusing, but some of the kindness behind them seemed to have diminished. "You can be honest with me, Dorothy. I shan't think worse of you, and I certainly wouldn't betray your confidence."

"I don't know what you're talking about." She was as defiant as her timidity would allow, but the voice which spoke the words was unable to prevent itself from trembling.

Lewton rose from his chair and came to sit beside her on the settee. "I know about the cottage, Dorothy. And I know that now that Lorrimer is dead, you'll be able to keep it."

She felt almost at once the angry prickle of tears in her eyes, and the sudden nausea of a secret discovered swelled within her stomach, so violently that the urge to retch was almost irresistible. It was as if he had encroached into her private world of agony and, rather than be grateful for the opportunity to share a trouble, she was outraged by his intrusion. And yet, his words were spoken with a definite empathy. She knew that there was no malice, that what he was doing was demonstrating that he knew about the one fear which had plagued her for weeks. He was not goading her, she realised; rather, he was taking away the burden of having to confess the truth of it herself. This realisation alone was all that prevented her from screaming at him in indignant humiliation, of scratching at his face, and of pushing him out of the door.

"You can trust me, Dorothy," he said, his voice as soothing as a priest in a confessional. "I wish you would accept that."

She slipped her hand out of his grasp and stood. She walked only a short distance, from the settee to the stone fireplace, but the silence in which she did it seemed interminable. She kept her back to him, her eyes closed tightly, and her teeth clamped together, as if the situation were causing her physical pain. "How did you know about it?"

"I overheard you and Lorrimer arguing a few days ago."

"Why didn't you say anything?"

"I was waiting for you to confide in me. Waiting and hoping," he added. "Now that everything concerning his death is over and done with, I saw no reason to wait any longer."

"How much did you overhear?"

Lewton got to his feet and walked slowly towards her. "Enough to understand that he was planning to sell the cottage. And enough to know where that would leave you."

Still, she did not look at him. Her head was turned away, but he doubted she was sobbing. The shoulders were still, and the breathing was regular. For that, at least, he could be grateful. He had the urge to place his hand on her shoulder, to show her that he was there to support her in every way, but something about the averted gaze suggested that it would not be a welcome gesture. As if to deny himself any temptation, he placed his hands in his pockets.

"I can only imagine the strain under which you've been living, Dorothy," he said. "Why didn't you think you could tell me what you were suffering?"

She had no answer to give him, only to rectify what he so clearly saw as a mistake on her part. "He had promised me a permanent lease on the cottage. He had always said I was welcome to consider it and treat it as my home. Then, without warning, he told me he had changed his mind."

"What had caused him to do that?"

"I don't know."

"Do you know whether he set any wheels in motion or whether it was just a decision he had made?"

"I don't think he had consulted Philip Ryman, no. Not yet, at least."

Lewton smiled. "That's something. If he hadn't got so far as to tell his own solicitor about it, there can't be any proof of his intention to sell."

She turned to face him now, and he saw that the tears in fact had begun, despite her stillness. They glistened against the skin of her cheeks, but she seemed herself not to notice them. Her hands were clasped together with such force that the knuckles had whitened, and, in that moment, Lewton felt as if he was being shown a glimpse of Dorothy's near-perpetual state since William Lorrimer had gone back on his word. Now, his previous optimism corroded by the sight, Lewton did not hesitate. He ignored any instinctive hesitation and took a step towards her, to take her in his arms. She fell against him, as if she had been waiting so long for him to make the move that her legs had given way under the strain of the expectation. Her head rested against his shoulder, and her arms hung loosely around his back. There was no pretence of love in the embrace, only an assured and much needed display of friendly support. For the moment, it was all that was necessary.

"If I'd known about it," Lewton said, more to himself than to Dorothy, "the verdict of the inquest might have been something entirely different."

She understood his implication immediately. "You mustn't say anything like that again, Thomas. You're not capable of it."

In the moment, she did not realise it, but later, she would understand that his reply troubled her. "You don't know what I'm capable of."

Gently, she pulled herself out of the embrace and wiped the tears away with the tips of her fingers. "I'm ashamed to say it, but I can't feel sorry that he's dead."

"Why should you? When you think of what his actions would mean for you, how could you be sorry that he isn't able to carry out the threat?"

"The sale might still go ahead," she said, voicing for the first time a fear which had deprived her of sleep from the moment she had heard about Lorrimer's death.

"True, but it won't be imminent, if it happens at all. His executors will have to be appointed, and they will have to decide what to do with the cottage. Did Lorrimer have any family?"

Dorothy shrugged. "I don't know. He never spoke of any."

Lewton seemed to take her reply as evidence of the truth of his point. "Whoever his executors are, they will have to decide what to do about this place, and they'll need probate to come through to do it. All that takes time, which we can use to sort something out for you. Assuming, of course, that you can't come to some arrangement with Lorrimer's executors and the estate."

The brightening of her eyes showed that here was a solution which had not occurred to her during any one of those sleepless nights. "You mean, they might let me stay, and I could pay rent to the estate?"

Lewton nodded. "It's possible. One must assume that Lorrimer's executors aren't as uncaring and disloyal as he was himself."

Dorothy sighed and sank down onto the settee. "Bless you, Thomas, I had given up all hope."

He smiled and lowered his gaze to the hearth rug. "Besides, even if the worst did happen, I wouldn't see you homeless."

"People would talk," she said. There was a vague suggestion of red around her cheeks.

"Only about how badly Lorrimer treated you. Their disgust would outweigh their shock."

His smile had widened, and it prompted her to do likewise. It felt enriching to her, a long-forgotten happiness displacing the more familiar misery, as if Lewton had somehow been able to deliver her from herself. "Thank you, Thomas. You've no idea what it means to me."

He had, but he said nothing. It would have been inappropriate, of course, but Lewton also had no desire to say so much that it would be too much. More often than not where Dorothy Parrish was concerned, he despised his own awkward hesitancy. Now, he was glad of it.

"Shall we have more tea?" Dorothy asked.

"Why not?"

He sat back down beside her and watched her pour the tea. He could not say that her relief was absolute, but he could tell from the widening of her eyes and the faint smile which crept along her lips that there had been a warming of her emotions. He hoped that tonight, at least, she would be able to sleep with a little more peace in her dreams than of late. He could have no way of knowing that later, when she was alone in the cottage, replaying the conversation in her head, Dorothy would come to realise that if Lorrimer's death had not been ruled as suicide, the sale of the cottage might have given her and, by extension, Thomas Lewton himself, a significant motive for murder.

And neither of them could have known that, in this, they were not alone.

Chapter Six

I
t was true to say that the majority of people of Little Marsham took it for granted that William Lorrimer had committed suicide. However, there were some who preferred to keep their minds open, even in the wake of the formal verdict of the coroner's court. As she sat in her living room, ignoring the pot of coffee which she had made for herself, Angela Ryman felt compelled to accept the verdict, fearing she had no other option, but it did nothing to alleviate any of those doubts which she had felt in the immediate aftermath of the man's death. It was not that she had any definite proof to the contrary, but Angela found that she was unable to say with conviction that Lorrimer had pulled the trigger of the gun himself. She had never voiced these concerns, of course. To do so would have been reckless, especially in the absence of evidence in support of her suspicion, but she was in no doubt that it would also have been damaging, especially as her doubts concerned her own husband.

She inhaled suddenly, the air hissing between her teeth, as though the thought had caused her some degree of unexpected, physical pain. She rose from the settee, the pot of coffee now abandoned completely, and walked to the small cabinet in the corner of the room. She took a glass and poured herself a generous measure of gin, adding ice and a small splash of tonic water. Ordinarily, she would not drink anything stronger than coffee in the afternoons, but she was unapologetic for this break from tradition. The memory of Philip's confrontation with William Lorrimer seemed to be sufficient justification for it.

Her mind drifted now back into the recent past. It had only been after the event that she had realised that the argument she had heard had not been the first altercation between them, but rather had been one more in a series of conflicts. She could recall Philip on the telephone on several previous occasions, his voice as lethal as a knife blade and the anger behind it barely suppressed. She could not have known who was on the other end of the line, naturally, but when she looked back over those calls, she could have no doubt that it had been William Lorrimer. There had been something about the personal confrontation she had witnessed, which had betrayed Lorrimer as the voice on the other end of the telephone in those earlier exchanges. Angela had not known what the specific cause of the disagreements had been, but she had assumed that it had been professional, since, beyond being his solicitor, Philip Ryman had no relationship with William Lorrimer.

Angela may not have been aware of why they had argued, but the quarrel had told her the consequence of the dispute. She recalled now her arrival at the offices of Ryman, Leith & Parkes in the high street, the familiar Tudor building with its latticed windows set into the black and white painted masonry. It had not quite been lunchtime, so that Angela had been surprised to see that Miss Grange, Ryman's plain but efficient secretary, was not at her desk. Angela had inferred at once that an early lunch had been decreed and, in that fact alone, there had been an element of suspicion on Angela's part. The door to Ryman's office had been ajar, so that she had been able to hear the voices coming from it but had not been able to see directly inside. She had walked softly towards the open door, leaning closely to it, so that the voices had become more distinct, just as now they seemed to amplify within her memory.

"It's about time people understood you for what you are, Ryman," Lorrimer had said. "How can I trust you to look after my affairs now, knowing what I do?"

"I'm telling you, Lorrimer, it isn't what you think," Ryman had replied. Even to Angela, the voice had sounded unconvincing, and she had doubted, then or now, that her husband had believed his own words.

"Don't compound one lie with another," Lorrimer had scoffed. "This village won't forgive multiple duplicity."

"I'm begging you, Lorrimer, I can put things right. I just need a little time."

Angela had been surprised by Ryman's subjugation. She had been conscious at once of a sense of disappointment in him, as if his submission to Lorrimer had been a form of personal betrayal of her. She had not expected him to be so easily defeated, and it seemed to be a facet of his character which she could never have anticipated. It was as if this one moment of weakness had been so acute that it had been capable of eradicating her previous impressions of his strength and determination. It had been an extreme reaction, no doubt, and she had no doubt that it had been unfair, but it had been no less emphatic for that.

Lorrimer himself had been unimpressed by it. "It's too late to put it right, Ryman. You've broken every level of trust between us. I shall be taking my business elsewhere."

"You can't," Ryman had protested.

"You've given me no choice."

"But people will ask why."

"Then you can tell them."

"It will ruin me."

Angela had not been able to see it, but something about Lorrimer's tone of voice had suggested that he was smiling when he replied. "And you deserve it."

There had been nothing more said. Lorrimer had pulled open the door, so swiftly that there had been no opportunity for Angela to move away, so that there had been no possibility of concealing her intrusion into the argument. Lorrimer had sneered at her as he passed her, but he had not spoken. Philip Ryman, when he had seen her framed in the doorway, had seemed both surprised and terrified, as if she were no longer his wife, but a predator which had cornered its prey.

"What are you doing here?" he had said.

"What's happening, Philip?"

"Nothing." The lie had been obvious, and neither of them treated it with any degree of credibility.

"What did Lorrimer mean about taking his business elsewhere?"

Ryman had heaved his shoulders and lowered his gaze to the floor. "Please, Angela, leave me alone."

She had waited for him to speak further, but he had denied her. His silence was, in itself, an evasion. "What have you done, Philip?"

Now, draining the glass of its gin, she seethed as she recalled his reply to the question, which had been to close the door slowly on her and turn the key in its lock. Her later attempts to elicit the truth from him had resulted in a variation of the same theme, his responses being, in turn, deflective and obstructive. Finally, she had abandoned any hope that he would confide in her or treat her with sufficient respect to tell her the truth, but she had not forgotten what she had heard. It had occurred to her to attempt to find something approaching the truth from Lorrimer himself, but she suspected that it would result in a similarly defiant closed door. To Angela Ryman, however, the prospect of disappointment was not something to fear.

Only a few evenings after the scene in Ryman's office, she had waited outside Lorrimer's cottage for him to return. She was about to abandon her plan, as the sun had begun to dip beneath the horizon, but at the very moment she had started to walk away from his gate, he had appeared before her. If he knew why she had been waiting for him, he gave no indication of it. His politeness, which she had felt must surely have been false, seemed to her to be almost villainous in its insincerity.

"How may I help you, Mrs Ryman?"

She had tried to demonstrate that she was not fooled by him. "What's the dispute between you and my husband?"

He had inclined his head, the gesture seeming to her to be one of malicious pity. "Wouldn't your husband be the best one to ask about that?"

"He won't speak to me about it." She had been determined to demonstrate her dislike of him. "If he did, I wouldn't have to degrade myself by asking you."

He had laughed, shortly but spitefully. "I don't think it is for me to speak for him, Mrs Ryman. It isn't my responsibility to divulge what he chooses to withhold."

"I want you to tell me what you know about him which could ruin him, Mr Lorrimer," she had insisted.

He had given her the impression that he was contemplating co-operation, which made his subsequent refusal all the more hurtful. "It is for him to tell you, not me. All I can say is that if he does not tell the truth, to you and to everybody else, the matter could be very damaging for him." He had said no more, other than to bid her a good evening, and one more door was closed in her face.

Less than a week later, William Lorrimer was dead. To Angela, her doubts rising almost immediately, it had seemed dangerously close to a horrific matter of cause and effect, a conviction which a verdict of suicide had done little to shake.

She watched Philip now, as he walked down their garden path, his head hanging low and his shoulders rounded, as if an albatross of defeat hung around his neck. She wondered why it was that his weakness inspired hatred in her rather than pity. She had never before thought it possible to despise him; she would not have married him if it had been even a remote possibility. But the change in him had appalled her, so that any feeling of tender empathy for him had turned into a malignant disgust. How much more impressive, even attractive, it would have been if he had thrown Lorrimer to the Devil rather than buckling under the weight of this oppression of unknown origin.

She listened to the latch of the door and the snap of the lock as he closed it behind him. He entered the sitting room like a shamed schoolboy entering a headmaster's office, his expression as humbled as it was embarrassed. He put his hands into the pockets of his trousers, but Angela had already seen their tremble, and the reaction of spiteful loathing had already risen inside her.

"Where have you been?" she asked.

"I went for a walk." He looked up at her, his pale blue eyes begging her not to argue. "I just wanted to think."

"About the verdict?"

He shrugged. "I suppose so. Isn't it a little early for gin?"

He regretted it as soon as it had been said. If he had feared an explosion of emotion from her, he was to be disappointed, but, in other respects, he would have preferred it. The sneering snort of air through Angela's nostrils and the sly smile across her lips were altogether more punishing.

"So, you're a hypocrite as well as a liar," Angela sneered. She turned back to the drinks cabinet and poured herself another gin, adding ice with an indignant clatter, twisting the lemon as if it were his neck, and adding a further dash of hostility before she drank some down, as if purely to spite him.

"I'm not a liar," he lied.

"You didn't tell the truth at the inquest." She said it without accusation, but merely as a statement of fact. "I don't suppose I should be surprised. You've been lying to me for weeks."

He sat down on the settee, placing his hand hopefully on the coffee pot. Like many other things in the house, it was cold. "Do we have to do this now?"

"I want to know, Philip. I want to know what it is about William Lorrimer which you're keeping from me and which you kept from the inquest."

"It was nothing important," he hissed, his teeth clenching in something approaching anger. "I've told you it was nothing, and I'm sick of saying it. Now, leave it alone."

She scoffed, drowning her bitterness with gin. "So, you still have some scope for emotion. Whatever your secret is, it hasn't drained you completely of your masculinity."

"I don't have to listen to this." He rose from the settee and marched to the door. He pulled it open, but stopped, turning back to face her. "If you want honesty, Angela, try starting with yourself."

"Meaning what?"

"You may have forgotten about Gerald Bowers and Mary Jerrold, but I haven't."

She threw back her head and laughed. "Don't be so bloody ridiculous."

"Am I being ridiculous?" His eyes narrowed. "If so, I'm not alone."

"You're talking nonsense, and you know it."

"Look," he spat, "why don't you say what's really on your mind?"

She glared at him for a moment, her lips pursed, as if they dared not open for fear of what might be said. His eyebrows raised confrontationally, taunting her into a reaction. She could feel the heat of fire returning to him, and she felt curiously impressed by it, as she wondered whether something of the man she had fallen in love with, the man who had dazzled her with his determination and decisiveness, was still somewhere beneath the sullen, broken frame of his present self. A hint of his strangely cruel allure returned to the pale eyes, and his shoulders seemed to swell with a shadow of their former certainty.

She put down the glass and walked towards him. "I'll say this, Philip. Whether the court's verdict was correct or not, regardless of whether Lorrimer shot himself, he's dead. Which means, I suppose, that whatever was happening between you might not be as much of a threat to you when he was alive."

"Are you accusing me of something, Angela?" he asked, his voice quietly contemptuous.

"All I'm saying, Philip, is that whatever was troubling you about Lorrimer, you must be pleased that he so conveniently killed himself."

"That's a wicked thing to say."

"True, nonetheless."

He shook his head. "You seem to be suggesting that the verdict was wrong. If you think Lorrimer was murdered, you'd better have proof before you voice your concerns."

"Is that a threat, Philip?" She was smiling, in mockery more than humour. "Perhaps you're more dangerous than I've ever thought."

Philip Ryman was not smiling in return. "You don't know what you're talking about. You'd better pull yourself together before you say something you'll regret."

"What I've said still stands, Philip," she replied. "Lorrimer is dead, and that appears to be very convenient for you."

"The man killed himself, Angela. I can't, and I won't, be blamed for it or for any consequence of it."

He walked out and closed the door behind him. Angela, her smile slowly fading, heard the door close and, through the sitting room window, she watched him walk away from the house. He did not look back at her, and she hardly expected him to. Slowly, she paced around the room, her mind wandering over the argument and the inquest. Gradually, she made her way back to her drink. She hardly felt the cold of the glass against the more deadly chill which had descended on the room in the last few moments. She raised it slowly to her lips, sipping at it but hardly tasting it, as if her tongue could detect nothing other than her own fears and suspicions and the bitter aftertaste of violent death.

II

PART TWO: MURDER

Chapter Seven

Gerald Bowers saw the strange woman again on the following morning. This time, she had not walked away from him, even when he had gently called out to her. She had remained motionless, staring down at the grave in front of her, and as he drew nearer to her, Bowers could see that the woman was beautiful.

Beneath the veil, the skin was a delicate pale, with only the suggestion of pink at the cheeks, but with lips which were so scarlet that they appeared to be splashes of blood on a freshly fallen snow. Her hair, pulled tightly into the nape of her neck, so that the angle of her jaw was clearly defined, was as black as her mourning dress, which she wore with such command that it suggested a respectful elegance as much as formal grief. Beneath the veil, the eyes were closed, and tears ran gently down the angular bones of the cheeks. Her mouth did not quiver, however, and her shoulders were motionless. She stood erect, with only her head lowered in deference to the dead, and a small, black bag was clutched in the gloved hands.

She sensed Bowers' approach before he had any chance of addressing her. At once, the spell was broken, and she stood back from the grave, one hand detaching itself from the bag and wiping away the tears with an almost frantic necessity, as if she had been discovered trespassing in a place in which she had no entitlement to be. Bowers held out a calming hand, and shook his head, as if to explain silently that he had no wish to intrude.

"Please, do not go," he said. "I have no wish to disturb you."

The woman did not speak, but she could not keep her eyes on Bowers. They flickered around the cemetery, like those of a schoolgirl caught in an act of rebellion but for whom the consequences were now due. Had she ever been aware of Dorothy Parrish's presence in the churchyard, she would now have realised that Dorothy had gone.

Bowers was smiling, both genial and trustworthy, but she did not respond. Something of her previous taciturnity was returning, and her eyes now were no longer damp with grief, but alive with something altogether more determined. Bowers could see that they were a deep shade of green, and he had a sudden impression of a feline attractiveness about the contrast between those bright, but powerful eyes and the darkness of her hair and clothes.

Bowers looked down at the grave at which she had been standing. He managed to suppress his surprise and, when he spoke, he hoped that none of it was evident in his tone of voice. "Am I to take it that you knew him?" He pointed to the grave.

The woman took her time in responding and, when she did, it was with a slow nod of the head. "I hadn't seen him for several years, though." Her voice was clear, unsoiled by any traces of sadness, but it was quiet, almost stifled by the breeze, so that Bowers had to strain to hear it.

"Did you know him well?"

She gave another slow nod, but now it was accompanied by a slight bite of the lower lip, as though the mild pain of the teeth against flesh would distract her from her sudden impulse to weep once more. She looked back at Bowers, her expression returning to one of calm detachment. "My name is Isobel Croft. Does it mean anything to you?"

"I'm afraid not."

She looked down at the grave beside them. "Did he ever mention any family to you?"

The question was so unexpected that the vicar was unable to disguise it. His mouth flapped for a moment with unspoken replies, and his eyes flickered with confusion. Isobel Croft, however, remained consistent in her composure, and he felt obliged under the spell of it to speak. "I'm afraid he didn't. Certainly not to me."

She did not give any reaction, so he was unable to determine whether she had expected the answer or not and, similarly, whether she had been offended by it. At last, after holding Bowers' gaze for a few seconds, she looked back down to the gravestone. "I can't blame him. Neither of us were particularly good at keeping in touch."

The implication was clear, and Bowers was struck by it. Almost needlessly, he said, "Am I to take it...?"

Isobel Croft looked back at him, a faint smile flickering around her scarlet mouth. "William Lorrimer was my brother."

It was not spoken with any sense of melodrama or intention to shock. It was stated as a matter of fact, a piece of information for which she expected no consolation or condolence, and her expression encouraged neither. She wanted no pity, Bowers could see, and she wanted no platitudes about grief or recovery from it. She wanted something else. Her presence here, the determination in her eyes, and the emotionless detachment, marred only by the very briefest of mourning, were so obvious that Bowers could draw no other conclusion. Suddenly, he became aware of a deathly cold along his spine.

"It is getting cold now," he said. "Would you like a cup of tea in the vicarage, Mrs Croft?"

She was not aware herself of any chill. It was an autumn morning, but not an exceptionally cold one. She found the vicar's suggestion otherwise strangely disturbing, but she was prepared to dismiss it, because the idea of tea was a welcome one. She had not had any refreshment since an early breakfast, and a cup of hot tea would, she knew, be sensible as well as invigorating. She nodded her thanks, and, with only a small display of reluctance, she allowed him to lead her away from the grave of her brother.

The tea was made swiftly. When Bowers returned with it, he found that she had removed her hat and gloves, seated herself in an armchair beside the fire, and was staring out of the parlour window. The view across the churchyard, he seemed to realise for the first time, served only as a reminder of one's own mortality. He wondered how much of a comfort it was when parishioners came to seek his advice and find solace in his words, to have this memory of their ultimate fate looming back at them. In that moment, he found his entire position in life something of a ridiculous failure.

Tea poured, they sat for a moment in silence. Now that he saw her face fully exposed, Bowers thought that he could trace some resemblance between Isobel Croft and William Lorrimer. It was not, by any means, anything to be taken for granted, nor was it so extreme as to be remarkable, but there was something about the profile, a suggestion around the shape of the eyes, the similarity of certain mannerisms which made the family connection clear.

"I suppose my appearance here has come as something of a shock," Isobel said without prompting.

Bowers nodded his head. "I would certainly say so. You say you and William were not in regular contact?"

"I have been living abroad for many years," she said, as if to explain it. "An occasional letter or postcard was the extent of our communication." Then, as if something had suddenly occurred to her, she sat upright in her chair. "I wouldn't want you to think that there was any discord between us. It was nothing like that."

"Of course not," replied Bowers, who had assumed exactly that. Knowing Lorrimer as he had, and taking his initial impression of Isobel Croft for granted, he would have understood entirely if she had distanced herself from her brother.

"Our lives took different paths, that is all," Isobel said. "I married an American financier, you see, so our life had to be in New York."

Bowers smiled. "A long way from Little Marsham."

She did not give any response. She sipped the tea slowly, her lips pursing into a kiss in order to blow air across its surface to cool it. The gesture reminded Bowers at once, painfully, of Mary Jerrold, who had done something similar.

After a silence, Isobel rose from her seat and walked towards the window, looking back over the churchyard. "Would you be offended if I said I was not altogether convinced about religion?"

Bowers placed his cup onto the side table and leaned back in his chair. He crossed his legs and made a steeple of his fingers, the tips of which he put to his mouth. "My offence or otherwise is of no importance. Your relationship with God is what counts."

"I don't think I have one."

Bowers kept his eyes on the nape of her neck, where the black hair was still pinned. "Perhaps not, but He has one with you, whether you acknowledge it or not."

Her head turned slightly, as if the words had made some sort of impression on her. "Why is there a change in God?"

"A change?"

Now, Isobel turned on her heel and faced him. Her face was hidden by the shadows cast by the light behind her, so that a blurring halo of light surrounded the top of her frame. It seemed to intensify the black of her dress, giving her the appearance of some black angel, whose intentions were either not understood or of a conflicting nature.

"The Old Testament God is vengeful, wrathful, ready to punish," she said. "The New Testament shows Him to be forgiving, loving, and protective."

"It is the same God, nevertheless," replied Bowers. "The God who revealed Himself to Moses, in the Old Testament, stated that He was the compassionate and gracious God. He says that He is 'merciful and gracious, slow to anger, and abounding in steadfast love and faithfulness, keeping steadfast love for thousands, forgiving iniquity and transgression and sin.'"

If she recognised it as a quotation, she gave no indication of it. "That God has never struck me as compassionate."

"But there is no distinction between them," insisted Bowers. "What you term the New Testament God was also capable of destruction. Thessalonians tells us that God will punish with everlasting destruction those who do not obey Christ. Does that sound compassionate?"

Isobel shook her head. "Perhaps not."

"What you must understand is that the God of wrath, as you call Him, is the same God of love. God is everything. If there is any distinction between the Old and New, it is that in the latter, God reveals Himself through Jesus, who comes to fulfill the prophecies and laws, not to abolish them. God, in the Old Testament, announced the coming Saviour, who would redeem

55

humanity through death and resurrection. Jesus is the living embodiment of that deliverance. But God Himself is still prepared to destroy those who do not accept the message."

Isobel turned back to the window, as if the explanation had served no purpose for her. "I prefer to believe in a God of vengeance."

Bowers understood now that there had been a point to this minor theological debate, a specific intention which had been buried beneath her initial question. He rose from his chair and walked slowly towards her. Either she did not hear him approach or she did not care about it, since she made no movement. He followed her gaze through the pane of the window and felt certain that she was looking at Lorrimer's grave.

"Why should you want to believe in a God of vengeance?" he asked.

Her reply was not what he had expected. "You buried my brother in consecrated ground."

"Of course. I sought my Bishop's approval, but he was happy to give it."

Now, she turned to glare at him. "And why did you do that?"

Bowers, suddenly aware of the intensity of those green eyes and of the blood-crimson of her lips, knew that she was capable of any form of vengeance. "Because of what he did, what the inquest said he had done."

Isobel Croft held his gaze for a long moment, before finally breaking it with a slow nod of her head, turning her gaze back to where William Lorrimer lay beneath the ground. She inhaled slowly, as if she needed all the air she could take in, to say the next words. Equally slowly, she began to shake her head. "My brother didn't kill himself, Mr Bowers. He was murdered."

The word seemed imaginary to Bowers, as if it was one which had never been spoken before, whose meaning, if any, was unclear. "Murdered?"

Isobel Croft turned to look at him. There was no trace in her expression of any disbelief in her own words. "Do you see now why I want vengeance?"

Bowers shook his head. "The inquest was clear, Mrs Croft. There was evidence."

"I have my own evidence."

"Your own suspicions, perhaps, but…"

She cut off his words with a raising of her voice. "Evidence!"

Bowers lowered his head, his hands clasping slowly behind his back. "Might I ask what evidence?"

But Isobel shook her head. "That doesn't matter for the moment. Rest assured, I have it, and I shall use it."

His frown deepened. "Use it?"

As she began to nod her head, a smile stretched across her lips. It was not malicious, he thought, nor was it spiteful. If anything, curiously, it was reassuring. "Yes. I know the murderer, Mr Bowers, and I shall have vengeance for my brother. With or without any form of God on my side."

Only now did she turn away from the window. She walked back to the chair which she had vacated, picked up the cup of tea, and drank slowly from it. Bowers watched her closely, now discomforted by her equanimity, which seemed to him should be in conflict with the thoughts which lingered in her mind. He saw now that her previous tears had been born as much from anger and retribution as from grief and pain. Her question about God had not been a result of any religious consultation, but a natural extension of her thoughts of revenge and murder.

"Whatever plan of action you have set for yourself, Mrs Croft," he said, "you must turn your back on it. No good can come of it."

She had replaced her coat, hat, and veil. Now, she bent forward and picked up the small, black bag. "And no good can come from soiling my brother's reputation with a finding of suicide against him."

"Whoever you think is responsible, please, I beg you, do not confront them."

"I have nothing to fear in that regard, Mr Bowers." She smiled gently at him, but the green eyes were defiant. "Thank you for the tea."

As soon as she had reached the door, he had moved to block her path. "Can I not dissuade you?"

She looked at him strangely, as if seeing him for the first time. "My brother must have justice, Mr Bowers. Of the Old Testament kind or otherwise."

It seemed to take an age for the sound of the front door opening and closing to reach him. When he finally heard the latch, it sounded like a death knell. He closed his eyes against it and walked back to the window. He saw Isobel Croft walking away from the cemetery, her step more assured than previously and her head no longer trying to vanish into her breast. Her spine was still erect, but her shoulders were square, as if they had been fortified by a newly found determination. Bowers, suddenly aware that he was in possession of a potentially disastrous secret, wondered whether anything he had said might have given her this new assurance. He closed his eyes, as if to erase the conversation and his memory of it, but he knew that it was impossible.

He found that he was holding his breath, and his lungs had begun to protest at it. He spat out the suppressed air and groaned with the effort. His shoulders heaved, and his breath hissed in his nostrils. His fingers clenched, and their nails bit into his palms, but the pain was not cathartic. It was barely noticeable. There was only one pain which could permit any sense of purifying punishment.

Turning away from the window, his thoughts as heavy as his step, Gerald Bowers walked out of the parlour and up the stairs, unbuttoning his shirt as he went.

Chapter Eight

Angela Ryman lay back in the bed and allowed herself a brief but pleasurable recollection of the lovemaking which had now come to an end. It had been forceful in its urgency and, more than once, she had felt his hand at her throat as he impressed himself upon her. His grip was strong, on occasion worryingly so, with the assurance that only a small increase in pressure would show it to be too strong, perhaps. Angela was not frightened by his proclivity for grabbing her neck, but the prospect of taking it too far was terrifying. And yet, she was not so dishonest with herself to deny that it was all the more thrilling for it.

She watched him now as he lit a cigarette, his back muscles shifting as he performed the task. He was a man who belied his age, the angles and musculature of his body those of a man closer to her own age than his. It was not that the difference in their years was dramatic, being little more than a decade, but it was an obvious one, nonetheless. And yet, his trimness of build, the broadness of shoulders, and the command of his presence seemed to Angela to be those of a much younger man. True, his hair, which was grey now more than his natural brown, was fading slightly on the crown of his head, in some sort of natural tonsure, but it remained thick elsewhere, now ruffled and disorientated from the effect of the grip of her fingers. The moustache, military in its perfection, hid most of what she suspected was a cruel mouth lingering beneath it. She found him physically attractive now, so that if she had known him as a young man, she knew that she would have found him mesmerising. And yet, her personal honesty continuing, she was well aware that the attraction was superficially physical. She doubted she would like him as a person. It was impossible to imagine walks through the woods, romantic meals in the seclusion of a corner table of a restaurant, or quiet drinks on the veranda of the marital home on long, summer evenings. Angela doubted he craved those things with her either. If he did, he would have said so now, instead of allowing the affair to proceed by these weekly trysts in whichever bed was easiest to find. And, with tedious regularity, that bed would always be hers. For it to be occupied otherwise would mean Philip Ryman would have to be at home and, if that miracle were granted, the secondary one of him showing any interest in her would be impossible to turn into a reality. The affair served a purpose, and Angela knew it. To induce it to try to be anything more would have been both foolish and fatal.

He lay beside her now and smoked in silence. She did not lean into him, having learned that such suggestions of intimacy were unwanted and unnecessary to him, once the purpose of his assignation with her had been completed. Instead, she lay with one arm stretched behind her head and the other, cigarette in hand, curled across her exposed breasts and stomach. She turned her head to face him.

"What time do you have to get back?" she asked.

"Soon."

"What does that mean?"

Arthur Corrigan looked across at her, but he did not return the smile she was giving him. "It means I have to be back soon."

"How soon?"

"Sooner than I thought if you keep on like this."

She laughed, but it was not entirely genuine. His casual attitude could offend her as frequently as it could enthrall her. It was not that she wanted more from him, but his directness, coming so often without warning, could be unsettling, so that it was easy to feel offence at what he had said. "Where has she gone this time?"

"Who?"

The question seemed to her to be bizarre. "Elsa, of course."

Corrigan turned to face her once again. "What does it matter, as long as she isn't here?"

Angela found herself incapable of arguing against the ruthless, yet somehow perverse logic. "She's no different to Philip, really. She doesn't care what you do or who you see, any more than he does about me. I wonder why we have to keep this thing between us a secret at all." She arched her body, so that her head was resting on her free hand. "Do you think either of them would care if we did tell them?"

"We're not telling them anything," Corrigan said.

"No, I know. I'm just saying, if."

He shrugged and took a long intake of smoke from the cigarette. "Perhaps they're doing the same thing as we are. Together."

It was clearly not a thought to have occurred to Angela. "Would that bother you?"

"No." His voice betrayed no sense of a lie.

"Do you think Elsa knows about us?"

"I couldn't give a damn." He looked across at her. "Does Philip suspect anything?"

She thought back to her argument with Ryman, in particular to his reference to Mary Jerrold and Gerald Bowers. "If he does, he doesn't see you as the man involved."

Corrigan smiled cruelly. "Who does he suspect then?"

Angela did not reply. Instead, she leaned back onto the pillows of her bed and stared up at the ceiling. She looked at a small crack in the plaster and fell silent. She wondered whether she would have been able to respond with such a determined clarity as Corrigan had done to the question of whether she cared if Philip knew about their affair. She tried to replay the scene now in her head, their roles reversed, and when the time came to express her lack of concern about the idea of Philip Ryman having an affair with Elsa Corrigan, she found that the definitive, single syllable of negativity which he had spat at her would not come. Instead, somewhere in the back of her mind, or perhaps the depths of her heart, there was a muffled, half-suffocated sense of betrayal and sadness. Suddenly, she wondered why she was lying there, shrouded in hypocrisy as well as in bedsheets and blankets, perfectly content to play her own games of lust and happy to convince herself that her marriage was dead, but equally unwilling to entertain the thought of permitting Philip to do likewise.

The cigarette now seemed to taste foul, and she leaned across the bedside cabinet to extinguish it in the glass ashtray which was set beside the reading lamp. She felt Corrigan move beside her, possibly enticed by the curve of her hips, feeling his hand snake across them, the familiar prelude to something else, but Angela shifted away from him.

"Something wrong?" he asked.

Angela threw her legs out of the bed and sat upright. She arched her back, stretching her spine, and Corrigan watched the muscles work. She ran her hand through her auburn hair, which, to him, looked so much more alluring when it was ruffled and unkempt from their time together, as if its untidiness was some sort of testament of his conquest of her. The thought made him smile. If she had seen it, the smile would have sickened Angela as much as his thoughts would have had she been able to glimpse into his conscience.

She turned to look at him over her shoulder. "There is something going on with Philip."

Corrigan was instantly bored by the topic, and he made no attempt to conceal the fact. Leaning back in the bed, he let out a contemptuous groan. "Whatever it is can't be of any importance."

"Is murder not important to you?"

The word seemed to seize him by his throat. He glared at her, his lips parting into a snarl, and the slow clenching of a fist struck her as both calmly menacing and unfailingly dangerous. He shifted his weight so that he was facing her completely and when he spoke, his voice was low, almost soft, but no less threatening for it. "What are you talking about?"

In the moment, Angela wished she had said nothing. His reaction was confusing to her, so intimidating that it was as if she had accused him of the worst of all crimes. As if in some childish need for comfort and security, she gripped the blanket and raised it to her chest, covering her nakedness from him. Suddenly, it seemed somehow inappropriate that he should be able to see her so exposed, so vulnerable.

"Nothing, it doesn't matter." She knew that the evasion was futile.

He moved so swiftly that she had no opportunity to avoid his grasp. His hands were on her shoulders, and she became aware suddenly that she seemed to be falling. He had pulled her backwards, simultaneously getting himself out of the way, so that she found herself lying back on the bed, and he had moved on top of her. He pointed his finger at her like a pistol, and his face loomed over her, but not in any pretence of passion. His deep, brown eyes were alive with a heightened but serious emotion, and flecks of spittle hit her face as he spat out his commands.

"Tell me what you meant, Angela. Don't make this end like our last quarrel."

She was not surprised that he referenced their last argument, but she had not expected him still to be able to make her feel as if it had been her fault, as if she had designed somehow for his hand to come crashing against her cheek. Once, twice, and a third time. He had told her that she had made him do it, and she had not replied. The reason for the argument had been lost to her, under the devastation of the moment, but the climax of it would be something she would never forget. And now, here was the potential for a repeat of it. And he had already absolved himself from blame for it so that, if it happened, it would be entirely of her own making. And she would believe it, for a time at least, and she would question why it was that she kept taking him to her bed, whilst simultaneously wishing he would arrange to meet, as if he were some sort of dangerous, addictive drug which held her in its thrall.

"William Lorrimer," she said, her voice hoarse from the effort of fighting back tears.

"He killed himself."

She closed her eyes, afraid to say anymore, but knowing that she had no choice. "I know, but he and Philip were having a terrible argument one day, and Philip said something about Lorrimer being able to ruin him."

"How?" Corrigan's eyes had narrowed, but the pistol finger had lowered, and he had lessened the weight on her hips.

She shook her head. "I don't know. But, not long after, Lorrimer was dead, and all Philip's problems seemed to disappear."

Corrigan thought about it for a moment before raising himself off her completely and moving off the bed. He stood before her, unabashed at his own nakedness, and his head held backwards slightly, looking down on her through half-closed lids. A smile was forming beneath his moustache. "Do you think Philip is capable of murder?"

"Doesn't that depend on how desperate he is?"

He conceded the point with a shrug of his shoulders. "Have you confronted him about this?"

"He denied it." A memory came back to her, and she sat up quickly. "And then he told me that I'd better get proof before accusing him of anything."

Corrigan walked slowly around the bed. "What did Lorrimer have against Philip, I wonder."

"Something to do with the business, I'm sure of that."

Corrigan nodded. "Dipping his hand in the cake tin, perhaps."

But Angela shook her head. "Why would he need to do that? We're not struggling financially."

"What else could it be?"

She had no reply to that. She watched him as he sat down on the bed and twisted his body so that he was looking her in the eyes.

"Listen to me carefully," he said, taking her chin between his fingers, but with a grip which was slightly, but suggestively, too strong for its purpose. "Don't breathe a word of this to anybody. Understood? Philip is right about one thing, for once in his life, and that is that you need proof before you start hurling allegations. So, don't."

A flicker of her eyes showed that she agreed. Corrigan did not release his grip on her, though, and his eyes had hardened once more. "Besides, if the gossips of this bloody hole of a village get wind of your suspicions, that'll be it. It's best if people just accept that Lorrimer killed himself. If there's any possibility of doubt, people will start asking questions, and then it'll be Hell. Leave the bastard buried. The sooner he's forgotten, the better."

She was looking at him now with a frown of concern. She said, "Of course", but something about his insistence unsettled her. This persistence that no suggestion of murder should ever be allowed to fester seemed to her to hint at some personal stake in the matter, as if the rumours would be as harmful to Corrigan as they would be to Ryman himself. It was a fanciful thought, perhaps, but something about his manner made it appear to be less ridiculous than Angela felt sure it was. She knew that any attempt to question Corrigan further would be futile, possibly even perilous, but the unsettled discomfort in her mind was impossible to ignore.

"Are you all right, Arthur?" she asked. "I'm sorry if my stupid talk about Philip has irritated you."

He shook his head. "Then stop talking about him."

And, as he moved closer to her, Angela Ryman complied with the command. Any thoughts she had conjured about Corrigan being frightened of any rumours of murder were forgotten, as she released herself once again to the dangerous, but fatally attractive allure of the man she hated as much as she loved.

Chapter Nine

Everett Carr sat in a quiet corner of *The Marsham Tuns* public house, sipping at a glass of red wine, which was far superior than he had anticipated or had any right to expect.

He had secured accommodation at the inn without difficulty, the landlord being both fulsome and efficient in his welcome. The room allocated to Carr was simple but comfortable. The bed, flanked by two small chests of drawers, a small lamp on each, was as soft as any public house mattresses could be expected to be, and the sheets were immaculate and suitably starched. Carr, a child of the late Victorian and early Edwardian era, was accustomed to surgical precision in the folds of his bedsheets and the stiffness of them was reassuringly harsh. There was a shared bathroom down the landing, but the room nevertheless had its own small, porcelain sink. It was not the Albany or one of the luxuriant hotels which Carr had been fortunate enough to frequent in the past, but nor did he expect or want it to be. It was a room which offered and provided a reassuringly warm, rural welcome, and Carr had accepted it with gratitude and pleasure.

He had unpacked at his leisure and, having washed his hands in the porcelain sink, made his way down to the main area of the public house, a cosy room with a warm fire and Tudor beams extending across the ceiling. It was old without appearing to be so, so that it appeared accommodating rather than antique. The arrival of a stranger to Little Marsham had been noted, but the stares were neither indiscreet nor intrusive. Carr had been offered a pint of the local brew, which the landlord had assured him was "the envy of the county," but Carr had never been swayed particularly by the allure of beer and the deep, rosy glow of the ale, which he saw in a number of glasses which surrounded him, did very little to alter his views. He declined politely, saying that the fault was his and not the local brewer's, and ingratiated himself by offering to buy a glass of the beer for anyone who might feel inclined to share a drink with him. For himself, he had said, a glass of the best wine in the house would be appreciated. Murmured, but honest and genuine thanks were passed to Carr, and very few of the local drinkers declined his offer. During the ensuing scramble to collect their share of the order, the drinkers did not notice Carr slip away from their throng and settle himself, with his wine, in that darkened corner of the inn.

He had been sitting there for perhaps half an hour when the woman from the cemetery walked into the bar. Carr was momentarily shocked into stillness, his glass half raised and the dark eyes widening. He had not expected to see her again, and he was forced to admit to himself that, in the hours which had passed since he had seen her standing at one of the graves in the cemetery of St Bartholomew's, he had forgotten about her entirely. Now, she stood with her back to him, at much closer proximity to him than she had been among the tombstones, and more vivid than she would ever have been in his memory, so that the funereal black of her dress, hat, and veil seemed all the more poignant to him. The men who had accepted Carr's offer of a drink stared, but there was nothing but respect and empathy in the eyes, and the silence which fell on the room when she entered was solemn rather than uninviting. Nevertheless, it seemed to unnerve her and, when the landlord enquired as to her choice of drink, she was unable to answer.

Carr rose from his seat, pushing himself up on his cane and using the varnished wooden table as an additional support. He limped as swiftly as possible to the lady's side and placed money on the bar. "A brandy, I think, landlord, is all that is required now."

The woman looked across at Carr, into those eyes as black as her dress, and smiled apprehensively. "Thank you, sir. Most welcome."

The brandy was prepared, and Carr handed over payment. He took the glass of brandy and indicated his small table in the corner. "Perhaps you would like to join me?"

She seemed unwilling initially, no doubt thinking that she would prefer to be alone, but there was something about Carr's eyes and the twist of a smile beneath the large moustache and Imperial which she found comforting. He was avuncular rather than interfering and somehow, she felt as if she would be able to sit with him, even in silence, and not be troubled by his company. "I may not be able to offer very much conversation."

Carr's smile intensified. "I can bear silence as easily as chatter. But we are both strangers in this little village, I think, so we have that in common, at least."

"Very well, and thank you."

They sat at the table, and Carr raised his glass to her. They sipped their drinks and sat for a moment in silence. She raised the veil and removed her hat before slowly pulling off the black leather gloves.

"My name is Carr," he said finally. "Everett Carr."

She took the hand he had offered politely but not firmly, taking hold only of the tips of his fingers. "Isobel Croft."

Carr looked into her green eyes, vibrant despite her grief, and at the scarlet of her lips and the black of her hair, all of which contrasted with the paleness of her cheeks. There was a delicate vulnerability, he saw now, about the slightly upward curve of the nose and the habit of gently biting the corner of the lower lip, which transcended any immediate suggestion of mourning or loss.

"If you will allow me to say so, Mrs Croft," said Carr, "I am sorry for your loss."

She looked at him, her expression surprised rather than offended. "How do you know I am married?"

He pointed to her hand. "You wear a ring."

Her pale cheeks flushed briefly, and she began to caress the diamond which glistened on the third finger of her left hand. "Of course. You must think me very stupid."

"Distracted, perhaps," said Carr softly. "By grief."

"I could be dressed in black as a personal choice," she argued.

Carr smiled. "Very possibly, but I doubt you would stand in a cemetery alone on account of a similar whim." She glared at him fiercely, as if he had intruded on her privacy in some way. He shook his head and waved a finger in gentle denial. "No, no, do not misunderstand me. I have not been spying on you, rest assured."

"What then?"

"I saw you in the churchyard earlier this morning," he said, his voice suddenly soothing. "I was visiting Mr Bowers at the church, and we saw you. I left when he went over to speak to you."

Her eyes flickered now, and her brows creased in a confused frown, as if a long-forgotten memory had recalled itself to her mind. "Oh, yes, of course. I didn't see you, Mr Carr. Only Mr Bowers. He was very kind."

Carr offered no reply. None was necessary, and he felt that anything he said would be either meaningless or fatuous. Instead, he looked down into the flames of the fire which burned in the grate beside their table. The warmth of it was obvious and welcome against his leg, so that the usual cold in his shattered knee almost seemed to vanish momentarily. But it could never vanish completely. Carr knew that his lameness was permanent, and he was at ease with the diagnosis. What he would never be able to reconcile to himself, however, was that the smashed bone and stiffness in his leg were similarly permanent reminders of the fact that Miranda, his beloved wife, had died in his place.

Isobel's voice intruded into his thoughts. "Do you know Mr Bowers personally?"

"Not at all. I have corresponded with him over recent weeks, but I met him for the first time this morning."

"I wondered why you were here."

The frankness of the comment startled him slightly. "I beg your pardon?"

She must have registered his surprise, because she stammered an apology, and the same flush of crimson flashed in her pale cheeks. "I'm sorry, but with you saying you were a stranger here…"

Carr gave a small laugh and preened his moustache. "I am, indeed, a stranger here but I am not in the village at the personal invitation of Mr Bowers. No, no." he leaned towards her, his voice lowering into a conspiratorial whisper, gently making her an accomplice in his machinations. "If I dare say so, I ingratiated myself into Mr Bowers' acquaintance."

She was smiling at this foolish, but charmingly genial man. "But why?"

"His church has been gifted a remarkable painting by a lesser-known Danish artist," Carr said, "and I very much wanted to see it."

"Are you an art critic?" Something about the lurid necktie and handkerchief, the skull lapel pin, and the flamboyant moustache and beard seemed to suggest as much.

But he shook his head. "Not at all. I like what I know, dear lady, and I know what I like. I can say no more than that. And this painting of Christ on trial before Pilate fascinated me. So, as I am a man of leisure, I thought I would come to see it."

"I see." She sipped some of the brandy, barely touched until now, and clasped her hands back into her lap. "Do you believe in God?"

The sudden shift in tone and topic of the conversation troubled Carr. His eyes narrowed, and he turned his head slowly to face her. "Do I take it that you do, my dear?"

She gave a slight, almost indistinguishable shrug of the shoulders. "I'd like to believe in a vengeful God. Mr Bowers says that the Old Testament God of wrath and vengeance is the same as the New Testament God of love and forgiveness."

"And that seems paradoxical to you?"

She nodded. "He tried to explain it, but I could not accept it."

Carr began to stroke the lapel of his jacket gently with the fingers of one hand whilst the fingers of the other drummed lightly against the table. "Is there a particular reason why you should wish to believe in a rancorous God?"

Her eyes had brimmed now with tears. She fought hard against the temptation to let them fall, to succumb to the emotional release of actual sobbing, but Carr could see from the deep inhalations of breath and the clenching of the jaw that the battle was a difficult one. He did not make any attempt to coax her into a response, knowing that to do so would not only have been unwelcome but less than gallant. Any premature effort to speak, he knew, would lead only to an onslaught of tears and those violent, wracking sobs which can exhaust as well as purify. Instead, Carr remained motionless, his still hand fixed on his lapel, his fingers now at rest on the table, and his eyes averted from Isobel's face, as if to look at her would have been to intrude into her.

"I have very specific business here in Little Marsham," she said at last. The voice was quiet but in control of itself, although Carr was compelled to incline his head towards her in order to make out the words. "Private business, I should say."

Whether she had meant it as a means of warning him not to intrude, or whether it had been a mild rebuke for any previous invasion of her privacy, he could not say. He hoped it was not the latter, as such an intrusion had not been his intent, but it might easily be the former. He bowed his head and said simply, "Of course, dear lady."

"There is something very important I must do," she added, "which I hope will not take long. Once it is done, by tomorrow morning, I shall leave the village and never return."

Carr smiled at her and raised his glass to her. "Then, whatever it is, I wish you well in it. And I hope you obtain the outcome you desire."

She nodded her thanks with a brief, curt movement of her head. Looking across at him, she could see that something of what she had said had intrigued him, but, likewise, she could detect in those dark eyes something approaching regret. "Please, Mr Carr, don't think that you have offended me in any way. You've been very kind to a stranger, and I do appreciate it."

"Not at all," he said, bowing his head.

"You seem to be a very kind man."

He smiled at her. "Kindness is an increasingly rare quality in the world, Mrs Croft. We must keep it alive as best we can."

She wondered, for a moment, not so much what he meant by it but what had prompted him to say it. The immediate anxiety in those dark eyes had vanished now, but she had the impression that there was something deeper, a darker sadness, behind their blackness. He had given her the courtesy not to pry, and she now reciprocated. And yet, something about him fascinated her, and she found herself wishing that she could meet him again, to come to know him better, but the idea was nothing more than a fragmented and momentary daydream.

She replaced her hat, veil, and gloves before rising from her seat. He did likewise. She held out her hand, and he shook it gently before placing his lips softly on the gloved knuckles. "Goodbye, Mr Carr."

"Mrs Croft."

He watched her walk out of the bar, but he did not look out of the window to see in which direction she chose to go. Instead, he sat down once more and remained in silent thought for several minutes, the only sound being the distant chatter of the pub and the crackle and hiss of the flames of the fire. He had picked up his cane, and now he turned it carelessly in his fingers, the lights of the inn glittering in the silver of the handle. Finally, he gave an impatient click of the tongue and eased himself up from his seat. He pulled on his long, dark overcoat with the velvet collar, placed his felt hat on his head, and wrapped a long, woollen scarf around his neck. He limped out of the bar, smiling a note of thanks to the landlord, and he made his way back to the Church of St Bartholomew.

There was no sign of Isobel Croft or the Reverend Mr Bowers. The church, silent and foreboding against the early evening sky, loomed out across the equally still stones of the cemetery. The silence was intense but peaceful, which made the sense of apprehension which crept along Carr's shoulders all the more alarming. He looked up to the top of the bell tower, thinking to himself that any peal of bells in this heavy quiet would seem to shatter the foundations of the Earth itself.

He walked into the cemetery as the wind began to rise around him. Carr was not a superstitious man, but there was something about this sudden gust of natural air in this place of the dead which struck him as being unnervingly apposite. He made his way along the narrow pathway of the churchyard, his gaze switching from the gravestones to the door of the church, in case Bowers should appear to greet him. But Carr was to remain alone there for the duration of his visit.

He could recall well enough where he and Bowers had seen Isobel Croft. Carr had not made any particular mental note of her position at the time, but he felt sure that he was now standing in the same spot as she had done. She had been standing in front of the stone on the furthest left of the front row, below an overhanging branch of one of the many, customary yew trees in the churchyard. The history of yew trees in churchyards was known to Carr, but it did not enter his head now. Instead, he was looking down at the modest, almost perfunctory inscription on the stone in question, with its tragically short timespan between the dates of birth and death. The name across the top of the stone meant nothing to Carr, and nor had he expected it to, but William Lorrimer must have meant something to Isobel Croft, he thought, and the relationship must have been close enough for her to come, in full mourning, to this small, seemingly insignificant village so soon after his death. The conclusion that she had been Lorrimer's sister had been reached almost as soon as Carr had read the prosaic inscription on the unprepossessing marker of death.

How William Lorrimer had died, Carr could not know, any more than he could know what business it was which Isobel Croft had to complete by the following morning. Carr could know none of it, but he could suppose, and he had no hesitation in supposing a connection between the two events. Curiously, he had a notion of a consequence of that connection, but it was an instinctive reaction only, and he could not be sure of its veracity. Nevertheless, he seemed to feel a sudden sensation of doom descend onto him, so heavily that he found himself rolling his shoulders, as if to relieve himself of it. He wrapped the scarf more tightly around his neck and turned on his heel.

He walked towards the church and stepped inside. It was empty. Moving as swiftly as he could, cursing his broken bones with silent oaths, Carr made his way to the vicarage. He knocked on the door, once, twice, three times, none of them eliciting any response. He looked up at the windows but saw no sign of Bowers. He supposed a vicar's duties were many and varied, and it was surely unreasonable, let alone naïve, for Carr to expect the man to be shackled to the confines of his church and home. Defeated, Carr limped back down the narrow path of the churchyard and left the place behind him. If he were to satisfy his instincts at once, he would have to do so without Bowers' immediate help. Isobel was staying at *The Marsham Tuns,* and she would surely need to return there at some point to sleep. It was a meagre plan, to sit and wait for her to return, or even leave word with the landlord that Carr wished to speak to her, but it was all his troubled mind could concoct for the present. By the time he was back in the centre of the village, no better plan had formed in his mind, and Everett Carr returned to his temporary place of residence in order to put the plan into effect.

Although he had no way of knowing it as he spoke to the landlord of *The Marsham Tuns,* however, had Carr looked back up at the top windows of the vicarage before leaving the churchyard, he would have seen Gerald Bowers, staring back down at him, the freshly bloodied whip hanging loosely between the vicar's fingers.

Chapter Ten

Early the next morning, Philip Ryman was seated at his desk in his office.

He had risen, dressed, and left the house before Angela had woken, so that the possibility of any further argument could be discounted without hesitation. As he had washed, he had looked at himself in the shaving mirror and wondered who the man staring back at him really was. It seemed not to be a face Ryman recognised, the features simultaneously the same but altered beyond recognition. The eyes were still blue, but they no longer held the vivid ambition of his youth; they were now heavy with anxiety and regret. Similarly, the mouth, once set in a seemingly permanently confident smile, now hung downwards, as if invisible weights of despair were suspended from the ends of it. His cheeks, never anything but thin, now seemed to have fallen in on themselves, giving an impression closer to that of a skull rather than a human face. Ryman thought back to the past, when he had been a handsome and determined young man, a country mile away from the defeated, desolate husk he was now. No wonder Angela despised him, although she could not hate him any more than he despised himself.

He sat now in the leather armchair which had been his father's, when the old man himself had occupied this same office. The memory of his father caused Ryman a pain which was almost physical in its intensity, so that he smarted against it. The old man would never have allowed things to get this far, of course, simply because he would not have permitted them to occur in the first instance. His father had loved his mother, Ryman had no doubt of that, but he would never have allowed her to dominate him. He would have refused her if he felt she deserved it. It was not that Ryman's father was a bully or unreasonable in complying with his wife's requests. But if he had felt that she was behaving unreasonably, he would have said so. He would have asserted himself when he felt it was necessary, and, in doing so, Ryman supposed that he would have garnered respect from the woman with whom he had chosen to spend his life. Similarly, in her own way, his mother would have resisted his father as far as she felt it necessary and, within reason, he would have compromised. It was, Ryman thought, what made the marriage not only a partnership, but a successful one.

And what of his own marriage? It was useless to compare the two, just as it was futile to liken him to his father. His father had taken a wife, but not at the expense of his own character. Ryman, conversely, had sacrificed his natural obligation to be true to himself for the sake of having the woman he desired. Just as she still was, Angela had been very beautiful when he had first known her, and he had been, in his own eyes, a stiff, awkward, and foolish young man. A starched shirt of professionalism compared to her flowing dress of freedom. Initially, therefore, he had not been able to believe himself worthy of her love. He had been certain that her attraction to him was transient, whereas his for her was profound, and he was keenly aware that she could abandon him for someone else without a moment's thought. It had not been as if there was a shortage of successors to his throne. And so, in those first, crucial weeks of courtship, Ryman had bowed to every whim, refused no demand, and denied no request.

The result had been obvious, although he had still not foreseen it. Once he had set the trend, she had come to expect it. Their union swiftly degenerated into a series of demands, insistences, and entitlements. Ryman's mother had been frugal, whereas Angela was a spendthrift. Dresses required replacing without reason and, with it, shoes and jewellery had to compliment. Refusal was an impossibility, not only because Angela had never come to expect it, but also on account of Ryman's own inability to deny her in any case.

As time passed, this paranoid protection of the relationship had developed into a habit and, like many habits, it had become destructive. Only now, years after the event, was it entirely self-evident that the course Ryman had chosen for himself had been a financially disastrous one. Angela's happiness, and his inability to deny it, had required money, of course, which had not been a problem at the outset. Later, Ryman came to realise how much he had spent on his wife and how little control he had exerted over that spending. Suddenly, he had found that there was far less in his reserve than he had thought. How easy it was to lose money and how difficult it was to replace. The legal practice was healthy, but it would not support the crisis alone. Ryman had found that additional funds were required, and it had seemed so easy to make the decision on how to obtain them. The initial race meetings had been a success, as had the first trips to the gaming rooms he had heard about in London. The allure of chance, the roll of dice, and the turns of cards had served him well, and his heart had swelled with hope. But, as his marriage had done, the initial necessity for money degenerated into a habit. And, as Philip Ryman had learned, when one has risen, one can only fall. The cruel irony of driving her away by trying so desperately to keep her happy was not lost on him. It was just one more source of agony.

It had been William Lorrimer, of course, who had caused the deceit to come close to exposure. How he had discovered what Ryman had been compelled to do, Ryman did not know, and perhaps it was irrelevant. What mattered was surely what Lorrimer could do with the knowledge. It made him as much of a threat to Ryman as those men in London whose names and faces Ryman could seldom bring himself to remember. Men like those he could expect to be as dangerous and malignant as they were, but Lorrimer had seemed insignificant by comparison, which seemed to make his particular threat to Ryman all the more terrible. There was something sinister about the insinuation of power which had accompanied Lorrimer's threat which struck Ryman as far more potent than any London threat of broken bones.

Angela had been right, of course. Lorrimer's death had been a blessing; because of it, Ryman would be able to continue what he had felt forced into starting, and, as a result, he might save himself from those other dangers as long as he could remain undetected. It was a strange sensation to have, this gratitude for another man's death, but Ryman could not deny it. He thought back to Angela's words a week ago, to her suggestion that Lorrimer's death had been perhaps too convenient for him. Her insinuation had been clear, but Ryman was not sure how seriously she took it. Without proof, how seriously could she take it?

It was this same absence of proof which had prevented him from voicing his own concerns about her. He had told her to be honest with herself, he recalled, but he had been unable to say more, not without proof to support his suspicions. It was curious, he thought, how something could be certain in one's own mind, so that it was nothing less than an absolute fact, but without any actual evidence in support of it, as if one's own instincts were corroboration enough of the point in question. And Ryman was absolutely convinced in his own mind that Angela was seeing someone else. There were several men in the village whom Ryman felt unable to trust, but only one whom he knew for certain to be a hypocrite. Only one for whom another man's wife was a temptation, someone whose calm and soothing manner would be easily seductive to a woman like Angela. Ryman knew already that his wife had a connection with the man concerned, just as Mary Jerrold had.

Ryman remembered the Jerrold scandal all too clearly, and his surprise had matched his disappointment when Gerald Bowers had not been removed from his post. Henry Jerrold's compulsion to leave Little Marsham in the wake of the rumours about his wife and Bowers, when the vicar himself had been permitted to remain in place, was nothing less than an insult. Certainly, if this history were about to repeat itself with his own wife, Ryman would not feel compelled to leave, but he would ensure, one way or another, that Bowers' hypocrisy in Little Marsham would come to an end.

His thoughts were interrupted by the sound of the telephone bell. The sound, shrill and unexpected, startled him, and he gasped in a sudden breath of air. He was expecting no calls and, as he reached out for the receiver, he felt an insidious sense of dread creep up his spine, like a prediction of inevitable doom. He spoke into the mouthpiece as calmly as possibly, but the tremble in his voice was impossible to disguise.

The voice on the other end of the connection, so familiar and so despised, wasted no time with any pleasantries. "You've not been in contact recently, Ryman."

The words transfixed him with the same terror as if a knife had been placed across his throat. His grip on the telephone tightened, and his tongue seemed to become too loose to form words properly. "I have had business to attend to."

"Only our business should matter to you."

Ryman could feel the beads of sweat forming on his temples and upper lip. "I will have a payment for you by the end of the month."

"The connection must be faulty," said the voice. "I thought you said by the end of the month."

Ryman closed his eyes. "I need time, but I can get the money."

"You've had time. If you can't take the strain, old boy, you shouldn't play with the bigger boys."

Ryman could hear the threat in the voice, the reference to schoolyard tugs of war games being all the more menacing for their evocation of childhood innocence. He seemed to feel the pain of the retributions they would mete out to him for his inability to meet his debts. How could he have ever imagined that the turn of a card or the throw of a die could be so deadly?

"But I was paying, wasn't I?" he said, his breathing laboured under the fear of the future. "I was sending you money regularly. It's just that something happened which forced me to stop."

"What?"

"Someone became an obstacle to me for a while."

"Who?"

"It doesn't matter."

"What sort of obstacle?"

Ryman struggled to find the words to respond. "He discovered what I was forced to do to pay you. That doesn't matter either. What's important is that he's no longer a problem for me."

"And why's that?"

It was obvious from the tone of the voice on the other end of the line that the answer had already been guessed. But Ryman complied in any event. "He's dead."

The chuckle which followed, low and malicious, was obscene. "Maybe we underestimated you, Ryman. It seems you're prepared to take the biggest gamble of them all."

Ryman shook his head, as if they were able to see his physical denial as well as hear his verbal one. "He killed himself."

"Whatever you say, old boy." There was a new quality to the voice now, an almost impressed note of camaraderie, as if the two men speaking down the telephone wires were now somehow linked by a common act of violence. Ryman had no doubt that this man was no stranger to murder. For people like him, as with all of the ones concerned with him, murder was a way of life. "How about I give you two weeks? For a fellow lover of the tables."

The words of gratitude, which fell clumsily from Ryman's mouth, were unctuous in their sycophancy, and he despised himself for them. More so, perhaps, than the villain on the other end of the line.

"Don't disappoint us, Ryman," came the final warning. "Much as I like a little country village like yours, I don't want to leave London just now. Take my meaning?"

"I take it," hissed Ryman, as the violent purpose behind the seemingly harmless remark made itself clear to him.

The call was terminated. Ryman placed the receiver back onto the cradle of the telephone and slumped down in his chair. His breathing was shallow, the temptation to give into futile sobs almost overwhelming, but he conquered it. A small victory, one which passed by him unnoticed. His mouth was dry, as parched as a shipwrecked sailor whose thirst would turn him eventually to seawater. Ryman perhaps was not quite so desperate, and a carafe of water and a glass were routinely placed on his desk each morning by Miss Grange. He reached for them now and threw back the water as if it were whisky. It quenched the thirst, but it did nothing to drown the fear.

Chapter Eleven

Edgar Corrigan accepted the cup of tea with a smile. "I'm so glad you invited me over. Is everything all right?"

Harriet Delaney nodded her head, a smile creeping across her lips. "Everything is fine. Am I not allowed to want to see the man I love?"

They were sitting on the settee in Harriet's cottage. Lunchtime had long since passed, but the afternoon sun was showing no signs of dimming, and the air was fresh without being damp, so that the day could have belonged to spring as easily as it did to autumn. Harriet had not been out of the cottage that day, preferring instead to remain indoors, but it was clear from the glow in Edgar's cheeks that he had been for a recent walk. Simply by looking at him, seeing the clear effects of fresh air and exercise, she felt exhausted. She had not slept well, her dreams being troubled and spasmodic, and she had risen long before her body had been ready for it. She had never been able to lie purposelessly in bed when unable to sleep, particularly when something specific was troubling her. Drowsiness had begun to descend on her immediately prior to Edgar's arrival, but Harriet knew that sleep would still elude her, even if she attempted to succumb to the definite sleepiness which her body told her she was feeling. By contrast, Edgar had clearly slept without trouble, and no matter how far he had walked, he was as full of energy as an excitable, newly-born puppy. She did not say so, and she rebuked herself for thinking it, but Harriet was close to finding his vigour as exhausting as her lack of sleep.

As if capable of reading her thoughts, Edgar said, "You look done in, darling. Are you all right?"

She nodded, smiling at his concern. "A bad night, that's all."

"Do you want me to go, so you can rest?"

Harriet shook her head and took hold of his hand, kissing his knuckles tenderly. "I wouldn't have invited you here if I felt like that."

"Good. And I'd much rather be here than up at the house."

She frowned. "Why?"

"Something strange going on with the old folks," said Edgar, his face suddenly serious and the eyes more intense than usual. The canine excitement in him had faded, as if burning itself out with its intensity.

"In what way?"

He shifted his position so that he could face her, placing his cup and saucer back onto the silver tray. "I was on the top landing, and I saw Father at the drawing room door, leaning towards it, as if he were listening to something going on inside. After a few moments, the door opened, and Mother stepped out. Father asked her who she had been talking to and she replied that she had been on the telephone."

"Nothing unusual in that."

Edgar conceded the point whilst simultaneously holding up a cautionary finger. "But there is something unusual about mother speaking in hushed tones."

"And was she?"

"So father said. 'Why were you whispering? Secret assignations, Elsa?'"

"What did she say in response?"

Edgar smiled. "She told the old devil to mind his own business. But he said that if she was telling someone on the telephone that she would see what she could do and that life was unbearable, he had a right to know about it."

Harriet made no effort to conceal her shock. "What did she mean?"

Edgar shook his head. "I don't know, but she must have said it. Father wouldn't make that up to her face, would he? Anyway, she told him that her private conversations were no concern of his. And then," he added, as if it had been an afterthought, "she said something very odd. She told him not to pretend he cared what she did when his interests lay elsewhere in the village."

Harriet stared at him, her mouth opened in a startled but silent scream, as the obvious implication settled into her consciousness. "She doesn't mean...?"

Edgar shrugged. "What else can she mean? I don't think I'd put it past him."

She tightened her grip on his hand. "Oh, darling, I'm so sorry."

"It's not him I worry about; it's Mother. I hate to think of her being unhappy, especially on account of him. If it is true, I wonder who the woman concerned is."

Harriet inhaled deeply and raised her eyebrows. She sat forward and picked up her tea. "Perhaps it is best not to know." And then, after some thought, she looked back at him. "Is that why you went for a walk? To get away from it?"

If it had been his motive for the walk, he did not seem to have recognised it as such. "Perhaps so, yes. Although I hadn't consciously thought of it."

She found herself gazing at him, as if seeing him again for the first time. She stared at those wide, imperfect eyes with their conflicting colours and the long nose whose tip flinched slightly as he pursed his lip to blow cooling air across the surface of the tea. "I've got a very silly face," he had once said to her, "but I can only blame my parents for it." She had laughed, freely and without any pretence, and she had known almost immediately that he was a man whom she could love. He might not be excitingly charming, still less dangerously alluring, but he was reliable, loving, and candid. She thought now, as she looked at him sipping the tea, that he was everything William Lorrimer had not been. Lorrimer had fooled her, by allowing what she now knew had been his natural spite and malice to lurk unseen beneath only the most fragile veneer of tenderness. Edgar had no such pretences. Harriet wondered how it could be possible to claim to love someone when the personality you exposed to them was itself a lie, as Lorrimer had done with her. And, when it came to it, who was the real victim of the lie? After all, Lorrimer had lied not only to Harrier but to himself. Surely, that was the most terrible deception of all.

"I thought we might drive into Fernchester this evening," Edgar was saying. "Have a meal out somewhere."

Harriet smiled but shook her head. "Do you mind if we don't? I told you I haven't slept very well."

His brow creased in concern. "You're not still worrying about people blaming you for Lorrimer killing himself?"

Harriet shrugged. "Partly, I suppose."

"What else, then?"

She lowered her gaze from him and began to scratch at a finger which did not itch. "Just ghosts, Edgar."

"You mean Lorrimer." He rose from the settee and walked over to the hearth, his hands in his pockets. "He's never out of your head, is he?"

"Not in the way you fear."

He smiled, but there was no humour in it. "Foolish, isn't it? To be jealous of a dead man."

She got up and almost ran to his side. "You mustn't be jealous of him. There's no reason to be. I didn't want him anymore. I wanted you. And I still do."

He accepted it with a brief nod of the head, but his eyes remained fixed on the hearth rug. "But he holds an allure for you which I can never hope to have."

She shook her head sadly. "I wish he didn't have it, believe me."

As if to miss the point intentionally, Edgar said, "You admit it, then."

She felt as if she had come to a dead end in a maze, but when she turned back to retrace her steps, she found only another dead end facing her. "You don't understand."

"I'd like to."

And she wished she could make him, but the necessary words would not come. Those which did seemed inadequate. "It's the shock of what he did, I suppose. The violence of it, the desperation of it, of knowing that there was no other option left but that one, terrible finality. I can't get it out of my mind, Edgar, and it frightens me."

However futile she might have thought the words were, they seemed to have the desired effect. In their wake, Edgar recognised at once the petulant selfishness of his petty jealousy, and he was instantly ashamed of it. He put his arms around her shoulders and kissed her lightly on the head, the blonde hair lightly caressing his cheeks.

"Never mind me," he said. "I just don't want to share you with anybody."

She didn't reply, but the apology was not dismissed. She remained motionless in his arms, her arms by her side. They remained locked in the embrace, with the silence between them lingering, until it was broken by the snap of the letterbox.

Harriet seemed to be startled by the sudden noise, and Edgar felt as if he, too, had been woken from a sleepless dream. She pushed herself away from him and walked towards the door, leaving him standing before the fire. She returned to the room with only one envelope in her hands, which she proceeded to open. She pulled out the single, folded sheet of paper, tossed the envelope onto the fire, and swiftly read the letter once and then, more carefully, a second time. Edgar watched her face, the blue eyes darting over the words and her lips moving slightly, almost imperceptibly, as she took in the meaning of the correspondence. He was surprised to notice a darkening of her expression, which suggested that the contents of the letter had been either unwelcome or unexpected.

"Is everything all right?" he asked, crossing the room to join her. He looked at the letter in her hands, taking in the detail of the embossed legend at the head of it, spelling out the name of a firm of solicitors, with an accompanying address in the centre of London.

Harriet nodded distractedly. "Yes, absolutely. Just something of a shock, that's all." She realised she was making no sense, and she shook her head, as if to dislodge any further opportunity for confusion or misunderstanding. "I'm afraid an old lady I once knew has died, and I have been left something in the will."

The news surprised Edgar perhaps more than it had shocked her, and he was unable to disguise the fact. "I thought you had no living family."

Harriet smiled at him and placed a hand on his cheek. "She wasn't a relative, although I did call her my aunt. She was just a kind old lady who befriended me when I was a little girl. I never knew why. I haven't seen her for years." A note of sadness came into her voice. "That was my fault. Not intentionally, you understand. Life just happened, like it does. I'm ashamed to say I'd forgotten about her. Poor Miss Liddell. She obviously hadn't forgotten me."

She was crying now and, once again, she felt his arms around her. His breath came out from between his teeth in soothing, comforting hisses, like the waves of the sea against rocks. The sobbing was silent and mercifully brief and, after only a few moments of it, Harriet pulled herself out of his embrace and wiped her eyes with the palm of her hand. Edgar, foolishly gallant, handed her his handkerchief.

"I'm sorry, Edgar," she said. "It is just one more shock on top of everything else."

"Of course, I understand."

Harriet pointed to the letter. "The solicitors want me to make an appointment to go to their offices in London to discuss it all. I suppose I'd better do it straightaway."

Edgar nodded. "I'll let you get on with it, then."

But Harriet shook her head and tossed the letter onto the settee. "It can wait. I want to clear my head first, try to forget everything which is racing through my mind. You're right, Edgar, darling. I've been cooped up in the cottage all morning and it isn't good for me. Let's go for a walk, and perhaps I'll let you persuade me to pop into *The Marsham Tuns* for an hour or two."

Edgar's smile was as full of pleasure as his heart. "There's nothing in there for me to argue with."

She laughed, and the sound exhilarated him. "I'll go and get my hat. Wait there."

As if there would be anywhere else he would prefer to go. Edgar watched as she ran to the hatstand and took from it a navy, brimmed slouch hat which he knew to be a particular favourite of hers. She paired it with a long coat of matching colour and presented herself to him as if she were on parade.

"Ready if you are," she said.

He offered his arm, and she took it. "Let's go and show the world how it's done."

When she smiled, she knew that she had never loved him as much, and she recognised that the long-forgotten sensation which now seemed to overwhelm her was a feeling of carefree, undiluted happiness. For the first time in what seemed like an age, death did not dominate the thoughts of Harriet Delaney, and for that, she could only thank Edgar Corrigan.

Chapter Twelve

Darkness had fallen without remorse when Bowers found the body.

He had spent the majority of the afternoon and early evening preparing his sermon for the following Sunday's service and, as the sun fell below the horizon, he had made for himself a tasty but frugal meal, which he had eaten in silence, with only his thoughts and a small glass of wine for company. The wine was both excellent and comforting, but the thoughts were nothing less than troublesome.

He had felt certain that Everett Carr had not seen him in the window on the previous day; if he had, he would surely have persisted in banging on the vicarage door or, more likely, by shouting up at the window itself, making it impossible for Bowers to ignore him. The fact that Carr had limped away from the church suggested that he had seen nothing. For that, at least, Bowers could be grateful. As if to remind him of the fact his back burned with a cathartic pain from the latest lashes across it, now in their initial stages of healing. Why Carr had felt the need to return to Lorrimer's grave was uncertain, but Bowers suspected that he had come into contact with the woman called Isobel Croft. If so, Bowers could not help but wonder whether Mrs Croft had repeated her concerns about the death of her brother to Carr himself. Certainly, if she had, it could not have failed to pique the man's interest.

After all, Bowers himself could not pretend that he had been able to put aside what Isobel Croft had said. On the contrary, her words seemed to echo throughout his mind with every thought he had for the sermon, and they seemed to reverberate from every verse of the Gospels which he read in preparation. Her words were persistently intrusive. What Isobel Croft could know about the death of William Lorrimer, which had escaped the court's notice, and that of Little Marsham itself, Bowers could not say, nor could he tell what it was about her knowledge which would lead her to the conclusion that her brother was murdered. The more he had thought about it, the less he had been able to accept that she knew anything at all. Surely it was more likely that her natural grief at his sudden death, and the violent nature of it, would cloud her judgement, leaving her unable to admit that Lorrimer had a reason or the will to kill himself. A blind refusal to accept what was obviously the truth, even in the wake of a coroner's verdict, was not an uncommon human reaction. People were, as Bowers was only too keenly aware, inclined to lie to themselves instead of admitting a more credible, but infinitely more terrible truth.

It had been with this train of thought that Bowers had consoled himself when his efforts to find Isobel Croft had failed. It had been only a brief moment of indecision on his part, but it had been sufficient to delay too long in retrospect. As matters had turned out, it was not until after teatime that Bowers had made his way to the village in search of Isobel. He had not known for certain where to find her, but there were not many places for a stranger to stay in Little Marsham, so that it was not unreasonable to assume that she would have found accommodation at *The Marsham Tuns*. She might have booked a hotel in Fernchester, he supposed, but Carr's return to the gravestone suggested otherwise. And yet, neither Carr nor Isobel Croft had been in the tavern when Bowers made his enquiries, which left the vicar with little option other than to return to the vicarage. To distract his mind from Isobel Croft, he had begun those preparations for his forthcoming sermons and, during them, he had begun to convince himself that Isobel was acting only under a delusion of grief. It did not explain why Everett Carr had come to look at Lorrimer's grave, however, but Bowers could solve that particular mystery by simply asking the man in question about it on the following morning, a course of action which Bowers resolved to take.

It had been when he made the decision that the vicarage telephone had rung. Bowers, unaccustomed to the disturbance at this time of day, had answered it with caution. "Hello, vicarage?"

Her voice had been frantic. "Can I speak to you? It's very important."

"Are you all right?"

"It's you I'm worried about."

"Me?"

"Please." There had been almost tears in her voice as well as, he had felt sure, in her eyes.

"What has happened?"

"I must see you in person."

"Very well."

And the appointment had been made. After it was over, when the words and the warnings had been spoken, Bowers walked slowly back to the church, his mind uneasy. The memories had been forced to resurface, and he had the terrible sensation of history repeating itself. As if to encourage his fears, the scars on his back, new and old, began to burn. His mind seemed to drown in recollections of he and Mary Jerrold, sitting in the vicarage parlour, either in companionable silence or in the deepest of conversations. Either circumstance was, for Bowers, a matter of pleasure and privilege. The memory of her sitting opposite him, and latterly beside him, closer than perhaps was prudent, was in turn enthralling and devastating, reminding him as it did not only of the feelings he had held for her, but also the painful absence of her from his present life. How strange it was, he thought, that such wonderful memories could be simultaneously so warm and yet so cold, how they could comfort and distress in equal measure, as if they were the tricks of a capricious spirit. And now, it seemed, the whole sorry story was in danger of being relived, but this time without any justification.

It was when he walked through the gates of the churchyard, at a little after ten o'clock, that he heard the noise. It was muffled, but it was unmistakably the sound of running feet, fleeing in the opposite direction to which he was walking. He looked out across the graves themselves, his senses seemingly heightened by his unease and anticipation of danger, but there was no sign of the intruder, whoever it had been. He now began to walk towards the rows of the stones of the dead, his anxiety rising and his breathing becoming increasingly shallow, like that of a man who had run for miles, even though he had taken only a few, hesitant steps. At last, the breath froze in his throat, as his eyes fell onto the horror.

Lying at the base of one of the graves, a grave which he knew instinctively to be William Lorrimer's, there was a mass of black. The lace-veiled hat was askew on her head, dislodged when she had fallen to the ground. Her legs were splayed at an unnatural angle, and the arms were spread out to the sides, as if she were waiting for some sort of hideous, morbid embrace. She was motionless and, even before he had pulled out his matches and struck a light, Bowers knew that she was dead. The stillness of her body, the immobility of the limbs, and the grotesque position of the body, the spine, and hips twisted in an abnormal curve, as if there had been no feeling as she had tumbled to the ground, showed that there could be no life.

The sudden fizz of the match and the seemingly blinding flash of light of the flame only served to confirm Bowers' fears. Death now lay fresh across the grass of the cemetery and, as if to herald it, the leaves of the yew trees hanging above the scene hissed in the night breeze. The front of the black coat now seemed darker, caused by the blood emanating from the multiple stab wounds to the area surrounding the heart. The eyes which looked up at the sky had the glossy, unreal stare of a doll. The red lips were parted, showing the top row of slightly misaligned teeth, and the naturally pale skin now seemed like the underside of a fish, its pallor no longer delicate or attractive, but cold and dead.

Bowers blew out the match only when the flame had begun to burn the tips of his fingers. The darkness which followed seemed supernaturally intense and, notwithstanding his shock at finding this horror in the churchyard, his first instinct was to seek the comfort of more light. He struck another match and forced himself to look once more at what lay at his feet, at this product of murder which stared up at him, the dead lying amongst the dead.

Isobel Croft.

She had said that the death of her brother had been murder. Now, it was she who lay at the grave of that same, dead brother, herself the victim of the very crime which she had come to Little Marsham to expose.

III

PART THREE: INVESTIGATION

Chapter Thirteen

Everett Carr looked down at what had once been Isobel Croft.

He was not shocked by the sight of murder, having seen its effects more often than he would have liked, but he was typically saddened by it. It had long been a mystery to him how any human being could ever feel the need to take the life of another. It resisted every instinct he had himself, subverting every emotional compulsion he held, so that whilst he might be able to comprehend a personal motive for murder, the execution of that impulse to kill remained inexplicable to him. It was a transgression of his firm belief that every human being, however saintly or sinful, had the right to live life to its natural end.

Bowers had telephoned *The Marsham Tuns* and insisted that the landlord wake Carr from his slumbers. Having heard the news, Carr had dressed swiftly and had hurried across the village to the churchyard.

"I am sorry," Bowers had stammered, his breath billowing from his lips like the smoke from a burning house. "I panicked, and I didn't know what to do. I wanted a friendly face to reassure me, I suppose. It is so awful. Oh God!"

Carr had made no reply. Instead, he had limped slowly over to the body which lay across the path of the gravestone, as if it had somehow risen from the soil and the moss only to fall down once more after exposure to the night air. "We must call the police at once."

Bowers, his eyes widened with tearful panic, and his hands wringing themselves together as much from fear as from a need to keep out the cold, had nodded. "How stupid of me. I didn't think. Stupid, stupid."

Carr had ignored this self-recrimination; indeed, he had barely heard it. "Telephone them now, Mr Bowers. Any delay will be fatal."

Now, alone, Carr knelt beside the body, his attention caught by one of the hands. It was barely visible in the darkness, but Carr had the impression of something poking out from between the fingers. He peered closer, taking a silver cigarette lighter from his coat pocket and passing the flame across the hand, slowly so as not to extinguish the light in the gathering gloom. There, held tightly in between the finger and thumb, he could see a small triangle of paper, a distinctive blue-purple colour, like that of a newly blossoming bruise. Carr's instinct told him that it was the remnants of a letter or an envelope. It might mean nothing, but it was a strange thing for a woman to have in her hands in a cemetery. Stranger still, though, was why only a fragment of paper and not the letter or envelope itself was present.

Carr extinguished the flame and rose to his feet, as the sound of Bowers' voice stirred him from his musings. "Our local inspector and constable will be here shortly. Do you think we could perhaps cover her? For dignity's sake, if nothing else."

Carr shook his head slowly. "We must touch nothing. I know it must seem heartless, even inhumane, but it is absolutely necessary."

Bowers shrugged. "I bow to your experience."

Carr acknowledged the concession with a small tilt of his head. "The grave is that of a man called William Lorrimer, as you know. Mrs Croft was his sister, I gather."

"Did she tell you that?"

"No."

"Then how did you know it?"

Carr shrugged, thinking back to his casual deductions when he had returned to this very spot himself after his talk with Isobel Croft. "How did Lorrimer die?"

Bowers was visibly unsettled by the question and, sensing it, Carr's interest was immediately pricked. The vicar, knowing that his expression had said more than he would have dared himself, took a deep breath and explained. "A week ago, if you had asked me that, I would have said he shot himself. Certainly, that was the verdict of the coroner's inquest."

"But now you doubt that verdict?" Carr felt a familiar crackle of anticipation pulse along his spine.

"I wouldn't have done if it were not for something Mrs Croft said."

Carr's eyes were now as darkly intense as the night sky. "What did she say?"

Bowers shook his head. "I put it down to grief, an inability to accept what her brother had done. I'm afraid I didn't take it seriously."

Carr's instincts prickled. "What didn't you take seriously, Mr Bowers?"

The vicar looked into those dark, persuasive eyes, so different from the gentle, almost avuncular voice. "Mrs Croft thought that Lorrimer had been murdered."

The word, once spoken, seemed to foul the air with its dread. Carr looked back to the body and considered it for a moment. Bowers was surprised that Carr was not more shocked than he appeared to be. It was as if he had known all along what had been in Isobel's mind and, further, as if he knew what had passed between her and the vicar.

"Did she have any proof of that?" asked Carr, his glare returning to Bowers.

"She said so, but she didn't elaborate. She said only that she wanted justice for her brother."

"The justice of a vengeful, rancorous God?" Carr smiled at Bowers' startled astonishment. "Do not be alarmed, my boy. I have not been eavesdropping or spying on you. Mrs Croft talked to me about the Old Testament, too, just as she had with you. Tell me," he said, after a moment's thoughtful pause, "why would William Lorrimer have taken his own life?"

Bowers thought carefully about whether to reply. "I'm not a man for gossip, Mr Carr, but I suppose you would be able to find someone in the village eager enough to tell you all about it. He was in love with a girl called Harriet Delaney. A pretty and vibrant girl, she is, and Lorrimer was lucky to have caught her eye. But, unfortunately for him, her attention swayed elsewhere."

"She fell in love with someone else?"

Bowers nodded. "Edgar Corrigan, the son of the man who gifted the Van Jansen painting to the church."

Carr seemed genuinely saddened by the tragedy of it all. "The affairs of the heart, my boy. They are the cruellest tricks of all."

Bowers said nothing for a moment. "You said that this poor woman, Mrs Croft, spoke to you about God. Did she say anything else, by any chance?"

Carr inclined his head, the smile under his moustache and Imperial widening. "Anything in particular?"

"She told me that not only did she believe that her brother had been murdered, but that she also knew who the killer was." Bowers looked into Carr's eyes and saw the expectant question lingering in their dark gaze. But Bowers shook his head. "I'm afraid she didn't say who it was."

If Carr was disappointed, he said nothing about it, but one hand balled into a fist, and the other tightened its grip around the silver handle of his cane. "We may draw an obvious conclusion, though, may we not? A woman comes to this sleepy village after the death of her brother. She does not believe in this formal verdict of suicide, believing instead that her brother was murdered. No sooner has she voiced her suspicions, she herself dies. And, this time, there is no doubt that it is murder. It would seem that her suspicions have been confirmed."

"Can you be so sure?"

Carr pointed to the body of Isobel Croft and, in a voice which was less amiable than usual, said, "Do you think this is a coincidence? I should say it is very much cause and effect."

The vicar shook his head. "They found a suicide note, written in Lorrimer's own handwriting, addressed to Harriet Delaney. It was read out at the inquest. A vitriolic and malicious farewell to the world."

Carr frowned. "Then there must be some other explanation for it, one which we cannot guess. The fact is that this poor woman has been murdered, only shortly after saying she knew the identity of her brother's killer. We must reconcile those facts somehow."

Bowers wrapped his arms around himself, as much to shield him from the terror of the situation as the cold of the day. "It's horrible. And in my churchyard of all places."

"It had to be here, on this very specific spot, that is evident."

"Why so?"

"What better place to confront the person she thought had murdered him? Mrs Croft arranged to meet with the killer at her brother's grave to force them to confront what they had done to him." Carr paused, as if speaking the words aloud had caused him to consider a point in its reality for the first time. "Might I ask, my boy, what you were doing in the churchyard at all, this late in the evening?"

For a moment, Bowers seemed not to have understood the question. Whether he was offended by it being put to him or whether it had startled him by coming without warning, Carr could not tell, but the suddenly alert expression on the vicar's face, with its immediate reflection of a cornered animal, was impossible to deny. "I was in the vicarage, working on my sermons for Sunday."

If Carr knew it was a lie, he gave no indication of it, although Bowers was far from soothed by the smile which crept across Carr's face and the voice which said simply, "I see," was amiably innocuous.

Bowers, not altogether convinced that Carr believed him, thought further explanation was required, and this part, at least, would be true. "I heard running footsteps in the churchyard, you see, and I came out to investigate."

"What time was this?"

"The church clock had just struck ten."

"Well, if it was the murderer you heard, that timing will be of immense assistance to the police. Did you see anybody, or did you only hear these running footsteps?" Carr watched the shake of the head which formed Bowers' reply. "Of course, it may not have been the murderer, but someone who stumbled across the body. An open mind is a sensible thing to have in such circumstances."

Bowers pointed to the left. "The footsteps were running in that direction."

"Away from the main entrance to the churchyard? Could anybody get out of here that way?"

"There is a gate in the eastern wall of the cemetery."

Carr nodded his understanding. "And, of course, to flee in the direction of the main gate would mean that they would have to pass the vicarage, so whoever it was would have run into you." Carr placed a finger to his lips. "So, whoever killed Mrs Croft must have known about that second gate. Someone who knows the church well."

Bowers was unsure. "I would think everybody knows about it."

Carr smiled. "I didn't."

Simple words, but somehow Carr said them in a fashion which seemed to Bowers to be accusatory. For the first time, Bowers thought he had witnessed some indication of how formidable this dandy little man might have been when bringing a courtroom to order. He suddenly felt less at ease in Carr's presence, as if any small detail might betray a secret to him and his quiet, deceptively sharp mind.

That mind was now chartering a different course. "If the motive for Mrs Croft's murder is seemingly apparent, we must ask ourselves who might have had reason to murder her brother. In order to solve one clear case of murder, we must solve another less obvious one."

"We must solve it?" queried Bowers, as if the words had somehow been distorted by the night breeze.

Carr chuckled cheerily. "Forgive me, a slip of the tongue. The police must solve it, I meant to say, of course."

If Bowers had wished to probe Carr further on the matter of whether a private investigation might be contemplated, the headlamps of a car, almost blinding in their sense of authority, prevented him from doing so as they broke the darkness of the night. The purr of the engine was in itself a reassuring sound of officialdom, an impression which was increased by the sight of the two large silhouettes of men who emerged from the car. The headlamps remained on, so that the two approaching figures were kept in unidentifiable darkness, although Carr recognised the purposeful gait and determined swagger of a country police inspector and his subordinate well enough. Whatever amateur investigation into this mysterious death Bowers might have envisaged, the official enquiry into the murder of Isobel Croft was about to commence.

Chapter Fourteen

C arr had given his short statement to the police first, having indicated that Bowers' testimony would be more beneficial to them than his own. He did not feel inclined to divulge any of his preliminary thoughts to the local inspector, a man called Dunn, who had ignored Carr completely, preferring instead to delegate the task of taking Carr's statement to a detective sergeant by the name of Barlow, who had taken down Carr's words with a pleasing and impressive efficiency. Carr had not taken up much of Barlow's time and, having given assurances that he would not leave the village for the foreseeable future, he had left the churchyard of St Bartholomew's and returned to the relative comfort of *The Marsham Tuns*.

He slept as well as he might have hoped, but the memory of the body he had viewed, still raw and fresh in his mind, invaded his dreams like a bitter enemy. When he awoke, he felt refreshed enough to face the day, but the same thoughts which had plagued his rest now infiltrated his consciousness. Whatever proof Isobel Croft might have possessed in relation to the death of William Lorrimer, it had made her own death necessary, which meant that it was surely more than rumour and suspicion. And it also meant, he had no doubt, that someone had been clever enough to make a murder look sufficiently like suicide that the suspicions of the authorities had not been aroused. All of which was more than sufficient to tantalise the curiosity of Everett Carr.

A quiet enquiry of the landlord provided Carr with the location of William Lorrimer's cottage, and a small donation to the landlord's private income had ensured his discretion. News of the murder of Isobel Croft would break soon enough, as Carr was only too keenly aware, but it did not have to be down to him and, whilst the village was ignorant of the violence which had been done within it, Carr hoped that some meaningful and inconspicuous enquiries of his own could be made.

The cottage which Lorrimer had called home was almost indistinguishable from those which both immediately surrounded it and extended beyond it along the single high street of the village. The similarity of the red bricks and thatched rooves of the dwellings was comforting rather than repetitive, as if the uniformity of the housing was a reflection of the personal solidarity which can be found so often amongst the neighbours of a village such as Little Marsham. Carr might have found it quaintly reassuring himself, were it not for the darker thought which immediately occurred to him that this same, peaceful atmosphere had bred beneath its surface the initial causes and the eventual chaos and disruption of brutal death. With the thought simmering in his mind, he was conscious of the darkness of his suit against the cheerful colours of the well-preened flowers in the procession of identical gardens which stretched out before him, as if he were himself some sort of darkly shrouded manifestation of the violence which had disrupted the stillness of Little Marsham's charming tranquillity.

He was not unduly surprised to find that there was no sign of the police at Lorrimer's cottage. Their attention would be focussed primarily on Isobel's room at the inn, on her personal belongings, so that the connection with Lorrimer would be of a secondary importance at present. It was a matter of priorities and, whilst Carr had no doubt that Gerald Bowers would have told them of Isobel's suspicions about her brother, his death was a matter of the past. It would be an important factor, but policework was routine, and Isobel's death was the present. Carr, however, had no such routine to follow, and, as such, he felt no constraints of priority.

He may not have been surprised at the lack of a police presence, but he was nothing less than alarmed when he saw that a glass panel in the front door had been smashed. The hole, with its uneven and jagged edges, was large enough for him to get his hand through, he estimated, but it was not of such proportions that it suggested any significant force had been behind it. It was foolish, but the suggestion was that the breaking of the glass had been somehow timid, almost reluctant. Carr pressed his gloved finger against the wooden door itself and pushed gently. The door swung open without resistance, and Carr stepped over the threshold, at once aware that he was acting unofficially. He had no concern about that, but the adjoining sensation of invading the privacy of a man whom he had not known was shaming. Carr felt an immediate self-loathing and, as if the weight of it was a tangible strain on his shoulders, he almost turned away from the room which confronted him and back out into the open air. It was no more than a sweeping thought, almost a perfunctory nod to propriety, one which Carr's natural politeness demanded but which his equally instinctive curiosity could not honour.

The burglar, whoever he might have been, had not been careful in his search. Carr was aware at once of a general devastation, whose particulars were initially buried under the impression of their whole. Drawers were upturned, the contents forming haphazard piles of intrusion by the casual manner in which they had been discarded. The cushions of the small settee were pulled out of place, left now in a position which gave them the appearance of an untidy, ill-prepared Eastern divan. The flooring was as much scattered paper as it was the rugs placed carefully over the exposed boards, which had been treated with varnish. Paper folders and various files had been emptied and discarded, lying now like cardboard effigies of shot birds left with outspread wings. As far as Carr could tell, the papers were personal to Lorrimer: bank statements, various bills, invoices, and receipts. They would form part of the police enquiry, no doubt, but a cursory glance at them suggested that they were of little interest to Carr.

The mess aside, the room reflected the tastes and requirements of a man who made no apology for either. The paintings on the walls were a blend of modern and classical art, none of which belonged alongside each other. Their collective ugliness could not disguise their individual expertise, but the overall collection seemed to Carr to be one of an eclectic but indecisive mind, as if all the pieces were admired but at the expense of any tasteful selection of them. The rugs on the exposed wooden floors, too, neither complimented nor augmented the colour and style of the settee and chairs. The furniture was traditional, carved from oak in the Victorian fashion, but the lightshades and table lamps were incongruously modern. These juxtapositions were jarring rather than intriguing, although Carr wondered whether it was his own tastes which were altogether too stringent and conservative.

His eye was caught by a small table which had not been upturned. This fact alone, amid the wreckage of the rest of the room, made it conspicuous. Lying on top of it, the pages facing downwards, as if it had been placed to one side after reading of it had been disturbed, was a heavy, leather-bound volume. The lettering on the spine was gilt, but some of it had withered away with the passing of time, although the meaning of the words had not been entirely eroded: *Gemmel's History of Human Disease.* A heavy, ponderous medical tome, a textbook of sorts, designed for the official medical student and any layman who might take a passing interest in the history and mechanics of surgery and pathology. Frowning, Carr lifted the book gently and peered at the pages revealed to him. Whatever disturbance had interrupted Lorrimer's reading, it was clear that he had been immersed in a study of the causes and effects of injuries to the human brain. In particular, there was a section devoted to the research of James Ewing in America. The name meant nothing to Carr, but even the most cursory glance at the text suggested that Ewing's work was authoritative in terms of diagnosis and treatment of both benign and malignant tumours. Carr's frown intensified. It seemed an unusual topic to have interested Lorrimer. Had it been a tragic and personal interest? If so, did it mean that Isobel Croft was wrong? A disease which would fall within Ewing's expertise might be sufficient cause for a man afraid of pain and inevitable death to end his own suffering. Carr shrugged, replacing the book as he had found it, but not before he had taken note not only of the fact that it was a library book from Fernchester, but also the date upon which it had been taken out.

He continued with his search. There was a small, varnished bureau set into one alcove of the fireplace, in front of which was a stern chair, whose wooden seat and upright back gave the impression that the bureau was for work, not comfort. The drawers of the bureau were open, but their contents were not unduly disturbed, as if the intruder at last had found what he was looking for. Carr saw nothing of immediate interest himself: a collection of pencils standing upright in a small, wicker basket; personalised stationery in a variety of exclusive colours and designs; an ornate letter opener, sharp like a dagger, with a carved dragon's head on the hilt; a gold fountain pen and matching inkpot, set into a wooden case especially designed for their display. They were all necessary implements, but there was something arrogant about them, as if their functionality were not enough but had to be enhanced by a personal display of flamboyance.

It was not until he looked amongst the discarded papers on the blotter that Carr became interested. Initially, it was a curious phrase scrawled across the blotter itself which caught his attention. The writing appeared to be Lorrimer's own, if the other examples were to be taken in comparison, but there was something less formal about the script, as if it had been written in haste, so that the usual care taken in the construction of the words was lacking. Carr understood: it was an *aide* memoir, a note for Lorrimer's use only, something which had occurred to him at some point in the past and which he had felt needed instant immortality on the blotter. Carr peered closely at the words themselves, making sure that he was in no doubt about them, even if their meaning remained impossible to determine. The phrase was simple but so irrelevant that it might have been the ramblings of a madman: *the snake isn't real.*

Without further evidence, Carr had no means of explaining the phrase, so he simply docketed it away in his mind and resumed his search of the bureau. Several pages, torn from a notebook or simply taken from a sheet of foolscap, were scattered across the top of the writing desk of the bureau, each of them filled with jottings which, although random, all seemed to be adhering to the same theme. They were similar to dedications often found in novels, expressing gratitude or acknowledging support, except these messages ranged from being sentiments of love to declarations of hate, with every emotion in between being depicted with some turn of vindictive or valedictory phrasing. They were apologetic, remorseful, malicious, murderous, tragic, furious. They were the rambling thoughts of a troubled mind, each apparently centred around the same person, since the same single name appeared time and again throughout the tempest of words. *Harriet.*

As he flicked through the loose pages, Carr came across a photograph, removed from its frame. It was the image of what Carr took to be Harriet Delaney herself, taken somewhere near the sea, with the outline of a beach and the faraway horizon blurred behind her. She was holding her blonde hair out of her face, suggesting a strong breeze had been blowing, but the naked arms peering out of the summer dress showed that it had been a warm wind rather than a perishing one. It had been a day of happiness, Carr presumed, from the line of white teeth showing from under the parted, smiling lips.

All of which made the slashes through the photograph, presumably by one blade of a scissors, all the more terrifying. They seemed somehow far more violent, desecrating what had obviously been a once fond memory. In its way, the violated photograph echoed the scrawled messages on the sheets of paper, reflecting as they did a happiness turned into hatred.

Almost without thinking, Carr placed the defaced photograph of Harriet Delaney into his coat pocket. He took one of the pieces of paper and secluded it beside the photograph, leaving the rest for the police to find. He hesitated for a moment, his thoughts fixating on nothing in particular, and his dark eyes narrowed under the heavy, white brows. His lips pursed under the sculptured moustache, and he gave a slight shake of the head. Something was troubling him, but his mind refused to focus on it. It was the forgotten lyric of a song, the face seen in the street which was recognised but whose name was evasive, the incessant teasing of a task which had to be completed, but whose nature was momentarily unknown. He had seen something which was important, but what it was or why it was of significance merely danced on the periphery of his mind. Snarling with frustration, Carr slammed the ferrule of his stick on the floor and limped away from the bureau.

It was as he reached the front door that he saw something which he must have noticed when he had entered, but whose details he had ignored in that moment, his mind no doubt distracted initially by the overall devastation of the room. He had glanced briefly over these bills and invoices, but he had not consciously taken note of the single newspaper clipping which had been mixed with them in the ransacking of the house. Now, the columns of print and the blurred photograph which accompanied the article seemed only too clear to him, to the extent that he marvelled at his previous neglect of their existence.

He lowered himself to the floor, not without difficulty, and picked up the article. Rising to his feet, Carr glanced over the contents of the newspaper story. It was one which he recalled, since it had caused something of a controversy when it had broken: Linacre House, an orphanage, forced to close down amid allegations of cruelty and abuse. Carr's recollection was flawed, because the scandal, like so many others, had been swift to rise and even swifter to dissipate. Nevertheless, in its brief yet intense existence, it had caused a great deal of outrage and debate. Lorrimer, it seemed, had an interest in it even now, years after the event, although Carr was at a loss to explain that interest. His natural conclusion was that Lorrimer had been a child at Linacre, which was not impossible but hardly conclusive. And, if he had been, Carr could not think that it was likely he would wish to be reminded of his time there in the form of these newspaper clippings.

A thought occurred to him with the sudden shock of an explosion. With the tip of his walking stick, he rummaged around the surrounding papers, but there were no more clippings. Lorrimer, it seemed, had not been so interested in Linacre that he had collected articles about the place. He had only this one. The article was like so many of its time: a brief history of the allegations and speculation about the vanishing of the brother and sister who owned the iniquitous place and the doctor who had, wilfully or not, aided and covered for them. It was no different to a dozen others printed on the same day in various papers across the country. Carr's eyes hardened with thought. If the article was not special in itself, it was more likely to form part of a collection of others of its type. And yet, only this one remained.

Which led Carr to a single, yet fascinating conclusion. That Lorrimer did have an interest in Linacre House, that he had collected various articles about it, and that those articles had been discovered and removed in the burglary, this single one being dropped and left behind in haste. And that, in turn, thought Carr, led to a very interesting idea about whether the cruel sibling owners of the orphanage had concealed their identities with respectability and buried themselves in the small, quiet village of Little Marsham.

Chapter Fifteen

Once he had sat down to read it in detail, the solitary newspaper clipping, whilst short on historical background, was sufficient to stir memories in the mind of Everett Carr. He had returned to *The Marsham Tuns* and ordered a pot of hot coffee, with which he now sat in contemplative silence, the extract of the article resting on the table in front of him. The public bar of the inn was almost empty, and Carr was grateful for the quiet and the privacy.

Linacre House, at one time, had been originally the Thomas Linacre Hospital, founded in the mid-19th century, and something of the discipline of the Victorian medical procedure seemed to have remained in its structures, long after the final operation had been undertaken there. Even as an abandoned ghost of its former self, as it had been for many years since its closure, the building had seemed capable of exuding a sense of clinical efficiency, despite the windows of wood, the overgrown lawns, and dead bushes of the grounds. Notwithstanding these obvious signs of decay, the building had managed still to retain something of its former pride, as if it were waiting only for the time when it could be restored to its former magnificence. It was with the purchase of the property by Edwin and Marjorie Pryce that steps had been taken to do so.

Pryce had been a former schoolmaster in the north of England, and his sister a governess to the children of a wealthy textile merchant. For reasons which now eluded Carr's memory, the Pryces abandoned their posts and moved to London, where the former Linacre Hospital was transformed, under their watchful eye, into Linacre House. Their own parents having died when they were infants, the Pryces were eager to care for children left in a similar predicament; hence, the building which had once been so proud to be a hospital became an orphanage. Over a period of time, Linacre House thrived and, to the world which looked upon its endeavours with admiration and respect, its charity and sanctuary saved many children from poverty, starvation, and death.

It was only later that the rumours began. How they surfaced seemed to have become buried under the weight of the scandal itself, but what had become rapidly clear was that Linacre House had offered not the salvation the public had believed but a damnation which that same public could never have imagined. Within only a few months, the stigma of disgrace had begun to infest the place. Stories of torture abounded, always denied by the Pryces. Carr could remember the story of one boy, no more than ten years old, who had complained that his bath water was too cold. The Pryces' solution had been to force the boy to stand naked in the grounds for fifteen minutes, his hands behind his back so that they could offer no warmth of their own. The month had been November. When he had been permitted to enter the premises once more, the boy's bones were so chilled that he gladly threw himself into the now tepid bathwater, which had itself, by that time, been used by a number of other boys. His next bath, cruelly but inevitably, had been one of scalding water, in which he had been forced to sit, the resulting burns to his skin taking months to heal and leaving permanent scars. Such tales seemed to be reported on a daily basis, along with those of beatings so severe that some bones never healed, mental and physical punishments, and humiliations, ranging from mild embarrassment to outright terror.

What the cause of the Pryces' sadism was, the reports had never seemed to know. Theories had passed from gentlemen's club to gentlemen's club, from office to office, and from tea shop to tea shop. The Pryces had become an obvious target for hatred and disgust. And yet, in this, they had not been alone. The orphanage had a medical supervisor, a general practitioner by the name of Dr Matthew Olson. If the Pryces were to be burned in effigy, Olson was to be pilloried. No medical advisor, it had been insisted, could have treated wounds or any other effects of suffering and not been aware of the horrors of Linacre House. If the Pryces were vicious, Olson had been no better; in his own way, he had been worse. If the Pryces' appetite for violence and abuse was to cost them all they had possessed, it would do no less for Matthew Olson.

An enquiry had become inevitable. Before it was launched officially, however, both Edwin and Marjorie Pryce vanished. When news of their disappearance became known, Matthew Olson had been left to confront their sins and to take them onto his own shoulders. Perhaps unsurprisingly, he must have seen the inevitability of it, because, when the authorities attempted to find him, Olson himself had fled. Investigations were undertaken to trace the three people held responsible for the terror of Linacre House, but those enquiries failed. Vague, unsubstantiated reports came to light, which suggested that one or all of them, in turn, had been seen in places as varied as Canada, Ceylon, or Rhodesia. Alternative information received suggested that one or all of them had died in various, but no more specific circumstances, from natural accidents to suicide.

In time, as so often happens, the Linacre House scandal died, overtaken by monstrosities of equal or greater proportions, or by events of more immediate relevance to the country and the world at large. As interest, morbid or compassionate, dwindled away over the weeks and months, the more the lawns and bushes of the grounds of Linacre House grew, the dirtier the windows became, and the more forlorn the building seemed. For the second time in its existence, the Thomas Linacre Hospital died of wounds which it could not treat, and which would never heal.

By the time these thoughts had settled in Carr's mind, his coffee had gone cold, although not as horrifyingly cold as the poor boy in the November evening air must have been. Carr picked up the clipping of newspaper and placed it back in his coat pocket, as if to look at it was to be somehow complicit in the crimes which it had reported. Nothing which he had read in the piece, nor any memory which it had prompted, seemed to have any relevance to the deaths of William Lorrimer or Isobel Croft, apart from the irresistible suspicion that either one or both of the Pryces, or perhaps Dr Olson, had resurfaced and was living now in Little Marsham. If so,

Lorrimer's possession of the article and the burglary suggested that he knew as much, which would certainly be a motive to silence him. And yet, there was a second hypothesis which Carr felt unable to ignore. Perhaps it was not the Pryces or Olson who were in the village, but one of the maltreated children, now having reached adulthood.

Carr shook his head free of these wild, unsupported theories. He grunted under his breath, preening the moustache and Imperial, his dark eyes darting from side to side, as he formed a decision in his mind. Finally, he rose to his feet and limped carefully towards the bar. He made his apologies about the coffee to the landlord and, in his most casual and ingratiating manner, enquired as to the address of Harriet Delaney. The information obtained, he walked back into the village's high street and began to walk slowly towards his destination. Somewhere in the near distance, the church clock chimed the hour. To Carr, it sounded curiously, but no less ominously, like a portentous tolling of death.

Chapter Sixteen

arr's initial impression of Harriet Delaney was that the photograph, regardless of its disfigurements, did her no justice. Her hair was golden blonde, and her eyes a deep, complementing blue, but both were much more vivid in their respective colours than he had anticipated. She was a beautiful girl, he was in no doubt about that, but he seemed equally positive that there was an intelligence behind the glamour, one of which she seemed to be acutely aware, and it was this which he found far more intriguing than any physical attribute which she otherwise might have possessed. He had introduced himself in a manner which was affable, but apologetic. "I have no wish to intrude, dear lady, but five minutes of your time would be greatly appreciated, and I assure you that I will not outstay my welcome."

Whether it had been his seemingly fussy politeness, or the assurance in his appearance that he was merely an eccentric but harmless older man, she could not say, but Harriet invited him into her cottage and offered him tea. On the contrary, she had been seized almost at once by a memory of her maternal grandfather, whose hair was a similar crisp white to Carr's and whose extensive beard had been, in its own fashion, as elaborate as the pristinely waxed moustache and Imperial which she now admired on this stranger's face. His manner of dress, dapper in black but with a lurid contrast of colour about the necktie and handkerchief, suggested a man not only of some social prominence, but also of a distinct and undeniable fascination. To Harriet, any suggestion that Everett Carr could be anything other than a kind, benevolent, and charming new acquaintance would have seemed too unlikely to be credible.

Carr was surprised, but not perturbed, to find that Harriet was not alone. Edgar Corrigan shook his hand with a polite but unnecessarily fervent zeal, and it struck Carr that this energetic enthusiasm was in such direct contrast to Harriet's assured presence that she might find it occasionally overbearing. And yet, this innate eagerness was narrowly prevented from being the overriding quality of Edgar Corrigan by the more bewitching and subtle effect of the young man's eyes. Carr had never met anybody with heterochromia before, although he was aware that Goethe had suffered from it, and he had read somewhere of an unsubstantiated theory that Alexander the Great was also rumoured to have been similarly afflicted. Whether these figures from the past had created a similar impression to their contemporaries as Edgar Corrigan now produced on Everett Carr was impossible to know, but the effect of the juxtaposition of light and dark in the irises of the young man was bewildering. Carr had become conscious that he was staring too intently, almost rudely, and he was both embarrassed and ashamed into looking away too suddenly, so that his unwitting discourtesy was incapable of denial.

If Edgar had been offended by it, he gave no indication, and it might have been that he was accustomed to such reactions. Certainly, he made no effort to ignore it. "A caprice of nature, Mr Carr. Who knows how these things happen?"

Carr bowed. "I am sorry, you must think me very rude. I had no intention to offend."

Edgar laughed. "You certainly haven't offended me, Mr Carr, although I suspect you have outraged yourself, which I suggest is to your credit and honour."

Harriet, handing Carr a cup of tea, smiled at him. "Edgar's eyes were the first thing which attracted me to him. So fascinating, and so alluring."

The young man rolled his eyes. "Don't get sentimental, Harriet. You might embarrass Mr Carr, and you will certainly embarrass me."

Carr gave a nod of his head. "It is true that when there is something clearly different about a person, one either has to accept that people will stare or else one will begin to resent those very natural reactions."

Edgar murmured his agreement. "And I find one far less destructive than the other. Surely people ask you about your leg, for instance, Mr Carr. I can't help but notice you're lame."

"Edgar!" cautioned Harriet.

But Carr waved aside the remonstrance. "Mr Corrigan is quite right. People do ask about it, sometimes with careful politeness and sometimes with intrusive insolence. How one responds depends on which attitude prompts the question. Which is all the more reason," he added, glancing at Edgar, "for me to reprimand myself for my insensitivity."

"Think nothing of it, please."

Harriet, her eyes fixed on Carr's outstretched leg, had formed the obvious question in her mind, but the hesitancy in the blue eyes suggested that her lips were reluctant to shape the words. Carr watched her carefully and smiled to himself. In a frank but welcome change of subject, he turned to look at Edgar. "It is your father, I believe, who has made a gift of the Van Jansen to St Bartholomew's."

The young man nodded. "A rare gesture of goodwill on my father's part, designed entirely to make himself feel important. His benevolence doesn't extend much further than his own needs. I don't know why he's done it, frankly, since he hasn't the slightest interest in art."

"I understood he was working closely with a local artist on the project," said Carr.

"Laurence Fisher, yes." Edgar shrugged his shoulders. "I don't know the intricacies of it all, but I know Fisher is an expert on this Danish chap, and my father can smell a business opportunity from thirty paces. So, I suppose the arrangement suits them both equally."

"Have you seen the painting, Mr Carr?" asked Harriet.

"It is the reason for my staying in the village, Miss Delaney." He looked at the surface of his tea. "It is a remarkable piece. Your father's generosity perhaps deserves more recognition and less cynicism."

Edgar snorted. "I'd find that easier to accept if I didn't know him so well."

Harriet shifted in her seat. "Forgive me, Mr Carr, but the painting might be the reason you're in the village, but I don't think it explains why you're here specifically."

Carr sat upright in his chair, as if the remark had been a rebuke, and he placed his cup on the wooden table beside him. For a moment, he sat in silence, his fingertips together and the silver-handled cane resting lightly against his damaged leg. "I'm afraid I am here on some delicate business. I hope you will appreciate what I can only say is a friendly warning."

He had not intended to be so melodramatic, and he at once regretted the words. Their effect on both Edgar and Harriet was to steal their voices for a long moment. They glared at him in unison, breaking it only for the briefest of moments to glance at each other, after which their eyes returned to Carr's own.

It was Edgar who spoke, his natural amusement replaced by something altogether more serious. "Dear me. You sound positively ominous, Mr Carr."

Carr looked across to him and then, more deliberately, to Harriet. "Tragic, rather than ominous. I'm afraid that, at some point today, you can almost certainly expect a visit from the police."

Harriet's eyes remained fixed on him. "The police?"

The simple nod of Carr's head was somehow filed with portent. "Last night, there was a terrible act of violence in the village. A young woman was killed. Murdered, in fact."

Edgar sat down slowly. "Murdered?"

Carr nodded sadly. "It is a matter for the police to tell you as much or as little as they wish, of course, and I must be careful how much I say myself. Suffice it to say, however, that there may be more questions about the suicide of William Lorrimer."

Harriet's eyes would have frozen flames. "What sort of questions?"

"The dead woman, Isobel Croft," said Carr softly, "was William Lorrimer's sister."

Edgar stirred in his chair, as if this revelation was the more shocking of the two which Carr had delivered. "I didn't know he had a sister."

Harriet stood up and walked over to the mantel piece and took a cigarette from a silver case there. "She went to live in America after she married, almost ten years ago. They hardly spoke in the meantime."

"Did you ever meet her?" asked Carr.

Harriet shook her head. "No. She had emigrated long before I met William."

Edgar was becoming impatient. "Why would the police be coming here, Mr Carr?"

"That is something the police will have to explain to you," replied Carr. "When they come, however, they will certainly want to know your movements last night. I would encourage you, as strongly as I am able, to tell them the truth."

A moment passed between Edgar Corrigan and Harriet Delaney, but it appeared to be nothing more than a matter of curiosity. Carr, whilst registering the exchange of glances, made no effort to extract any further information from them. To have made the attempt would have been so obviously inquisitive that it would have failed to extract any useful information. As it was, he allowed his words to stand, to be digested, and to emphasise their own importance by the silence which followed.

It was Edgar who broke it. "Are you saying there is a connection between these two deaths?"

"It is something the police will have cause to consider. I wished only to prepare you for it."

Harriet gave a small, bitter cry. Her eyes had watered with tears of frustration, and her voice was a quivering blend of outrage and spite. "Everybody thinks I more or less murdered William, so they may as well say I killed his sister."

Edgar threw himself out of his chair and strode to her side. He placed his arm around her, but she showed no sign of being comforted by the gesture. "Easy, old thing, you mustn't talk like that."

Harriet looked down at Carr. "I wasn't responsible for either death, as it happens."

Carr, not about to pass judgement, simply smiled gently and bowed his head in apparent acquiescence. Slowly, he rose from his chair and walked to the window, to stare out onto the small patch of garden which adorned the front of Harriet's cottage. "Was Mr Lorrimer in good health?"

The question seemed to surprise her. "As far as I'm aware."

"You had no reason to think that he had any specific medical troubles?"

She was smiling now, as if these apparent irrelevances and her ensuing confusion were matters for baffled levity. "None at all. Why do you ask?"

Carr shrugged. He had no intention yet of divulging any information about the textbook he had discovered in Lorrimer's cottage. "Idle speculation, dear lady. I'm afraid it is an irritating trait of mine."

Harriet shook her head. "If William was ill, he didn't say anything to me about it."

Edgar had been thinking. "Perhaps it would explain why this estranged sister of his turned up after ten years without warning."

Carr simply smiled at the conclusion and allowed it to pass by unanswered. "Do you know anything about his parents?"

She shook her head. "They are both dead, I believe. He was brought up by his maternal grandparents."

"Did he never stay, for any length of time, at an orphanage?"

She gave it a moment's thought. "Not that I know of."

"Does the name Linacre House mean anything to you?" Carr turned to face her swiftly, but if she had recognised the name and was now about to dissemble, he could see no trace of it.

"I've never heard of it."

"You don't recall, from a number of years ago, an orphanage in London being closed down on account of terrible abuse of the children?"

"No."

Edgar, however, was nodding vaguely. "I seem to remember something of the sort. A brother and sister, as I recall?"

Carr nodded. "Did Lorrimer ever give any indication that he was connected with the place? Or, perhaps, that he knew someone who was?"

Harriet was adamant. "Never."

"Have you ever heard anybody else in the village mention the name?"

Harriet shook her head in confusion. "May I ask what the point of these questions is?"

Carr shrugged, a careless movement designed to suggest nonchalance. "Nothing sinister, I assure you, dear lady. I tend to have foolish ideas which I cannot ignore. You mustn't think anything of them. They are the fancies of a silly old man."

If she was dissatisfied with the response, she did not say so. Instead, she gave him a brief, humourless smile and inhaled deeply on her cigarette. "You say you have come here to warn me, Mr Carr. May I ask why you felt I deserved such consideration?"

"Because I know you are already a much-tried woman, Miss Delaney," was his reply. It was spoken calmly, with an equal blend of empathy and sympathetic compassion. It reminded her of the priests of her childhood and their gentle tones of encouragement to confess. "You said yourself that you were blamed for Lorrimer's death and that you may as well be blamed for this latest atrocity. Perhaps I am old fashioned enough not to believe in a justice which is so conveniently simplistic as that."

"Are you an idealist or simply naive?" The question was not intended to be as offensive as the words suggested.

Carr gave a slight shrug of his shoulders. "Perhaps a little of both, I cannot say."

"You don't know me, Mr Carr," said Harriet. "Why would you wish to protect me?"

"Because I have sympathy for you, Miss Delaney. And," Carr added softly, "I think you may need a friend who can help you."

"What do you mean?"

In reply, Carr walked towards the centre of the room, his head bowed, stopping only when he was by Harriet's side. Slowly, Carr reached into his pocket and took out the slashed photograph of her. He held it out to her. She looked down at her own defaced image, her eyes widening in horrified shock.

"Where did you find that?" she whispered.

"It came my way." Carr replaced the photograph in his pocket. "You don't seem surprised by it."

She shook her head. "Sadly, I'm not. William took the end of our relationship extremely badly. He hated Edgar and me for it." She held out her hand to Edgar, and he took it, a sign of supportive union.

"And so, he took his own life?" Carr's voice was low.

Harriet threw her cigarette into the grate of the fire. "I never wished for any of this to happen."

Carr seemed not to have heard. His eyes were narrowed, and his lips pursed in thought. "Damaging a photograph of a lover in that fashion speaks to me of malice rather than grief."

"I think he was consumed by both," said Harriet.

Edgar, as if to reassert his position in her life, stepped forward and held Carr's gaze. "Very possibly, but more so by malice than anything else."

Carr was interested, and the dark eyes widened slightly. "Is that your impression only, Mr Corrigan, or is it shared by anyone else?"

"If people are honest with themselves, they'd say they agree."

"Edgar, please," sighed Harriet. "Don't let's go down this road."

But he was immune to reproach. "You may say I'm biased, Mr Carr, but I can assure you that I can be objective about William Lorrimer. And I have no doubt that he pulled the wings off butterflies and the legs off spiders when he was a child. He was that sort of man."

"How interesting," muttered Carr.

Edgar was more intense now. "He would telephone Harriet and shout obscenities down the line at her. At me, too, calling me every name you can imagine, although he preferred to call me a vile, little snake, a serpent, a reptile, and similar things. His words, I assure you. Some may call it a reaction to grief, Mr Carr, and perhaps you will yourself. But I call it spite, pure and simple."

A memory of the meaningless message scrawled across Lorrimer's blotter flashed across Carr's mind: *the snake isn't real.* "He specifically called you a snake?"

"More than once." Edgar sniffed. "He couldn't see that he was the only snake around."

Harriet sighed heavily. "William's dead, Edgar, for God's sake. Whatever we thought of him, whatever he did to us, whoever called whoever what names…none of it matters now. Don't speak ill of him now that he cannot defend himself."

To Carr, she suddenly seemed exhausted. Her eyes had become heavy, the shoulders slumped, and her cheeks now seemed almost unnaturally pale. She stood, motionless, her arms hanging uselessly by her sides, with the demeanour of a woman around whom life was flowing and she could play no part in its ebbs and currents.

"I have taken up too much of your time, dear lady," Carr said. "I shall leave you in peace. I wanted only to warn you of a visit from the police, and I have done so."

With a smile, he turned his back on them. He took his hat and coat from the stand and opened the front door. Before leaving, however, he called out Harriet's name. When he had her attention, he smiled warmly at her, but it did not extend to those dark, persuasive eyes.

"Remember me," he said, "if you feel you do need a friend who can help."

Allowing a moment of seriousness to pass, he smiled once more, offered a final wave, and left them in peace. They would have been able to see him walk down the small garden path and out onto the high street, but they could not have seen that his expression had darkened, the lips had tightened, and the eyes had narrowed in anticipation of some unknown, but still discernible danger.

Because, to Everett Carr, the sensation of impending wickedness and the certainty of murder and blood seemed almost palpable, as if a serpent had coiled itself around this pastoral reflection of Eden.

Chapter Seventeen

I t was the purest chance that Carr was able to secure an audience with Dorothy Parrish. Having left Harriet's cottage, his mind consumed by his thoughts, he walked slowly down the high street, balancing ideas and theories, when he saw Dorothy coming out of the village shop. She, too, looked as if her mind were seized by concerns, her head sunk on her breast and her stride quickened by anxiety, as if she was desperate to get home and being outside was somehow exposing a secret which she wished to remain closely kept. She was so enthralled by her own thoughts that it was simple for Carr to change his direction without her noticing and to engineer a small, but useful collision. As Dorothy walked into him, she gave a shrill, involuntary shriek, and, for his part, Carr gave a reassuring but apologetic laugh.

"My most sincere apologies, dear lady," he said, a guileless smile on his lips and a warmth rising behind the dark eyes. "So careless of me; I'm afraid I wasn't looking where I was going at all."

"It's quite all right," she replied, rather breathlessly. "I think it was my fault, in any case."

Carr's smile widened. "Then perhaps we shall say that we will share the blame."

Despite herself, Dorothy laughed. "Very well."

He held out his hand, and she took it, albeit reluctantly. "My name is Everett Carr."

"Dorothy Parrish," she reciprocated.

"I was just heading to the little tea shop across the way for a cup of coffee and a muffin," Carr declared amiably. "Perhaps you would care to join me?"

Dorothy hesitated. There was something irresistibly ingratiating about this little man that the invitation, made so unexpectedly, seemed impossible to decline. And yet, despite his manner and obvious kindness, she did not feel in a particularly garrulous mood.

"I'm afraid I might not be very good company," she said. "I've had something of a shock, you see." The words were silently cursed as soon as they were out of her mouth.

"Dear me," said Carr. "Perhaps it would help to talk about it?"

Dorothy shook her head. "I'm afraid not."

"I see." His voice had lowered, its tone heavily tainted by his apparent disappointment.

Dorothy felt suddenly wicked, believing immediately that she had offended him by her dismissive responses to what she had taken to be his purely innocent, polite remarks. Now, as if to compensate, and entirely unaware of the crude, psychological manipulation he had performed on her, she smiled at him and placed her hand on his wrist.

"Forgive me," she said, "I'm being uncommonly rude. Perhaps you would like to come back to my cottage for coffee? As a form of compromise."

Carr inclined his head in acceptance. "I would be honoured, dear lady."

"I can't offer you muffins, though."

Carr bowed. "I can live without muffins."

Her cottage was a little distance away, at the other end of the village to Harriet's, and closer to the Church of St Bartholomew. In structure, it was almost identical to its neighbours, with its thatched roof and whitewashed stone walls, and it struck Carr once again that the regularity of appearance of these dwellings was so comforting that the sudden, terrible intrusion of murder into its heart was all the more disturbing.

Inside, the cottage was neat without being fussy. The furniture was traditional, in both structure and design, and the stone hearth promised a welcoming glow of heat when required. The settee and chair, to which Carr was directed, were comfortable, and he could imagine a pleasurable evening with a book, the heat of the fire at his legs, and the soothing warmth of wine in his throat. There was a scattering of paintings on the walls, mostly landscapes of village life or sketches of churches, all framed and placed in such a position that they provided just enough decoration to make an impact but not enough of one to appear too busy or elaborate. Carr had the impression that the framing of them had been carefully considered and was entirely deliberate. Above the fireplace, where he might have expected a mirror of some sort, Carr saw a portrait of Christ, resembling the *Christ Salvator Mundi*, although even Carr's untrained eye could discern that it was not the da Vinci work. Beneath it, somehow altogether more powerful for its simplicity, was a plain, wooden cross. It had no adornment, as if its message was plain enough without any further comment being required. It struck Carr that any embellishment on the two small beams of the cross would have seemed like a flamboyance, which would have both eradicated and scoffed at the meaning of it.

Dorothy arrived with the coffee and placed it on the small, round table which was set before the fire. Carr leaned forward in his chair and moved a folded newspaper from it, making room for the tray. Casually, he looked at the paper in his hand and saw that Dorothy had completed the crossword, although the series of letters crossed out in the margin of the paper suggested that some of the anagrammed clues had proved torturous for her. He watched her pour the coffee, and he accepted the cup with a gracious politeness.

"Do you live alone?" he asked.

The question was a potential probing into her privacy, but she did not seem to be offended by it nor did she appear to be reluctant to reply. "Yes, I do. I never married. Did you?"

"My wife died," Carr replied, a saddened smile creeping across his lips. His hand went instinctively to his shattered knee.

"I'm sorry." The words, although heartfelt, seemed fatuous after the embarrassed silence which had preceded them.

Carr bowed his head and took a sip of the bitter, black coffee. It was good, as warming as it was stimulating. "You may not realise it, Miss Parrish, but I have seen you somewhere before."

Dorothy frowned slightly, the comment taking her unaware. "Really? I'm afraid I can't think where it might have been."

"In the churchyard, the day before last."

Dorothy was shaking her head, not in denial but in a failure to recollect. "I'm sure I would have remembered you, Mr Carr."

This veiled reference to his appearance, one which suggested she found him either alarming or outrageous, did not offend him, since he barely registered it. "You didn't see me, of course, but I saw you. From a distance, you understand. You were watching the vicar, Mr Bowers, in conversation with a woman."

Dorothy's eyes were fixed on him, but the lids were gently flickering, as if from her effort to maintain her composure. The small, almost indistinct clearing of her throat seemed to have the effect of suggesting that she somehow had choked on her own surprise. She waited a long moment before replacing the cup on its saucer, lest the rattling of china against china betrayed the simmering shake of her hand.

Carr presented her with the image of a man entirely unaware of her suppressed distress. "I mention it only because the lady herself is now dead."

The flickering of Dorothy's eyelids stopped instantaneously, and the lips, which had until now been pressed together, slowly parted. "Dead?"

"Murdered, I'm afraid."

A quivering hand went to her mouth. "Dear Lord. Does that mean what she said was true?"

It was Carr's turn to replace his cup carefully on its saucer and without betraying the sudden emotion which swelled within him. "I wondered whether you would have been able to hear it."

Dorothy looked over at him. "You know what she said?"

Carr nodded deliberately. "Mr Bowers told me."

"If she has been killed, it must mean that she was right." Dorothy rose from her seat, if only to have something to do, but it gave the impression of a subconscious desire to flee. "William Lorrimer was murdered."

"Would that surprise you?"

She shook her head. "He was an unpleasant man."

"The woman you saw was his sister. Her name was Isobel Croft. Did you know of her?"

A shake of the head. "He never spoke about his family to me."

Carr nodded. Her reply was at least consistent with what Harriet and Edgar had said. "The police will know from the vicar that she confessed her suspicions of murder to him. It would be wise of you to explain how you came to know about it, too."

She looked at him with a wild fear behind her eyes. "You think the police will want to speak to me?"

"To everyone in the village." He rose with difficulty from the chair. "Isobel's death suggests that she was right about the death of her brother. That means the police will want to find out who had a reason to kill him."

She inferred from the statement an accusation which he had not made. "I didn't kill him."

Carr closed his eyes and nodded. "Nobody has suggested that."

His calm demeanour seemed to influence her. She froze, as if seeing him for the first time, and his polite, kindly smile seemed to seduce her back to reason. Her eyes flickered, as if she were waking from a long and confusing sleep and was momentarily unaware of her surroundings. Her lips trembled into speech, but only to the extent of muttering, "Of course, of course," repeatedly under her breath. She walked slowly back to the settee and lowered herself onto it. Carr leaned forward and lifted her untouched coffee, passing it to her with a smile, for which she thanked him and sipped the drink carefully. Carr remained standing at the hearth, leaning on his silver-handled cane and looking down at her like a doctor might assess a patient who has taken the first dose of medicine.

"Are you calmer now?" he asked.

She nodded. "Much, thank you. I'm sorry. What must you think of me? It was just the shock."

"The reality of murder is always unnerving," Carr said. "Any words one uses to describe its effects are inadequate."

Further discussion on this point of philosophy was prevented from being undertaken by a swift knock on the door and the sound of the latch. Carr watched as the door was thrown open, and, without invitation or consent, a man stepped into the room. His eyes were wide with excitement, and he was already speaking, his voice coming out in rapid gasps. He at once stopped, however, when he saw that Dorothy was not alone, his expression changing to that of a guilty schoolboy caught talking out of turn, and he mumbled a derisory, perfunctory apology.

Dorothy waved him into the room and pointed to a seat and the coffee pot. "Mr Carr, this is a dear friend of mine, Thomas Lewton. Thomas, this is Mr Everett Carr, whom I met outside the shop a few moments ago. He's staying in the village."

Lewton rose from the chair to shake Carr's hand and sat down once more, having done so. "You're not here for the sights, surely."

Carr gave a short laugh. "In a manner of speaking. I came to view the new painting in the church."

If Lewton thought this a futile and irrelevant reason for being in Dorothy's cottage, he did not express it. "The painting was news yesterday, perhaps, but not today. The police are all over the village. Inspector Dunn himself, no less. The scaremongers say it is a case of murder."

Carr lowered his gaze. So, the rumour mill had begun its work already. He told himself that he shouldn't be surprised. In such a place as Little Marsham, a suspicious death would hardly be something capable of prolonged containment. It was a symptom of that peculiar blend of human instincts which allowed people to be simultaneously appalled and thrilled by such an atrocity. To Carr, it had always seemed a perverse predisposition, one which could not be said to enhance the human psyche, although he was not so hypocritical as to deny his own predilection towards it.

"A woman has been killed," he said. "I'm afraid there is no doubt that it is murder."

Thomas Lewton looked up at him, his eyes suddenly cautious of this stranger in their midst. "You know about it already, do you? And do you know who the woman is?"

Carr nodded. "Her name was Isobel Croft."

Before he could explain further, Dorothy Parrish spoke. "She was William Lorrimer's sister."

When Carr looked at her, he was surprised by her expression. She was glaring at Lewton from under her lids, which no longer quivered with emotion; now, both the lids and the glare from under them was like granite. Her lips were compressed together, as if in a sense of fury, and Carr found himself entranced by her expression. He looked to Lewton and found that he, too, was mesmerised by her stare, although his eyes betrayed no fascination but profound anxiety. It was as if an unspoken discovery had been made and, of the three people in the room, only Carr was unaware of it.

"How appalling," said Lewton.

"That's not the worst of it," said Dorothy.

Lewton was quick to turn to face her. "What do you mean by that?"

Carr felt it best if he intervened. "Miss Parrish will tell you this, even if I caution her against it, so it seems inevitable that you will find out. Mrs Croft confided in the vicar that she had reason to believe that William Lorrimer had not committed suicide."

Lewton glared at him. "But the man blew his brains out, straight through the sphenoid. They read out his suicide note to her at the inquest, for Heaven's sake."

Carr smiled. "That is not so serious an objection to the theory of murder as you might think it is, Mr Lewton. It is quite easily explained, in fact."

"Really?" If he understood Carr's meaning, he did not demonstrate it. "It seems to me proof that Lorrimer killed himself."

He looked at Lewton, his eyes as serious as his voice was gentle. "His sister says not and, within a day of saying so, she herself is killed. Does that coincidence not strike you as odd?"

"Only as a coincidence, in the absence of proof."

Carr bowed his head. He was not about to argue with the man. "Whether it is chance or not, the police will treat it as a pertinent line of enquiry. It will be as well to be sure where you were last night."

Lewton frowned. "You think we will be questioned?"

"If you had any dealings with William Lorrimer, certainly," said Carr. "Even if you did not. This is not a large village, and a woman has been deliberately murdered in it. Everyone will be spoken to, I can assure you."

Dorothy placed her coffee cup on the tray. "I was here, all evening. I didn't go out."

Lewton stared at her and, for a moment, there was something about the flicker of his eyes and the nervous twist of his mouth, which suggested to Carr that Lewton had not believed her. He waited for Lewton to say something, but nothing came, and Carr doubted that whatever it was would be divulged if he pressed Lewton on the point. Instead, and in a voice as nonchalant as he could muster, Carr asked, "And were you at home, also, Mr Lewton?"

Perhaps to Carr's surprise, there was no resistance to the enquiry. "As a matter of fact, I wasn't. I fancied some fresh air, so I went for a walk. Not far, you know, just to the fringes of Marsham Woods. I say, I wonder if that fire was connected to what happened."

Carr felt his skin prickle, as if something had crawled its way along the nape of his neck. "Fire?"

Lewton nodded. "As I was walking along the path which runs alongside the woods, I could see flames a little distance off. Quite a bonfire somebody had made."

"What time was this?"

"A quarter to ten. A little later, perhaps."

"Did you see anybody else around?"

Lewton gave it careful consideration but, ultimately, shook his head. "No, I don't think so."

"Did you investigate?"

"No." Lewton's tone of voice gave the impression that he thought the idea a stupid one. "It was none of my business. But," he added, "it must be easily verifiable. I'd hardly think the people in the houses opposite the woods, the Rymans, for instance, could have failed to notice the fire."

"I see." Carr smiled, as if to demonstrate that he had meant no offence by his enquiries. "I wonder if I might ask one more question. Taking it for granted that Mrs Croft's belief that Lorrimer had been murdered, why might someone have done it?"

It was Lewton who replied, but Carr's attention was fixed on Dorothy Parrish. She was glaring once more at Lewton, her lips again compressed in suppressed fury and her eyes burning with anger. Her hands were clasped so tightly together that her fingers must have been registering pain, the knuckles whitened by the pressure. Lewton, however, was making a point of not looking at her, and it was this refusal which Carr found most interesting of all.

"Lorrimer was not a popular man," Lewton said. "A terrible thing to say, in the wake of his death, but it's true. He was a spiteful, malicious man, and I doubt he had a real friend in the village, but I can't say anyone had a reason to kill him."

"Miss Parrish?" said Carr.

Dorothy shook her head. "I can't think of anyone."

Carr allowed a moment to pass. "Well, I must be on my way. Thank you for the coffee, Miss Parrish. A pleasure to meet you, Mr Lewton." He shook both their hands, bowing politely as he did so. Then, with a hardening of the dark, opaque eyes, he added a word of caution. "Be honest with the police, I beg you."

Lewton felt a sudden annoyance. "Are you suggesting we've been less than honest now?"

Carr quietened him with a wave of the hand and a pursing of his lips. "I simply offer advice, Mr Lewton. You are free to ignore it, if you wish. Good day."

He gave a courteous bow and walked out of the cottage. The silence which followed his exit was brief but uncomfortable. Lewton walked to the fireplace, his hands behind his back, and Dorothy remained leaning against the door she had closed on Carr. After several moments, Lewton looked across at her.

"He's right, though, isn't he?" he asked. "We weren't honest."

Dorothy pushed herself away from the door and walked with purpose towards him. "Are you accusing me of something, Thomas?"

Lewton held her gaze. "I did go to Marsham Woods, but only after calling here first. On my way back, I called again. On both occasions, I got no reply. You weren't at home last night, Dorothy."

"Are you daring to lecture me on honesty, Thomas, when you've been lying to me from the moment we met? And," she added with a dose of malice, "you know full well that Lorrimer's death wasn't suicide, because you had a good reason to kill him."

"What are you talking about?" His voice was more cautious than confused.

"Stop lying, Thomas," she hissed. "I know what you did."

The accusations developed into an argument which burned fiercely, before eventually subsiding into sobbing, mutual confessions. At no time during the intervening period did either Dorothy Parrish or Thomas Lewton, look out of the small front window of the cottage. Had they done so, they would have seen the figure of Everett Carr in the near distance, watching from far enough away to be discreet, but close enough to be able to witness the argument between them, with its pointing fingers and flailing arms, like a silent parody of an exotic dance, although his natural compassion and decency compelled Carr to turn away before the final, tearful reconciliation had taken place.

Chapter Eighteen

Fernchester was not a town which Carr had visited before, but he had known many others like it. Built on an ancient Roman settlement, whose walls remained in place, in part at least, the town was served by a single railway station, at which Carr alighted from a slow, somewhat grimy train. It was only a short walk into the market town itself, which consisted of a noble but solitary church, quaint lattice-windows shops, and a bandstand, in which a small throng of amateur musicians was playing *Guide me, O Thou great Redeemer*, with a confidence and ease which belied their lack of professional status. Carr was taken aback momentarily by the music, so he stood and listened, his soul briefly uplifted by the hymn.

The library of Fernchester was on the corner of a narrow street, opposite a small bakery. The smell of fresh bread and baking pies drifted on the air as Carr approached, and it struck him that an early lunch might not go amiss. For now, however, his attention was fixed on the library itself, an unprepossessing building which resembled a church manse rather than a working library. The walls were stone and the slanting, slate roof formed a large but ungainly gable above the small red door, which served as the entrance. Inside, however, amid the solemn, reverential silence of such places, Carr found that the deficiencies of the exterior were ameliorated by the pleasures of the interior, with its peculiarly alluring smell of antiquated books and old leather bindings. The shelves were formidably stocked, so that the place seemed to be larger than it was. The volume of books and the neatness of their categorisation seemed to swell the dimensions of the building itself. A small, elderly woman was the only librarian visible, seated behind the large wooden structure which served as the checking out desk. She smiled brightly as he passed her and wished him a cheery if fussy good morning, which he reciprocated, with a slight bow in addition.

"I wonder if you could help me," said Carr. "I'm looking for a specific book on human disease by a man called Gemmell. Would you happen to have it?"

"I am sure we have," said the woman, flicking through the pages of a reference ledger. "Ah, yes, although I am afraid it is out."

Carr clicked his tongue in mock disappointment. "A pity. I don't suppose you could let me know when it is due to be returned."

The woman raised her eyebrows in mild displeasure. "I'm afraid it is overdue."

Carr clicked his tongue in feigned annoyance. "I wonder if you might contact the man who has borrowed it. I would so very much like to consult it, you see."

The lady shook her head. "It was a woman, actually."

"A woman?" Carr's surprise was evident.

"According to the records, yes."

"Such a nuisance, as I'm only in town this morning. I must return to Little Marsham this afternoon."

The librarian's eyebrows rose further, and a smile broke out upon her face. "The lady lives in that village."

Carr was pleased with his guile rather than surprised by the news. "What a coincidence! I don't suppose you'd be able to give me her name, just so I could ask her if I could consult the book. Unless, of course, it is my old friend, Dorothy Parrish, who took it out?"

"No, it…"

"Harriet Delaney, perhaps?" Carr was effusive. He was speaking rapidly now, so that the librarian had trouble keeping up with or registering the words properly. "A very charming young woman. I was speaking to her only the other day. And to Dorothy this morning, actually. If I had known she had taken out the book, I would have looked at it there and then. How annoying."

"But it wasn't her," said the woman behind the counter, "it was Mrs Elsa Corrigan."

The words were spoken before she had been able to prevent them. She stared at him now, her eyes open with alarm, but her mouth clamped shut in tardy discretion. She cursed herself for allowing his rapid, seemingly vacuous prattle to work its magic on her and, looking into his dark eyes, she knew that she had said too much. He was smiling at her with comfort, though, and there was no trace of malice or mischief in his expression. She doubted that he was a man who would betray a confidence, even if she had done so herself.

"You won't let on it was me who told you, will you, sir?" she whispered. "There's matters of confidentiality to be thought of."

Carr, leaning over the counter so as to be able to hear her, shook his head and placed a finger to his lips. "Think nothing of it, dear lady, and do not worry. You have done a great service, so console yourself with that."

"I don't see how," she felt obliged to say.

Carr smiled. "Rest assured, you have."

In order to avoid giving her the impression that he had come to the library solely in order to extract from her the information he had received, he asked for the art section. It took him perhaps half an hour to find any book which made mention of Meryk Van Jansen. The Dane, it seemed, had made little to no impact in his chosen field, so that almost every major work of art critique was sure to overlook him. What reference to him he could find told Carr that the man had died in poverty, his life and pitiful career destroyed by drink, and Carr was overwhelmed with a sense of sadness that such an obvious talent could be consigned to obscurity because of the very man who possessed it. It seemed somehow perverse that Van Jansen could have been the author of his own misfortune, not to say the artist of his own despair, on account of his natural weakness for the allure of alcohol.

Carr turned the page of the reference book and found a reproduction of *The Trial Before Pilate.* An involuntary sigh of admiration escaped from his lips as his eyes drifted once more over the figure of Christ, surrounded by the sadistic guards and their malicious intent, at Pilate's judgemental finger and Procla's pleas against it. The reproduction was well done, and the image was no less powerful for being copied into the book, but nothing could compare with seeing the original, certainly not with seeing it mounted in the very house of God. Slowly, Carr closed the book and replaced it on the shelf from where he had taken it. He found that he was frowning now, and he had the familiar feeling that he had heard or seen something in this library which was important, either by its absence or its presence. His mind was often uncooperative, and experience told him that, eventually, he would remember it; for now, he could only wait for matters to run their natural, if annoyingly slow course.

By the time he had caught the train out of Fernchester and arrived back in Little Marsham, the detail remained beyond his reach, and Carr at last abandoned any attempts to prise it free from his memory. Instead, he walked slowly up the hill from the railway station and towards the row of cottages which looked across at Marsham Woods. The walk was a slow one, his knee raging from the effort of the necessary climb so that, more than once, he had to pause for respite. As a consequence, it was close to lunchtime before he arrived at the woods themselves, and he wished he had stopped somewhere for a cup of coffee and something to eat. Finding his breath, he dismissed his regrets, however, and crossed the country road which separated the woods from the cottages opposite, stepping into the brambles and overgrown grass which bordered the expanse of trees which now loomed over him.

The woods were impressive. Carr was no expert, but he knew that the leaf and bark giants which towered over him were a mixture of deciduous species, comprising, he thought, oak, ash, and chestnut. The high, green crowns of the trees gave a natural shade from the autumnal sun, whilst, below it, the ground was almost entirely clear. As he moved further into the heart of the woodland, Carr had the undeniable sensation that time was abandoning him. Little Marsham itself was far enough away from the roar and commotion of London, but even the little village seemed somehow to be an intrusion into this area of natural splendour. Here, there was no way of marking time other than the rise and fall of the sun, nor was there any immediate trace of the existence of modern humanity. If he had been a more religious man than he was, or if his faith had been more certain, Carr would have felt closer to God here, in this soothing wilderness of nature, than in any stone temple or church built by man.

He could not say how long he had been in the woods before he found it. It was, perhaps, the merest chance that he did see it, and he wondered how much of his success was down to the fact that he was looking for signs of scorching, makeshift kindling, and the like. The smell of fire would have long since evaporated, of course, but the physical debris was still evident at his feet: the charred remnants of leaves, the square patch of black where the base of the fire has taken, now looking like a dark stain of mischief. Looking back over the path he had trod, he could barely make out the rows of cottages which looked out onto the woods. Thomas Lewton had said that the inhabitants of those cottages must have been able to see the fire he had himself witnessed; from this point of view, Carr had a moment of doubt about it, until he remembered that Lewton had said that the fire had been fairly extensive. In darkness, these trees and bushes would appear impenetrable, so that a sudden flare of orange flame would certainly stand out against the black of the woods.

Carr turned back to look down at the remnants of the fire. They were extensive enough to justify Lewton's suggestion of a bonfire and Carr found himself wondering how long it had raged before it had finally lost its fuel, heat, or oxygen. With the tip of his cane, he poked around the crisp, blackened leaves and burnt grass, all the time trying to understand what it was which had been burned and, more importantly, why it had been destroyed.

Eventually, rummaging around the ashes, he discovered something which alerted his instincts. With a hiss of effort, he lowered himself to the ground, his useless leg stretched out to the side, and picked up a small fragment of cloth. It was dirty, but it was impossible to tell whether the filth was already present when the garment, whatever it was, had been burned or whether it was the result of the smoke and flame. Carr smelled it, but only the lingering odour of fire was evident, although, holding it close to his face, he could now tell that the fabric was linen. Its edges were singed, but the centre was relatively untouched by the flames and, as he peered at it closely and turned it over in his fingers, Carr felt a shudder pass through him. On one side of the linen, there was a rust-coloured stain, not quite red and not quite brown. It might have been a fruit stain, or it might have been a rust stain.

Equally, it might have been a blood stain.

He placed the cloth in his coat pocket and returned his scrutiny to the ground beneath his feet. There were unburnt pieces of wood, little more than kindling and fuel, he thought initially, but the discovery of the small clasp of metal made him wonder whether he was wrong. He picked up the small, misshapen chunk of metal and examined it closely. It was almost impossible to tell what it was, but it would have been difficult to convince Carr that it was anything other than a small clasp or hinge, although from what it had been wrenched was not immediately apparent. With a bitter curse, Carr pulled himself to his feet and placed the clasp in his pocket with the stained linen.

For a moment, he remained standing there, gazing down at where the fire had burned, his mind aimlessly walking down its own roads without ever reaching specific destinations. Idle thoughts and theories occurred to him, but they reached no further than the certainty that something of importance had been burnt and the offerings had included a linen garment which might have been stained, just possibly, with blood. It was possible that Isobel Croft's killer had murdered her and burned his clothes, stained with betraying blood, in order to disguise the evidence, but it was little more than speculation. All the ashes and remnants of the fire proved was that Thomas Lewton had told the truth about seeing it. That truth did not mean he was innocent of murder, however. Witnessing the fire blazing and committing the murder were separate incidents. As an alibi, the fire was worthless.

With a sigh, Carr turned on his heel and made his way out of the woods. He was not far from the edge of the trees when he heard the gentle sound of a woman sobbing. Following it, his dark eyes alert to the sight of its origin, he came at last across Harriet Delaney, sitting on the trunk of a fallen tree, her hands clasped in her lap, her knees pulled together, and her head slumped on her breast. The handkerchief she held was performing no purpose, as the tears were falling freely from her eyes.

Chapter Nineteen

He approached her quietly, so as not to startle her, but his efforts were in vain. Either she had heard a noise which he was unaware he had made or else she had sensed him moving on the edges of her consciousness. Her immediate reaction was one of childish guilt, as if she had been caught in the execution of a minor misdemeanour; her second, almost simultaneous one was a mild anger that anyone should intrude into what was obviously a private moment. Carr was aware of both these reactions, however hard she tried to conceal them in the moments afterwards, and his instinctive reaction was to take a step backwards in apologetic retreat.

She held out a hand to stop him. "It's all right, Mr Carr. You don't have to leave. I was just having a moment on my own."

"Then I have no wish or right to intrude, dear lady," he replied with customary politeness.

Harriet was insistent. "Please, don't go. I feel I've had enough of my own thoughts."

Carr walked slowly towards her and, having placed a handkerchief across the bark of the trunk, sat down beside her. For a moment, neither of them spoke and the only sound, apart from the usual rustle of leaves and the far-away cries of country birds, were the infrequent but delicate sniffs, which Harriet gave into the handkerchief. She dabbed at her eyes and gave a few short intakes of breath before lowering the handkerchief once more. She breathed in deeply, and Carr watched as a smile slowly returned to her lips.

"It is amazing how being close to nature can soothe one's soul," he remarked.

She looked at him. "I love it out here in the woods. So peaceful, so restful, so comfortingly far away from people."

"People who have been unkind to you?"

"Exactly."

Carr smiled sympathetically. "I know only too well how wicked people can be, whether it is justified or not."

"I sometimes think it is justified. Other times, I am sure it is not. I'm sorry," she added with a weak smile, "I'm not making any sense, am I?"

Carr patted her gently on the forearm and leaned in towards her, as if to honour some private conspiracy between them. "Enough sense for an old man like me."

Her laugh, involuntary but heartfelt, warmed him. "You're not an old man, Mr Carr."

"I feel older than I am, believe me, my dear," he replied. "Old enough, certainly, to wish I had as much of my life ahead of me as you have of yours."

"My father would have said I was being self-indulgent, crying about my problems, like this." The memory of the man, now long since dead, seemed to harden her voice.

Carr kept his eyes on her, cautious not to enrage or derail her with his response. "In that case, he doesn't strike me as having been a compassionate man."

"Religious," she said, as if that explained the point without any further comment being needed. "My upbringing was devout, to the point of obsession. We had no money, of course, because my father thought that possessions were a sin. Always going on about camels and needles, instead of telling his daughter that he loved her."

It was spoken casually, but Carr could still detect the sting of bitterness behind the words, the embers of the once much more profound acrimony of a child who felt unloved. Her tone of voice was now resigned to the past, to a situation which, as a child, she could not have changed, and which was beyond any reparation now that she was an adult. And yet, in moments such as these, it was clear to him that those childish hatreds and frustrations could still rise to the surface, like a drowned corpse inevitably drifting back to the surface of a lake.

"Were you an only child?" he asked.

Harriet nodded. "I didn't even have the luxury of being able to share the loneliness with someone who could have understood."

"And you have sought a substitute for your father's love ever since, perhaps?" asked Carr.

If there were any capacity for offence in his words, it was so diluted by his gentle, caring tone of voice that she was unable to summon any hostility. "I've never thought about it like that, but I suppose it must be right. Looking back, perhaps it's the only explanation for beginning a relationship with William Lorrimer."

Carr's eyes fixed themselves on the autumn leaves at his feet. "Did the police come to see you?"

She nodded, and tears returned to her eyes. "That is why I'm here. I couldn't face anybody after them. Not even Edgar."

"Was their visit as difficult as all that?"

She shifted her position on the trunk of the tree. "They have a way of making you feel guilty for everything. As if I didn't feel guilty enough about William already."

"Did they say anything about his death?"

She looked at him, her eyes heavy with tension. "You knew what they were going to say, didn't you? That there's a suspicion now that he was murdered?" She watched him nod his head slowly. "Why didn't you say anything when you came to the house?"

He gave a shrug of the shoulders. "It was not for me to pre-empt a police interview with details such as those. I had hoped that what I did say might be sufficient to put you on your guard."

"By saying the police might suspect a connection between the two deaths," she said. "Yes, I could see after they had gone that was what you had tried to do."

"Did the police ask for your movements on the night Isobel Croft was killed?"

"As a matter of routine enquiry," she said in a gently mocking tone of voice. "I wonder whether anything is truly routine with those people."

Carr offered a conspiratorial smile. "They are a breed of their own, these police detectives. They lack subtlety, certainly, but they do have their procedures. One cannot be too delicate when one is restricted by official constraints."

"They were very official, certainly."

"Were you able to satisfy them about your movements?"

The question was asked so mildly, without any suggestion of inquisitiveness or importance, that she replied without hesitation. "I told them that I was at home writing a response to an urgent letter I had received yesterday morning. An old lady I once knew has died and left me a small legacy. Her solicitors wanted me to make an appointment to discuss it."

"Surely the police would say that you could have received this letter and written a reply at any time?" Carr tried to maintain an element of delicacy in his voice.

"Yes, but Edgar was there when it was delivered, as I told them, and I showed Inspector Dunn the endless drafts I'd discarded." She smiled coyly. "I found it rather hard to know what to say. He said it must have taken me a couple of hours."

Carr smiled in sympathy. "And earlier in the day?"

"I was with Edgar. We went to Fernchester, then to see his parents, and we had an early dinner together. He left me just before ten o'clock to go to the village pub for a drink, and I sat down to write my letter."

"Ten o'clock, I see," said Carr. "That is the time of death, is it?"

"Around then, yes, according to Inspector Dunn."

Carr fell silent for a few moments, his fingers tapping lightly against the silver handle of the cane. "Did the police ask if you could think of anybody who would have reason to murder William Lorrimer?"

"Yes."

"Did you provide them with any suggestions?"

"Apart from me, you mean?"

Carr stared at her. The response both alarmed and disturbed him. "Did you have reason to kill him?"

She dabbed at her eyes with the handkerchief, although Carr could no longer see any tears which required attention. "I hated him. Not at first, but towards the end. So much so that I could imagine killing him, yes. I suppose that is a very wicked thing to say but, unless you knew him as I did, you can't understand, not really. Edgar gave you some idea of how he could be. Malicious, overbearing, always looking for an outlet for his spite."

"Was he ever violent towards you?" Carr's voice, quiet and heavy with emphasis, suggested that he was more than a little afraid of the answer.

She shook her head. "I cannot say that. Not physically, at any rate."

"Violence against the mind is just as damaging as it is against the body," observed Carr.

Harriet thought about the idea for a moment, and then, with an element of sadness, she nodded her head. "In that case, yes, he was violent towards me."

"And so you walked away to another, better man?"

"Yes." Her tears now began to pool in the corners of her eyes once more.

Carr placed a soothing hand on her forearm, for a moment only. "Surely that means that it would be Lorrimer with the motive to harm you, not the other way around?"

Her eyes fixed on the leaves at her feet, as if their natural tints of brown and orange were somehow confirmation of the conclusion Carr had put to her. "I suppose it would."

Carr touched her hand. "You must not allow these people who blame you for his death detract from your happiness with Mr Corrigan. You, and everyone, is entitled to find love and to revel in it. It is not a right which anyone can take away from you."

Her tears were falling freely once more as she looked at him through their blurring prisms. "You're so kind, Mr Carr. I wish my father had been even a little like you."

He shrugged off the compliment, but she noticed that the rosiness in his cheeks, until now only a product of the chill of the air, had deepened. They sat for a moment in an easy silence, neither of them unnerved or disturbed by the lull in the conversation. To Harriet, this quietly spoken, kind old man's company was like a warm bath on the coldest of nights, and she felt comfortable, if not safe, in the solace of it.

"But the fact remains that William killed himself," she said.

Carr's fingers snaked around the silver handle of his cane and unfurled again, the action being repeated several times. "The death of his sister, which undoubtedly was murder, makes no sense if what she claimed about his death was not true. Lorrimer's suicide robs Isobel's murder of any motive."

"But he left a suicide note," persisted Harriet.

"Addressed to you, I understand."

She gave an embarrassed nod of the head. "More of William's spite."

"Was the note signed?"

"No, but it was in his own handwriting."

Carr raised a cautionary finger. "There is absolutely no doubt of that?"

"None." She shuddered gently. "I testified as much at the inquest. As did several other people in the village. He wrote that note, nobody else. And why would he do that if he was not about to kill himself? It must have been suicide."

Carr nodded. "There is an alternative theory, one which is quite obvious."

"I can't see it."

"The note was found at the scene of Lorrimer's death?"

"Beside his body, yes."

Carr gave a bark of triumph. "Then that is the answer. There is no direct evidence that the note had any relevance at all to the death of Lorrimer. A direct connection was taken for granted only because the letter was found by his body. Once you realise that, the mystery of it vanishes completely."

"I don't follow."

"Let us say that whoever murdered Lorrimer had a secret of their own," Carr said, "one which he had discovered. So, he was killed to keep him silent. By chance, the murderer discovers Lorrimer's note to you, written for purposes of his own, and sees an opportunity to make it appear as if he has killed himself. Later, when Mrs Croft arrives in the village, with her declarations of murder and knowledge of the culprit's identity, our murderer sees only one option open to him to protect himself."

Harriet stared in dazed amazement. "What a way you have of seeing things, Mr Carr."

He seemed not to have heard her. "You have not answered my earlier question, dear lady. Did you suggest anyone to the police with cause to murder Lorrimer?"

Harriet felt his dark eyes on her. "I couldn't say too much, Mr Carr, because I have no evidence in support, but I didn't tell the police everything I know. You see, there is one particular person I'm concerned about."

"Yes...?"

"A few weeks ago, I heard a tremendous argument here in the woods. I recognised William's voice at once, of course, and I knew only too well the malevolence within it."

"Did you see with whom he was arguing?"

She shook her head. "Not at first. William was shouting something about a theft."

"A theft?"

"He said something like, 'It's theft, and you know it! And I'm not going to stand around and do nothing about it.'"

"Anything else?"

Harriet's eyes narrowed in concentration, but she shook her head. "Nothing that I remember for sure. Although I thought I heard something about a snake, I may be mistaken."

"A snake?" Carr, his dark eyes flickering with fascination, turned himself to face her.

"I can't be certain, but I think so." Harriet's tone was filled with caution.

Carr nodded slowly. "And what happened then?"

"I watched William emerge from the woods and march off in the direction of the village." She frowned at the memory. "I could tell from his pace that he was furious about something. I thought about running to catch him up, but something about his attitude made me think it would be a dangerous thing to do."

"I think you were wise to show restraint, dear lady," muttered Carr.

Harriet did not offer any direct response. "And then, after a few moments, the other person appeared from the woods and stepped into the clearing. Then, I could see who it was very clearly. They stood still for a while, just watching William walk away, and then they did something which, at the time, seemed very odd. Now, it seems all too chillingly obvious."

Carr's moustache twitched with curiosity. "What did they do?"

As she replied, Harriet performed the gestures herself. "They raised one arm out in front of them, the fist balled, except for the index finger, which was outstretched, and the thumb which was raised. Like a gun, Mr Carr. Then, they mimed firing a shot in the direction of William. It was all done so slowly that it was terrifying."

Carr pushed himself to his feet. Replacing the handkerchief in his pocket, he took two painful steps forward. For a moment, he stood with his back to her, and his head bowed, like a strange, forbidding bird with a black plumage of dread. Then, slowly, he turned to face her. His expression now was grave, the eyes darker than ever, and the white of his moustache and Imperial more judicial and serious than before.

"This other person," he said grimly, "was it a man or a woman?"

Harriet tried to avert her eyes from his, but she found that she was unable to do so. "It was a man."

Carr spoke delicately. "I want you to think very carefully, dear lady, and tell me the truth. You will remember Edgar Corrigan told me that Lorrimer had called him a snake during an altercation. Was it Edgar you saw emerge from the woods?

Harriet shook her head, a smile creeping over her lips. "I do recall what Edgar said, Mr Carr, but it wasn't him I overheard arguing with William. It was someone else entirely."

"But it was a man you recognised?"

The nod of her head was definitive. "Oh, yes, Mr Carr, I know who it was. You see, it was the painter, Laurence Fisher."

Chapter Twenty

I t was late afternoon when Carr arrived at the Corrigan house. The discreet, but ultimately unsatisfactory enquiries which he had made into the whereabouts of Laurence Fisher had proved fruitless, beyond a common understanding in the village that the young artist had been compelled to visit London and was not expected back in Little Marsham until, at best, the early evening. Carr had accepted the disappointment with equanimity and had consoled himself with a plate of mutton and vegetables, accompanied by a small glass of the excellent red which *The Marsham Tuns* offered. The food had been serviceable, but Carr had treated it more as a matter of function than of any particular source of pleasure. The meal over, and a second glass of the wine contemplated but dismissed, Carr stepped out into the high street and made his slow but determined way towards the large house on the edge of the village.

He had seen it every day during his visit, of course. It was impossible to miss, no matter how far away from the heart of the village it seemed to be. It loomed with a definite sense of majesty, above the high street, as if it were the protective guardian of the small network of streets and lanes which lay latticed beneath it, or else on account of some desire on the part of its architect, long since dead, to demonstrate the social hierarchy of the residents of the manor and those people confined to the lesser cottages beneath it. As Carr turned into the driveway, he could see that the house itself was a typical Georgian sandstone building, with three floors, each designated by rows of latticed windows across the front of the property. A porch framed the arched entrance, flanked on either side by Italian cypress trees and crowned by a coat of arms and a Latin dedication, which time and corrosion had rendered almost illegible. Two annexes were set on either side of the main block of the house, and Carr supposed that these were servants' quarters or similarly functional sections of the property, which were not to be considered part of the main structure. Overall, it was an attractive residence, if somewhat formal in its construction, and its symmetry, whether by design or accident, was both natural and reassuring.

Carr's peal of the bell was answered promptly by a butler whose appearance was as efficient as his service. He showed Carr to the drawing room, where he was advised that Mrs Corrigan would join him in due course. It was a large, airy room, tastefully but not ornately furnished, with a view of the front lawns extending beyond the two, broad and latticed panes which were separated by a narrow, wooden window seat, across which were several cushions, tossed in a decoratively careless fashion. Carr did not presume to sit, preferring instead to stand by the marble fireplace, above which hung a large, gilt-framed mirror, whose glass reflected the main portion of the room, so that it appeared much larger than it was.

Elsa Corrigan did not smile when she entered the room, nor was her expression one of overt hostility. Carr was impressed by the noble, stoic features, and he was struck suddenly by the similarity in bone structure to Edgar. Mother and son shared the same long nose, sloping away from the similarly intelligent eyes, and the hair was the same shade of burnt yellow, which was too dark to be considered blonde. It was clear to see where Edgar's somewhat androgynous beauty was rooted, and yet, Carr thought, there was something in Elsa Corrigan's blue eyes which told of an unspoken sadness, as if her life belonged somewhere else, and there was a touch of distance in her expression, which suggested that she was always looking out towards that other life and pondering how it might have transpired.

"Mr Carr?" she asked, offering her hand, which he took, giving a small bow of greeting. "I don't believe we've met before."

Carr shook his head. "No, but I trust you will forgive this intrusion. You have a very beautiful house," he added, looking around the drawing room. "Georgian, I think."

Elsa nodded demurely. "It has been in my husband's family for hundreds of years."

Carr smiled. "So much more attractive than these modern monstrosities which seem to be the fashion nowadays. All glass and no charm," he added, with a hint of genuine sadness in his voice.

Elsa, not quite knowing how to respond, merely smiled. She made a gesture, indicating Carr should sit down, and he complied. Elsa sat on the settee opposite him, her hands clasped in her lap and her eyes fixed on him in a silent, but not hostile expression of enquiry. Carr, seemingly for the first time, was embarrassed by his position, and he smiled as a reaction against it.

"I am fully aware of how strange this must seem to you, Mrs Corrigan," he said, "but I come here in good faith. I am afraid it is only a matter of time before Inspector Dunn, of your local constabulary, comes to visit you."

The faint, quizzical smile across Elsa's lips faded swiftly, and the blue eyes grew cautious, like those of an animal who has suddenly sensed danger. "The police, coming here?"

"Perhaps you have not heard of the tragedy which occurred in the village last night?" Carr watched her shake her head. "A woman was killed, stabbed to death in the cemetery of St Bartholomew's Church."

"What has this to do with me?"

"Perhaps nothing, perhaps everything. The woman was William Lorrimer's sister, so there is, as you see, a direct connection to you."

Elsa took his meaning without argument. "An indirect one only."

"A connection, nonetheless." Carr smiled, as if to assure her that there was no intended confrontation in his response.

Elsa returned the smile. "I doubt my son's relationship with Harriet Delaney will feature much in any police investigation. You say this unfortunate woman was Mr Lorrimer's sister. Surely, then, the matter is more likely to be connected with the Lorrimer family than mine."

It was a good point, and she had made it succinctly and well, a fact which Carr acknowledged with a bow of his head. But his dark eyes had become impassive. "There is reason to suppose that Mr Lorrimer did not take his own life."

Elsa almost betrayed no reaction, but the subtle flicker of her eyes showed that the news had derailed her more than she might wish to convey. "But the inquest -"

"The verdict may yet be overturned," said Carr softly. "So, you see, any connection to Mr Lorrimer is likely to be of interest to the police. Might I ask," he added, his tone aiming for conversational cordiality, "how well you knew him?"

She shrugged her shoulders. "Not especially well. He came to the house on occasion, to garden parties and suchlike, which we hold from time to time for the village, or for various dinner engagements. This was before my son became involved with Miss Delaney, you understand."

"And after that?"

"He came less frequently, of course. On one occasion, he came here, threatening to assault Edgar. My husband, Arthur, dealt with that, as only he could." Her expression said as much as her tone of voice about how much she disapproved of the manner in which her husband had dealt with it.

"There was a scene?"

Elsa shook her head. "I'd prefer not to discuss it, Mr Carr."

He gave another consenting bow of the head. "When was the last time Mr Lorrimer came here?"

"A month or so ago."

The lie came instantly to her lips but, if she were surprised by it, she did not demonstrate it and nor did Carr show that he was aware of it. The library book on medical treatise exposed the lie by its dates: assuming Lorrimer had removed it from the house, he must have been there as recently as a few days before his death, since that was when Elsa Corrigan had taken it from the library in Fernchester.

"Did you know if Mr Lorrimer was suffering from any illness?" asked Carr delicately. "A brain tumour, perhaps?"

Elsa's shifted in her seat, as if a current of electricity had been passed through her. Her recovery was swift, but it came too late to be wholly effective. "What makes you ask that?"

Carr stroked his damaged knee. "I think you know, Mrs Corrigan."

"I'm sure I don't."

"Do you take many books out of the library in Fernchester?"

The question, seemingly innocent enough, might have been an accusation. "What are you saying?"

Carr leaned forward in his chair, his voice mellifluous and his dark eyes now assuming their most kindly shimmer. "I have no wish to cause you pain, dear lady. But the fact is that I know you took out a medical textbook from the library a few days before Lorrimer was killed. You will understand my confusion when I tell you that I found that same book in his own cottage."

"His cottage?" The words seemed to make no sense to her.

Carr felt compelled to persist. "Might you be able to explain why it was there?"

"No." The reply was little more than a barely intelligible croak, muffled by the effort of resisting the tears which were forming in her eyes.

Carr leaned back in his chair. It was no real mystery, after all. Lorrimer must have taken the book on one of his more recent visits to the house, perhaps when he came searching for a confrontation with Edgar Corrigan. It would have been easily smuggled out of the house. What puzzled Carr was Lorrimer's reason for taking it, which, in itself, was as tantalising a question as why Elsa Corrigan had borrowed it in the first instance.

"Why did you wish to consult the book, Mrs Corrigan?" he asked.

"It is a personal matter," she said. "To do with a close friend. Yes, he has a brain tumour, but really, it is very sad and extremely personal."

Carr made no comment. He searched her face for any indication that she would offer more information on the point, but she was resilient. When she met his gaze, it was as if she were daring him to probe further, and Carr knew, from his experiences as a judge and in over five decades of life generally, that some matters were best left unresolved for the immediate moment.

"On the night Mr Lorrimer died," he said instead, "can you say where you were?"

She did not need to give the question any depth of thought. "I don't see that it is any of your business, Mr Carr."

He conceded the fact with a raising of his hand. "Indeed not, my dear lady, but is it such a secret that you cannot indulge an old man?"

He had not taken the success of this psychological trick for granted, but he was pleased to find that it had succeeded. Elsa's defensive attitude weakened as she came to realise that any refusal to answer might now appear to be, at best, petulant and, at worst, a suggestion of deceit. In the moment, for all his calm kindness, she found that she was now perhaps a little frightened of this extravagant but mildly manipulative stranger. And yet, despite her compulsion to tell him the truth, Elsa did not consider herself obliged to confide completely in him. Her drawing room, she noted bitterly, was not a court of law.

"I went for a walk," she said, "down to the village and across the heath."

"Did you meet anybody?"

She shook her head. "I had not realised I would need to provide an alibi."

Carr recognised her discomfort, and he knew that she was offended by the questions. If he had been in any doubt about it, her words and the manner in which she spoke them, would have eradicated it. "I realise this is unpleasant, Mrs Corrigan."

Either she was uninterested in his acknowledgment of the fact, or she had not heard it. "I did see some lights in Mr Fisher's painting studio."

Carr's eyes hardened with interest. "Mr Fisher?"

"Our local artist." Elsa looked across at Carr. "My husband is working with him at the moment to resurrect the career of some other, equally unknown artist."

"I'm aware of that and of the gift your husband gave to the church," said Carr. "I have seen the painting itself. It is remarkable."

Elsa smiled, but it was out of politeness rather than humour. "I'm afraid art is an undiscovered country to me."

Carr returned her smile, as if to demonstrate that there was no adverse judgement to her confession. "Did you see anybody in Mr Fisher's studio?"

She shook her head. "But I suppose he must have been in there, or else there would be no need for the lights to be on."

"It was not torchlight you saw, then? The light was not moving around?"

"No."

"You took it to be Mr Fisher himself, then?"

She smiled in bewilderment. "Naturally, as it is his studio."

"Did you approach it?"

"No." The brief silence which followed seemed to demand more from her. "I didn't stay long at all. I noticed the light, and I moved on. It was none of my business."

"Of course not," replied Carr. He rose slowly to his feet. "I think I have taken up too much of your time, dear lady. I thank you for your hospitality and your patience. I shall see myself out."

Elsa Corrigan took Everett Carr at his word and watched him step out into the hallway. Almost as soon as the door was closed behind him, she sank back onto the settee, cradled her head in her hands, and allowed the silent tears to fall slowly but freely down her cheeks.

Chapter Twenty-One

"My wife is a liar, sir," said Arthur Corrigan. "I do hope you realise that."

Carr had not yet reached the front door when he was stopped in his tracks by the voice. He turned to find Corrigan leaning against the frame of the library door, his ankles crossed and his arms folded. He was smiling, but the stretching of the lips was malicious, and the deep, brown eyes, which stared at Carr, were glazed with a subtle cruelty. There was an insidious arrogance about the man, which Carr found instantly distasteful. He was not a man to make impulsive judgements about people, but he was conscious immediately of a strong dislike for Arthur Corrigan, an aversion which seemed to prickle and infiltrate his skin like an infection. Despite it, Carr held out his hand and gave his name, by way of introduction. Corrigan, with an almost palpable disdain, pushed himself away from the door frame and walked casually towards Carr, taking the offered hand and giving it a firm shake. The grip was too forceful for the occasion, as if to display a fundamental need on Corrigan's part to exert his superiority. Carr, unimpressed, simply smiled.

"You mustn't believe anything she tells you," said Corrigan, nodding his head towards the drawing room.

Carr's smile remained in place. "I must say, she didn't strike me as being a liar."

Corrigan laughed, a guttural and condescending noise. "You don't know her, though, do you? Not like I do."

Carr conceded the point with a raise of his eyebrows. "Is there a reason why you say she is a liar?"

Corrigan placed his hands in his pockets, making the gesture seem almost threatening. "About that library book, for one thing."

Carr lowered his gaze, like a teacher expressing disapproval at a wayward pupil. "You were listening at the keyhole, Mr Corrigan."

Corrigan was unrepentant. "She hasn't got a friend who is so ill that Elsa needs to consult a medical textbook about it, let me assure you."

"Indeed?"

"That's proof she's a liar."

Carr shrugged. "Perhaps it is proof only of a friend about whom you know nothing, sir."

Corrigan shook his head. "Don't you believe it. My wife is full of her secrets. Only yesterday, I overheard her plotting on the telephone, making secret arrangements, talking about how bad her life here is."

"Perhaps to this friend?"

"There is no ill friend," insisted Corrigan. "If there were, I would know of it."

"Did you ask your wife about this conversation you overheard?"

It was clear from his expression that Corrigan thought the question was a stupid one. "Of course, I asked her about it."

"And what explanation did she give?"

"Lies!" Corrigan barked. "That's what she gave. Which is why I'm warning you about her. Whatever it is you want from her, and whatever she's told you, don't be too quick to believe her."

It was only his own suspicions that Elsa Corrigan had lied to him which prevented Carr from dismissing these warnings as foolish melodrama. Nevertheless, although she may have lied, Carr could not envisage Elsa Corrigan as the manipulative deceiver her husband sought to portray. If anything, Carr felt compelled to treat Arthur Corrigan himself as the more likely liar and cheat.

"Do you make a habit of eavesdropping on your wife's conversations, Mr Corrigan?" he asked. If he felt any awkwardness about the question, he did not display it.

Corrigan's eyes narrowed. "I do what I like in my own house."

Carr did not give the response any credence by way of a further reply. "The police will want to know where you were last night, Mr Corrigan, as you will have heard me warn your wife."

"Then I'll tell them," came the untroubled reply. "I was here."

"Alone?"

"Except for the servants, yes."

"No doubt they will corroborate your version of events."

Corrigan shrugged. "I doubt it. I didn't see any of them, and I didn't ring for any of them."

"I see." Carr spoke the words with a solemn but artificial regret. "Can you think of any reason why anyone would wish to harm William Lorrimer?"

"Harm him?"

Carr clicked his tongue in disappointment. "You listen at doors, Mr Corrigan. Let's not pretend you don't know what I mean."

The rebuke, all the more powerful for its calm delivery, had irritated rather than worried Corrigan. It was evident that he was considering a refusal to answer, but the thought was only a temporary one. "I can think of several people who disliked Lorrimer, but I'm not sure any of them would go so far as to kill him. I include myself in that." The final words, little more than an afterthought, were so obviously a routine assertion of innocence as to be meaningless.

"Not Laurence Fisher, for instance?"

Now, the supercilious arrogance wavered, and a flicker of concern glimmered in Corrigan's otherwise antagonistic eyes. "What's Fisher to do with anything?"

Carr gave a simple shrug of his shoulders. "I understood Mr Fisher had an argument with Mr Lorrimer a few days before his death."

"I don't know anything about that."

"Did Fisher not mention it to you?"

Corrigan shook his head. "Why should he?"

"Given your close working relationship on the Van Jansen restoration, I thought he might have confided in you."

Corrigan laughed now, his poise returning. "Fisher and I rarely discuss anything other than the Van Jansen project, Mr Carr. We're not as close as you might assume. To be honest, I am not sure that Fisher is capable of forming any close relationship with anybody. He is very cautious about people, you see. A product of his childhood, I suppose."

"In what way?"

"He's an orphan. His parents were killed in a railway accident near Crewe when he was a baby. He was brought up in a variety of orphanages, and, as I gather, they were not always happy experiences."

A memory was stirring in Carr's mind. "Has he ever mentioned the name Linacre House?"

Corrigan frowned. "Seems familiar, but perhaps I've heard it somewhere else. Possibly from Fisher, yes, but I couldn't say for certain."

"Your wife says that she saw lights on in Fisher's studio last night. Would you know anything about that?"

"No." The denial came easily to Corrigan's lips, but Carr was not fooled by it.

"Does Fisher often work at night?"

The second lie came with an unctuous smile. "I really couldn't say."

"I see," said Carr for the second time and with the same inflexion of regret in his voice. "What was your own personal feeling towards William Lorrimer? I believe you had cause to throw him out of this house."

"Only after suitable warning."

"He was making a nuisance of himself, I take it?"

Corrigan nodded. "He couldn't come to terms with the fact that Harriet Delaney had ended their relationship and taken up with my son. It brought about a change in Lorrimer. Until that happened, I don't think anybody knew quite how malevolent he could be."

Carr gently brushed his impressive moustache. "That appears to be a common theme."

"When he blew his brains out, he did the village a service." Corrigan seemed to be unaware of the callousness of his words. Then, suddenly, he pointed at Carr. "Except, now, we don't think he did kill himself, do we?"

"Possibly not."

Corrigan was nonchalant. "Whoever killed him, then, did the village a service."

Carr's eyes seemed to grow darker than their natural shade. "And his sister? Was her death also a benefit to the community?"

The insensitivity in Corrigan's expression thawed. His lips slowly parted, as if he were about to speak but could find no words to express his feelings, and his eyes seemed to shift their focus, as if seeing both Carr and the tragedy of death for the first time. No apology came, and nor did Carr expect one. Men like Arthur Corrigan, he had no doubt, would view such admissions of wrongdoing as an inherent weakness. For Corrigan, the silence which passed between them, lingering long enough for its effect to be made, served as sufficient contrition.

"Have you got all you came for, Mr Carr?" asked Corrigan at last.

Carr raised his finger. "Just one more point. Your donation of the Van Jansen to the church—was that a simple act of charity? To do the village a service, shall we say?"

Corrigan smiled scornfully at Carr's twist of the knife. "Nothing more than that, Mr Carr. Fisher and I felt it would be appropriate to honour the church with a gift."

"Such a selfless act," said Carr. "And, dare I say, good for publicity elsewhere?"

Corrigan's smile widened, but it still lacked any trace of genuine humour. "What a cynical man you must be, Mr Carr."

Carr shrugged. "A realist, perhaps."

Corrigan held his gaze for a long moment before looking over Carr's shoulder towards the door. "Is that everything, Mr Carr?"

Carr bowed politely and tipped his hat. He turned on his heel, and Corrigan followed him to the door. Pulling it open for Carr, he offered a word of farewell. Carr reciprocated and stepped out onto the driveway.

He walked slowly back to the road, his head sunk on his breast and the cold wind biting at his shattered knee. He tried to empty his mind of the less-than-satisfactory trip to the manor house, but snippets of the conversations kept flashing in his mind like intermittent electric bulbs being turned alternately on and off. Only one of them seemed to stay lit for longer than the others, and that solitary sphere of light was the fact that Laurence Fisher was an orphan and the very real possibility that he had been a victim of Linacre House. Carr's mind returned to the newspaper clipping which he had found in Lorrimer's cottage, the same clipping which seemed to suggest a connection between Lorrimer and the orphanage and, by extension, between the orphanage and Lorrimer's death. Earlier, it had been little more than a fledgling idea. Now, with the revelation of Fisher's parentage, it seemed to be only a few pieces of information away from being not only a certainty, but also a compelling motive for murder.

Chapter Twenty-Two

Although it was only a little before six o'clock, the time of year meant that it was already dark when Carr arrived at Fisher's studio. The sky had the same blue-black gloom as a fresh bruise, and the stars were freckled about like small droplets of discarded paint beside the brighter, silver disc of the moon, which peered out from behind a cloud like a scared child looking for monsters from beneath the bedsheets. The wind had risen and whilst not violent, it was cold enough to make Carr wish for an open fire and buttered muffins.

The studio itself was little more than a dilapidated garden shed, but Carr supposed that it was sufficient for an artist's purposes. The windows were small and strangely fragile, the wood of the frames showing the first stages of rot. The panes were smeared with dirt and grease, so that any natural light which infiltrated the interior would be so minimal as to be almost futile. The paint had once been green, Carr guessed, although now it was the derelict grey of abandonment, but only in those places where it had not flaked away entirely. The door was functional but not imposing, its handle rusted by the continuous onslaught of the elements. As he looked down at it, Carr could see that the lock had been forced and had yet to be replaced, so that the door hung loosely on its hinges. No doubt this was the work of the person who had required the lights which Elsa Corrigan had seen, which meant that whoever that person was, he was not Laurence Fisher, who would surely have no cause to break into his own studio.

Carr pushed against the door and let it swing open, its hinges straining with the effort, their scream unnaturally loud in the almost silent night.

Carr was anxious not to alert any passer-by to his presence in the studio, so he dared not risk any light, either by the electric switch on the wall inside the studio or from the engraved, silver cigarette lighter in his pocket, so he waited a moment for his eyes to become accustomed to the darkness of the interior. As they did so, Carr became aware of the silhouetted outlines of a chair and desk, boxes, and what he took to be small filing cabinets. Along a windowsill, to his left as he entered, there were vases and old jam jars, filled with a variety of paintbrushes, chewed pencils, and wooden rulers. There was an unmistakable smell of damp inside, which forced Carr to take out his handkerchief and cover his mouth and nose with it, a small cough of distaste simultaneously barking from his throat.

As his eyes adapted to the gloom, Carr became aware at once of something missing. He was no artist, but he supposed that certain trappings might be expected to be associated with every painter: easels, canvases, sketchbooks, smocks. In this almost derelict den of Laurence Fisher, however, there was nothing of the sort. Carr walked to the desk and pulled open the shallow drawers on either side. He found only discarded pencils, their points broken, a haphazard ball of old twine, and some loose coins. Turning away from the desk, he walked further into the studio, to where a small stool was set to one side, presumably the one which Fisher used when he was working. Once again, the absence of any evidence of such work struck Carr with some force. He glanced to the door, recalling its broken lock, and he made the natural assumption that Fisher had been the victim of burglary, possibly by whoever it was Elsa Corrigan had seen. Carr shook his head irritably. The idea was nonsense: burglars, he told himself, did not turn on lights. They would act very much as he was doing now, stealthily and in darkness.

And yet, the lock was broken, and all trace of Fisher's art was gone. It was surely impossible to deny a connection.

Carr nodded slowly as realisation dawned on him. Elsa Corrigan had seen a light, yes, and she had stated that it was motionless. But she had also confessed to looking at the studio for a moment only and paying very little attention. She might well have mistaken a torchlight, held still whilst something was examined, for the ceiling lights of the studio. The presence of a torch would sit far more easily with the facts of the broken lock and stolen property, but if a burglary had taken place, it led to the secondary mystery of why anyone would wish to steal Fisher's work. The brief murmur of an idea that Fisher might have painted something incriminating drifted into Carr's mind, but it was only a fleeting, unsubstantiated thought.

Carr looked once more around the studio. In the far wall, there was a small fireplace, which would surely provide only a scarce source of heat. Now, its grate was as cold as the grave, both to the touch and to the eye. Carr knelt down in front of it, his damaged leg stretched out to the side. He took out his cigarette lighter and sparked it into life. Using the ferrule of his cane, he poked in the long-extinguished ashes. There seemed to be nothing of value, however, and he was about to smother the flame when he saw it. Amongst the black and greys of the burnt wood and ashes, the vivid blue-purple of the small piece of paper seemed vibrantly incongruous.

More striking than its contrast, however, was its familiarity. Carr picked it out of the grate and rose to his feet. He was suddenly eager to make sure of his recollection. He had no doubt now that he had seen this type of paper twice before: once, in the dead hands of Isobel Croft and, on the second occasion, in Lorrimer's cottage. He remembered clearly his frustration at being unable to recall something in the cottage which had struck him as important. In Lorrimer's cottage, Carr had made a mental note of the dead man's personalised stationery, of its variety of exclusive colours, but in that moment, he had been unable to forge the link with the small scrap of such paper which Isobel had gripped in her final moments of life. Now, here it was again, having been partly burned in Laurence Fisher's studio fire.

The connection struck Carr almost as heavily as the blow to the back of his knee. He felt an immediate, searing pain erupt in his shattered leg, and he was aware suddenly of the foolishly delicate clattering of his stick to the ground, which contrasted sickeningly with his own startled, animalistic howl of agony. He was aware that he was sinking to the floor, morbidly compliant in his inability to retaliate. Within half-seconds, he was on his hands and knees, his head slightly turned to look behind him, in the hope that he might see the fact of this unknown assailant. But all Carr saw was darkness. He had not registered the raised hand of the person behind him, and nor did he seem to hear the grunt of effort as the attacker lunged forward with a sickening speed and determination to hurt. Carr saw and felt none of it.

In that moment of pain and dread, all his world consisted of was the sudden impact of something hard against the back of his head. There was a hideous, deadening sound, which seemed to him to be both unnatural and terrifying. Sudden and simultaneous wishes not to be dead or, alternatively, not to have to live with any permanent damage to his brain seemed to overwhelm him, but this moment of panic was not prolonged. Almost immediately, it was overtaken and subdued by a second blinding explosion of lightening pain in the back of his skull. His mind raced across his life, and none of it seemed to make any sense to him. All that mattered to him now, it seemed, was the increasing severity of his pain. But the light faded as quickly as it had come, and Carr felt himself slump to the floor, his lungs expelling a groan of air as he lay on the flagged stone of the ground, its cold somehow soothing, despite being so intense that it seemed to be the ice of his grave.

Then, as the dull, black of unconsciousness came to sweep him away, Everett Carr felt nothing more.

Chapter Twenty-Three

He was conscious of noises, but their nature was uncertain. They might have been voices, but the words were indistinguishable, too protracted to be intelligible, and their pitch was too low, so that they were little more than prolonged, deep sounds with no meaning. There were lights, too, although he was not sure whether they were behind his eyes or all around him, but they were piercing, maliciously bright, whatever their source. His mind was weighted down by a dull but persistent ache emanating from the base of his skull to his frontal lobes, cruel in itself, but courteous enough to leave no fraction of the skull untainted by its presence. The stone floor was no longer against his cheek and the sudden realisation of the fact seemed to start a fire under the skin of his face. His lips had the faint taste of brandy across them, so that a similar fire raged on them, but it was cleansing, revitalising his senses slowly but assuredly, so that he was aware now that he was seated and there was an arm around his shoulders. Beyond these small indications of life, his principal sensory perception was pain, and he took a moment to succumb to it, as if to normalise it and thereby make it tolerable.

More brandy passed his lips, and he coughed in ineffective retaliation. He passed a hand across his face, once, twice, and with force on the third time, as if in an effort to pull the pain from out of his head through his physical features. The comforting sensation of the hair on his face against his palm was more soothing than the taste of alcohol, however medicinal, and the vain but reassuring stroking of his elaborate moustache, followed by the loving caress of the Imperial beard, was as much of a remedy as any tonic or hospital prescribed bed rest.

Everett Carr opened his eyes and seemed to see the world in colour for the first time. As he looked on, those brittle, mildewed windows in their slowly rotting frames, at the rickety wooden desk, and at the glass jars filled with the wooden stems of brushes and pencils, Carr found himself marvelling at the vibrant colours of the decay. What had seemed previously to be drab and disreputable, now seemed vivacious and palatial, like the first spring morning after the coldest of winters. It was a transitory, even fanciful idea, and he knew that it was his eyes and mind deceiving him as they returned to their normal functions, but the effect was no less dramatic, or indeed welcome, for that.

"Thank God you're all right," said a voice to his side.

Carr turned, conscious at once of a brutal lance of pain across the back of his skull, and found himself looking into a pair of kindly, concerned eyes which peered out behind the lenses of a pair of circular, tortoiseshell spectacles. The cheeks beneath were freckled, giving them the appearance of freshly laid eggs, and the unruly tangle of ginger hair curled across the forehead and over the ears, so that the man still retained something of his childish naivety. Carr became aware at once of an enthusiastic innocence, which would have been the pride of a benevolent grandparent but the prey of a schoolyard tormentor.

Carr tried to stand, but the young man coerced him gently back onto the stool. "Don't try to stand. You've had a nasty knock on the head. I've sent for some medical help."

Carr fought hard to find the voice for the words, which came out in a thick, coarse whisper. "Very kind, thank you."

"More brandy?"

Carr waved away the ornate, silver flask with its cork-lined bayonet cap and inscription. "No, thank you, Mr Fisher."

The young man stared. "You know my name?"

"I know this is your studio, and I knew you were due back from London. I made my guess. My name is Everett Carr," he added with a bow of his head and an offer of his hand.

Fisher accepted the hand and shook it tentatively. "I don't know what you were doing in my studio, Mr Carr, but evidently, someone didn't take kindly to it."

Carr waited for the inevitable assurance of Fisher's own innocence, but it did not come. Perhaps the artist felt it would have been otiose, or, Carr supposed, he might have known how hollow a reassurance it might have seemed.

"I don't recall very much of what happened," said Carr. "Someone kicked my cane away from me and struck me on the back of my bad knee. I'm lame, Mr Fisher," he added, by way of explanation. The words, which he so seldom spoke in any circumstances, seemed both incongruous and suddenly tragic to his own ears.

Fisher might have been aware of the older man's embarrassment, for he did not make any direct response. "I came through the door and found you flat out in front of me. Whoever it was hit you twice on the back of the head."

The memory of the second blow, surely unnecessary unless it had been designed to kill, caused a wave of nausea to break over the shores of Carr's senses. "Perhaps I will have another dash of brandy after all."

Fisher obliged, and Carr sipped at the drink with gratitude. After a moment, allowing it to take its effect, he handed the flask back to Fisher. "Family heirloom?"

"Sorry?"

Carr pointed to the flask. "It is very exclusive."

Fisher lowered his head, his freckled cheeks singing slightly. "I don't have any family, Mr Carr. No, this was left to me by an old friend, who died. He was an artist, one of the inspirations in my life. This was the last thing of value he had and when he died in poverty, he left it to me. I shouldn't use it, really. You must blame an artist's vanity, Mr Carr."

"Perhaps I should blame an understandable sentimentality," said Carr gently.

Fisher smiled sadly. "I prefer that explanation."

If this sudden vulnerability was an act, it struck Carr as a particularly skilful one. "I should explain what I was doing here."

Fisher laughed. "Don't worry, Mr Carr. I doubt very much you're the man who robbed me."

"Robbed you?"

The artist waved his arm around the room. "Look at the place. Anything of any use or value has been stolen. My easels, my sketchbooks, my canvasses. Months of work gone."

"I noticed as much when I came in here," said Carr, now remembering. "Where were you last night, Mr Fisher?"

The look he gave was quizzical but not offended. "At home."

"And you have been in London all day today?"

"Yes."

"Might I ask what you were doing?"

Fisher shrugged. "Some research at the British Library."

"Further investigations into Van Jansen?" Carr watched the young artist nod his head. "What time did you leave?"

"I caught the seven o'clock train. Why?"

Carr ignored the question for the moment. "When was the last time you were here, at the studio?"

Fisher gave it a brief moment of thought. "Yesterday afternoon, at around six."

"And now is the first time you've come back here since then?"

Fisher was, perhaps understandably, becoming irritated. "What are you getting at, Mr Carr?"

"You must forgive me," smiled Carr, pulling himself to his feet and gesturing for his cane, which Fisher passed to him from the floor. Carr was surprised at how relieved he felt simply to have it back in his hands, to have its faithful reassurance by his side once more. "I must be making no sense at all to you."

"Not much," agreed Fisher.

Carr took some moments to catch his breath. The effects of the attack had not been ameliorated by his desire to stand. "Last night, there was a report of a light in here. I believe it was a torchlight. Now, as you say, your work is missing. It is not too difficult to imagine a connection, and for my sins, I came here to try to prove it."

"Why?"

Carr dismissed the question. "A far more important point is why anyone would wish to steal your work, Mr Fisher."

The young man sighed and looked uselessly around the wreckage of his creative haven. "In that, I'm as much at a loss as you, Mr Carr. It pains me to say it, of course, but my work isn't worth stealing any more than it's worth buying."

Carr has suspected as much, but his natural politeness prohibited him from saying it. Instead, he made an alternative suggestion. "What about a connection to the Van Jansen restoration?"

Fisher's eyes glazed, as if transfixed by the idea, and his short gasp of a laugh gave the impression that he had not thought of it before Carr had spoken. "Of course, it must be that."

"Did you have anything in here, relating to the project, which might have been valuable to a thief?"

"My research papers." Fisher ran to the small desk and pulled open the drawers. He swore bitterly when, as Carr knew, his eyes had fallen on the old twine and discarded coins. "There were journals in here, filled with notes about provenance, contact details, valuations from independent experts. Prints and platelets of Van Jansen, his letters, his receipts, almost everything you might need to piece together his drunk, failed life."

"Would they be valuable?"

Fisher laughed, but it was a malignant sound. "The irony is that until Arthur Corrigan and I began work on reintroducing Van Jansen's work, the answer to that would have been no. Now, they may well fetch a high price. Do they call that being the author of one's own misfortune?" He sniffed. "Or should that be the painter of one's own demise?"

Carr offered a bitter smile at the joke. "Who would know that you had these documents here?"

Fisher shrugged. "Everyone in the village knew I was working on the project with Arthur Corrigan."

"Might he have been responsible?" When Fisher looked at him in confusion, Carr shrugged simply. "In an effort to remove you from the process?"

Fisher shook his head. "Corrigan has a business head on him, Mr Carr, but not an artistic one. He can't do this without me, so what's happened here will affect him as badly as it does me."

"I see," murmured Carr. "Why would anybody steal the easels and the canvasses?"

"To make it appear to be a common burglary, perhaps?"

"To disassociate the burglary from Van Jansen specifically, you mean?" Carr, his eyebrows raised, gave a slight bow of his head. "It's a possibility."

Whether it was or not, Fisher seemed uninterested. He had been leaning against the fragile wooden desk, with its empty drawers, and now he pulled out the chair and sat down with a grunt of failure. He removed his spectacles and sent them clattering across the top of the desk before running his hands through the ginger curls and down the sallow, mottled face.

"I suppose it was inevitable," he said, replacing his spectacles. "I've never had much luck in the past. No reason why the present should be any different."

Carr had a brief vision of a child with flaming hair, suffering at the respective hands of Edwin and Marjorie Pryce, expecting but never receiving help from Dr Matthew Olson, but perhaps finding solace in sketches or childishly crude attempts at landscapes of places far away from Linacre House. Whether that child had existed, Carr could not say, but, if he had, it was not a difficult leap of the imagination to see his adult self as being something like Laurence Fisher. If Carr had the desire to ask the question, he was not to satisfy himself of it. The time for that enquiry, if it ever came, would be later.

Instead, an alternative question intruded into Carr's mind. "Did you know William Lorrimer?"

It startled Fisher, and he was unable to disguise the fact. "What's he got to do with anything?"

Carr's smile was polite, but his voice was insistent. "Did you know him?"

"Vaguely." There was a hint of cautious derision in Fisher's tone.

"I believe you argued with him a few weeks ago. Not long before he died, in fact."

Fisher was now glaring at Carr, but it was not clear whether he was trying to understand how Carr knew about the argument or what relevance it might be to the man himself. "So, what if I did?"

Carr noted the lack of any denial. "He made an allegation of theft; is that not so?"

Fisher was shaking his head, almost immediately. "No, not at all. You have been misinformed, Mr Carr. Gossip can easily become a twisted version of the truth."

Carr gave an impression of humility, placing his hand on his breast. "A thousand apologies, Mr Fisher, if I have been given false information."

"You have," declared Fisher.

"I was told such dreadful things about Lorrimer saying he was going to expose this theft, do something about it, about him calling you a snake, and Heaven knows what."

Fisher's face had paled, but his indignation remained as intense as ever. "If you must know, Mr Carr, there was an altercation between Lorrimer and me, that much is true, but it was nothing to do with me. It was about Edgar Corrigan and Harriet Delaney."

It was Carr's turn to glare. "Indeed?"

"If you listen to village gossip, you may have heard that Lorrimer was accused of making anonymous threats to Miss Delaney and Corrigan on the telephone, of dogging their movements, and making their lives a general mess."

Carr nodded. "I have heard something of the sort."

"Right, well, I thought it was a pretty poor show. So, I told Lorrimer so. We came across each other in the woods, and I told him what I thought."

"How did he react?"

"With a rude, but defensive suggestion that I do something unpleasant to myself." Fisher laughed, despite himself. "If you'd known Lorrimer, that would not be as shocking as it might appear now."

CHAPTER TWENTY-THREE

"And what happened?"

Fisher gave a roll of his shoulders, as if recoiling at the memory. "I told him he should leave the two of them alone, that they'd done nothing wrong, and he would do himself no good in carrying on like a petulant schoolboy."

"But he refused to oblige?"

Fisher smirked. "That's putting it mildly. He told me to mind my own business and asked what it was to do with me. I told him, I have no special affinity for Corrigan or the Delaney girl, but decency is decency. And that's when Lorrimer said Corrigan had stolen the girl from him."

Carr looked up at the ceiling. "And that was the theft concerned?"

Fisher spread his palms in agreement. "But there was no mention of a snake. Whoever overheard us must have mistaken something else for that. Unless I called Lorrimer a poisonous little snake. I may well have done. I really can't remember."

"Or vice versa, perhaps?" ventured Carr.

"Just possibly," conceded Fisher with a smile. "The truth is, Mr Carr, very few people in Little Marsham liked William Lorrimer. If I didn't know Lorrimer had shot himself, I'd have said Philip Ryman would have killed him outright."

Carr felt his blood turn to ice in his veins, and the rhythmic pain in his head seemed to increase its pace. "The local solicitor?"

Fisher shook his head. "I'm not going to chastise you for gossiping about me, Mr Carr, and then indulge in the same malice against Ryman. I just know he had cause to hate Lorrimer, that's all."

Carr, with a show of being humbled, bowed. "Your morals do you justice, my boy. And you are quite right to reprimand me. I am an old, lonely man. When you are likewise, Mr Fisher, you might find yourself falling for these snippets of interesting conversations, regardless of whether they are true or not. If you do, no matter how much they may brighten your dull days, you must remember this moment and follow your own advice."

Fisher laughed. Despite the slight awkwardness of the past few minutes, he found himself liking this little man with the impressive moustache and the dark, persuasive eyes. "How's your head now, Mr Carr?"

Carr touched the base of his skull. "I fear it shall be worse tomorrow than it is now, my boy. I think a bowl of soup and an early bed are in order. For now, I thank you indeed for your kind attentions. You have been very obliging to a nosy old fool."

Fisher lowered his gaze. "Not at all. A pleasure."

Carr limped towards the door, Fisher following closely behind. Carr pointed to the broken lock of the door. "You should attend to that immediately, perhaps."

"I shall."

Carr smiled and stepped back into the late evening air. It was refreshingly cool, but its sudden, cold vitality seemed to intensify the pain at the base of his skull. He wavered for a moment, his step more unsteady than usual, but he dismissed Fisher's attempts to assist. Slowly, he made his way away from the studio and back towards the village. He did not look back towards Fisher but, if he had, he would have seen the young artist slumped back at the desk, his head buried in the crook of one arm and the fist of the alternate hand slowly but fiercely banging down on the wooden surface of the table.

And if Carr had retraced his steps back to the studio and interrupted this moment of barely contained fury, he would first have heard Laurence Fisher's voice, hissing out between clenched teeth, as it whispered a hostile and vehement refrain.

"Bloody Lorrimer…better off dead…just bloody better off dead…"

Chapter Twenty-Four

On the following day, Carr's head felt no worse than in the immediate aftermath of the attack. He had retired to bed early, with a stiff brandy and soda inside him, and had slept better than he felt he had any right to expect. The early morning glare, which greeted him when he cautiously opened the curtains of his room at the tavern, was painful but not immobilising. Carr was not accustomed to malingering; he had been raised to bear discomfort and pain with fortitude, and his parents, being typical of both their class and their era, had seldom permitted any childhood illness to persist. A brief period of recuperation, with associated sympathy, would have been expected, but so would a determination to leave the sick room and continue with one's duties at the first sign of improvement. Now, nursing the back of his head with a soothing palm of his hand, Carr felt a similar obligation to persist.

He abluted and dressed, rather slower than might ordinarily have been the case, and attended to the daily obligations to his moustache and beard. Once completed, he looked at himself in the plain but honest mirror, which hung above the small fireplace in his room, and nodded his approval at the image which stared back at him. Washing and dressing had somehow made the throbbing ache at the base of his skull bearable, as if the simple formality of morning routine had served as a tonic against it, if only by restoring something of his dignity. The dark eyes were alive, even if the cheeks were a little paler than normal, but the face which looked back at him was not that of a defeated man, and, on account of that, Everett Carr was both grateful and galvanised. His knee still seared with pain, but that was nothing new to him, and he knew that it was little or nothing to do with the previous night. The cause of that agony was altogether more difficult to bear.

He descended to the main area of the inn and ordered some hot, strong coffee, together with toast and marmalade. Breakfast was not a meal which had played a serious part in Carr's life, but, intermittently, he felt it was prudent to indulge and that morning seemed to be such an occasion. The coffee was what he craved, however, and the pot was reassuringly hot and the black liquid inside suitably powerful and bitter. The toast was serviceable, if functional, although the marmalade was as good as any, he had sampled in London. Human resilience and even the most basic of breakfasts had done much to suppress the pounding in his head and, as he rose from his breakfast table, Carr felt ready to confront the day.

He stepped out of *The Marsham Tuns*, but found that his path was blocked. The man standing before him was large, although he carried both his height and heft with an easy authority. He was young, perhaps a shade under forty than over it, although his face had already begun to show signs of his responsibilities. There was a permanent crease between his eyes, and similar lines extended from the side of his nose to the corners of his mouth. The nose was broken, but had been re-set at some point, as successfully as such self-inflicted operations can ever hope to be. One ear was misshapen, swollen almost beyond recognition, so that the man's days playing rugby were plainly legible. The flaws were not sufficient to detract from his otherwise handsome face, however, and the eyes, so pale a shade of brown that they appeared almost amber, displayed a suave intelligence.

"Mr Carr," he said, by way of greeting.

Carr bowed his head. "Detective Inspector Dunn."

The young detective was startled, but he was quick to suppress it, the reaction swift enough for him to retain his impassive professionalism. "You're quick at identification, sir. For the sake of formality, perhaps I should confirm it."

Carr smiled. "I have had some dealings with policemen over the course of my life."

"Nevertheless…" said Dunn, holding out his professional identification for examination. Carr, eager not to offend, made a show of studying it and declared himself satisfied. Dunn pointed to a second man, standing a little distance off. "I believe you know Detective Sergeant Barlow."

"Vaguely."

"You were present when we arrived on the scene of Isobel Croft's murder," said Dunn.

Carr nodded. "I gave my statement to Sergeant Barlow, yes. I think you were otherwise engaged, Inspector."

It was a rebuke, albeit delivered politely, and Dunn took it with courtesy and aplomb. "There was much to ascertain, as you can imagine. Sergeant Barlow is a very capable officer."

Carr smiled. "Of that I have no doubt. As are you, I am sure, Inspector."

"I like to think so, Mr Carr," said Dunn. He was smiling, but it appeared to be an obligation rather than a pleasure. "Which is why I'm here now. I need a word, sir. You see, I'm a little concerned to hear that you appear to have been making—shall we say?—enquiries of your own."

"I beg your pardon, Inspector," said Carr affably, "and no offence meant, I can assure you. I can only blame a force of habit on my part."

Dunn nodded, but it was evident that he was far from satisfied. "I don't like the suggestion that I can't be trusted to do my job, Mr Carr."

Carr was quick to assuage such fears. "Inspector, a man who has risen to your rank in the criminal investigation department at such an early age should have no fears on that account. I have no wish whatsoever either to give that impression or to hinder you in your investigation."

Dunn was not impressed by the flattery. "You've been questioning people, Mr Carr. Surely, you'd know I would find out."

"I certainly made no effort to conceal it," smiled Carr. "It seems to me, Inspector, that something very wicked has taken place in this beautiful village. You have spoken to Mr Bowers, I know, and I am sure he has told you what Mrs Croft said to him about her brother's death."

Dunn nodded. "Yes, but—"

"You're a man of intelligence, Inspector; that is obvious," said Carr. "You're not going to say that Mrs Croft was mistaken, because you know that her death makes no sense unless she was telling the truth. Her brother was murdered, just as she was, and she knew who the murderer was. She confronted him at her brother's grave and…" He found that he could not say the words. Any way of finishing the sentence seemed, on reflection of the tragedy, too trite to be credible. Carr found his breath once more. "What we must do is find out why William Lorrimer was killed."

"I'm aware of that," said Dunn patiently. "And I was thinking along those lines, it's true."

"Excellent," interrupted Carr. "Now, do you not think that two heads will be better than one? Pardon me," he added, glancing over at Barlow, "three heads."

There was something quizzical in his tone of voice, a note of mischief which Dunn found both irritating and irresistible, despite his frustrations. If he was any judge of character, and he thought that he was, Dunn understood what it was which Carr had not yet said aloud. "Are you saying you've discovered something, Mr Carr?"

Carr put a hand to his breast and nodded slowly. "I believe so."

But Dunn was immune. "You have a duty to tell me what it is. You know that, I'm sure."

"If I were you," said Carr, his voice now losing some of its amiability, "I'd have one of your boys look into the scandal surrounding a place called Linacre House."

Dunn's expression showed that the name was unfamiliar to him. "And why would that be?"

"I think Lorrimer had discovered that somebody connected with the place is living here in Lower Marsham."

"Why would that be a reason to kill him?" Dunn's voice carried within it no twist of irritation, only a sudden, genuine interest.

Carr's eyes darkened, and the previous affability drifted out of his expression, being replaced by an unmistakable shadow of sadness. "It would be a very good reason to kill him, believe me, Inspector, but it is important that I do not cloud your judgement. You must learn about it with as few preconceptions as possible. Nevertheless, if anyone connected to Linacre House is living here secretly, they would certainly not wish the association to come out."

"And it would be a motive to silence Lorrimer?"

Carr nodded. "Unquestionably."

Dunn found that he was absorbed, however reluctantly, as he placed his hands in the pockets of his coat. "Anything else, Mr Carr?"

Carr shook his head. "Nothing, although I would ask Mr Fisher about the burglary at his studio, and it would be as well to bear in mind William Lorrimer's personal stationery. And, yes, whilst I remember, you should investigate a fire in the woods on the night of Mrs Croft's murder." He reached into his pockets and pulled out the metal clasp and the stained linen.

Dunn took both items and examined them carefully. "Is that blood?"

"Possibly, but it will need much closer examination than we can give it here."

"What was in this fire?"

Carr shrugged. "At this point, I cannot say for certain."

Dunn looked back at him from under a raised eyebrow. "But you have ideas?"

Carr preened his moustache and beard. "Always, Inspector."

"Don't you think you should share them?"

It was obvious from the inspector's voice that he thought so, but Carr was more cautious. "Sometimes, the ideas aren't very good, Inspector, and they must be given time to ferment before they are of any value at all. But I shall keep nothing from you, on that you have my word."

Dunn handed the piece of metal and linen to Barlow. "I think it would be best, Mr Carr, if we spoke again later this evening. I'd be interested to know when these ideas of yours have fermented." His eyes were amused, but there was a serious authority coating his words.

Carr bowed. "I would be honoured, Inspector. And thank you for indulging me."

Dunn held up a hand of caution. "I'm not sanctioning any sort of private investigation, Mr Carr, you must understand that, but I can't stop a member of the public from gossiping, however much I may discourage it."

Carr's eyes narrowed. "I object to the word gossiping, Inspector, if I may say so. Other than that, I note all you say. Good morning."

As he tipped his hat in a polite gesture of farewell, stepping past Dunn and Barlow into the main street, the inspector called after him. "What word would you prefer, Mr Carr?"

Carr stopped in his tracks and turned on his heel. "Assisting, Inspector. Much closer to the truth."

Dunn's smile might equally have been a sneer. "Where might you be assisting next, sir?"

"I find I need some legal advice, Inspector," said Carr, tipping his hat once more and turning away from them.

The two detectives watched him limp down the street, and he was out of sight before Barlow looked across at his senior officer. "We're not taking him seriously, are we, sir?"

Dunn shrugged. "I'm reserving judgement, Jim. Have a look into this Linacre House he mentioned. If there's something in what he says about it, let's give him the benefit of the doubt. If not, we'll warn him off." He pointed to the metal and the linen. "Either way, those are a priority. Let's find out if that is blood. Ask around, see if anyone recognises the metal clasp as being part of something."

Barlow pocketed the items. "What do you think that old lunatic meant about Lorrimer's personal stationery?"

Dunn shook his head. "You heard what I did. Let's take Mr Carr one step at a time. Linacre House first, writing paper, second. And, Jim," he added, his voice now rigid with seniority, "don't call anybody a lunatic or anything else derogatory in my presence again. If you can't manage that, reconsider your position."

Barlow, humbled, gave an obedient nod of the head. "Yes, sir."

"We'll part ways, Sergeant," declared Dunn. "You go back to the station and docket those pieces of evidence. Get that wheel turning, and then get yourself to the archives. Start digging into Linacre House."

CHAPTER TWENTY-FOUR

"What will you be doing?"

"Speaking to Laurence Fisher." Dunn looked back to the pub. "We'll meet back here at noon. You can buy me a Ploughman's and a pint."

Barlow smiled. "You're on, sir. But I still say it's medical advice this chap Carr needs, not legal."

Dunn gave no further reply, but his contemplative expression suggested his mind thought otherwise. The inspector was still young, but he had seen enough of life, both as a man and as a police detective, to take nothing for granted. And that, he told himself, included Everett Carr.

Chapter Twenty-Five

Sitting across from him, Everett Carr was unable to decide whether Philip Ryman was a frightened man or a guilty one. There was something about the eyes, like those of a man who has spent his life chasing the gallows, which suggested that either possibility might be true. They were unnaturally wide, which might have denoted fear, but there was a furtive dread behind their blue, which suggested the inexorable guilt of a hidden secret. They were restless, never settling on Carr for longer than a few seconds, preferring instead to dart around the professional luxury of the office, as if desperate for some means of escape. The fingers were similarly mobile, turning a pencil around themselves with a dexterity which only a nervous man can exhibit, and the unmistakable aroma on his breath of stale alcohol, mixed with fresh, suggested that his troubles were buried under daily excesses of the stuff.

"I don't know what you want me to say," he said.

Carr's voice was gentle, but uncompromising. "Is it true?"

Ryman placed the pencil down carefully on the desk. "Why should I discuss this with you, Mr Carr?"

"You're under no obligation to do so," Carr replied, "but it might save you from a visit from the police. I imagine you would prefer that. For a solicitor to be interviewed formally as a suspect in a murder investigation would be professionally awkward, I daresay. Certainly, in my day, it would have been," he added with a smile.

Ryman's eyes narrowed. "You're a solicitor?"

Carr shook his head. "A barrister, and I sat as a judge for many years.

Criminal matters, though, not civil. I'm retired now."

Ryman watched Carr's hand drift automatically to his shattered knee, and something about the sudden sadness which filled the dark eyes under the heavy white brows suggested to the solicitor that there was a connection to be made. Similarly, it gave him the impression that any enquiry into the matter would be both unwelcome and ignored. Ryman leaned back in the leather chair and contemplated Carr for a quiet moment. The man had not made an appointment, but had entered the offices of Ryman, Leith & Parkes with an ingratiating politeness which had prevented Ryman from refusing to see him. Carr's demeanour and manner had been so courteous that to deny him an audience would have seemed churlish and, Ryman was compelled to admit, oddly cruel. Now, looking at this brief but unmistakable sadness in the dark eyes of his visitor, those same feelings of obligation returned to him. Angela, he had no doubt, would consider them a weakness and force him to feel ashamed of having them.

"It's true that Lorrimer and I didn't see eye to eye," he said, trying not to hear the words as a confession, "but I had nothing to do with his death. If Laurence Fisher is saying anything to the contrary, he needs to be careful. We still have laws of slander in this country."

Carr did not look at him; instead, he kept his eyes fixed on the floor beneath him. "Why would he suggest that you had a good reason to kill him?"

"People are vicious."

Now, Carr did raise his gaze. The statement had been so intensely spoken, the words so laced with venom, that the honesty of it was almost blistering. It struck Carr that it was a curious thing to say, so bleak in its paranoia and yet so petulant in its apparent self-indulgence. "What makes you say that?"

Ryman must have felt that he had said too much, because the shake of his head was so vigorous that it seemed as if he were trying to erase the memory of his words from his mind by shaking them loose from it. "I'm sorry, I shouldn't have done."

Carr allowed a moment to pass before speaking once more. "From what people have told me about him, I can believe that Mr Lorrimer himself was vicious. Or perhaps it would be more accurate to say malicious."

"I can't argue with that." Ryman rose from his desk and walked over to a filing cabinet, from which he took a file of papers. He threw it on the desk and sat down once again. "That is just one of the files I have regarding William Lorrimer. He was a client, but I suppose his entitlement to confidentiality will be breached when the police come, so I may as well breach it. Keeping his secrets always made me feel contaminated anyway."

Carr felt similarly contaminated by Ryman's bitterness. "What's in the file?"

"His instructions to sell a cottage he owned. The sale was only in the initial stages and not finalised, so I don't consider myself duty-bound to execute it."

Carr was frowning. "Is there a reason, beyond personal dislike, that you would not wish to do so?"

Ryman nodded, his lip curled in disgust. "Because it would mean that a perfectly respectable and harmless woman would be left homeless. I happen to think that is a disgrace, but Lorrimer had no compunction about it. If you want to know what sort of man he was, there you have it."

Carr's frown had deepened. "Which woman?"

"Dorothy Parrish."

Carr froze, except for the most discreet flicker of interest in the corner of one eye. His mind returned to the cottage where he had talked with Dorothy, recalling its neatness and its pride, the religious devotion displayed in it, and he wondered now how it would have felt to her to learn that her future in it, and her continued ability to call it home, was not only jeopardised but coming to a very definite end. Carr could almost hear the tears of rage and taste the natural panic at the prospect of sudden homelessness, and he could imagine only too keenly Dorothy's dangerous frustration at being unable to do anything about it.

"Did Miss Parrish know about Lorrimer's plans?"

"Not officially," replied Ryman carefully. "But I wasn't surprised when he told me he'd explained the position to her. On the contrary, I would have been amazed if he hadn't. I very much doubt he found the task at all unpleasant."

"Would Miss Parrish have been able to contest his plans?" Carr suspected he knew the answer, but the question seemed appropriate in any event.

Ryman shook his head. "Not at all."

Carr was thinking of Isobel Croft. "What if any of Lorrimer's surviving relatives had wanted to carry out his wishes over the sale of the property?"

Ryman gave the same response. "Dorothy would be homeless."

Carr let the information come to rest in his brain. The truth of the matter was inescapable. Dorothy Parrish suddenly had a motive for ridding herself not only of William Lorrimer but also his next of kin. Carr felt his throat tighten, as if the strength of his conclusions was so damning that it was strangling him. "Did you come straight to the office this morning?"

The sudden change in topic seemed to disorientate Ryman momentarily. "Yes."

"And last night? Were you at home?"

Ryman shook his head. "Not all night, no. I worked late here, then went to the pub for a drink before going home."

"Presumably, you would be able to verify that, if the police asked."

"If I had to." Ryman was becoming visibly impatient. "The place was full, so plenty of people would have seen me."

"And what time did you get home?"

Ryman paused before answering. "I stayed rather longer than I anticipated. I got home at a little before eleven. My wife will verify that to the police, assuming she tells the truth. Now, why are you asking all this?"

Carr had been about to question the comment about Mrs Ryman's honesty, but Ryman's insistence for an explanation was so forceful that to ignore it would have seemed evasive. When he spoke, Carr's voice was low, serious, and laced with foreboding. "Have you heard about the events in the village of last night?"

Ryman's instincts had ignited, and he replied with caution. "What events?"

"A woman has been killed," Carr explained. "There's no doubt that it is murder, but her death calls into question the verdict that Lorrimer committed suicide."

Ryman frowned. "How? There can't be any uncertainty about that, surely."

"The woman was his sister." If Carr expected a reaction to that, he was not to receive it. "She confided that she had proof that her brother was murdered."

"What proof?" Ryman was unable to disguise his skepticism.

"We don't know," confessed Carr, "but she also claimed to know the identity of the murderer. So, you see, her death means that we must take what she said seriously."

Ryman nodded, but it was obvious that he remained far from convinced. "I see that, but the idea is fantastic."

Carr lowered his gaze to the clenched hands in his lap. "Perhaps, but you'll see how important what you have just told me about Miss Parrish now becomes."

Ryman's understanding of the situation, and his outrage at it, was clearly defined in the widened stare and the disbelieving, parted lips. "Dorothy wouldn't do anything like that. She couldn't kill someone, for God's sake."

"She has a powerful motive for both murders, Mr Ryman."

"I won't believe it of her. You've got it all mixed up if that's what you believe."

Something clicked in Carr's mind, like a silent and invisible trap being sprung, and he visibly started at it. It was a connection, a memory of something he had heard or seen which had not previously made sense but now was explained, but when he tried to bring the thought into focus, it drifted away from him, like fog in a strong wind. Carr was used to these frustrating, but common lapses in his ideas, and he closed his mind to this present example with a private sigh of resignation.

Ryman had been watching him carefully, but, once again, it seemed to him that any enquiry as to the cause of Carr's sudden realisation would be futile. Instead, he leaned forward in his chair and asked, "Where was this woman killed?"

Carr, suddenly aware once more of his surroundings, smiled apologetically. "The churchyard. Mr Bowers found her."

The change which came over Ryman's expression was as startling as it was swift. Until the mention of the vicar, the eyes had been inquisitive, and the lips pursed in interest. Now, in the briefest of moments, the eyes had narrowed, the brows creased, and the lips had tightened into a snarl.

"Bowers?" The word came from his lips as a violent hiss.

Carr was instantly on his guard. The edges of his nerves felt like pulses of electricity throughout his body. "That's right."

Ryman got up from his chair and paced towards the window. "Do you know Bowers well?"

"Not especially." Carr waited for a further comment from Ryman, but it was not immediately forthcoming.

Ryman turned away from the window, and Carr saw in his eyes a degree of anger, which was as much to do with sorrow as with fury. "The man's a hypocrite and a liar."

Carr was shocked, not so much by the words but by their incongruity. They seemed so inappropriate as a means of describing the man Carr had met at St Bartholomew's that, for a moment, he was unable to understand them. They seemed to be discordant, like a bow across an untuned violin.

"I must say that he does not strike me as such," Carr felt obliged to reply.

Ryman sneered. "You can take my word for it."

Carr inclined his head. "I should prefer to have some grounds for doing so."

Ryman looked across to Carr with a degree of antagonism. "Ask him about Mary Jerrold, Mr Carr. Get him to tell you how he abused his position with her. His behaviour towards her was, at least, something on which William Lorrimer and I could agree."

Carr's eyes narrowed. Ryman had been discreet enough not to provide specific details of what had happened between Bowers and this lady, but the sordid implication was only too clear. "William Lorrimer was aware of what was happening?"

"He was one of the people who confronted Bowers about it," said Ryman. "As I did myself. Bowers refused to admit anything of the truth, of course, preferring instead to hide his hypocrisy behind his sanctimonious preaching."

"How far did you and Mr Lorrimer take your protestations?"

"How far?" Ryman frowned in perplexity.

"Did either of you threaten to report him to his bishop, for example?"

"Lorrimer did suggest it might be an option."

The inference was an obvious one to draw. Now, almost sadly, Carr was forced to accept that Bowers himself almost certainly had as much cause as anyone else to wish both Lorrimer and Isobel dead. He rose to his feet, his cane clattering against the wooden legs of the chair. "I must be on my way."

Ryman did not protest, walking towards the door in silence, in order to show out his visitor. Carr moved slowly across the carpeted floor of the office, although his mind was racing at speed. He nodded a gesture of gratitude to Ryman and stepped out into the reception area. Ryman had half closed the door when Carr turned back to face him.

"One last question, Mr Ryman, if you would indulge me," he said. The raise of Ryman's eyebrows was going to be the only prompt to continue. "Why did you suggest that your wife would not be honest about your movements?"

Ryman appeared not to understand. "I'm sorry?"

Carr smiled an apology, as if it were he who was mistaken. "I beg your pardon. When we were talking just now, you said that you had worked late and gone to the local inn for a drink. You said you got home later than you had planned."

"That's correct."

Carr nodded. "Yes, but then you said your wife would verify it, assuming she told the truth. I just wondered what you meant by that remark."

Ryman glared at him, as if he had been caught up in a lie of some sort and that it was his own honesty which was questionable. A flame of anxious red engulfed the side of his neck, extending to his cheek, and the breaths seemed to come with difficulty to his lungs. He did not answer immediately, and Carr had the impression that he was debating internally with himself about what that reply should be. Finally, he smiled, a malicious and disconcerting stretch of the lips over the teeth, and the eyes glimmered with a spiteful intensity.

"Perhaps you should ask Mr Bowers about that, too, Mr Carr."

And with that, the door was closed in Carr's face with a forceful snap of the lock. It left him in no doubt that the interview had been terminated.

Chapter Twenty-Six

Not unexpectedly, Carr found Bowers in the church, sitting on the front pew, before the carved representation of the instrument of torture which, through the centuries, had become an incongruous symbol of faith and hope. From the back, the vicar seemed to be at peace, his head bowed as if in prayer, but there was something about the slope of the shoulders which suggested defeat rather than sanctuary and Carr had the sudden impression that it was not solitary mediation which dominated the scene before him, but a pervasive sense of loneliness. He listened carefully, but, whilst he would not have been surprised to have heard tears, he did not. The silence in the nave was absolute, but so eerie in its intensity that it was neither comforting nor harmonious, and yet the gentle sound of Carr's footsteps, uneven on account of his limp, still seemed intrusive, the volume unnaturally intensified by the stillness around it. Carr expected Bowers to react to the sudden noise, but the head remained sunk on the breast, and the shoulders made no movement, so that the vicar was either unaware of the disturbance or untroubled by it.

Carr sat down beside him and, for a moment, made no effort to speak. Instead, he looked up at the cross before him and attempted to find a silent solace from it. As a construction, it was plainly carved, free from any form of adornment or ritualistic decoration, and it struck Carr in that moment that the simplicity of the representation was somehow more powerful than any elaborations could have been, as if the message conveyed by the cross beams was more potent by its simplicity. Carr, not a man to denounce God but, equally, a man whose experiences had left him unable to be entirely assured of His presence, felt strangely closer to Him in that silent moment of contemplation than he could ever previously recall. It was an indication of the power of faith and, suddenly, Everett Carr felt humbled by it.

"Did you wish to speak to me, Mr Carr?"

Bewitched by his thoughts of divinity, Carr initially did not respond. He bowed his head in apology and turned to face the vicar. The face he saw looking back at him was almost that of a stranger. Bowers' youthfulness now seemed weathered, the darkness of the brown eyes matched by the shadows beneath them, and the solemnity of the mouth suggested a sadness which was disproportionate to the number of his years. It was, perhaps, the effects of murder which had taken their toll. Carr had witnessed it many times; as well as destroying every confidence, the crime of murder was capable of eliminating youthful hopes and optimism, like a famine across a troubled continent.

Softly, Carr cleared his throat. "There was something I wished to discuss with you, yes."

Bowers seemed not to have heard. "I find that I spend longer in here now than before. I come to find peace, forgiveness perhaps, but I tend to find only silence. What am I to make of that, Mr Carr?"

The older man shrugged. "It isn't for me to advise you on that. You must find your own answer."

"If God is no longer listening to me, how can I hope to do that?"

"Only you can know the answer to that."

Bowers shook his head. "I've prayed for answers, Mr Carr, but they're never answered."

Carr looked towards the cross once more. "My father used to talk about the test of the shaving mirror. When a man shaved, he would say, he was forced to look into his own eyes, and if he was lying about anything in his daily life, he would know it by his own reflection. A man can't ever lie to himself, and shaving is a daily reminder of it."

Bowers allowed himself a small smile, but it did nothing to lift his mood. "What is it you're trying to say, Mr Carr?"

Carr looked across to his companion. "Perhaps you are denying God's responses to your questions, because you don't feel worthy of them."

Bowers' spine stiffened, an involuntarily defensive movement. "I don't know what you mean."

Carr flexed his fingers around the silver handle of his cane. "Tell me about Mary Jerrold."

It had not been a confrontational demand, but a friendly persuasion to confide. When Bowers looked into Carr's dark yet kindly eyes, he saw no evidence of recrimination or judgement, only an invitation to share a burden. And yet, despite Carr's obvious amiability, Bowers was unable to divorce himself from the suspicion that there was an inherent wish to invade his privacy and condemn him for the past.

"So, you have fallen prey to the gossips and the malicious, Mr Carr," he said, his disappointment obvious, despite his external politeness.

Carr raised a finger of protestation. "Not at all. It is not my intention either to pry or to upset, only to understand. I believe William Lorrimer attempted to make your life difficult on account of your relationship with this lady."

"Who told you that?" spat Bowers.

Carr ignored the question and its indignation. "Is it true?"

"No." The lie was an immediate, nervous spasm, and Bowers was at once aware of it. He eradicated it straightaway with a nod of his head. An exhalation of air exploded from his lungs, as if he were exhausted from keeping the secret within him and was now finally released from the effort.

"Lorrimer threatened to tell the bishop that there was something immoral in your relationship with this woman?"

Bowers nodded, but when he looked at Carr, there were tears in his eyes. "There wasn't, I swear it."

Carr laid a hand on the vicar's arm, a soft but definite assurance of discretion. "Tell me."

Bowers rose from the pew and walked towards the altar. The cross now loomed high above him, the Van Jansen painting resplendent beneath it. Bowers seemed to have no interest in either of them in the present moment, although he stood with his head lowered in supplication, as if praying for the strength and honesty needed in order to explain matters to Carr. For himself, the older man likewise took no notice either of the cross or the painting, his eyes remaining fixed on Bowers' long, thin back. Slowly, Bowers raised his head, whispered a brief prayer of thanks, and turned to face Carr. Not a believer in miracles, nevertheless Carr had the sudden impression that Bowers had once more been able to hear answers to his prayers.

"Do you believe it is possible for a man and a woman to have a close relationship which has nothing to do with love, Mr Carr?" asked the vicar. "And, by love, I mean both spiritual and physical."

"Of course."

"That was all there was between Mary Jerrold and me." Bowers clasped his hands together, and Carr watched the knuckles whiten with the pressure applied. "For her, at least."

Carr made no immediate response, but his frown and the slight nod of his head, so gentle as to be almost impossible to see, showed that he had understood. It seemed suddenly fitting that this conversation should be taking place in the cold stoicism of the church itself, rather than in the warm comfort of the vicarage, and the reversal of their roles struck Carr with a brutal irony. Here was the vicar confessing his sins to the unanointed, before the God in whom only one of them could be said truly to believe.

"I never once abused my position," said Bowers. "I never even confessed to Mary what my feelings towards her were. Perhaps I didn't need to."

Carr shook his head. "Perhaps not."

Bowers began to pace before the altar. "Her husband was a tyrant. Ask anyone in Lower Marsham about Henry Jerrold, and you will hear nothing but good. If you could ask Mary about him, you would hear what I did. Something quite different, I assure you. The clothes she wore, the way she dressed her hair, the food she ate, the opinions she held – all dictated by him."

Carr closed his eyes sadly. He had come across such people, oppressive and oppressed, bound together by something the law and the public decreed was love, but which was as far away from it as it was possible to imagine.

His mind turned to Miranda, to the life they had shared before it had been taken from them, and he knew that nothing in that relationship had been anything other than mutual respect and a respective desire for the other's happiness. They had shared a life without allowing it to dominate either of their individual existences. For one or the other to have dominated would have been to ruin the partnership and to have distorted what had brought them together. Murder had intervened and broken the union, and Carr knew that nothing but such violent wickedness could have done so. And yet, for every marriage like his own, he knew that there were many which were aberrations of that ideal. He felt a sudden sadness overwhelm him, and an abrupt fire of grief exploded in the shattered knee.

"She confided in you?" he asked now, his mind returning to the present.

Bowers nodded. "She said she had nobody else she could trust with her secret. You must remember, and try to understand, how esteemed Henry Jerrold was in this village and the county. He was a JP, a philanthropist, and a picture of respectability. Any criticism of him, even the slightest hint of impropriety, would have been dismissed as incredible, if not slanderous."

Carr stroked his knee. "There is no better camouflage than respectability."

Bowers sighed. "What chance did Mary have? The church, and the vicarage, slowly became refuges for her. She could have no way of knowing how torturous her visits were for me, and I would never have dreamed of telling her. What mattered wasn't my feelings, but hers. If I could offer respite from her prison for a few hours each day, I was happy to do so."

Carr raised his eyebrows. "But it led to gossip?"

Slowly, Bowers nodded. "And what do facts matter then?"

There seemed no reason for any direct reply. "Would Lorrimer have made good on his threat to tell the bishop?"

Bowers seemed to need no time to consider the point. "Very probably. Even after Henry Jerrold took the matter out of his hands."

"By taking Mary away?"

Bowers sat down once more and buried his face in his palms. It was answer enough. "I swear to you, Mr Carr, that I never once acted on my emotions and never once acknowledged them."

Carr contemplated the vicar for a moment and, with an instinctive assurance that something was not being said, he wondered what Bowers was withholding. For his part, Bowers could feel the memory of the bitter sting of the leather as it lashed his back, as keenly as if he had whipped himself in the last few minutes, and the lie about acknowledging his sin seemed to burn his tongue with an equal ferocity. His back was latticed with those scars of acknowledgment of his sins, but he saw no reason to explain as much to Everett Carr.

The older man sat in thoughtful silence, his gloved fingers tracing their way across the waxed moustache and stiff, Imperial beard. His dark eyes were narrowed in concentration, the lips pursed in thought, but no words came from them. Bowers, grateful for the silence which followed his admissions, fell into a session of private prayer. Carr, once aware of this, did nothing to interrupt, and he only spoke once more when it was clear that Bowers' benedictions were at an end.

"Thank you for your candour, Mr Bowers," he said. "I do not pretend to be unaware of how difficult confiding in me must have been."

Bowers shook his head. "Perhaps I have been thankful for the opportunity to explain it to someone with a sympathetic ear."

Carr ignored the compliment. "I fear my intrusion into your private affairs doesn't end with Mary Jerrold."

"I don't understand." Perhaps he did not, but the vicar's eyes were fixed on Carr with an intensive, almost haunted glare.

"Tell me now, about Angela Ryman."

The words were spoken without emotion, but their intent was only too evident, and Bowers could not fail to recognise it. If Carr had expected some sort of indignant response, he was not to receive it. Instead, Bowers gave the stifled laugh of a defeated man who has come to realise that his objections to a given argument are and have always been in vain.

"You've obviously spoken to her husband." Bowers watched Carr nod in purposeful confirmation. "If I tell you that the man is paranoid, for reasons I cannot begin to know, it will sound as if I am prefacing my response with an excuse. Nevertheless, it is true. Philip Ryman is frightened of something, and I have no idea what it is, but it has warped his view of my connection with his wife."

Carr spoke softly. "Does lightning never strike twice?"

"I have no feelings for Angela Ryman, any more than she has for me." Bowers looked the older man in the eyes, as if daring him to contradict his words. "She and I are friends, I admit, but there is nothing more to it than that. Any suggestion to the contrary is an ill-founded rumour."

Carr inclined his head doubtfully. "You can see how it might seem as if history were repeating itself, Mr Bowers. The coincidence is impossible to deny."

Bowers' stare was defiant, even as he looked up at the cross. "But it exists, nevertheless."

"Philip Ryman seems convinced that his wife would betray him and that you might be the reason for it." Carr took no pleasure in saying the words, but they were necessary.

Bowers shook his head. "I have told you, Mr Carr. Ryman is a man with his own troubles. Whatever they are, they are nothing to do with me."

There was something emphatic about the singling out of Bowers alone, which made Carr's nerves shimmer with curiosity. "But it might be to do with his wife?"

Bowers rose from the pew. "I shall not engage in speculation with you, Mr Carr. And nor will I betray any confidences which are not my own."

Carr smiled to himself. "Perhaps Mr Ryman's paranoia has a more secure foundation than even he realises."

"You must ask him that."

"If Ryman suspects his wife of being unfaithful," Carr persisted, "might he have mistaken you for William Lorrimer as the man in question?"

If Bowers was shocked or otherwise amused by the question, he did not show it. "Why on earth would you think that?"

Carr was thinking of Laurence Fisher. "It has been suggested that Ryman might have had cause to wish Lorrimer harm."

"By whom?"

Carr smiled. "Perhaps you will allow me my own confidences."

CHAPTER TWENTY-SIX

Bowers shook his head. "I know nothing about that."

"Mrs Ryman has not confided in you about anything of the sort?"

"Not about William Lorrimer."

Carr's eyes hardened. "Then about whom?"

But Bowers said nothing more. Instead, he turned his back on Carr and knelt on the altar steps. Carr watched him, only partially aware that his presence during this new stage of prayer might be invasive. His mind was caught in a net of its own making, the thoughts and ideas holding his concentration captive, so that he was almost unaware of anything around him. At last, however, he pulled himself to his feet and approached the kneeling figure. Gently, he placed his hand on the vicar's shoulder.

"I shall leave you in peace, Mr Bowers," he said softly. The vicar offered no reaction. "I leave you only with this word of caution. The police will be able to discover what you have told me, be assured of that. It would be as well not to try to hide any of it from them, even if it may seem to incriminate someone you care for. Or, indeed, for that matter," he added cautiously, "yourself."

And now, Bowers did react. His lips ceased moving in silent prayer, and he glanced back over his shoulder, the brown eyes burning through the lenses of his spectacles. "Incriminate myself? What in the name of God do you mean by that?"

Carr patted him soothingly on the shoulder. "You must face facts, Mr Bowers. Lorrimer's threat to report your relationship with Mrs Jerrold, however innocent it might have been, could be construed as…"

"A motive for murder? I assure you, Mr Carr, it was no such thing."

Carr smiled back at him and took a step back. "I offer it only as a word of caution. Good day."

It was not until he was halfway down the aisle of the nave that Carr heard Bowers call his name. He stopped in his tracks and looked back towards the altar. Bowers had risen now and was facing Carr directly, his hands clasped in front of him. Slowly, he unfurled his fingers and held his arms wide.

"This is the house of God, Mr Carr," he declared. "In here, the truth is what matters. I am in no doubt that the murderer of William Lorrimer and Isobel Croft will come here in due course and make peace with God. Whatever else I may doubt in life, I am sure of that."

Carr did not respond. Bowers seemed about to say something more, but no words came. If they had, Everett Carr would have been left in no doubt as to the truth of the murders in Little Marsham. As it was, he merely turned on his heel and walked slowly out of the church, his footsteps and silver-handled cane tapping unevenly on the stone floor of the nave.

Chapter Twenty-Seven

Angela Ryman had stopped crying by the time Carr knocked on the door of the cottage. If he had called five minutes earlier, he would have found her racked with sorrow, unable to speak, her throat hoarse with the severity of her sobbing. He might even have been able to make out the gasped, but ultimately empty promises to herself that she would have revenge for the humiliation she now felt so keenly, or the venomous oaths of hatred at the man she had known she never loved but on whom her life seemed to have become dependent. Only now, the affair torn to pieces and left in tatters at her feet, did she realise how little she had meant to Arthur Corrigan, and she had learned it only by the casual ease with which he had ended their covert relationship.

He had not been such a coward as to do it on the telephone and, for that, she had to give him some measure of credit. Equally, part of her wondered whether he had broken off their affair in person out of some perverse pleasure in seeing her reaction to the news. He would have known how badly she would take it, and she understood now that he was cruel enough to enjoy her tears, if only because they would be a sign to him of the power he held over her. For him, her misery would have been a badge of honour, like a vicious mockery of the medals awarded for valour, and to witness it would have entertained him. It was strange, she thought, how differently she saw him after the event. Before, she had only glimpsed his capacity for cruelty, and never had she anticipated that she would be on the receiving end of it.

She cursed herself now for smiling when she had opened the door to him, just as she was sickened by her naïve expression of delight when she saw him on the threshold. "What a lovely surprise."

His reaction had been entirely contrary to hers. "I can't stay long."

He had walked into the cottage without invitation, as if it were his domain and not her own marital home. She had checked the lane outside, satisfying herself that there were no witnesses to the visit, and she had closed the door swiftly, to preserve their privacy. He had not entered the main sitting area of the cottage, but had remained in the small hallway, his hands in his pockets and his eyes fixed on her with a grim expression. Looking back, catastrophe was inevitable but, in the moment, she had no sense of foreboding.

"We're not due to meet today," she had said, stepping towards him and putting her hands on his shoulders.

He had anticipated the planned kiss, and he had recoiled immediately. "Look, I haven't much time, and I don't want to prolong this any longer than I have to. We've got to stop seeing each other. There's no easy way to say it, so I may as well be straight with you. That's just how it is."

Her instinct, even then, might have been to cry, but her confusion, blended with her natural panic of discovery, momentarily overwhelmed her grief. "Has Elsa found out about us?"

"What?" Corrigan had seemed genuinely baffled. "No, of course not. It's nothing to do with her."

"Then why?"

His reluctance to tell her the truth had been obvious. "It's just best to keep our distance, Angela, that's all."

"I can't do that." She knew, then and now, that this was no understatement.

"You'll have to," he had snapped. "The police have been to the house asking about this woman who was murdered. They're digging up the Lorrimer business, too."

"We had nothing to do with that," she had said, but the words somehow had seemed more certain than she had felt.

Corrigan had clenched his jaw. "Of course, we didn't, but having the police poking around makes me nervous, and it should make you nervous, too. We're not exactly behaving in a respectable fashion, are we, Angela? I'm not prepared to give the police any ammunition."

"What ammunition could you be giving them?" she had asked. The idea, it had been obvious, had made no sense to her.

"I'm just being cautious." Corrigan had begun to pace. "Besides, it isn't just the police. There's a persistent old bastard sniffing around the village. Name of Carr."

"And?"

"I've just got a feeling that he might be more dangerous than the police." He had stopped moving and had looked her directly in the eyes. "The less interest he or the police show in us, the better, so let's not give them any reason to think about us. Right?"

She had shaken her head. "I don't understand. Why are you so frightened? Have you done something I should know about, Arthur?"

But Corrigan's impatience had intensified. "For Christ's sake, woman, just do as I say! It's over and done. For now, if not forever, so just get used to it and accept it."

In some ways, she should have expected the explosion. His attitude, the aimless wandering on the spot like an animal behind bars, and the glaring eyes widened by panic ought to have been enough to alert her to the possibility of an outburst, as should the uncharacteristic nature of it all. And yet, when the flecks of spittle hit her cheeks, and the roar of his voice forced her eyes to flicker in fear, she had been unprepared for it. She had stood motionless in its wake, not daring to respond immediately, as if to do so would have been to unleash a more violent rage from within him. She seemed to be aware of nothing but the rasping breath in his nostrils, more feral than she had ever experienced in him, which had made her wonder whether he was waiting for her to respond and was preparing himself for it. Worse, she had wondered whether he was hoping for it, so that it might give him an excuse to unleash this stifled fury which had become so evident in him.

When it had become obvious that she was not about to speak, his breathing had calmed and, when he spoke, his voice had been restrained.

"I've said what I needed to. I should go."

She had heard the door open, and she had envisaged it closing behind him, as he walked away without any further challenge from her. Shaking her head, as if to banish the image from her mind, she had quickly resolved to refuse to allow him to have the final word.

"You're not going to do this to me."

They had been simple, frank words, but he had not expected them, so that when they had been said, their effect was to hold him back. In that respect, they had been more powerful than any tirade of emotion. She had heard the door close slowly once more.

Angela had turned to face him. "I won't let you do this. You're not going to pick me up, use me for your own amusement, then toss me aside."

He had looked at her with something approaching a sorrowful fondness. In retrospect, she would recognise it as a snide amusement. "That's exactly what I'm doing."

The arc of her hand in the air and the sudden sound of her palm against his cheek, like the cracking of a whip, had startled her as much as it had Corrigan and, in its immediate aftermath, he had stared at her as if seeing her for the first time. Instinctively, she had gasped and thrown her hands to her mouth, as if distancing them from him would somehow atone for the attack. If she had expected him to retaliate, she had not recoiled from him in anticipation of it but had remained expectant of whatever punishment she felt might come to her. And yet, his response had not been any form of physical reciprocation, nor had it been any verbal display of anger. Instead, and somehow far more cruelly, he had rubbed his cheek and slowly began to laugh.

"If I'd had any doubts about ending this sorry little liaison," he had said, "you've just put an end to them."

Her tears had flowed with impunity. She had heard herself, as if from a distance, wailing at him for forgiveness, her arms reaching out to him in a plea for salvation. He had grabbed her wrists, more tightly than necessary, and dragged her arms to her sides, so that she had been unable to move of her own accord. His face had been close to hers, and she could smell the stale tobacco and coffee on his breath. When he had kissed her, she had found it repellent for the first time.

"For old time's sake," he had sneered. Turning away from her, he had pulled open the door again and had stepped out onto the narrow garden path.

"I'll break you for this, Arthur," she had shouted through her sobs. "I'll ruin you!"

The words had been hollow, and she had known it, just as he had done. She had no power over him, not in that moment, not in the last six months of their affair, and at no time in the future. He had smiled back at her, as if to reinforce what she already knew to be true.

"You silly bitch," he had said before the door closed on her.

How long she had sat crying, she could not say. It might have been hours rather than minutes; she had no way of knowing. What she did know was that when there was the gentle tapping at the door, her immediate thought was that Corrigan had returned. Her tears had stopped and, when she pulled open the door, her expression was defiant. She had expected an argument, and she had felt ready to engage with it. But the sight of the small, dapper man in black, with the contrasting white Imperial beard and immense moustache, forced Angela to pause. She looked into the kindly eyes which stared back at her with a politeness which belied their darkness.

"Mrs Ryman?" he said.

Angela nodded, bewildered still by the shock of not seeing Corrigan standing there. It was a foolish confusion; she ought to have known that he would never return to her. If there were to be any crawling for reconciliation, it would be her on her knees. Corrigan would expect it and, unless she could resist her instincts, she would oblige. She felt her teeth clamp together in a determination not to humiliate herself any more than she had already allowed.

The little man on the doorstep must have noticed something of her internal turmoil. "Are you all right, dear lady?"

Angela nodded. "Thank you, yes. I'm quite all right. Sorry, but who are you?"

He removed a black leather glove and offered his newly exposed hand. "Everett Carr, dear lady. I wondered if I might have a few moments of your time."

Everett Carr. Initially, the name meant nothing to her, but then a vague memory of Corrigan's words came back to her. He had mentioned the name Carr to her, and it had seemed to be a name which troubled him. Looking at this elegant yet faintly ridiculous man in front of her, Angela found Corrigan's unease all the more difficult to understand. Without quite knowing why, she pulled the door open and permitted him to enter. She was surprised to see that he limped over the threshold, and whilst she had noticed the silver-handled cane by his side, she had taken it as an anachronistic item of fashion rather than a medical necessity. She wondered, albeit idly, what the damage to his leg was and how it had come about, but she said nothing to further the enquiry.

"I was about to make some coffee," she said. "Would you like some?"

He bowed in gratitude. "That would be most welcome, thank you."

She pointed to the living room. "Please, do sit down. I won't be a moment."

Carr walked over to one of the floral-printed armchairs and lowered himself into it. For a moment, he sat in thoughtful silence, wondering primarily what had happened not so long before his arrival, which had caused this young and attractive woman to be reduced to a violent fit of sobbing. The redness around the rims of her eyes told its own story, and Carr, as a man of the world, thought he knew well enough what the matter had been. However, since Carr himself had been with her husband not too long ago, it was evident that he was not the cause of the grief. Similarly, and for the same reasons, Carr knew that Bowers could not be responsible, which might vindicate the vicar's picture of their relationship. With a raise of his eyebrows, Carr wondered which of the other men in the village Mrs Ryman had been involved with until that very morning. Speculation was idle, of course, but it was likewise prevented by the lady's return with the coffee.

Angela poured, and Carr accepted the cup offered to him with a smile and a bow of the head. It was good, strong and bitter, and a tonic to the cold outside air of the morning. Angela watched him sip the coffee and dab at the luxurious moustache with his handkerchief. She ignored the cup which she had poured for herself, preferring instead to concentrate on her visitor, but Carr did not seem to be in any hurry to explain his presence. As the moments passed, Angela became increasingly impatient.

"How can I help you, Mr Carr?" she asked at last.

He seemed to have forgotten that he had any purpose there at all. "Forgive me, Mrs Ryman, I should have explained. But it is so cold outside, and I am so grateful for the warmth of this coffee, that I forgot myself."

"That's quite all right," she replied with a forced smile. "I suppose it's about William Lorrimer."

Slowly, Carr placed his cup on the small table beside his chair. "Why would you say that?"

Angela was not about to divulge Corrigan's warnings to the very man who was the subject of them. "Village rumour is a powerful tool, Mr Carr. Might I ask what business it is of yours? I suppose you're not a policeman, since you haven't shown me any identification to prove it. Besides, you don't look much like one either."

Carr smiled. "No, I am not a policeman. My interest is merely casual."

"Is that so?"

"We are all members of the world, dear lady. In times of common distress, we all need some sort of support, even if it is from a stranger."

"What common distress?"

Carr held her eyes with his. His smile remained in place, but the voice which came out the same lips was so serious that it was somehow ominous. "There has been a murder in the village, Mrs Ryman."

"Murder?" The word seemed alien to her, as if her mouth and voice were incapable of forming or expressing it.

"A woman called Isobel Croft. She was Lorrimer's sister." Carr lowered his voice. "It is almost certainly true to say that the inquest was wrong. It wasn't a case of suicide – he, too, was murdered."

Something about the flicker of her eyes suggested to Carr that Angela Ryman was not surprised or shocked by the news. There was none of the usual outrage, no startled widening of those same eyes, and no futile refusals to believe the news. Instead, her eyes rolled to the ceiling, as if what he had said had confirmed a private belief or provided an answer to a question which she could not resolve herself.

"You don't seem surprised," Carr ventured to say.

"Lorrimer was a very unpleasant man," she replied.

"Your husband said he thought the man could be vicious."

Her eyes flashed to him, as if he had insulted her directly. "You've spoken to Philip?"

"Earlier this morning."

"What did he say?"

Carr was struck at once by the suppressed desperation in her voice. "What he said is of less interest than what others did."

"I don't understand."

"It has been suggested to me – and to the police, no doubt – that your husband might have had reason to kill Lorrimer personally."

There was a moment of frightened silence before the obligatory denial was muttered through her clenched teeth. "That's ridiculous."

"Is it?" Carr asked the question in a low voice, loaded with irony. "I wonder if you truly believe that, Mrs Ryman."

The memory of the arguments between Ryman and Lorrimer came crashing through her mental defences once more, carrying with them those earlier private suspicions that Lorrimer's death had seemed to be convenient to her husband. In a momentary lack of control, Angela almost found herself giving a voice to them once again to this small, extravagant, but politely dangerous man. Now, for reasons of delay rather than thirst, she picked up the coffee and sipped at it eagerly.

"What was the bitterness between your husband and Lorrimer, Mrs Ryman?" asked Carr.

"I don't know." Angela did not regret the unhelpful reply; it was, she told herself, the truth after all.

And nor did Carr consider her response to be untruthful. What troubled Angela Ryman, he thought, was altogether more personal than a disagreement between her husband and a dead man. Slowly, he leaned back in the chair, and he looked away from her, into the cold grate of the fire. "Were you at home on the night before last?"

"As a matter of fact, I was. I was in this very room, reading. Is that when this girl was killed?"

Carr nodded. "Did you see anything suspicious or out of the ordinary?"

Angela shook her head. "No."

Carr waited for a moment, in case she had anything further to say. It seemed she had not. "Where was your husband that night?"

"Working late at the office, as usual." These last words were laced with spite. "He came home at about eleven o'clock, reeking of alcohol. Again, as usual."

Carr nodded. This part of the Rymans' involvement in the matter was at least consistent. "You did not leave the house at all?"

"No."

Carr looked across at her and smiled kindly. And yet, as before, the amiability was not reflected in those dark, meaningful eyes. "I'm aware that things are not entirely well with you, Mrs Ryman. If you will confide in me, I shall not betray your trust. But if you cannot do so, then please accept a word of caution instead—do not conceal anything from the police in a case of murder."

She ought to have been offended, he thought, but she seemed more terrified than upset, as if the possibility that Carr might know something of her life was more unbearable than any other horror which she might have to face. But slowly, the fear seemed to turn to anger and, when she spoke, her voice betrayed the struggle of the two emotions within her. "What has Philip been saying to you?"

He turned his head to face her. "You do your husband a discredit, dear lady. The redness of your eyes says more to me than your husband ever would."

Without thinking, she wiped the palm of her hand across her cheeks, as if the traces of her previous tears were still evident there. "I'd ask you to mind your own business, Mr Carr."

Carr placed a hand over his heart. "I shall do so. But my offer of a friendly confidence remains. I know Mr Bowers, my dear, and I know what your husband fears. Equally, I know that those fears are misguided."

If she had expected herself to be incensed by this invasion into her privacy, Angela was surprised to find that the opposite was the case. Once again, she had the urge to tell him everything, but she refrained from doing so. Instead, she rose from her chair and walked over to the window, as if to distance herself from the conversation. "I suppose Gerald has told you everything in such a way as to make himself seem like the villain. He is fond of viewing himself as a martyr."

Carr made no direct response. "Your husband's vision of the world is tainted by the Mary Jerrold scandal."

"Twisted by it, rather than tainted," replied Angela. "To him, and to William Lorrimer, Gerald Bowers is nothing more than a predator, preying on young, married women under his care."

"In the Jerrold case, was that not partly true?" Carr's voice was saddened, and she could hear it.

"He never acted on his feelings." It was evident that, to Angela, this was a vindication. "And there is no question of anything like it between us. We are friends only. I trust him." She laughed. "That is not an easy thing to say about anybody in this village."

Carr smiled. He rose from his chair and limped slowly towards the window. For a moment, he looked across to the woods in which he had found the stained fabric. "Your husband's fears are not entirely unfounded, though, dear lady. There is someone else, is there not?"

Angela felt the tears form in the corners of her eyes and trace their cold path down her cheeks. She made no effort to stop or conceal them. "It isn't Gerald Bowers."

"I know that." Carr waited for her to speak once more.

"As a matter of fact, Mr Carr," she said, accepting the handkerchief which he had subtly and gently offered to her, "there is nobody else anymore. He ended it this morning, just before you arrived. The bastard wants nothing more to do with me. Strange, isn't it, how you only realise later what a fool you've been making of yourself?"

"His name?" prompted Carr in a whisper, although his instincts provided the answer before she supplied it.

"Arthur Corrigan." Angela's eyes had hardened, but the tears continued. "If Philip knew, I think he'd be even more appalled than the idea of me being with Gerald."

Carr was barely listening. He could hear only the cymbals of ideas crashing together in his head. "Does Mrs Corrigan suspect anything about your relationship with her husband?"

Angela shook her head. "Elsa Corrigan has never loved Arthur. They were together because she was under pressure to marry, and Arthur is a persistent man when he has his plans set out in his mind. Elsa wouldn't care if he slept with every woman in the county."

"How sad," was all Everett Carr could find to say.

Angela turned to him. "At least she's honest with herself, Mr Carr. How many of us can say that?"

"Honest with herself?"

There was a nod of the head. "Oh yes. You see, Mr Carr, Elsa Corrigan wouldn't care about her husband having affairs, because she was sleeping with someone else herself."

Chapter Twenty-Eight

It was Edgar Corrigan who answered the door. He could not have been expecting Carr to visit, and yet he exhibited no sense of surprise or alarm at seeing the older man on the doorstep. On the contrary, he offered a cheery smile and stepped aside to allow Carr to enter. His manner was affable without being fulsome, and the contrasting-coloured eyes were warming in their welcome.

"How nice it is to see you again, Mr Carr," he said, taking the visitor's hat and coat. Carr was struck by the fact that Edgar did not seem to consider this task to be exclusively one for the servants, although he doubted Edgar's father would have a similar opinion.

"How is that lovely young lady, Miss Delaney?" asked Carr. "She is well, I trust."

Edgar nodded. "Bearing up, I believe, is the phrase. I don't suppose any of us are truthfully all right at the moment. With everything which is going on, I mean."

Carr's expression was serious. "Murder is intrusive. It will always leave its mark on a community as well as on an individual. Things in the village are not likely ever to be the same again."

Edgar's natural vitality could not help but be clouded by the bleak but honest prediction. "Gives a chap pause for thought."

Carr smiled at him. "Miss Delaney spent the day William Lorrimer died with you, I believe."

Edgar's expression lightened. "Yes. We went into Fernchester, came back here, had dinner together. I left her at about ten o'clock. She had a letter she needed to write to some solicitors in London. Harriet's been left some money or something from an old aunt."

"She told you that?"

Edgar nodded. "I was there when the letter was delivered."

Carr bowed. "My apologies, dear boy. She told me as much. And you? What did you do after you left her?"

"Am I being questioned, Mr Carr?" laughed Edgar. The older man waved away the query with a smile and a swipe of his hand through the air. "I went to the local pub, as a matter of fact. I wasn't ready to come home, and one can always find a game of cards or chess on offer in the *Tuns*. You're staying there, I understand?"

Carr did not reply. "Did you see anybody in there you knew?"

Edgar required only a moment's thought to provide Carr with the answer he had expected. "Philip Ryman was there. Had been for some time, by the look of him."

"He was drunk?"

Edgar rolled his eyes. "As usual. Rumour has it that Ryman has some very big problems."

Carr's eyes darkened. "Financial?"

"Aren't they usually?"

It was doubtful that Edgar Corrigan had experienced or could understand financial problems, so that this tone of resignation with which he spoke the words seemed comical rather than sympathetic. And yet, something about them gripped Carr's interest with a strength which was almost tyrannical in its power. He thought back to his conversation with Angela Ryman, who had talked about some sort of feud between Lorrimer and her husband. A connection, vague and uncertain, forged itself nevertheless in Carr's brain and, as it did so, he was plunged involuntarily into a long silence, his dark eyes gazing abstractedly into an unseen point in time. Edgar, noticing this sensory distancing, was unsure whether to interrupt or not, but his dilemma was solved by the sound of a door opening breaking the spell on Carr of its own accord.

"I heard voices, Edgar," said Elsa Corrigan, as she stepped into the hallway.

Carr looked across at her. He knew that he could remember both the clear blue of the eyes and the burnt yellow of the hair, together with the elegantly patrician nose, but now, seeing them afresh, he was struck by how intense each of those qualities were, so that she seemed more beautiful than his memory had given credit for.

"Mother, this is Mr Everett Carr," announced Edgar.

"We have met," said Carr, stepping forward and offering his hand.

Elsa shook it politely but briefly. "I confess I hadn't expected to see you again, Mr Carr."

He smiled amiably, as if anxious to show her that he was not offended by her words and that, if it had been her intention to offend, he would not have been put off by it. "I shan't intrude on you longer than I must, dear lady, but I do wish to have a quiet word on a somewhat delicate matter."

Elsa looked into his dark eyes, as if hoping to find some clue as to why he was here and what it was he wished to say, but they remained impassive, although kindly, and the smile beneath the opulent moustache and trim beard was so persuasive in its geniality that Elsa found herself incapable of denying it.

"Edgar, perhaps you would arrange for some coffee," she said.

It was a dismissal as much as a request, but her son seemed neither fazed nor insulted by it. He agreed with a smile and went about the task without complaint. Elsa pointed Carr towards the sitting room, followed him inside, and closed the door behind them. Carr did not speak immediately. He was conscious that his presence was not a welcome one, although he had an intuition that it was not animosity which Elsa Corrigan felt towards him, but more a sense of caution. It was not an entirely unfair mistrust, he supposed: he was, after all, probing into private affairs where he had no authority to do so, and he doubted that she would understand or be interested in his personal motives for these enquiries. His morality and his personal deficiencies were, she would no doubt say, a matter for him and no concern of hers. Making any effort to explain to her why he had felt compelled to investigate these two deaths, or any attempt to elucidate his private demands for justice for others where he had lost it for himself, would be of no interest to her. And, for that matter, she would be correct to say that they were no business of hers. Private justifications such as these were for the individuals concerned, just as personal secrets and affairs were. Intrusion into one in order to satisfy the other was surely hypocritical, and Carr could understand why Elsa Corrigan might refuse to speak to him on those grounds. But an anticipated rejection was not sufficient cause to prevent him from trying to gain what information he could from her. To walk away would have been to betray himself, something he could never allow himself to do.

"You have something to say, Mr Carr?" Elsa said, her lips smiling but her eyes holding their defences.

Carr's voice, when he replied, was lowered by the seriousness of his tone, and, similarly, for the first time, she found herself disturbed by the darkness of his eyes. "I know you think you have no reason or obligation to speak to me about anything, Mrs Corrigan, and I give you my word that I shall walk out of here now if you insist on it. But I must assure you that I wish you no harm, and I am not here to seek out salacious or malicious gossip."

"Then why are you here?"

"Because two people are dead." The words seemed almost like an accusation. "Two people have had their lives taken before their natural end. I may be old-fashioned, Mrs Corrigan, but I think we all have a duty to ensure that justice is done in such circumstances."

Elsa held his gaze. "That is the police's duty, Mr Carr, not ours."

He bowed in concession, but those eyes remained blackly defiant. "Theirs is a professional duty, madam. I talk more of a moral one."

The arrival of the coffee, brought by a maid, prevented any response in the moment. The maid placed the tray on a low table, her offer to pour being politely declined by the mistress of the house, and nothing was said until the girl had left the room. Elsa did not move to sit or pour the coffee and Carr reciprocated, standing before the fireplace with one hand behind his back and the other clasped around the silver handle of the cane.

"I understand what you're saying, Mr Carr," said Elsa, now walking towards him. "But really, I cannot see what I can do to assist you. I had very little to do with William Lorrimer, and I certainly didn't know this poor woman who was killed."

"I have not said that you did, dear lady," Carr pointed out, "but you may know things which have a bearing on their deaths."

"I cannot see what."

"A certain library book, for instance?"

Elsa's teeth clenched momentarily. "I told you before that I don't know why it was in Lorrimer's cottage."

Carr smiled, as if she had finally bitten the cheese in his trap. "I am sure you do not know, dear lady, but I am equally certain that you might suspect why. After all, one can guess a thing without actually knowing it."

Her blue eyes were frozen on him. "You're suggesting that I might have an idea why Lorrimer had taken my book?"

Carr nodded slowly. "From what I have learned about the man, Lorrimer must have taken it for a reason, and I would go so far as to suggest that this reason would be something to his advantage."

Elsa, with an effort of will, kept her voice under control, but she could feel herself shaking internally, as if she had suddenly stepped into a cold and inhospitable room. She looked across at Carr, but there was no direct warmth to be taken from him, although she could sense something like encouragement behind his eyes.

"Are you hinting at blackmail, Mr Carr?"

"A dirty word, dear lady." He shrugged. "Perhaps he was seeking verification of an idea he might have had about something."

But Elsa was not about to betray herself so easily. "Something like what?"

Carr was unable to camouflage his disappointment. He had hoped that she might offer the information voluntarily, thereby sparing him the embarrassment of having to confront her with his theories and suspicions. Her intransigence was forcing his hand, however, which he felt could only cause the two of them discomfort. And yet, the truth was of paramount importance, and none of his discomfort or reluctance could hinder the seeking of it.

"I wish you would spare us both the unpleasantness," Carr said, "but you leave me with no alternative. You talked to me yesterday of a friend who is ill, suffering, in fact, from a brain tumour."

"This is none of your business," Elsa cautioned.

Carr ignored her. "I think you wanted to understand his pain as best you could before it was too late."

She did not reply. He watched her closely, but there was no suggestion that she was about to respond or react to his words. She sat down on the settee and silently poured the coffee, politely waiting for him to continue. Carr did not take a cup from the tray. Instead, he stood before her and looked down at her, as if in judgement.

"I think Lorrimer took the medical book from here on the occasion your husband threw him out," he said, "perhaps so he, too, could understand the condition concerned. I imagine that a man like Lorrimer would want any information he thought might be relevant."

Elsa smiled and shook her head dismissively. "He could have taken the book to research any number of topics within it. Really, Mr Carr, don't you think you're stretching a point?"

But Carr was not ruffled by her arguments. "No, dear lady. You see, when I found that library book in Lorrimer's cottage, it was open on a page about brain tumours. You yourself had told me that a close friend was suffering from such a condition. It is too much of a coincidence to assume that Lorrimer would be researching the same illness independently."

Elsa's eyes widened slightly, but enough to show that she was disturbed by his words. She had the suggestion of a cornered animal staring down the barrel of a hunting rifle, and it was Carr's finger which was about to squeeze the trigger. As if in defiance, however, Elsa leaned back on the settee and crossed her legs. "You seem to have more to say, Mr Carr."

Carr inclined his head in admission. "Assuming that you did take out the medical book in order to understand this friend's condition better, Mrs Corrigan, what does it suggest? Many things, perhaps, but certainly a specific desire to appreciate this person's particular agony. And that, to me, suggests a very close bond between you and this friend, one which demands more than a casual sympathy."

"Perhaps you should say what you mean."

Carr, with Angela Ryman's revelations ringing in his memory, sat down slowly in the chair opposite her. "You're in love with this man, whoever he is. And you have been for years."

Elsa was no longer looking at him, her eyes averting their glare to the empty grate of the fire. For a long moment, neither of them spoke, but it was evident that Carr expected Elsa to explain the position. With a small sigh, like an inhalation of courage, she obliged.

"His name is Edmund Draper," she said. "I knew him from many years ago. It was my husband who introduced us, and the attraction between us was immediate. For three months, Edmund and I were lovers. I have no doubt you think it very immoral, not only to commit adultery but to admit to it so easily."

"It is not for me to judge you, dear lady."

Now, Elsa did look at him. "Are you a married man, Mr Carr?"

His hand rested on the broken knee, and his reply was some time in coming. "My wife is dead."

"I'm sorry." Elsa, perhaps embarrassed by his confession, gave him no further opportunity to elaborate. "You must know what it means to be in love. You have experienced it. For my part, I always thought I knew what love was, but it was only when I met Edmund Draper that I learned that I had been wrong. What I felt for my husband was nothing compared to what I did for Edmund."

"I can understand well enough," said Carr gently. "Are you aware that your husband denies the existence of any friend with a brain tumour? He says you are a liar."

Elsa sneered. "That tells you more about Arthur than it does about anyone else. He sees no purpose in my life, so he can't believe anything which might suggest one."

"You said your affair with Mr Draper lasted for three months. Am I to assume that it was never rekindled?"

She shook her head. "Edmund went abroad for business. As so often happens, real life intervened into a private paradise. We lost touch."

"Until recently?" Carr guessed.

Elsa noticed only in that moment that she was crying. She reached under her sleeve for a handkerchief, but there was nothing there. She looked around in vain, her gestures seeming to be disproportionately frantic, as if exaggerated by her embarrassment. Carr pulled the gaudy handkerchief from his breast pocket with a flourish and handed it to her, the movement both gallant and elaborate. She took it from him with a word of thanks and dabbed at the corners of her eyes.

"Edmund wrote to me," she said between sobs. "He said he wanted to see me again before it was too late. My instinct was to refuse, Mr Carr, as God is my witness. It had been almost thirty years since we had been together, and I was worried that it had been too long. People change, after all, and I didn't want my memory of him to be tarnished by a reality. That makes me sound selfish as well as stupid."

Carr shook his head. "It does nothing of the kind."

She smiled at him. Her previous animosity now seemed to her to be foolish, and she saw Carr now only in terms of kindness. "Well, as you'll no doubt have guessed, Mr Carr, I did go."

"And did reality tarnish your memory?"

She made a sound which was something caught between a laugh and a sob, the hint of a smile lingering across her lips. "No, and I knew at once that it had been stupid to think it. He had barely changed at all. Older, of course, and frailer on account of the illness, but his essence, his heart, was unchanged. His smile was the same, his voice, and his eyes..."

Her tears began to fall once more, and Carr allowed her a silent moment of grief. At last, she looked up at him, and she seemed to him to have altered, as if recalling her feelings for this man Draper had somehow galvanised her. Her eyes were filled with an optimism now, and her cheeks flushed with excitement.

"It was as if I had fallen in love with him all over again," she said. "I flatter myself that he had a similar reaction to seeing me."

"I have no doubt of it," said Carr.

Elsa did not react to it. "And yet, seeing Edmund again was not an altogether happy experience."

"How so?"

She let the tears fall silently down her cheeks. "Because it reminded me of what a waste my life has been."

Carr found that he had no words to say. The confession had been brutal in its honesty, and it seemed to him that Elsa Corrigan had not realised the entire truth of her situation until she said those words aloud and heard them ring in her own ears. In this moment of private grief, Carr felt he understood more about the woman sitting opposite him than he could have learned from years of her acquaintance. Furthermore, he found himself dismissing as a malicious rumour Angela Ryman's suggestion that Elsa Corrigan was having a physical affair with another man. What Elsa was experiencing, Carr understood now only too well, was not the sordid infidelity in which Angela Ryman and Arthur Corrigan had indulged themselves. It was something much more profound, much more real, something not only far more powerful than Angela and Corrigan's affair, but also far more devastating. Carr felt a strong and empathetic sadness, not only for the life Elsa Corrigan felt she had lost, but for one she had lived, and finally for the woman herself.

Elsa had now begun to control her weeping, and she was once again dabbing Carr's handkerchief against her cheeks and into the corners of her eyes. "I'm sorry, Mr Carr. It's just that I hadn't realised how lonely I was until just now. I'm afraid I've made a fool of myself."

Carr shook his head slowly. "I would say that you have done quite the opposite, madam."

"I've never loved my husband," she said. "I think I've always known that. And I am sure he has never loved me."

Carr once again found himself thinking about Angela Ryman, but his natural tact prevented him from mentioning either her or the relationship with Arthur Corrigan. Instead, Carr employed his delicacy in another direction. "Is it possible that William Lorrimer knew about your feelings towards Edmund Draper?"

Elsa shook her head. "I can't see how."

"And yet he was looking into brain tumours, just as you were. How are we to interpret that fact if we assume he did not know about you?"

She gave it a moment's thought. "I suppose you must be right."

"How many times have you visited Draper?"

"Several times, over the last couple of months."

"Your husband told me he heard you plotting on the telephone, making arrangements. That would have been with Mr Draper, arranging one of your visits?"

"I had no idea Arthur had overheard." She seemed horrified, but it was soon replaced by indignant resignation. "He cares so little that he has never once tried to ask what it is I am arranging. Even if he knew, I doubt he would care, unless it was to be angry with Edmund for betraying him as a friend."

An idea had occurred to Carr. "On the night of Isobel Croft's murder, you told me that you had gone for a walk across the heath."

She could read his inference from his tone of voice. "I think you know that was only partly true."

"You were, in fact, returning from the railway station after one of your visits?"

"Yes." She confessed it in this single, guilty syllable.

"Perhaps Lorrimer might have followed you on one of those occasions?"

Elsa frowned in confusion. "Why would he do such a thing? I bore him no ill will. Why would he want to blackmail me? He never once approached me for money or with any hint of a threat."

Carr fell into silent thought for a few moments, stroking his moustache idly, his dark eyes darting around the room in a contemplation of ideas. At last, they came to rest on Elsa's face once more. "I have an impression of Mr Lorrimer as being a spiteful, vindictive man. Malicious, someone has called him. Is it possible that he might have been planning on telling your son about these feelings you had for a man other than his father?"

Elsa's cheeks paled, and her eyes suddenly began to flicker. "I suppose it would be an explanation."

Carr watched her closely. "Perhaps the only explanation?"

"Very possibly." She made a show of checking the time against the small wristwatch which she wore and the clock on the mantel. "Forgive me, Mr Carr, but I do have some calls I need to make this afternoon."

Why she had chosen this moment to dismiss him, he could not say, but he found the timing fascinating. He was suddenly beguiled by the notion that silencing Lorrimer about her relationship with Draper would be a powerful motive to drive Elsa to murder. He looked across at her, wondering whether he could believe her capable of it and, almost instantaneously, disliking the conclusions he drew. He rose from his chair and took back his handkerchief. As he replaced it in his pocket, he looked back towards her. "A final question, dear lady, if I may. Was anyone else aware of your relationship with Draper, either now or before?"

Elsa seemed embarrassed by the enquiry or, perhaps, by her answer to it. "A week or so ago, Mr Bowers found me in the church. I'm sorry to say that I was crying."

Carr sought to keep his interest under control, but his eyes were alive with curiosity. "You told him the whole story?"

She nodded. "Most of it, certainly. Like you, Mr Carr, he was very kind about it. I am grateful to you both."

Carr bowed in response and limped slowly towards the door. She followed him and opened it, to allow him to exit. Before he did so, he turned to face her. "You are entitled to be happy, madam. Do not waste any more of your life. Be happy, before it is too late."

She was surprised by how touched she was by the remark. She swallowed hard in an effort to suppress the urge to weep once again but the moment which passed between them, the understanding, which shimmered between those eyes fixed on each other, was sufficient to show that she was moved. Carr simply smiled and inclined his head.

"I shall see myself out," he said. She took him at his word and, once he had left the house, she closed the sitting room door on herself and sat once more in silence, with only her own thoughts and secrets for company.

For his part, if Everett Carr had looked back towards the house, his eye might have drifted up to one of the windows on the upper floor, and then he might have seen Edgar Corrigan looking down on him through the pane of glass. The distance between the two men would have been too great for Carr to be certain, but it was surely possible that he might have been able to discern something of the hostility in the young man's eyes, even if he might not have been able to detect the fury and venom which burned within them.

Chapter Twenty-Nine

The sun was fading when Inspector Dunn found Everett Carr sitting in solitary contemplation, at a table in *The Marsham Tuns*, an untasted glass of Muscadet and a barely touched supper of poached trout with vegetables in front of him. Carr's eyes were fixed on a point in the distance, the brows furrowed, and the lips pursed in concentration beneath the impressive moustache and pristine beard. In front of him, there was a large reference book, leather-bound, which Carr had evidently been studying and whose contents, Dunn supposed, had been the cause of the deep concentration in which he had discovered the older man. For a moment, it seemed to Dunn to be a shame to disturb Carr, but the inspector was not a man to allow polite sensitivity to obstruct professional duty, however unfair it might be. As it transpired, Carr smiled at the disturbance and accepted the official detective at his table with a sociable word of welcome.

"I shall not embarrass you by inviting you to join me in a glass of this excellent wine, Inspector," said Carr, "not when you are on duty, but some coffee, perhaps?"

Embarrassed nevertheless, Dunn smiled awkwardly. "A pot of tea, if I may, Mr Carr."

Carr signalled for the landlord. The order given and delivered, Dunn took out his notebook and pencil, placing both in front of him in readiness for what he viewed as a secondary interview but which, he felt sure, Carr would take as being more of a consultation. For that reason, Dunn felt it was both prudent and necessary to take the lead in the conversation.

"Perhaps you'd like to tell me exactly what you've been doing today, Mr Carr," he said, smiling with his lips, but letting the seriousness of his eyes show that the politeness was an obligation as much as a natural or even professional impulse. "Before that, I should ask how your head is."

Carr smiled, rubbing at the back of his head. "You have spoken to Laurence Fisher, I see. No other way you could know about my little mishap. I must confess that it is still rather painful. In cheap thrillers, of course, Inspector, a chap gets up from a knock like that and carries on regardless."

"I suspect you haven't allowed it to slow you down either."

Carr's smile graduated into a small, affable laugh. "Fortune favours the brave, Inspector. I suppose it is too early to know for certain whether the stain on that piece of half-burned material I found was blood or not?"

"The preliminary view is that it isn't."

"I am coming round to that way of thinking myself, Inspector. The more I think about it, the more convinced I am that the metal clasp I found explains what the stain is."

"I don't follow."

Carr seemed not to have heard. "Did Mr Fisher tell you about this burglary at his studio?"

Dunn nodded. "I can see no connection with the death of either Lorrimer or Isobel Croft."

Carr sipped now at the wine and murmured a word of appreciation. "You know, Inspector, the wine in this little inn is better than some of the most fashionable restaurants in London. It alone is worth a journey to this lovely village. But, I digress," he apologised, "forgive me. Before I was attacked in Fisher's studio, I found a small scrap of writing paper in the fireplace. Only a scrap, you understand, but I recognised it easily because I had seen it twice before."

"Where?"

"Once in William Lorrimer's cottage and once in between the fingers of Isobel Croft."

Dunn nodded. "We found the paper in the dead woman's hands, and, of course, we were able to match it to stationery found in Lorrimer's cottage. I'll send someone to Fisher's studio to retrieve the fragment from his grate."

"The significance is obvious, of course, and the fragments prove that Lorrimer wrote to both Fisher and Isobel Croft. The question is whether he wrote to them about the same matter."

"According to Mr Bowers, Isobel Croft knew the identity of Lorrimer's murderer and had proof of it."

"The letter taken from her hand was that proof," said Carr. "At least, it was proof of whatever secret it was which led to Lorrimer's murder. Isobel brandished it at the killer when she confronted him. Very naturally, the killer removed it once he had silenced her."

Dunn was frowning. "But Lorrimer would hardly have warned his killer that he had betrayed him to his sister."

Carr inclined his head. "It is so unlikely as to be ridiculous. I think it far more reasonable to suppose that Lorrimer wrote to the killer requesting a meeting. At that meeting, the truth came out about whatever it is we have yet to discover, and Lorrimer was killed. The letter to his sister was an insurance policy."

Dunn clicked his fingers. "Of course! 'If anything happens to me, here's what I have found out.' That sort of thing."

Carr was smiling at the youthful eagerness exhibited by his companion, like a child on a festive morning of surprises. "That sort of thing, my boy, yes."

"Laurence Fisher," sighed Dunn. "But why? What was the motive for killing Lorrimer?"

Carr did not respond immediately. His fingers drummed lightly on the cover of the reference book on the table between them, the sound seeming somehow in rhythm with the beating of Dunn's excited heart. At last, Carr smiled again and looked across at the inspector. "Mr Fisher is not the only one with questions to answer. Mrs Ryman, the solicitor's wife, is lying about where she was on the night Isobel Croft was killed."

Dunn glared at him. "How do you know?"

But Carr's attention seemed to be elsewhere, so that the tone of voice of his reply was distracted. "Because she said she was at home and saw nothing unusual that night."

Dunn shifted in his seat. "Forgive me, Mr Carr, but—"

Carr slapped his hand against his knee. "And yet, I still come back to Laurence Fisher. You remember, Inspector, that I referred you to a place called Linacre House?"

Dunn's reaction was instinctive. He seemed to recoil, as if he had touched a burning hot surface, his hands leaping into his lap, clasped together, and his shoulders hunching as he lurched back against the back of his seat. His face paled, and his eyes dimmed with a reaction of a dark dislike. His expression became aggressive, like that of a sullen schoolboy cornered at last by unwanted discipline against which he was determined to fight, as if he had been forced to take a punishment which Carr had tricked him into receiving.

Carr was at once aware of the sudden change in demeanour and his voice softened in the sort of concern which an amiable stranger can only ever have. "My dear inspector...?"

"I'm all right."

Carr signalled to the landlord whose experience, in observing the scene, knew exactly what medicine was required. Despite his initial refusal, Dunn found the brandy, for which the landlord insisted there was no charge, both refreshing and soothing.

"I'm sorry," he said, cradling the glass. "I should be stronger than that."

Carr sat quietly, his hands clasped around the silver handle of the cane and his dark eyes shining with empathy. "The best of us can be overpowered by the things which touch us. Perhaps even by the memories of our own experiences," he added deliberately.

Dunn smiled, suddenly looking exhausted. "I suppose I shouldn't be surprised that you seem to know everything."

Carr shook his head. "It is not knowledge, my boy, only instinct."

Dunn sighed and shook his head. "It's not quite done you proud, Mr Carr. My disgust at Linacre House isn't quite down to my own experience or memories. Rather more by a sudden understanding of how things could so easily have been for me."

"You were orphaned, though, Inspector?"

Dunn nodded. "But instead of going to a place like that, I was sent to live with an aunt in Fernchester. She brought me up. I was one relative away from being a victim of a place like Linacre House."

"There but for the grace of God…" Carr began to quote.

Dunn threw back the remainder of the brandy and ordered a second, his professional duty momentarily forgotten. "When you think what those poor children suffered, Mr Carr… I don't even think Sergeant Barlow has uncovered the majority of it, but I've read more than enough to know I don't want to read much more of it."

Carr nodded, his mind drifting back over the stories of cold and scalding bathwater, the broken bones, the scarring burns, and the other, darker type of abuse which no doubt had been prevalent. His reply was so feeble against the reality of the terrors of the orphanage that the voice was barely strong enough to speak the words. "What the Pryces did was indeed monstrous."

Dunn sipped at the second glass of brandy. "There is no question of that. It's the doctor concerned who haunts me."

"Matthew Olson," said Carr.

"How could he let it happen?" Dunn seemed genuinely in need of an answer, and his eyes pleaded with Carr to satisfy it. "He was a bloody doctor. Did they stop taking their oath at some point, and I never knew?"

Carr could understand the sneering anger manifested in the cruel sarcasm of the words, but he saw neither the benefit nor the wisdom in feeding it. Instead, he leaned forward and placed his hands back on the book which sat between them on the table. "Is Sergeant Barlow trying to find any names of the children who were in that place, who might be of an age now to match anybody living here?"

Dunn, now faced with a procedural and professional question, seemed to rejuvenate. The sadness, the traces of guilty relief at his own fortunes as compared with those less privileged than himself, dissipated from his eyes, and his jaw clenched in an official determination to proceed. "I tasked him with that, yes."

"Excellent," said Carr. "You see, Inspector, Laurence Fisher is an orphan. And we know, do we not, that William Lorrimer was taking an interest in Linacre House. We also know that Lorrimer had written to Fisher on at least one occasion, and we may deduce from the fact that Fisher burned that letter that its contents might be sensitive."

Dunn was nodding. "So, if Fisher was at Linacre House as a child and Lorrimer found out, there might be some sort of motive arising from it?"

Carr made a gesture of non-committal acknowledgment of the possibility. "If so, Inspector, it may not be Mr Fisher's only reason to want Lorrimer silenced. You see, I am not at all sure that Mr Fisher's sin is confined to him alone."

"What do you mean?"

Carr shrugged. "I doubt he burgled his own studio, for example."

Dunn frowned. "But the burglary might not be connected to the deaths."

"That remains to be seen, my boy, but there is more to be explained than the deaths alone. We must explain the studio burglary, the fire in the woods, and the stained cloth, for example."

"But they may not matter if they are not connected to the murders," protested Dunn.

Carr held up a warning finger, and his eyes were heavy with caution. "In order to be certain of the truth, dear boy, we must first identify and eliminate those matters which are inconsequential."

"Surely that is wasting time, Mr Carr."

"The young are so swift to action. Have you never heard of the tortoise and the hare, Inspector?"

Dunn rolled his eyes. "Yes, of course, but..."

Carr did not permit him to continue. "Once we have explained these smaller, perhaps less significant mysteries, Inspector, we will be left with the central problem, which will then be evident to us without any extraneous details to obscure it."

Dunn drained the second brandy, no longer for its medicinal qualities but purely because he felt he deserved it. "I would like to say that I am in charge of this investigation, Mr Carr, but I get the impression that it would do me no good."

Carr leaned forward, his hands resting now on the cover of the reference book. "Tell me, Inspector, when you examined Lorrimer's cottage, did you find anything which struck you as particularly strange?"

"Apart from the obvious burglary, you mean?"

"I mean, specifically, the blotter." Carr watched Dunn shake his head, but it was clear that the inspector was aware that, by doing so, he was admitting a deficiency. Carr did not feel compelled to castigate him for it, either in jest or in seriousness. "There was a very definite phrase amid the usual jottings and splashed of ink: *the snake isn't real.*"

Dunn's eyes were heavy with confused fascination. "It makes no sense."

Carr murmured a gentle word of agreement. "I confess that it didn't to me. Then, I heard various tales of arguments people had with Lorrimer, during which he called the people concerned snakes, vipers, serpents, and the like. And that," he added with a note of self-disappointment in his voice, "diverted my mind for some time. Until, Inspector, I heard about a very definite disagreement between Lorrimer and Mr Bowers. I was thinking things through before you arrived just now, and I think I have it—the solution to one of those inconsequential mysteries I mentioned just now."

"I don't follow you at all, Mr Carr."

Carr gripped the inspector by the arm and stared into his eyes. "The intruder in the studio, the fire in the woods, the metal clasp, and the stained material, my boy. I can explain them all, and I can do so simply because the snake isn't real."

"But which snake?"

Carr's voice lowered with intensity, and his dark eyes burned with a seriousness which echoed what struck Dunn as the sinister implications of the older man's reply.

"In the church, Inspector," whispered Carr. *"The snake in the church isn't real."*

Chapter Thirty

"Y ou're saying Bowers is somehow a fraud?" said Dunn.

Carr smiled enigmatically, his eyes closing slowly for a moment. "Mr Bowers is a man with his own troubles, I have no doubt, but he is not the snake in question. Let us go to the church now, Inspector. Between this book and the church, you shall see all there is to see." He tapped the reference book in an almost loving fashion.

Dunn might have preferred to have been shown the light in that moment, but he put up no argument. Perhaps he knew that doing so would end in disappointment. It was unlikely that Carr would have obliged. Dunn was growing keenly aware that this dapper little man seemed to enjoy his moments of mystification and the inspector suspected that denying Carr the privilege ultimately would benefit neither of them. With only a show of reluctance, therefore, Dunn got to his feet and stepped out from behind the table. He paused, turning to face Carr, and stood his ground, as if he felt somehow bound to reassert his official authority.

"I'm allowing you some leeway here, Mr Carr," he stated. "I trust I won't be disappointed or otherwise regret indulging you."

Carr bowed. "As do I, Inspector. I very much hope that my little ideas won't embarrass either of us. I'm sure they won't," he added, a flush of shame at his own immodesty reddening his pale cheeks.

It was obvious that there was to be no more reassurance than this, so Dunn let the matter rest. He watched Carr shuffle out from behind the table and waited patiently for the old man to limp past him and lead the way out of the pub, following closely behind at a suitably measured pace. Outside, the darkness had descended with a greater intensity and had brought with it a chill wind. The skies were free from clouds, however, so that there was no prospect of rain, and the stars were able to glitter like scattered pearls. Neither Carr nor Dunn spoke, although the silence was not awkward but determined, as if both men felt as if speaking would somehow delay their arrival at the church. Time seemed to stretch away from Dunn, however, and it occurred to him that they might never reach their destination, and with every step, his impatience seemed to make the country lanes seem indefinite. The illusion did not seem to be shared by Carr, whose benign and tranquil expression suggested a mind at peace with both the situation in which they had found themselves and the wider circumstances of the enquiry upon which they had embarked.

As they turned into the churchyard, Dunn had a momentary sense of foreboding which, later, he would be convinced was stronger than it had been. In the moment, it was a flash of trepidation, without either foundation or cause, nothing more than an inexplicable human impulse that something was wrong. It might have been the darkness of the evening or the anticipation of the promised exposure of a secret which ignited the inspector's imagination but, despite his later assurances to the contrary, it was not any form of precognisant instinct that they were walking into tragedy. And yet, as they stepped into the church itself, it was tragedy which confronted them.

There were two other people in the church, and both of them appeared to be dead. Gerald Bowers was lying on his side across the altar steps. The legs were bent at the knees, partially folded underneath him, and the hands seemed to be clutching at his chest. The face was pressed against the marble of the steps, the eyes open and staring sightlessly into the distance, and the mouth was hanging loosely open as if in some hideous mockery of surprise. The spectacles had fallen from the vicar's face and now lay helplessly and pathetically to one side, a pitiable crack evident down the centre of one of the lenses. A brass candlestick lay beside the body, tossed aside like an afterthought, its base stained by the terrible crimson colour which could only ever mean one thing. The blood was extensive, so that it seemed almost as if the place were drowning in the stuff. The terrible wreckage of the back of the vicar's head was a violent testament to the origin of the stains on the candlestick and, as if to reinforce the suggestion that blood dominated the church, a hideous scarlet stain had spread out across the fabric of the cassock and surplice, making the defacement seem crudely insulting instead of appallingly tragic. Similar but smaller flecks of blood had spattered the altar steps. To Carr, it seemed almost as if death had never been so violent or so chillingly absolute.

No less than two feet from the corpse lay the body of Dorothy Parrish. She was on her back, her legs and arms splayed like those of a broken doll, and her head hung crookedly against her shoulder. Her face was pale, but there was a flicker of movement around the nostrils, which showed that she was still breathing. Once he had realised it, Carr could see also that her stomach was rising and falling, as shallow and weak breaths were taken.

Dunn must have recognised life in Dorothy as swiftly as Carr, for he raced around her body and ran down the aisle towards the undeniably dead Bowers. Carr tossed his reference book onto the nearest pew and let his stick clatter to the stone floor as he knelt down beside Dorothy and took her in his arms, cradling her head and gently slapping the cheeks in order to break the spell of shock which had consumed her. He repeated her name, urging her to wake up, but his attention was fixed more on Dunn and the vicar's corpse than on Dorothy's slowly murmuring mouth and flickering eyelids.

"You don't think she killed him?" asked Dunn.

Carr was quick to shake his head. "From the position of her body in relation to his, I should say she came in here, just as we did, and approached the body, possibly to see if Bowers was still alive. When she saw the full horror of it all, she fainted. And no wonder."

Dunn nodded agreement. In that, at least, he and Carr had reached the same conclusion. "He's not been dead long, if I am any judge. No more than an hour, but we shall have to have it confirmed. But why? What did the killer fear from Bowers?"

Carr did not reply. As soon as the question was asked, Dorothy Parrish's eyes snapped open and, as her memory of the evil she had witnessed returned to her, she began to scream. In the stillness of the church, the wails of anguish were magnified, both in their volume and their ferocity, so that they seemed disturbingly to be barely human. Carr sat her up and kept his arms around her, counteracting her screams with soothing noises of his own, like a parent comforting a child coming out of a nightmare. Dunn ran into the vestry and was relieved to find, as he hoped he would, a carafe of water and some glasses. He filled one and rushed back to Carr, who took the glass and forced it between Dorothy's lips. She spluttered with the initial few attempts, water spilling down her chin and onto the lapel of her coat, but she began to take larger and more controlled gulps of it, once her mind had registered what it was and the good it would do. Slowly, breathlessly, she began to focus, and her eyes drifted around the church, as if seeing it for the first time, until, at last, they came to rest on Everett Carr.

"Dead," she stammered. "He's dead."

Carr nodded calmly, his eyes looking down at her. "It's all right, dear lady, we're here to deal with everything. Don't worry anymore."

She was staring into those kind eyes as if pleading with him to believe her. "I came here for some privacy. I found him... I didn't... It wasn't me."

He held her close to him. "There's no suggestion it was. None."

"He was just lying there. Just lying... Oh God!" Her eyes were now brimming with tears. The words were swallowed by a sudden wail of distress, and the tears flowed with a vengeance.

Carr signalled to Dunn. "Help me get her onto a pew."

The inspector and Carr each took her by an arm and forced her to her feet. She struggled, as if they were moving her without consent, but she was too weak for her impulsive protestations to have any real meaning. Dunn fetched more water, and in a moment of almost unrecognised compassion, he placed himself in such a position that his body shielded her from the horror and violence which had intruded into this sanctuary of hope and salvation. Dorothy did not acknowledge it, any more than she had noticed it, but she would have expressed her gratitude and appreciation if she had done either. Carr pulled himself onto a pew across the aisle and rested his cane across his knees.

"What time did you get here?" he asked.

"Perhaps half an hour ago, a little longer."

"It is now half past seven," said Carr, having checked his own watch and now snapping shut the case and replacing it in his pocket. "That should be of some assistance," he added, looking up at Dunn. The inspector nodded. He had done the same calculation: if Bowers had been dead no more than an hour and Dorothy had discovered the body at around seven o'clock, the time of death was easily fixed. Carr looked back to Dorothy Parrish. "What made you come to the church this evening, Miss Parrish?"

Despite her fear and shock, it was evident that the question unsettled her. "I wanted some time alone to think about things. Private things."

"I see," said Carr. He was smiling, and, for a moment, Dorothy wondered whether he knew what those private things were and, if so, how he knew. "Did you see anybody else when you arrived here?"

"No."

Dunn cleared his throat. "There was nobody in the church or the churchyard? You're certain?"

"Positive."

"No chance someone was hiding, and you didn't see them?"

Dorothy thought for a moment only. "I suppose that's possible. All I know is that I saw nobody."

Carr was stroking his moustache. "Was the vicarage in darkness when you arrived?"

"Yes."

Carr glanced towards Dunn. "That is a very important point, Inspector. I had anticipated it when we walked through the churchyard just now. Bowers would have turned off the lights in the vicarage if he had felt the need to come into the church himself or, more importantly, if someone had asked him to be with them in here."

Dunn nodded in order to show that he had followed the reasoning. "And Bowers is dressed in his formal robes. He was clearly kneeling at the altar, presumably in prayer, when he was killed."

"Which perhaps tells us almost all we need to know," murmured Carr, more to himself than to anyone else. The words were spoken so softly that Dunn almost missed them. When he looked back to Carr, he saw that the old man's eyes were fixed on the body of the vicar. Their glare was intense, and it struck Dunn that something important must have revealed itself to the little man.

But Carr seemed unaware that he had spoken at all. He had risen to his feet, and he was now walking slowly down the aisle, back towards the altar. His attention now had drifted from Bowers' body to the Van Jansen painting, which hung above the altar. Dunn waited purposelessly, watching Carr's back in anticipation of further action or comment, but, frustratingly, neither seemed imminent. At last, however, Carr gave a small chuckle of satisfaction and turned on his heel.

"Inspector, we must get this poor lady home," he said. "She has had a serious shock, the full extent of which has not hit her as yet, I fear. Perhaps we could send word to Mr Thomas Lewton. He and Miss Parrish are close friends, and she may be trusted in his care."

Dorothy had sat upright, her face now a mask of trepidation and fear. "No! I don't want to see Thomas. Not now, not ever."

Carr walked slowly back towards her, the ferrule of his cane tapping like a hollow heartbeat against the stone floor of the nave. His eyes were hardened, darker than ever in their seriousness, but his lips were still stretched in a thin smile of reassurance. When he sat down beside her, Dorothy seemed to feel an immediate calm descend onto her and her agitation seemed at once to subside. Carr's voice came to her with a gentle, almost melodic sense of soothing.

"I understand, madam," he said, "and I know why you are troubled, but everything will work out for the best."

She stared at him, simultaneously fascinated and curiously afraid of him. "You can't know."

The warmth of Carr's smile now extended to his eyes. "But I do. I know more than you think, dear lady, which is why I can give you my word that all will be well. You must trust me, and you must forgive Mr Lewton."

Now, Dorothy's fear exceeded her fascination. "You know what he did?"

"I know it all."

"How can you?"

But Carr shook his head. "Now is not the time. I shall speak to you and Mr Lewton in the morning. For now, you must have rest, and you must put all thoughts of Mr Lewton out of your mind."

Dorothy would have protested further, but something in Carr's face demanded that she take him at his word. He was smiling gently at her, his eyes both encouraging and supportive, and she was overcome with an irresistible urge to trust him. A glance from him compelled Dunn to take control of the situation, and the inspector went about his business. There was a telephone in the vicarage, Carr assumed, and Dunn was to use it to contact the station, upon which a car would be dispatched to take Dorothy home. Dunn also gave the order that Barlow was to be contacted, and the formal process of a murder enquiry was to be set in motion. Dunn's call was swiftly answered and, in under half an hour, he and Carr were alone once more in the church, pending the arrival of Barlow and a pathologist.

"We have work to do whilst we wait," Carr said, picking up the reference book from the pew where he had left it. "Come with me, Inspector."

They walked towards the altar, ignoring as best they could the horror which lay before them. Carr pointed towards the Van Jansen painting. "What do you make of it?"

"It's well done, I suppose," Dunn said without emotion, "but I'm afraid I can never see in these things whatever quality it is which makes them worth admiring."

Carr smiled as he continued to flick through the pages of the book. "Let me see if I cannot increase your appreciation of this particular piece of art, at least, my boy. The other day I was at the library in Fernchester and I found this book. It is a history of art generally, but it contains one of the few reproductions of the very painting you see before you, which you will recall is the original."

Carr had found the desired page, and now he brandished it to the inspector, who stared at it for a moment and then looked back to the painting above the altar. He glanced from one to the other once again before speaking. "What am I supposed to be looking at?"

"When I saw the image in this book," said Carr, "I had the sudden realisation that something was amiss. I couldn't place it. But then I was reminded of William Lorrimer's strange message on the blotter in his cottage."

"The snake isn't real," quoted Dunn.

"Precisely," whispered Carr with some excitement. "Come with me."

He walked up the remaining steps of the altar and approached the painting with Dunn at his heels. Carr held the book so that the image of the painting was in front of them, and he pointed to the various details in the book and their reflected images on the painting before them.

"You see? All the elements are here: the condemned Christ, Pilate, his wife, the sadistic and malevolent soldiers." Carr pointed to the various depictions in both the book and on the painting. "The two appear identical. And yet," he added, lowering his voice, and pointing to the legs of Pilate in both images, "they are not."

And now, Dunn understood. On the painting above the altar, there was a serpent coiled around the governor's foot and calf; in the book's representation of the painting, there was no such serpent. Almost inaudibly, Dunn said, "The snake isn't real."

Carr snapped the book closed and pointed to the painting above the altar. "A forgery."

Dunn narrowed his eyes. "Or the image in the book is one."

"Not so. A reference book like this would be seen by far more people than a painting hanging in the church of a small, isolated village in England. The existence of a forgery in a book like this would be much more likely to be detected than one on display in here."

"For that matter, Fisher must have noticed it."

Carr laughed. "I have no doubt of that, Inspector, since it seems clear to me that Fisher put the snake there himself."

"Fisher?"

"It is a very simple little operation, I suspect." Carr was staring at the painting, as if seeing it now for the first time, although his admiration now was not for the beauty of the image but for the skill in the execution of its fraud. "Fisher forges an obscure old painting, sells the copy to a collector on one side of the world for a fortune, but then sells the original to a collector on the *other* side of the world for a similar amount."

Dunn had recalled a point which Carr had made. "You said Fisher was not alone in his sins."

Carr shrugged. "The Van Jansen project was financed by Arthur Corrigan, was it not? And I cannot imagine Mr Corrigan being easily fooled. The scheme as I have described seems to me to be much more his idea than Laurence Fisher's. In fact, my intuition is that Fisher panicked and got cold feet."

"Because Lorrimer had found out about the fraud," said Dunn eagerly. "*The snake isn't real.*"

Carr beamed. "And wouldn't you say that such knowledge would be a very good motive to murder Lorrimer?"

"What about the burglary at Fisher's studio?"

Carr shook his head. "There was no burglary. What would a burglar think would be of value in such a ramshackle place? No, no. Fisher emptied the studio himself and burnt all evidence of the fraud in the woods. That was the fire Thomas Lewton saw on the night Isobel Croft was murdered. The small metal clasp we found was part of the hinge of an artist's easel, I suspect, and the burnt cloth will no doubt be shown to be the remnants of a smock. You said yourself that the preliminary view of the experts was that the stain was not blood."

Dunn was nodding. "It was paint."

Carr bowed his head. "I very much fear it was."

"But the studio *was* broken into," Dunn argued.

Carr nodded slowly. "By Corrigan, no doubt, in an attempt to make sure that Fisher had not carried out his threat to bring the fraud to an end. I imagine that there was a rather heated argument when he discovered Fisher had kept his word."

"And the attack on you?"

Carr shrugged. "Corrigan again, I should say."

Dunn gave a bitter curse. "Fisher has made sure we can't prove a word of it."

"I wouldn't say that, Inspector," purred Carr. "I should think a simple but effective trap can be easily set and very likely fallen into."

"A trap?"

Carr shook his head. "Now is not the time for Corrigan and Fisher, my boy. We must allow your men to do their work here, and I would like to have a look around the vicarage, if you would permit it."

Chapter Thirty-One

Whilst he was alive, the simplicity of Gerald Bowers' existence might have seemed honourable, or even noble, but in the wake of his death, it struck Carr as little more than tragic. The vicarage did not seem to embody any sense of life. There was no evidence of Bowers' tastes, of his life away from the pulpit, or of his particular individuality. There were books, naturally, but they were scholarly rather than entertaining, all reference books and theological journals, without any hint of novels or poetry. The pictures on the walls were generic landscapes of indistinct places, chosen for functionality rather than for any special appeal, so that they were so generic as to be bland. The parlour was neatly but modestly furnished, although its simplicity caused it to lack any real sense of warmth. It was small, but not cosy; comfortable, but not welcoming. The kitchen, likewise, was nothing more than functional and the small dining room offered no suggestion of memories of amused diners or exhilarating conversation. And yet, there was nothing particularly surprising about the vicarage as a whole. It looked as such places should, but it said nothing about the man who had lived in it. A stranger would have known nothing about him as a man, only as a vicar. Nothing that is, thought Everett Carr sadly, except the obvious loneliness which seemed to be the overwhelming sense of the place.

Carr's investigations into the downstairs rooms revealed nothing of any particular interest beyond these sober, almost gloomy impressions. There were discarded drafts of sermons in a small wastepaper basket, chequebooks and statements for a modest but well-managed banking account, and several letters from the bishop. Only one of these was of any interest to Carr, however, namely written confirmation of a personal meeting between the two men, in which the bishop approved Bowers' request to bury William Lorrimer in consecrated ground. Carr smiled gently, almost fondly, at the implication of the letter that Bowers had been so curiously antiquated in his views about the acceptability of the burial of suicides. It was an oddly comforting discovery, an indication that the young vicar had felt it necessary to observe, or at least to contemplate, the older values of his faith and profession. Carr found it strangely touching that so young a man could respect older traditions so venerably.

He walked out of the parlour and slowly climbed the narrow staircase to the upper landing. It was narrow, and only a small number of doors led off from it. There was a bathroom, over which Carr gave only a cursory glance, a small airing cupboard containing towels and fresh flannels, and two bedrooms. The smaller of these was evidently a guest room, and it was furnished as such, but the faint yet distinctly musty odour emanating from it suggested that it seldom performed its duty. Carr closed the door slowly, as if anxious not to disturb the room's eternal silence, and stepped next door to the main bedroom. It was sparsely furnished, with the same impression of functionality as was so clearly defined downstairs. There were enough items in the room to suit a bedroom's purpose—a small bedside table, a wardrobe, and the bed itself—but there was no more than that, nothing to indicate a personality either of the room or its occupant.

Carr felt the same sense of oppressive loneliness which had affected him in the parlour and dining room. Perhaps, Carr wondered, it had done exactly that, and the loneliness, the drabness, and the pessimism of the place had been glimpses into the man who preached every Sunday and listened with a divine patience to the troubles of others after all. Who listened to the troubles of Gerald Bowers himself? Maybe the dowdy vicarage was not a result of parsimony, but of an indication of a belief that Bowers personally did not matter. What good would it have been furnishing the house with bright pictures, literature, and memories of his life if that life itself had no meaning of its own?

These thoughts drifted through Carr's mind like ghosts amongst the graves of the dead. It was getting late, and he thought about abandoning his search and heading back to the village and his bed at the inn. He caught sight of his reflection in the pane of the bedroom window, seeming as clear as a mirror because of the darkness of the sky outside, and he was surprised to see that he didn't look as tired as he felt. The moustache and beard were still smartly fixed in place, and the eyes, from what he could make of them through the grime of the window, seemed alert and intense, if somewhat hardened by his mood.

It was when he turned back to the door that he saw it. An invisible hand of ice gripped him by the back of the neck, its cruel cold extending down the length of his spine. It was so harsh that it seemed to take away his breath. He walked slowly towards the door, his eyes fixated on the small hook which was screwed into place on the back of it. He walked with caution, as if he were approaching a coiled cobra, ready to strike, and when he extended his arm, he was not surprised to see that it trembled. His fingers curled around the leather handle of the obscene object, and he held it away from himself for a moment, as if touching it was in itself a form of defilement. The thongs of the whip hung down impotently, so that they almost seemed harmless and futile. Only the dark stains of dried blood showed where they had carried out their cruel, stinging work.

Carr glared at the thing as if he could not fathom either its nature or its purpose. His mind tried to imagine the pain of the whip across flesh, the tearing of the skin and the terrible noise of the strands of leather as they snapped through the air. Looking around the room, Carr could imagine the vicar, standing in the centre of the room, methodically and brutally bringing the whip across his back. Carr could see the tears in Bowers' eyes, just as he could see the sweat on his temples and the grimacing spasms of pain. Carr could see it all.

Everything, apart from any reason for it.

Numbly, he walked to the bed and lowered himself onto it. The whip lay across his lap, inert but no less deadly for that. His eyes fell on the small cabinet beside the bed, on top of which was a small and modest reading lamp, a copy of Hardy's *Tess of the d'Urbervilles*, and an old, cracked-leather edition of the Bible. Carr pulled open the top drawer, not for any particular investigative purpose but simply out of an almost involuntary curiosity. He found very little of interest at first: a notepad and pencil, a box of matches, some candles, and a small, green piece of stone which had been carved into the shape of a scarab. Carr was about to close the drawer once more when his eye caught something at the back of it, pushed further into the space than the other items, as if in a half-hearted effort to conceal it. Carr leaned forward slightly and pushed his hand into the narrow space, dragging out the object with the tips of his fingers.

It was a framed photograph, and, in Carr's mind, not only was a conclusion drawn, but a connection was made. The photograph was of a woman of exceptional beauty, and Carr could not look into the smiling face and the bewitching eyes without being sure that he was staring at the face of this Mary Jerrold, of whom he had heard. His mind recalled what Philip Ryman had said about the relationship between Bowers and Mary Jerrold, of its sequel, and of the village's condemnation of Bowers as a hypocrite. But he also remembered Bowers' honesty with him, his confession that he had been in love with this woman but that he had suppressed his feelings for her sake.

Suddenly, the choice of the Hardy novel, with its own themes of forbidden and suppressed love, seemed to Carr to be tragically easy to explain. Bowers may not have succumbed to the feelings he had developed for Mary Jerrold, but that would not be sufficient redemption for him. Here was a man who sought permission to bury a suicide in consecrated ground. What Carr had previously admired about this observance of older traditions he now took to be evidence not only of Bowers' reverence but also his devotion to God. If he was devout enough to question Lorrimer's burial, he would surely consider those feelings he could not deny as sinful. Carr could envisage him now, praying that God would remove the feelings or show Bowers how to dismiss them, but receiving no response whilst those sinful feelings deepened. And he could imagine Bowers' devotion to his faith suggesting that there was only one method of purging his soul. Carr looked from the blood-stained whip to the old, leather Bible, and a quotation from the New Testament, one which he had been startled by as a child but which he had thought long forgotten, came back to him:

"Indeed, under the law, almost everything is purified with blood, and without the shedding of blood, there is no forgiveness of sins."

The whip was evidence of Bowers' shedding of blood in return for forgiveness, and Mary Jerrold's photograph was the reason he was compelled to seek that forgiveness. Carr felt an overwhelming sadness engulf him. He closed his eyes, as if to blind himself against the images which formed in his mind of Bowers' purification of blood. His teeth clenched in an effort to suppress the feeling of futility which was rising within him.

And yet, the sadness was soon replaced by something much darker. Anger now began to burn in his chest, a fierce and ignoble anger fuelled by the injustice of interfering minds. How many of the lashes Bowers inflicted on his back were prompted by his own conscience, Carr wondered, and how many by the words thrown at him by the friends of Henry Jerrold? How much of the blood and pain was caused by men like Philip Ryman and William Lorrimer or any others who felt as they had? Carr could understand Bowers' own private shame, just as he could understand his attempts to rid himself of the sin, but it would only have been prolonged and intensified in his mind by the goading of those men who believed him to be a hypocrite. The thought made Carr's knuckles whiten, and his limbs tremble with fury.

He placed the photograph in one of the pockets of his coat. Into the other, he placed the purifying whip. Having either of them in his possession made his gorge rise, and he was compelled to swallow the sensation of needing to vomit. As he stepped out of the room and closed the door behind him, Carr knew that if any justice was to be served for the personal torment with which Gerald Bowers had lived, these tragic and terrible items he had removed from the room would be needed.

Chapter Thirty-Two

I f Angela Ryman had been impressed previously by the kindness of Everett Carr's dark eyes, she was now struck by their hardened intensity, and she was conscious that the lips beneath the waxed smile of the extravagant moustache were set in a fierce determination. Nevertheless, despite his obvious anger, he retained something of his natural politeness, since he bowed and tipped his hat in greeting. When he spoke, however, his voice was laced with something which struck Angela as unsettling, if not dangerous.

"May I come in, madam?" He said it without any expectation of a refusal.

She had been drinking, and her eyes had begun to glaze over with the glassed arrogance of the intoxicated, which was diluted only by a general suggestion of sadness behind those slowly freezing eyes.

"My business is urgent, dear lady," Carr said, "or else I should not be here at all." There was something about the polite formality of the words which made it seem impossible for her to refuse entry, and she stepped aside to do so. Carr murmured a word of thanks and, removing his hat, stepped over the threshold of the cottage. "Is your husband at home?"

Angela nodded. "For once."

"I would like to speak to you both." Again, there was no suggestion that his wish would not be granted.

Angela called to her husband, and, when she received no reply, she marched towards the back of the house, leaving Carr alone in the sitting room. He stood before the fireplace, waiting in patient silence, his eyes fixed on the floor beneath him.

"What do you want here?" asked Ryman, as he stepped into the room, Angela following closely behind.

Carr placed his hands in the pockets of his coat, feeling the photograph of Mary Jerrold in one and the bloodied whip in the other. "I want to talk about Gerald Bowers."

Ryman scoffed. "Then I have nothing to say to you nor you to me."

"Stay where you are!"

The command was shocking, and, as far as the Rymans were concerned, it was sobering. Perhaps it was all the more so because it had come from this otherwise quiet, softly spoken, and polite stranger to the village. Now, the glare from his dark eyes was as savage as the bark of his voice, and Angela found herself wondering about still waters and how deep they might indeed run. Ryman, too, stopped in his tracks and turned back on his heel.

Carr seemed to be unaware of the effect he had made on either of them. "We shall talk about him, and we shall do so calmly. And," he added with emphasis, "we shall do so truthfully."

As if not to appear defeated, Ryman shrugged. "In that case, I shall need a drink. What about you, my dear? Fancy one?"

Angela was watching Carr carefully. "No, I don't think I will."

Ryman was uninterested. "And you, Mr Carr?"

"I think not, thank you."

As he blasted a dash of soda into his large glass of whisky, Ryman merely shrugged. "Please yourselves."

Carr waited for him to sit down in one of the armchairs placed on either side of the fire, and, once he had done so, Carr glanced to Angela and gestured that she might wish to do likewise. She hesitated, her eyes now free from any alcoholic glaze and alive with a fearful premonition of disaster, but the insistence of Carr's own expression forced her to comply.

"I wish to make one thing clear from the outset," said Carr, his voice now back to its usual serene amiability, "and that is that I am not here as your enemy. Nor more am I here to interfere or to gossip. I wish only to help."

Ryman scoffed once more. "Then get out and leave us alone."

This time, it was Angela whose temper bit like a snake. "Would you just shut up, Philip? Just shut up and listen for once in your life."

Ryman glared at her and consoled himself with a mouthful of whisky. The sneer on his face was not petulance but something much closer to hatred. If Angela was troubled by it, she gave no indication of it.

Carr allowed a moment to pass. Then, deliberately and almost ominously, he removed one hand from his pocket and placed the photograph of Mary Jerrold on the table before them. Neither Ryman nor Angela needed to lean forward to take a closer look at it. They both knew who it was and, more importantly, perhaps, what importance the image held.

"Where did you get that?" asked Ryman.

"Everything in its correct order, Mr Ryman," said Carr. "You recognise her, of course?"

"It's Mary Jerrold," said Angela.

Ryman lit a cigarette. "Am I to presume that you took my advice, Mr Carr, and asked Bowers about her?"

"In a manner of speaking," said Carr. "Mr Ryman, I am aware of your fear that history is repeating itself."

"What do you mean?"

Ryman's attempt to appear ignorant was both obvious and futile, and Angela felt it more keenly than either of the two men. "Stop pretending, Philip. Just stop! We can't go on like this. We're not going to survive if we're constantly fighting the truth."

Ryman barked at her. "And who are you to preach about the truth, Angela? I know what Bowers is, and I know what he wants. You've been waiting for an excuse to walk out on me for months. Well, he's given it to you, hasn't he? So, why don't you go to him. I won't stop you. I'm not Henry Jerrold, so I'll just give up and let you go."

She stood up and threw her glass against the wall, shattering it into slivers of crystal. "I don't want you to let me go. Damn it, Philip, I don't want you to let me leave!"

Carr had closed his eyes during the exchange, but now, as Angela's sobs began to break the silence, he opened them slowly and turned to look at Ryman. He was staring at his wife, his brows furrowed and his mouth hanging open uselessly, as if he had just been shown that the world was not how he had known it to be and that the realisation had stalled his capacity to understand anything else.

Carr spoke. "You were both right and wrong about Gerald Bowers, Mr Ryman. He was in love with Mary Jerrold, but he never once acted on his desires. You see, she did not feel the same way about him."

Ryman glared up at him. "How do you know?"

"Bowers told me. I may not have believed him initially, but I have since had cause to do so."

"What cause?"

"You and William Lorrimer called Bowers a hypocrite and a liar," said Carr, struggling to keep the venom out of his voice. "You told me yourself that Lorrimer had threatened to write to Bowers' superiors about the Jerrold matter, and I have every reason to believe, just as you do, that he would have carried out that threat. That might have given Bowers a motive to murder William Lorrimer, but I have no reason to think he did. Just as I have no reason to believe that he had set his eyes on your own wife."

Ryman shook his head. "You'll forgive me if I can't share your optimism, Mr Carr."

"But you will, Mr Ryman," said Carr. "You see, what you and Lorrimer couldn't possibly have known is that Bowers shared your views of him. He not only shared them, but he believed them far more profoundly than either you or Lorrimer did."

Ryman's brows had creased in confusion. "I don't understand."

"Bowers knew that he was a hypocrite, and he knew that he had betrayed not only his faith but God Himself. All your antagonism towards him achieved was to reassure Bowers of that guilt which he had already admitted to himself."

Ryman sipped the whisky. "And are you taking his word for that, Mr Carr? I hadn't imagined you were so naïve."

"I'm not taking his word for it," said Carr sadly. "I have more terrible proof."

Slowly, Carr pulled his other hand out of his coat pocket, bringing with it the whip and all its traces of punishment. It seemed to reveal itself like a snake from amongst the grass. Carr lay it down on the table, beside the photograph of Mary Jerrold, beauty beside the beast. He heard Angela Ryman gasp in horror, her tears suddenly frozen on her cheeks by fear, and he looked over at Philip Ryman, whose expression paled in shock as the eyes widened in disbelief. Carr said nothing, allowing the leather thongs and their blood-stained history to speak for themselves. Ryman threw back the whisky and got to his feet, striding back to the drinks' cabinet, and pouring another liberal measure. He added no soda. Then, slowly and deliberately, he lit another cigarette and took a slow, purposeful sip of his drink. He refused to look at the whip.

"He used that thing on himself?" he asked.

"Yes." Carr said the word softly but not without emotion. "All you achieved, Mr Ryman, was an assurance that Bowers would punish himself for his transgression even harder than he was doing already."

Angela roared. "It's horrible."

Carr kept his attention fixed on Ryman. "You see the real significance of this, do you not? Bowers was using this thing on himself in order to seek forgiveness from God for his feelings towards Mary Jerrold. He kept this photograph not as a keepsake but as a reminder of his sin. Do you think, Mr Ryman, with those sins on his conscience and now knowing the terrible means he took to cleanse himself of them, that he would actively *repeat* those sins with someone else?"

Ryman's eyes could find nowhere to settle. "I…"

Carr was relentless, now leaning into Ryman's face. "Of course he wouldn't. You were wrong about him and Mary Jerrold, Mr Ryman. Wrong then about their relationship and wrong now about any relationship between Bowers and your wife."

Ryman smoked for a long moment. "I had no way of knowing what he was doing to himself. You can't blame me for it, nor can you blame me for thinking he was going to treat my wife the same way he had treated Mary Jerrold."

Carr sensed that Angela was about to speak, but he held up a finger and prevented her. His eyes bored into Ryman. "You believed that so strongly, didn't you, Mr Ryman? You were so wild with jealousy that you almost knew for certain that Bowers had set his malignant sights on your wife."

Ryman was defiant. "Yes! And you can't tell me I didn't have cause."

"If you did have cause, Mr Ryman," cautioned Carr, "it would not serve you well."

Now, Angela walked towards them, unable to remain silent. "What do you mean?"

Carr glanced at her briefly and then back to Ryman. "Gerald Bowers was murdered earlier tonight. Someone battered him to death in the church."

Angela gave a shriek of horror. "No!"

"I'm afraid so," said Carr. "And you, Mr Ryman, have just provided yourself with a very definite motive for that murder. Laurence Fisher told me that you also had good cause to wish William Lorrimer dead. I cannot help but wonder if he was correct."

It was not Ryman who replied, although he appeared to be on the brink of doing so, but rather, it was Angela who spoke. "Mr Fisher is correct, Mr Carr. William Lorrimer's death was very convenient for my husband."

"Angela, for God's sake!" hissed Ryman.

But she shook her head. "No, Philip. It is time for the truth. I've asked you time and again to tell me what the argument with Lorrimer which I overheard was about. This time, I won't let you walk away from it. Now, I want, and I will get the truth." She paused and knelt down beside Ryman's chair. She reached across and put her hand on his knee. Tears fell silently and without fuss down her cheeks. "And then, I will tell you the truth."

Chapter Thirty-Three

Carr thought he knew what truth it was which Angela Ryman wanted to tell her husband and he felt that his presence when she did so would be an embarrassing and intrusive one. Knowing about Angela's affair with Arthur Corrigan before her husband would place Carr in an invidious position, especially if Ryman were to discover that prior knowledge and Carr knew that he would be unable to deny it, if asked directly. The business between Angela and Corrigan was not linked to the murders, Carr felt sure of it, and so it was no direct concern of his. There was still the lie, which he knew Angela had told about her whereabouts on the night of Isobel Croft's murder to be resolved and, for that truth alone, he knew he would have to stay. Beyond it, however, Carr promised himself that he would leave the Rymans alone, if not in peace.

For Ryman's part, he looked over at Angela and found himself seemingly seeing her clearly after a long period of emotional confusion. Her eyes looked at him now not with suspicion or contempt, but with what he thought was encouragement. She looked tired, more tired than he could ever remember, and he knew that she must have looked exhausted for a long time, but he had never noticed it, realised it, or, shamefully, cared about it. Now, seeing the silent tears roll down the pale cheeks, Ryman knew that he was the cause of them. He stared at the glass of whisky in one hand and the cigarette in the other. He slammed down the drink on the table, pushing it away, and fiercely extinguished the cigarette. He took hold of Angela's hands and kissed them. This gesture of closeness had been the most intimate they had been in months, and both felt it as keenly as the other. The hands fell still, and the mutual grip intensified, as if in some physical representation of the renewed strength of their relationship.

Ryman looked up at Carr. "I didn't kill either of them."

"Tell me everything," replied Carr gently. He limped towards the chair opposite Ryman and lowered himself into it.

Ryman looked at him for a moment and then at Angela. Slowly, he released Angela's hands and leaned forward for the whisky. Rising to his feet, he walked with the drink to the fireplace and stood in silent contemplation for a while longer.

"I suppose the best way to do this is to come out and say it," he declared at last. "The truth is that I owe money to some very dangerous people and, God help me, in recent months, I've been forced to use client money in order to try to pay it back."

Hearing the words spoken out loud, Angela was surprised to find that they did not come as a great shock to her. It was as if she had always known but had turned a blind eye to it, and perhaps subconsciously, she had. Hearing it laid bare like this, she remembered Arthur Corrigan's remark to her about Ryman. *Dipping his hands in the cake tin...*

"Lorrimer knew," Ryman was saying. "He was a client himself, you see, and he threatened to leave and go elsewhere because of what I'd done. He said he would make sure people knew I couldn't be trusted. If it got out that I was taking money from clients, the firm would have been ruined." There was a pause. "*I* would have been ruined. If he had ruined me, I would certainly have had no money to pay off the debts. But they wouldn't be written off either, would they? I didn't dare think what would happen in that case. It would have been an end to all the misery, I suppose," he added with a solemn voice. It left neither Carr nor Angela in doubt as to what the repercussions were, which Ryman feared.

"These people are professional criminals?" asked Carr.

Ryman shrugged. "They're certainly at ease with threatening violence. I've never had any reason to assume they wouldn't carry it out."

"You stole some of Lorrimer's own money, of course," said Carr.

Ryman's eyes closed, almost involuntarily. "Perhaps my biggest mistake of all."

Angela rose to her feet and approached Ryman. "How did it all start?"

Ryman drained his glass. For a moment, he contemplated another but, to his surprise and that of his wife, he placed the glass on the mantelpiece and slowly put his hands in his pockets. Angela looked up at him. She saw in him now, something of the man she had fallen in love with all those years previously. It had been a simple choice he had made, to face the truth without the protective comfort of alcohol, but it had demonstrated a small but significant step to regaining control of himself. It was no great leap towards solving their problems, but it was an indication that Ryman had prepared himself for the journey towards redemption. A feeling she recognised as pride, long since forgotten, swelled within her.

"It began, and it'll end, with my own stupidity," Ryman said, looking at Angela. "You'll think I'm blaming you, but I'm not. It was all my fault. I never felt I deserved you. That's the truth. I was so happy when you showed an interest in me that I couldn't believe it was happening. It was like being let out of a cave and seeing the world for the first time. I never wanted to be put back in that cave, and I was determined not to go back. So, I made myself a promise that I wouldn't ever deny you anything."

Angela could not prevent the frown from forming on her brow. "What are you saying?"

"I was frightened," Ryman continued, seemingly as if she had never spoken. "Frightened that you'd leave me at any moment, scared that someone would come along who would dazzle you and take you away. So, I gave you everything you wanted and anything you asked for. Dresses, diamonds. Anything."

Carr was watching Angela with a silent, serious glare. Her reaction to this confession would, he felt sure, dictate their future as a couple. Ryman's honesty, whilst necessary, would strengthen their marriage or destroy it utterly. And it seemed to be dependent on the reaction of the woman sitting opposite him.

Ryman seemed aware of it also, and he was swift to justify himself further. "It's not your fault, Angela, and I never blamed you for it. Well," he added awkwardly, "not unless the whisky was talking. It was me, you have to understand that. Me and my own inadequacies, my own paranoia. My fear of losing you. It twisted my idea of who you were, and I didn't have the courage to refuse you. I thought if I had, you would have left me. So, I gave in to every demand."

Carr was nodding. He felt he could understand Ryman's dilemma. "Even when the legitimate money had gone?"

"Even then," said Ryman with a nod.

"So, what did you do?" asked Carr.

"Borrowed and gambled." Even in Ryman's own ears and even when spoken by himself, the words seemed like the final bullets being fired into his heart.

"Oh God, Philip," shrieked Angela with such force that it seemed as if a storm had broken.

Ryman walked over to her and kneeled before her, taking her hand in his, as if in some inappropriate parody of a marriage proposal. "There's no justification for it, and I offer no excuse, other than to say that it was a naïve, childish, and selfish thing to do. Without saying a word, I was insulting you, by assuming that you cared for the money more than me. I realise that in trying to make sure I held onto you, I may have achieved the opposite. If that's what has to happen, I'll accept it. And I'll understand it."

Angela had not removed her hand from her husband's grasp, nor did she fall into his arms in an embrace of forgiveness. The tears fell in silence and without any hysterics. "If Lorrimer exposed what you had done, the firm would have closed."

"Yes." And in disgrace, he thought, but there was no need for it to be said.

"Without the money you were using from the firm, you couldn't pay off these people."

Ryman knew that she had avoided saying that he had stolen the money; for that, at least, he was grateful. "No."

Angela now withdrew her hand from his grasp. "After the inquest, I said that Lorrimer's death was convenient for you. I was right."

"Yes." Then, when the realisation dawned, he added: "But I didn't kill him,

Angela, and I didn't kill his sister. I'm a liar, a cheat, and a thief, but I'm not a murderer."

Angela's tears fell silently and unnoticed. "How could you be so stupid? All these years, everything we've had has been a lie."

"I'm sorry. So bloody sorry."

"Being sorry alone can't fix this, Philip. We have to do something to pay it all back and to settle whatever these debts are."

Carr cleared his throat politely. "How much money have you taken from the firm, Mr Ryman?"

"Not enough to make any significant dent in the overall debt. I hadn't been doing it for long, as I said."

"Could you replace the money fairly swiftly if that other debt was taken away?"

Angela stared at Everett Carr, barely able to understand what he was saying and daring not to hope that he might have either the generosity or guile to offer a solution. Similarly, Ryman was staring at him, both confused and concerned at what might be passing through the older man's mind.

"Within a couple of months, perhaps," he said.

Carr pulled himself out of his chair and stood over them. Ryman rose to greet him, as if he were a schoolboy appearing before a teacher who had suggested a more lenient punishment for some transgression than might have been expected.

"You will need courage if I am to assist you in this," Carr warned. "Perhaps more courage than you have previously shown in your life."

"What do you want me to do?"

Carr reached into his inside pocket and took out a pencil and a small notebook. He handed them to Ryman. "Write down the names of the gambling establishments you visited, the names of the owners, and those of the men from whom you borrowed money. I have some connections at Scotland Yard and, with your information, perhaps they can work towards bringing some charges against them. But it will mean a formal statement from you and possibly an appearance at Court to give evidence. Can you do that?"

Ryman held the older man's gaze. "Why would you help me like this?"

Carr's dark eyes were more serious than Ryman had ever noticed before. "Because, within reason, I believe everybody deserves forgiveness and a second chance, Mr Ryman."

Ryman's eyes flickered, but Carr offered only a small smile of appeasement. Angela appeared by her husband's side, and Carr watched her hands fold around those of her husband. There was a quiet dignity in her nod of thanks.

"Thank you, Mr Carr," she said simply.

"You have no need to thank me, dear lady."

"You have given us a chance to survive all this."

Carr lowered his gaze. "Then perhaps, you might do me the honour of telling me the truth about where you were on the night Isobel Croft was murdered."

Angela offered no denials, nor did Carr expect any. She gave a brief, defeated closing of the eyes and a humourless smile. "How did you know I was lying?"

"You told me that you were at home on that night. In this very room, in fact, reading. I asked you if you had seen anything out of the ordinary. You said no." Carr pointed out of the sitting room window towards the trees and bracken opposite the cottage. "On the night Isobel Croft was murdered, there was a large fire in those woods. Thomas Lewton witnessed it and I found the ashes."

Angela lowered her head. "I see."

Carr looked over to her. "Indeed, dear lady. If you had been sitting here, as you said you were, you could not have failed to notice the flames. When you said you had seen nothing unusual that night, I knew you were lying."

Angela was looking at him, but her eyes were not focused on him. Carr had the idea that she was staring at him without seeing him, as if she were concentrating on something far away from the sitting room, or Carr, or her husband, or even herself.

"I was with Gerald Bowers," she said, her eyes now shifting into focus.

Her hands balled into fists as she said it, as if she had some irrational idea that she might have to defend herself physically. She knew it was neither a realistic nor a sensible threat, but her fingers remained clenched, so that she wondered if it was some sort of internal effort to retain her own composure rather than any instinct to defend it. She became aware of Ryman as he walked past her, this time submitting to the alcoholic support of the whisky decanter. Angela was shaking her head, even though her husband could not see it, as if doing so would somehow emphasise the truth of her next words.

"Not for the reason you've always thought, Philip." Angela snorted in frustration. "Well, perhaps it was, but not in the way it seems. I'm making no sense; I know it. I'm just trying to explain, but the words won't come out the way I want them to."

Her voice was not plaintive so much as frustrated. Carr thought he understood what she needed to say, and for that matter, he thought he could fathom why the words would not form properly on her lips. So many denials about her relationship with Gerald Bowers, whilst simultaneously telling so many lies to hide her affair with Arthur Corrigan, so that now, when the time for truth had come, she had almost lost her ability to recognise and to tell it.

"You went to see him in order to warn him about your husband's suspicions regarding the two of you," he said calmy, more for Ryman's benefit than that of his wife. "Your husband's increasingly erratic behaviour was beginning to alarm you. Is that not right?"

"Yes," mumbled Angela.

"And you thought Bowers was close to being in danger," continued Carr. "And so, as a friend, you went to warn him."

"I telephoned the vicarage that evening," Angela said. "I arranged to meet Gerald at the end of the lane, just before the Fernchester Road. I told him about Philip's drinking and his secrecy, that I was sure he was planning to do something desperate."

Ryman shook his head. "I wasn't. Not about Bowers, at least."

"I didn't know that," argued Angela. "I was worried. I didn't want Gerald getting hurt for nothing, for something he hadn't done." Her words stopped suddenly, cut off by a choking sob, as she remembered Carr's previous news. Her eyes fell on the whip, and her eyes began to water, as if she had been struck by those terrible leather strands herself. Defeated, she sat down on the settee.

Carr was looking out of the window. "And that is why Bowers was not at the vicarage on the night of Mrs Croft's murder. He found the body on his way back from his assignation with you."

Her tears were stronger now. "I suppose he must have done."

Carr turned to face her. "Did you come straight back here afterwards?"

"Yes."

"Did you see anybody?"

"No."

"You're certain?"

She gave a violent nod of her head. "I saw nobody, I swear. I got back home, and I stayed here. Not long afterwards, Philip returned from the pub."

She looked into Carr's eyes, pleading for his acceptance. He looked back at her kindly and, although not religious herself, Angela was conscious suddenly of what it must be like to look into the eyes of a priest after confession. Carr smiled and nodded his head in an arc of assurance.

"All is well, dear lady." He walked across to Philip Ryman. "Do you hear me, sir? All is well." Ryman did not look at the older man. There were tears in his eyes, and, although his mouth tried to make some reply, all he could do was shake his head.

Carr sighed gently. He limped over to the table and picked up the whip and Mary Jerrold's photograph, replacing them in his pockets. He knew that there were more truths to be told, but his presence was not required for them. Angela, as if sensing his thoughts, nodded and rose from her seat. Carr held up a finger, his eyes brightening, as if some thought had occurred to him and shown him a way out of a darkened forest. He turned and faced Ryman.

"Mr Ryman," he said, his kindly voice still hardened by authority, "your wife has promised to tell you the truth, and she will find the courage to do so, just as you must find the same strength to listen. Neither of you are entirely blameless in your present unhappiness. Accept that, and all will be easier to bear and to forgive."

Ryman turned to face him. "What do you mean by that?"

Carr smiled and pointed to the whisky glass. "Less of that, Mr Ryman. Now is the time for clear thought and consideration."

Ryman tossed the remainder of his whisky down the back of his throat and replaced the glass on the silver tray of the cabinet. He took two steps forward, as if to demonstrate that he was ready and willing to listen. Carr gave a low expression of satisfaction and looked back at Angela Ryman.

"The truth now and all of it," he cautioned. "I shall leave you both in peace, and I thank you for your assistance and candour. I repeat, all will be well." He took Angela's hand swiftly and bowed politely to kiss her knuckles. It was softly but deftly done, but she found it no less gallant for that. He looked back into her eyes and smiled.

"One last word before I go," he said. "It may give some comfort now and in the future."

"What is it?" asked Angela.

"Something which you would both be wise to bear in mind." Carr paused for a moment before responding further. "I think it is unlikely that Arthur Corrigan will be part of this village for very much longer. You have my assurance that he will not be around to hurt or manipulate anybody for many years to come."

Ryman walked forward. "What has Corrigan to do with anything?"

Angela knew that she was shaking, just as she knew that Carr was telling her something not only of importance but for her personal benefit. "What's going to happen?"

"Simply this," said Everett Carr. "Tomorrow morning, it is certain that Arthur Corrigan will be arrested and charged with a very serious crime, and it is equally certain that a lengthy prison sentence will follow."

IV

PART FOUR: ACCUSATION

Chapter Thirty-Four

On the following morning, Carr and Dunn breakfasted together at *The Marsham Tuns*. As was his habit, Carr satisfied himself with coffee only, having never had much of an early morning appetite. Dunn, contrarily, was regular in his eating habits and he was both ready and grateful for the plate of hot ham and eggs, as well as the toast and marmalade which followed. He ate the meal with enthusiasm, uttering spasmodic grunts of appreciation between mouthfuls, a habit of which he was both aware and mildly ashamed. For his part, Carr sipped elegantly at the strong, bitter coffee, dabbing away any stray drops, imaginary or otherwise, from his moustache with a lurid, emerald handkerchief, which, as was his custom, matched the ornately knotted necktie around his throat.

Once Dunn had emptied his plate and more coffee had been ordered, they began to talk in earnest.

"Are you sure about your facts, Mr Carr?"

Carr nodded slowly. "There is no room for doubt, Inspector. I told you that I had a simple but effective trap in mind. Once we spring it, however, we shall see whether my little ideas have been accurate or frustratingly wide of the mark."

"And what about proof?"

"The proof shall take care of itself, Inspector."

Dunn was frowning. "This business between Fisher and Corrigan, do you think William Lorrimer knew about it?"

"I have no doubt that he did."

"If so, it gives the pair of them a strong motive for murder."

Carr had taken a sip of his coffee and at the inspector's words, he slowly replaced his cup on its saucer. "Possibly."

"You don't sound sure."

Carr offered the younger man a warm smile of assurance. "There are still many things to be cleared up, Inspector. We must take them one at a time."

Dunn shuffled in his seat, leaning forward as if in some conspiratorial discussion. "Do you know who the killer is, Mr Carr?"

Carr took his time to reply, as if he were unsure how to respond at all. He had ideas, certainly, but none of them seemed to have formed into any conclusive solution to the murders at Little Marsham. There were glimmers of the truth, which flickered around the periphery of his mind, like the dusty wings of moths round a candle, but he was finding it almost impossible to trap them in the jar of his imagination. He felt sure, and had done so for some time, that he had already come across the vital clue and that he held in his hands the key to the mystery, although he was not altogether sure precisely which lock it fitted. And yet, he was convinced that something important, something which could erase all doubt about the matter, had been said and that he had heard it, but it remained as elusive to him now as it had ever been.

He was suddenly conscious of Dunn staring at him, and he realised that the inspector's question remained unanswered. Carr smiled and gave an irritated click of the tongue. "Forgive me, dear boy, I was a slave to my own thoughts. You must think me very rude."

"Do you know who the killer is?" Dunn asked again.

"All in good time, Inspector. For the present, we have other prey in our sights."

"But the murderer…" began Dunn.

Carr held up a silencing finger. "Will not strike again. I am in no doubt of that."

Dunn may have felt that a further explanation was both required and expected, but it was not to be provided. Instead, Carr smiled broadly and took out his notebook from the inside pocket of his jacket. From it, he tore two sheets, and with the use of Dunn's pencil, he wrote a brief message on each. He handed the pencil back to the official detective and folded the two sheets of paper into neat squares, before replacing them in his jacket pocket.

"Now, Inspector," he said, "it is time to set our trap. I should be most grateful if you would be at Mr Fisher's art studio in two hours. Then, we shall clear up at least one of the mysteries of this little village."

Dunn made an effort to speak, but Carr dismissed him with a kindly yet emphatic wave of the hand. He repeated his instructions regarding their later *rendezvous* and limped eagerly but uneasily out of the tavern.

Having delivered his messages, with the assistance of the local butcher's boy and at the expense of a shilling, Carr spent a relaxing and peaceful couple of hours in the village square. The morning was brisk without being cold, so that the scent of the flora and fields which surrounded this quiet corner of England drifted to his senses with a delicate determination. He watched people pass him by, engrossed in their own pursuits: schoolboys chasing a ball, couples walking towards the woods to refresh themselves after breakfast, and a small brass band in the bandstand, tuning instruments and playing stray bars of popular pieces. The smell of baking bread came suddenly to him, and he remembered a similar smell from the small kitchen in his grandmother's house, recalling now the excitement of his infant self as the smell of the baking turned into the sight and taste of the fresh loaves. Somewhere in the distance, he could hear the playful barking of a couple of dogs and, all around him, the low hum of collective human voices, coherent individually but no more than an indistinct murmur when taken as a whole. Amid it all, Everett Carr sat in silence, watching and listening to life as it existed in all its forms. A smile, contented and serene, stretched the ornate moustache and neatly trimmed Imperial beard below it, and he felt his dark eyes close, as if to allow these sounds and smells of simple, honest existence, so far removed from violent death and crime, to intensify. In such moments, Carr was reminded of why it was that he considered life a gift, one which everyone had a right to enjoy to its natural end. Not only a gift, but a privilege. Carr was grateful for both.

He ate a small but satisfying lunch at a tearoom in the village and possessed his soul in patience. The omelette and coffee had been sufficient for his needs, and the various displays of cakes and sponges went unnoticed. Carr had neither the appetite nor the taste for such indulgences. At last, he finished his pot of coffee, gestured for and discharged the bill, and, with a bow of thanks to his waitress, he walked slowly out of the tea shop and back across the main road of Little Marsham.

As he approached Fisher's dilapidated studio, Carr immediately saw Dunn lurking at the back, like some sort of inefficient music hall villain.

"I take it we're not too late," whispered Dunn once Carr had joined him.

"No. We have five minutes to wait, no more."

To Dunn, it seemed as if less time than Carr predicted had elapsed before they saw Fisher walking at speed across the fields towards the studio. He was moving erratically, his pace quickened with anxiety, and at intervals, he would break into a spontaneous but futile run, as if he felt that walking was taking too long to reach his destination. Carr reached out a hand and closed his fingers around Dunn's forearm, a gesture designed to demand silent caution but also to suggest satisfaction at the manner in which Carr's plan was playing out. They kept out of sight behind the studio, their eyes fixated on the sky above them and their breaths frozen in their lungs. They listened as the clatter of metal against metal betrayed Fisher's nervous handling of the key in the lock of the studio door. Carr heard the squeak of protest from the rusted hinges and the young artist pushed open the door and, as soon as he heard the door close once more, Carr gestured to Dunn. They stepped out from behind the studio and moved swiftly to the door. Carr paused, his hand on the knob of the door and his dark eyes dancing with anticipation. At last, with a smile at Dunn, he turned the handle and pushed open the door, stepping inside swiftly and purposefully.

Laurence Fisher was standing in the centre of the room. At the sound of the door opening, he whirled around, his eyes wild with panic. He had begun to speak, but the words seemed to dissolve on his lips when he saw that it was Everett Carr standing in front of him. The change in his expression, from frightened panic to an assimilation of polite enquiry, was swiftly and capably done, but it was neither quick nor complete enough to be entirely convincing.

Carr stepped forward and bowed his head in greeting, although his eyes remained fixed on Fisher's. "A happy coincidence that we find you here, Mr Fisher."

"I just came to collect some things, and then I am leaving," stuttered the young artist. "I'm in rather a hurry."

Carr placed a hand on his breast as if to show that he was sorry for any intrusion or inconvenience. "Of course, and I shall not delay you for long. I would like to have a quiet word, that is all."

Fisher smiled, but it was less than amicable. "Anything I can do."

Carr smiled in gratitude, but those dark eyes remained impassive. "I only have one question, really. Why did you burn all your materials and work from this studio in the woods on the night Isobel Croft was murdered?"

The words were like a blow to Fisher's stomach. The air seemed to explode from his body, and he gave the impression that he was suddenly gasping for air. Still, he was able to replace his smile, and a shake of the head suggested some degree of confused innocence. "What are you talking about?"

"Come, come, my boy," purred Carr, "it will not do. The fire was witnessed, and I, myself, found certain remnants of its contents. A metal hinge from an easel, for example, and a piece of stained linen, which had not properly burnt. It was clearly part of an artist's smock."

"It is nothing to do with me," insisted Fisher.

"I shall have the proof," cautioned Carr with a solemn gravity, "and, with it, shall come the truth."

Fisher's eyes widened momentarily, and in their movement, there was a flicker of panic. By contrast, Carr's expression remained unmoved, as if resigned to the inevitability of his prediction. Under Carr's glare, Fisher seemed to buckle, and his lips moved silently, as if in some effort to produce a silent confession of his guilt. Despite the appearance of any such attempt, however, no words came, and the young man turned away from Carr, as if to shield himself from any further effects of his accusatory stare.

Fisher, his back turned, reached into his pocket and produced the folded piece of paper whose contents Carr knew only too well. "You wrote this?"

Carr gave a slight bow of his head. "I'm afraid so."

"And the proof you speak of?"

"Will be here within the minute."

Fisher's shoulders slumped, and a low, miserable, mirthless laugh rolled out from his throat. "You sent two of these notes. I see it all now."

Carr shrugged. "A simple trick, I'm afraid."

Fisher looked over his shoulder, the eyes now heavy with defeat. "But effective, no doubt."

"I believe so," said Carr, "but we shall have to see if my little deductions are accurate."

"Do you have any reason to doubt they are?" asked Fisher, displaying for the first time the sneering attitude of a guilty but cornered man who has been discovered.

Beyond a brief smile, Carr offered no reply. Even if he had been inclined to respond, Carr would have been interrupted by the sudden sound of the studio door being thrown wide and the impetuous snarl of a coarse greeting.

"Fisher, what's all this—"

But Arthur Corrigan said no more. The sight of Carr and Dunn cut short his words and left him simultaneously surprised and outraged. He looked at Carr, his eyes twitching with suspicion, and to Fisher, as if the artist might himself have been privy to the deception which now seemed so evident and just as fatal to Corrigan.

"What is this?" he hissed. "What's happening here?"

Everett Carr stepped forward towards him. "It is for you to tell us that, Mr Corrigan."

Corrigan smiled, but the eyes were unaware of any humour. "Tell you about what?"

"Theft, forgery, and fraud."

There was a snort of derision from Corrigan, and a spiteful curse escaped from his lips. He made a movement towards the door, as if to leave the studio behind once and for all, but Dunn had evidently foreseen the tactic, since he had already made his way to the door and placed his back to it. He stood now, his weight balanced equally between his feet and his arms folded in professional impassivity. A slight and confrontational raising of his eyebrows was the only movement he permitted himself.

It seemed to be enough for Corrigan. "You'd better explain what you mean, Mr Carr. Just so I know what to tell my solicitors in case of any slander."

Carr's smile broadened, just as his glare darkened. "I should choose what words you say to your solicitors very carefully, Mr Corrigan. You will need their assistance far more keenly than their advice."

Carr's words had not frightened Corrigan, but he had hardly expected them to. Corrigan was too strong a personality to be troubled by a man he considered unimportant, and for his part, Carr was not perturbed by any failure to intimidate. It was not his intention to scare. When confronted with people like Arthur Corrigan, Carr had always felt a measure of satisfaction and, he was forced to admit, a degree of pleasure at seeing their punishment meted out.

"You are the recognised authority on Meryk Van Jansen, Mr Fisher," said Carr, turning to the artist. "You had worked hard to investigate both his life and work. Van Jansen's own isolation and his failure as an artist in his own lifetime meant that he was not well known and, hence, examples of his work are rare. Hence, they are extremely valuable."

"Yes," Fisher felt obliged to say.

Carr smiled. "Now, it occurred to me that Van Jansen's own professional obscurity would mean that his paintings might not be easily found, either in their original form or in reproductions. Would I be right in saying that?"

"Yes," muttered Fisher.

Carr's smile broadened. "In other words, if a collector purchased a Van Jansen painting and had its provenance authenticated by you, Mr Fisher, there would really be very little he could do to verify your word."

"And why would he do that?" interrupted Corrigan.

Carr turned to face him, with a polite glint in his dark eyes. "Why, indeed? If I may continue, Mr Corrigan, it seems equally certain that Van Jansen's

lack of exposure might also mean that his paintings might easily be forged."
He said the word carefully, as if desperate not to offend.

Fisher pulled a chair towards himself and sat down, the air exploded from
his lungs in a long sigh of regret and recrimination. It was not a confession,
but it was almost as valuable. Carr looked across at Corrigan and saw the
malevolent glare of warning in his eyes, although Fisher seemed unaware
of it. Even so, neither man spoke, and Carr felt obliged to continue.

"I have heard it said that all artists possess a vanity which compels them
to sign their work, either with their name or with a particular characteristic
of their own," he said. "For you, Mr Fisher, it was naturally impossible
to assign your own name to these forgeries, but you were able to add a
small detail to each of them, a detail which would not show on the original
paintings, but one which was in keeping with the overall tone and subject of
the piece in question. In the case of the painting in the church, for example,
it was a snake coiled around Pilate's leg."

Dunn was quick to respond. "The snake isn't real."

Carr nodded. "Precisely, Inspector. Lorrimer had written that phrase
down and it is proof that he, at least, was aware of the deception and of the
fraud."

"And you think one of us killed him because of that?" snapped Corrigan.
"You'd better have proof."

Carr ignored him, keeping his attention on Fisher. "The scheme, I
presume, was that you would forge Van Jansen paintings, pass them to
Mr Corrigan, who would secure a potential sale to a rich client from
abroad. A guarantee of provenance would be given by an assessment from
an independent expert. In each case, that would be you, Mr Fisher. And
a worthless painting would be sold for the usual high prices which we so
often read about for newly discovered rare works by forgotten masters.
And, naturally, the fee would be split between the two of you."

Fisher removed his spectacles and ran his hands down his face, as if it were
possible to erase his guilt and shame by doing so. "How did you know?"

"They have to prove all this, Fisher!" roared Corrigan.

The reaction was as startling as it was unexpected. Fisher leapt from his chair and grabbed Corrigan by his lapels, pulling the older man close to him. Their faces were inches apart, Corrigan's blanched by the surprise of the attack as much as Fisher's was reddened by it. Dunn took a step forward, but Carr held out a hand to stop him.

Fisher was shouting, specks of spittle flecking Corrigan's cheeks. "They can prove it, you bloody fool. Don't you understand what's happened?" He reached into his pocket and pulled out the note which Carr had sent. He shoved it into Corrigan's face. "Read it, you bastard. It says that the art scam has been exposed and that a meeting here is vital. And you had one yourself, didn't you? Saying exactly the same thing."

Corrigan's eyes were fixed on Everett Carr. "You sent it?"

Fisher's voice was growing in intensity and disgust. "Of course he did! And because we both turned up here, they know we were involved in it together."

"An innocent person would have ignored the message as being meaningless," said Carr quietly.

"So stop being so bloody clever and stop bleating about proof," said Fisher. With all his might, he pushed Corrigan away from him. The older man stumbled against a table and stared dumbly back at his confederate. Now, suddenly, Corrigan seemed isolated and alone, but there was no sympathy in the room for him.

Fisher turned back to Carr, his eyes heavy and his face suddenly seeming exhausted. "How did you know?"

Carr lowered his head, as if embarrassed by the minor violence which had been enacted. "When you revived me in here, you did so with brandy from a flask. You claimed an old friend had left it to you. Even in my daze, I could see that it was expensive and inscribed."

"You careless little bastard, Fisher, by God in Heaven," muttered Corrigan, his voice heavy with disgusted disappointment.

Carr continued. "This studio is almost falling down, and forgive me, Mr Fisher, you are not well-known enough to make a fortune from your own art. I had to account for that brandy flask, and when I realised the truth of Lorrimer's reference to a snake in the church's painting, coupled with the fact that you alone are the expert on Van Jansen, the explanation of the flask seemed rather obvious."

"I wondered afterwards whether you had noticed the flask."

Carr smiled gently. "When I confronted you about your argument with Lorrimer being overheard, you tried to suggest that his mention of a theft was to do with Edgar Corrigan stealing Harriet Delaney from him. That was a lie."

Another shameful nod of Fisher's head. "He said that any money we took for the forgeries was theft and he was going to make sure people knew. You've known all along, Mr Carr, how spiteful he could be, just for the sake of it."

"Indeed," replied Carr. He cleared his throat, almost apologetically. "As a final point, I must say, if you will forgive me for doing so, that your partnership with Mr Corrigan seemed to me rather too unlikely to be entirely genuine."

Fisher looked at him with a frankness in his eyes which had not been evident until that moment. "For Corrigan, it was all about the money."

"And for you?"

Fisher smiled weakly. "A bit of spiteful, petty revenge."

Carr pulled a chair towards him and sat down, easing his leg out before him. "You'll have to explain that, Mr Fisher."

The artist seemed consumed by an overwhelming exhaustion. "I haven't always been a cheat, Mr Carr. I was once a promising artist. All I have ever wanted was to have a career as a painter, to exhibit my work, and to see it appreciated. The closest I came was a small exhibition in a gallery in London some years ago. I had seen it as being the first step towards realising my ambitions and, as luck would have it, some influential dealers and critics were there."

Carr felt sure that he could predict the story. "I see."

Fisher seemed to discern the inevitability in Carr's expression. "Instead of receiving the plaudits I felt I was entitled to, I was ridiculed out of the exhibition. Do you know what one review said?" He recited the words which were etched into his memory with a cruel and shameful finality. "*Mr*

Fisher is an accepted authority on a forgotten, failed artist by the name of Meryk Van Jansen. It is fitting, perhaps, since Mr Fisher himself seems destined for failure and obscurity in his own right."

Carr's expression was serious. "One of the worst cruelties of all is when people think they are being clever by it."

Fisher was now silently weeping, but nobody acknowledged it. "I wanted to get back at them for their snobbery and their malicious arrogance. The more I thought about it, the more I came to realise that I could use Van Jansen to my advantage, to make fools of them all. If I couldn't make money by my own reputation, I would make it by enhancing his. It sounds foolish saying it out loud now, but it was as if he and I could help each other across the centuries."

"It doesn't sound foolish," said Everett Carr softly. "But Lorrimer found out about the forgeries."

Fisher nodded dumbly. "He had found an etching in the public library of the painting in the church."

"Quite so," said Carr. "I found a scrap of burned paper in the grate of your fire, which matched stationery I had found in Lorrimer's cottage. You would not have had cause to burn a letter from Lorrimer unless what he had written was dangerous to you."

Corrigan felt he had been silent for long enough. "None of which proves we murdered him. If, indeed, he was murdered at all."

Carr looked up at him. "Perhaps not, Mr Corrigan, but it provides you with a very strong motive."

It was Fisher who pleaded with him. "We didn't kill him, Mr Carr, I swear to you."

"Can you be sure of that, Mr Fisher?" asked Carr. "Perhaps you know of your own innocence, but can you vouch for Mr Corrigan's?"

"I didn't kill anybody," said that person with venom in his voice.

Carr pointed his stick towards Corrigan, with as much antipathy in the gesture as was in his voice. "Really? You have a violent streak, though, do you not, Mr Corrigan? You threw Lorrimer out of your house on one occasion, after all, and I have no doubt that my little accident in this very studio was on account of you."

Dunn spoke for the first time. "You came here to see whether Fisher had indeed destroyed all your work."

Corrigan growled, but it was the fierce yet frustrated roar of a defeated animal. "Don't think for a moment I'm sorry about knocking you on the head, Carr, you interfering little mountebank. But I didn't kill Lorrimer."

"That remains to be seen," cautioned Dunn. "But William Lorrimer was murdered, Mr Corrigan, and Isobel Croft knew who the killer was, and she had proof of it."

"What proof?" snarled Corrigan.

Dunn smiled slyly. "I'm not at liberty to say, sir. You shall have to take my word for it that it is true. Mr Carr will back me up on it."

Corrigan turned to Carr. "Will you?"

But Carr seemed uninterested in the change in conversation, and he gave a dismissive wave of his hand. "These are all matters for another time. For the present, if you will permit me, Inspector, I should like to ask Mr Fisher one last question." He turned to the young man. "You are an orphan, I believe?"

Fisher frowned. "What has that to do with anything?"

"Did you ever spend time at a place called Linacre House?"

Fisher shook his head. "No, I've never heard of it."

Carr seemed delighted by the answer. His lips stretched into a wide smile, and his dark eyes seemed to dance with satisfaction. "Thank you, Mr Fisher, you have made things much clearer in my mind."

There was no more to be said. Carr smiled at the three men, bowed politely in farewell, and made his excited but uneven way out of the studio.

Chapter Thirty-Five

When she awoke, Dorothy Parrish found Thomas Lewton slumped in the rocking chair by the bedroom window. It was motionless now, but it must have rocked him to sleep, for his head was inclined to the side and supported by a hand under the chin, itself supported by an elbow resting on the arm of the chair. His long legs were splayed in an awkward and ungainly position, and his stomach rose and fell in the gentle rhythm of slumber. She spoke his name in a hoarse, urgent whisper, but he did not react. When she hissed it more loudly, however, his eyes flickered, and a few mumbled, incoherent words tumbled from his mouth. His spectacles were pushed back onto his head, and he fumbled with them now, bringing them clumsily down onto the bridge of his nose. He rose from the rocking chair and walked swiftly to Dorothy's bedside.

"Are you all right?" he asked. "Lie back, and I will go and make you some tea."

"I don't want any tea," she replied.

He bit his lower lip, like a scolded child unfairly reprimanded for a minor indiscretion. She had spoken too brusquely, and she knew it, but she did not apologise. Somehow, to have done so would have seemed demeaning.

"You gave me something last night to make me sleep," she said.

He nodded unapologetically. "Just a little barbital. You needed rest."

She offered no argument. "I keep seeing Mr Bowers, lying in front of me, with his head…"

But she could not finish the sentence, and she shook her head in defeat.

A carafe of water and a toothglass stood on the dressing table, and Lewton poured some for her. She accepted it gratefully, and the water, although tepid, was alarmingly refreshing. She had not appreciated how dry her mouth was until it was cleansed by the drink. She handed the glass back to him, and he poured a second, which she sipped in a rather more controlled fashion.

After a moment, Dorothy looked up across to Lewton. "Everett Carr knows."

Lewton frowned. "Knows what?"

"Everything," she whispered. "About you, about Lorrimer."

"How can he know?"

Dorothy wondered whether the strident tone of Lewton's voice, was a result of incredulity or panic. "What does that matter? The point is that he does."

He looked at her. "You must be mistaken."

"He told me himself," she snapped. "He said he knew everything."

"Has he told the police?"

She shrugged. "I've no idea. He was with Inspector Dunn when he arrived at the church, so it's possible."

Lewton cursed under his breath and removed his spectacles, rubbing his eyes vigorously, as if to erase the scene unfolding mercilessly in front of him. He sat down in the rocking chair and buried his face in his hands. For a moment, Dorothy thought that he was weeping, but he was not, although he did seem to be trembling with anxiety.

"We have to think about what we are going to do," she said.

He shook his head. "They'll hang me. If Carr knows all about it, he'll know that Lorrimer had discovered the truth, too. What else can they do but put a rope around my neck?"

"They have to prove you killed Lorrimer before they can do that."

But he seemed not to have heard. "I can't stay here. I have to leave, and right away. Start again somewhere else. That's all there is to it." He looked up at her, but he did not replace his spectacles, so that he would not see clearly her inevitable refusal of his next plea. "Will you come with me,

Dorothy?"

The question was not unexpected, and she took no time to respond. "Fleeing isn't the answer, Thomas. We have to let matters take their course, and we must do it with courage."

His eyes were wild with panic, and they pleaded with her to change her mind. And yet, despite their frantic glare, he did not display any other evidence of his anxiety. On the contrary, he gave a short, mirthless laugh and shook his head. "Courage? When have I ever shown any of that?"

Dorothy looked back at him, and her eyes were as calm and soothing as his were desperate and agitated. "You showed courage when you confessed what you had done to me."

For a long moment, he seemed incapable of speech. "I thought you had abandoned me. From the moment you walked out, I thought I'd lost you."

She smiled, and she would have replied to him, saying that she had needed only space to come to terms with his guilt and shame and that she had never intended to abandon him, that even if she had wanted to do so, she would have felt unable to do it. She would have told him all that and more, that she had finally come to understand what it meant to love and perhaps to be loved, and that she had come close to forsaking any hope that she might ever learn that particularly human lesson. She would have told him so much, but she was prevented from doing so by a knocking on the cottage door. She looked at Lewton in confusion, and he reciprocated.

"Who could that be?" he asked unnecessarily.

Hastily, Dorothy threw on her dressing gown and got out of bed. Lewton rose and followed her out of the bedroom and down the stairs. A second knock at the door greeted them both as they reached the foot of the stairs.

"Go into the living room," said Dorothy. "I'll get rid of whoever it is."

She watched Lewton obey and waited until he was out of sight before she pulled open the door. Almost simultaneously, she gave a short gasp of shock when she saw who it was, standing on her doorstep.

Everett Carr tipped his hat and smiled politely. "Good afternoon, dear lady."

"What are you doing here, Mr Carr?" Dorothy asked the question politely, but her eyes did not possess the bland affability of her voice.

"To see how you were feeling, dear lady," purred Carr. "I see that you have had some rest, at least."

"Yes," said Dorothy, "I am much better, thank you."

"A great shock it must have been," sympathised Carr.

Dorothy stiffened and folded her arms in an almost defiant gesture. "I hope you haven't come here to question me, Mr Carr."

"Not at all. Purely a friendly visit to make sure you were well. Your experience was a serious one, after all, and one from which many people never properly recover."

She smiled, suddenly aware that she was both exhausted and cold. "Thank you, I am much better. I have slept very soundly, I can assure you."

"Splendid," said Carr, looking over her shoulder to Lewton. "I suppose Mr Lewton gave you a sedative of some kind."

"A little barbital, I think."

Carr nodded, satisfied. "I expected as much."

Dorothy spoke almost without intention, as if it were an instinctive spasm of her mouth. "I'm glad you're here."

Carr frowned. "Indeed?"

"I've remembered something which I think might be important. I wondered if you would advise me as to whether I should tell the police. I would hate to waste their time."

Carr bowed. "If I can be of assistance to you, dear lady, I shall be."

She took a moment to gather her thoughts. "When I got to the church, Mr Bowers was still alive."

Carr's eyes hardened with fascination, and the familiar freezing of his spine took hold of him. "Alive?"

"He was trying to speak."

Carr felt his fingers tighten around the silver handle of his walking stick. "Could you make out what he was saying?"

Dorothy shook her head in a moment of indecision and uncertainty. "That's just it, I'm not sure. I know what it sounded like."

Carr remained patient, but the smile across his lips was one of frustration rather than encouragement. "And what was that dear lady?"

Dorothy thought for a moment. "I thought he was saying something like, *'She knew...it was wrong'*."

Carr did not reply. His eyes flickered to a point in the distance of which only he was aware, and his expression was one of such enlightenment and understanding that he might have witnessed the presence and arrival of a deity personified. His lips slowly parted in a smile of amazed realisation, and he began to shake his head slowly, as if in disbelief at his own failure to recognise previously whatever point it now was which seemed so obvious to him.

"Mr Carr?" prompted Dorothy.

He bowed in apology. "Forgive me, dear lady, I was thinking of something else entirely. You asked for my advice, and it is this—do not mention this to the police. I shall do so on your behalf."

"Is it important?"

Carr shrugged. "Who can say? But you do not need to trouble yourself with the police. You should rest instead and leave all other matters to me. One last point before I go, if I may," he added. "Would you and Mr Lewton do me the honour of attending a little meeting at William Lorrimer's cottage tomorrow evening?"

Dorothy frowned. "For what purpose?"

Carr's smile widened. "I have a little idea, and I need your help to corroborate it, if I may impose on you. Shall we say eight o'clock?"

Whether he had anticipated a refusal and did not wish to provide an opportunity for one, Dorothy did not know, but Carr had bowed and turned his back on her before she could provide any negative response to his request. Slowly, she closed the door, her head hanging heavily with confusion and anxiety.

When she walked into the living room, she found Thomas Lewton pacing before the fireplace, his face twisted in nervous anxiety. "What's all that about tomorrow evening?"

"He wants us to meet him next door."

"At Lorrimer's?" Lewton watched her nod her head. Then, sighing heavily, he slumped against the door frame. "He's going to expose me, isn't he? He's setting a trap for me, and I'm going to have no choice but to walk into it."

She walked towards him and held out her arms to him. Now, his fears overtook him completely, and he began to weep. When Dorothy Parish tightened her hold on him, he felt no comfort from the embrace. To Thomas Lewton, the arms around his neck felt altogether too much like the hangman's noose.

Chapter Thirty-Six

Elsa Corrigan had breakfasted alone and was sitting in the drawing room, ostensibly reading a novel, but her concentration and interest had long since dwindled. The book lay open on her lap, and her slim fingers played with the corners of the page, in anticipation of turning it over, but her head was tilted to the side, and her eyes were so obviously fixed on the lawns beyond the window that any pretence to be reading was too negligible to be convincing.

Her mind drifted reluctantly back over the conversation with Edgar on the previous evening, although she knew that it had been more of a confrontation than a conversation. It had been the day of Everett Carr's visit, perhaps an hour or so after the little man had left. Elsa had met Edgar coming down the stairs a little while after she had taken a solitary tea in the sitting room. She had known at once that something was amiss. Her maternal instincts, which allowed her to know her son better than he knew himself, were alerted immediately to the absence of his customary smile and the darkened brows which had replaced his usual jaunty and childishly amiable expression. Reflecting on it now, Elsa realised that she might well have known something was wrong with him, but her personal defences had prevented her from addressing them with an almost equal vigour and, in the moment, she had disregarded and ignored those same instincts which had betrayed his mood to her.

"Edgar," she had said, "I thought you had gone out."

"No," he had replied, curtly but not impolitely. "What did Mr Carr want?"

The question had been as unwelcome as it had been unexpected. Elsa had known at once that she could not tell the truth. To do so would have been to betray the secret of Edmund Draper, and yet, there was a determination in Edgar's eyes which showed that complete evasion was both impossible and unwise.

"He seems to be prying into matters which don't concern him," she had replied, "and which are properly matters for the police."

"What matters?"

She had shaken her head. "Really, darling, they were not important."

"Then there is no harm in telling me about them."

She had contemplated her son for a long moment. The confliction of colour in his eyes had seemed so vibrant now that she had only then realised how much she had taken it for granted previously. There was an entreaty in the juxtaposition of their colour, a plea for her to confide in him with honesty and respect, and she had wavered for a moment, feeling herself succumbing to his wishes, before she had reasserted herself and had looked back at her son with a motherly dominance which she had no intention of relinquishing.

"He was asking about the time your father threw William Lorrimer out of this house," she had replied. "On account of Harriet, if you remember."

Edgar's eyes had flickered, and his fingers had begun to twitch, flexing and relaxing in a rhythmic but nervous motion. "What has that got to do with anything?"

Elsa had shrugged. "Nothing, as far as I can tell, which is precisely what I told Mr Carr."

Edgar had thought for a long moment. "Did he ask anything else?"

She had almost mentioned the library book, as if entirely confident that Edgar would not appreciate its importance or the connection with Lorrimer's death, but she had resisted the temptation equally swiftly. "Nothing which struck me as being of any importance."

"Did he ask about me or Harriet?"

And it had been this question which had shaken her the most. She had felt her throat tighten, and, in her mind, her eyes had widened in trepidation, and she had begun to shake with anxiety. For the first time, she had the idea that Edgar had heard every word of her conversation with Carr, but she had known that asking the question to confirm it was something which she would never be able to do. Instead, she had twisted it into another one, which was more evasive, perhaps, but far less dangerous.

"What would he have asked about you?" Elsa had said.

Edgar had shrugged. "I don't know, mother, that's why I'm asking."

"He didn't mention you at all," she had replied.

But he had caught her momentary hesitation. His eyes dimmed, and he shook his head slowly, almost unbearably sadly. "I never thought you could lie to me, mother."

The words had crucified her, each one like a nail through her flesh, and for a moment, she had been unable either to understand him or to reply. She had been uncertain which lie he meant and momentarily, she had been terrified that he had discovered all her lies and was now expecting her to have the courage to confess them. Again, the suspicion that he had been eavesdropping on her interview with Everett Carr raged in her brain, but Elsa had continued to deny it a voice.

"I'm not lying to you, darling," she had managed to say.

He had shaken his head. "If Carr was asking about Lorrimer and about the time Father threw him out of this house, he must have talked about me and Harriet. Why else would he be here? The whole village talks about me and Harriet when they discuss Lorrimer's death. They think we're the reason for it. Does Carr think the same?"

And in his fury and rage, Elsa had found an incongruous and shameful relief. So, after all, it had been Edgar's private paranoia which had caused his unusually depressed mood, rather than any suspicion which he might have held against Elsa herself. It had been reassurance which he had sought, rather than any explanation or demand for the truth from her. If she had been appalled by her own gratitude that her secrets were safe, even at the cost of her son's peace of mind, she had been equally comforted by it. She had taken Edgar's hand in hers and had kissed him lightly on the cheek.

"You're such a sensitive soul, darling," she had said. "You must learn to ignore gossip and rumour. Be happy with your life, Edgar. You only have one chance at it."

And then he had said something both unexpected and concerning. "Are you happy, mother?"

Now, sitting alone in the drawing room, she could not remember exactly what her response had been. She fancied that she had smiled at him, kissed him once more, and offered some platitude of assurance, although the precise words had vanished from her memory. Whatever they had been, they must have been sufficient for his purposes, for there had been no further discussion on the topic, and Elsa had permitted her son to walk away with her lies masquerading as the truth in his mind.

And they were lies. It seemed to Elsa as if her entire life had been an existence of lies. It was not altogether fair, she appreciated that. Her childhood, whilst not especially privileged, had been happy and peaceful, and she could not remember any spectre of untruth casting its shadow across it. It was only later that things had changed, when lust and dominance had manipulated her into mistaking them for love and driven her into a marriage which would now never release her, but from which she had come so close to escaping.

And whose fault was it? It was easy to blame Arthur Corrigan; perhaps it was just as convenient to blame Edmund Draper for disappearing from her life so suddenly. But Elsa knew that if she were to begin to be honest about herself, it would be as well to accept at last that the lies had begun with her. It had been Elsa herself who had persisted in them and kept them alive by not having the courage to look the truth in the eye and to let it have its day. It was Elsa who had permitted those lies to dominate and control her life, leaving her in the position in which she was now imprisoned and forcing her to live with the mistakes she had made and the suffocating guilt which they had imposed upon her. What had happened, all of it, had been a result of her own shame, cowardice, and attempts to conceal the truth. Slowly, she wiped the silent tears from her eyes.

No more lies. It seemed to her that there must come a time when a liar's tongue could coil itself around the truth and constrict the life out of it no more, when the lips could no longer form false words, and when the mind could create and sustain no further dishonesty. Eventually, she thought, matters must always be put right. In that instant, words from her childhood came back to her, from a play whose name she could not place immediately:

"...truth will come to light; murder cannot be hid long; a man's son may, but at the length truth will out."

As a child, she had understood the meaning, but it had lacked context for her. Now, it seemed to ring with all the clarity of church bells on a Sunday morning. Only now, after everything which had happened, did Elsa see the very real and terrifying connection between murder and truth, and only in that moment did she realise that she could keep neither of them buried any longer. Edgar had been smothered by deceit for long enough, and it was time that she released him from his bonds of dishonesty. The truth, Elsa Corrigan determined, deserved utterance, just as her son deserved to hear it.

She allowed herself a period of sobbing, refusing to believe it was an indulgence and convincing herself that it was necessary if she were to face her demons and her fears with courage. At last, she tossed the useless novel onto the table beside her chair and rose to her feet. Marching upstairs, dabbing at her swollen and raw eyes, she went into her bedroom. She remained in there for longer than she had anticipated, her courage momentarily deserting her. She pulled open the drawers of her dressing table and removed the familiar but tragic photograph from its hiding place at the back of the drawer. For a long moment, she stared the truth in the eyes, fighting back tears from forming in her own. At last, but strangely unable to replace the photograph in its secret place, she made her way back downstairs.

She was pulling open the door to the study, the letter she knew she must write already composing itself in her head, when there was a knock at the front door. It startled her and, for a moment, she was unable to move. Indecision and fear had gripped her with equal brutality, and her world seemed to freeze and plunge itself into darkness. There was another sharp bang on the door, which seemed to her to be so loud that it jolted her back into consciousness. She walked swiftly to the door and pulled it open.

Whether it was fear or amazement which struck her first upon seeing Everett Carr standing before her, she could not say, but she gave a short, horrified gasp, and she felt her spine stiffen with alarm. Carr could not have failed to notice it, but he said nothing and, Elsa supposed, she was grateful for it. Instead, with his natural politeness, he bowed and gently tipped his hat to her. When he spoke, his voice was comforting and affable, but those dark eyes showed that his business was serious.

"Forgive the intrusion, dear lady," he said. "I have come for a final discussion with you."

"Would you mind coming back later, Mr Carr?" Elsa asked, her breath struggling to fill her lungs and find the words. "I have some important business to deal with."

"I rather think I cannot," he replied. "I know everything about the deaths in this village, you see, and we must allow the truth to come out. If I may say so, Mrs Corrigan," he added with a voice laced with sympathy, "I think you have come to that conclusion yourself."

She glared at him. "What makes you think that?"

"I think you know, dear lady."

But she shook her head. "I do not, I assure you."

Carr took a step forward, and the seriousness of his dark eyes intensified. "If you will trust me and treat me as a friend, I shall justify that trust. If you cannot do that, I must proceed without your help, but I would warn you against forcing me to do that. Either way, Mrs Corrigan, it is time for the truth."

She was shaking her head, her breath now coming through her clenched teeth in coarse, rasping gasps. "What truth? What do you mean?"

Everett Carr took a further step forward and, with a curiously theatrical arc of a gloved forefinger, he pointed to the silver-framed photograph which Elsa Corrigan still held in her hand. As the tears fell down her cheeks once more, Carr gave a calm assurance that all would be well, and, with defiance, he stepped over the threshold and closed the door behind him.

Chapter Thirty-Seven

Ｎone of those people seated in William Lorrimer's sitting room that evening felt comfortable with the arrangement. It was as if the spectre of the dead man was standing next to Everett Carr at the stone fireplace, looking down on them in judgement of his death. The chair in which he would have sat was empty, as if none of them dared to occupy it, in case it was deemed to be some kind of affront to the dead. Instead, a small crescent of dining chairs had been arranged around the settee, and people had taken their places in those. A silence had fallen over the room, and Carr enjoyed it for a moment longer. He was dressed in his dinner suit, pristine and immaculate, the white carnation boutonnière in his lapel emphasising the darkness of the suit and tie. He resembled an elegant and extravagant professor attending before a nervous and disjointed class. He raised his head and smiled, the luxuriant white moustache and neat Imperial bristling as he did so, although his dark eyes were filled with anything but polite humour.

"My friends," he said, "firstly, may I offer my sincere thanks to you all for attending this little gathering of mine. I appreciate that it may seem somewhat melodramatic, but I can assure you that it is for the best. All of you are aware of how quickly and maliciously gossip can spread through a village such as this. My intention in calling this little seminar is to set out the facts of the deaths of William Lorrimer, Isobel Croft, and Gerald Bowers and to explain to you the truth of all that has occurred in Little Marsham over the past few months. In this way, I hope that none of you will be subjected to any unfounded rumours or suspicions, but instead, be protected against them.

"What I have to say is not pleasant. Indeed, in circumstances such as these, both explaining and hearing the truth can be difficult. One person in particular, I fear, will be affected more than anyone else. All I can say in rebuttal is that time will heal all wounds, and the truth will soothe what it once had hurt." There was an uncomfortable shuffling of fabric as people shifted their positions in their seats. The apprehension in the room, already acute before Carr's words, seemed now to intensify. Carr seemed keenly aware of it, for he raised a calming hand and patted the air, as if placating an invisible child in distress. "It is perhaps best," he continued, "if I told my story in my own way and began at the beginning of this tragic business."

There was a general murmur of agreement, and Carr, in deference to it, took a sip of whisky from a glass set on the mantelpiece, savoured it, and cleared his throat. He dabbed at his lips and moustache with his handkerchief and replaced it carefully in his top jacket pocket.

"In order to understand the truth of this matter, as I came to understand it myself," Carr said, "I must take you carefully through each of the points which seemed to me to be of importance. Once I have done so, you will see that, unfortunately, the facts point only to one person as being responsible for all three murders."

"You're absolutely certain that Lorrimer's death wasn't suicide?" asked Edgar Corrigan. "You have proof of it?"

Carr nodded and gave a slight bow. "Each point in its proper place, my boy, and you shall understand everything."

Edgar held up an apologetic hand and smiled briefly. Harriet Delaney, sitting beside him, took his hand and closed her own around it. Carr watched the gesture and smiled gently, allowing silence to fall once again.

"The mystery and also the truth behind it begins with William Lorrimer," said Carr. "When I talked to people in the village and to the people in this room who knew him best, the impression I was given of the dead man was that he was unpleasant. Edgar Corrigan described him as a man who, as a child, might have pulled the legs off spiders, and both Thomas Lewton and Harriet Delaney testified to Lorrimer's spiteful and malicious nature.

"And yet, this apparently malevolent and hostile man had taken his own life. An inquest had concluded as much. I confess that I had difficulty at once in accepting the finding of the coroner's court. The verdict had been that Lorrimer, heartbroken by Miss Delaney's termination of their relationship, had taken a gun and shot himself. But I ask you, my friends, would a man as vindictive and malicious as people told me Lorrimer had been have taken such a step? Or is it more likely that such a man who had taken some form of...*revenge?*" Carr spoke the word with a dangerous relish, which both shocked and unnerved the majority of those in the room.

"What sort of revenge?" asked Harriet Delaney.

Carr simply shrugged. "I don't know, dear lady, but is it not more conceivable that a spiteful and vindictive man would seek retribution for a wrong done against him, rather than allowing himself to become so consumed with despair that death was his only option? He had destroyed a photograph of you, Miss Delaney. Does that not demonstrate a destructive desire for vengeance?"

Thomas Lewton leaned forward, his brow creased in intelligent fascination. "Certainly, I can see your point, Mr Carr, but the man left a note. It was in his own handwriting."

Carr raised a finger. "Consider that note. I understand from Miss Delaney that it was addressed to her but not signed. Does that not strike you as curious? He addresses his last word to Miss Delaney, so that there should be no doubt that it was intended for her, but he does not sign his name to it. Why not? As a final farewell or, in Lorrimer's case, a final word of accusation against Miss Delaney, does it not seem strange that he would not complete the note with his own signature?"

Lewton, who had clearly not given this idea a moment's thought, leaned back in his chair. "Put like that, it does seem odd."

Carr bowed his head in agreement. "I learned from Miss Delaney that this note had been found by Lorrimer's body. It was perfectly possible, therefore, that the note had been deliberately placed there, to give the impression that it was a suicide note when, in fact, it was nothing of the sort."

"Then what was it?" asked Lewton.

"Unquestionably, it was a communication meant for Harriet Delaney. It occurred to me that the lack of a signature might be accounted for either because the note had not been completed before Lorrimer died or because *someone had removed a second page.* The former I thought unlikely: a man pouring out vitriol against a woman he believes has wronged him would not stop writing until his spleen was vented. I could not envisage Lorrimer breaking off his tirade before it was finished, but I could easily believe that a third person found the note and used it to give the impression that Lorrimer had committed suicide." He nodded slowly. "Yes, that I could believe very easily indeed."

Carr watched as those eyes which were fixed on him began to shift their perspective to each other, as the initial nausea of suspicion began to rise within the people concerned. For his part, Carr watched the person he knew to be the murderer and noted with a grim appreciation the ease with which the killer dissembled. To Carr, rather than any sense of suspicion or unease, there was only a sense of inevitable regret and, just possibly, an ache of fierce determination to see justice delivered.

"I had come to these conclusions almost as soon as I heard about Lorrimer's death," he continued, having refreshed himself with another sip of the whisky. "My suspicions about the veracity of the suicide verdict only became certainties, however, when Isobel Croft was killed. In her case, of course, there was no doubt that her death was deliberate murder, and it was equally certain what the motive had been. It is common knowledge by now, I think, that Isobel Croft was Lorrimer's sister and that she had confided in Mr Bowers that she believed her brother's death had not been suicide but murder, and she claimed to have evidence of the fact. When Isobel Croft was killed, it was immediately clear to me that her claims had been true and that Lorrimer had indeed been murdered. In order to discover the truth, therefore, it was necessary to investigate William Lorrimer's death. By doing so, the killer of Isobel Croft, I was sure, would be identified easily."

Carr began to pace before the fireplace, not in any attempt to unnerve his audience, but to give relief to the shattered bone of his knee, which had now begun to ache from lack of exercise. His head remained bowed, and his heavy brows were drawn together over the onyx eyes, in a frown of intense concentration.

"My personal investigation into Lorrimer's death began where it will end," he said, "in this cottage. It was here that the first indications of the truth came to my notice. The cottage had been burgled, but, whilst I had no way of knowing whether anything had been stolen, I was still able to discover some points which I thought might be of interest. The first was some very particular stationery, which you can still see is stacked neatly at the corner of this writing bureau." He pointed to the desk set in the corner of the room. "You will see that Lorrimer favoured a specific shade of blue-purple notepaper and envelope. That was, I thought, a matter of some interest."

Edgar Corrigan held up a hand. "May I ask why?"

Carr smiled gently at him. "Because a torn piece of it was found in the hand of Isobel Croft. Evidently, therefore, Lorrimer had written a letter to his sister, a letter which she, in turn, had thought necessary to have with her on the night of her own murder. The deed done, the killer tore the letter from the dead woman's hand, leaving behind a tell-tale fragment of it. That letter is, I suggest, no longer in existence, but it is undoubtedly the proof which Isobel Croft claimed to have that Lorrimer had been murdered.

"The dead woman's hand was not the only place I found that blue-purple stationery either. I noticed a burnt portion of it in the grate in the art studio of Laurence Fisher." Carr turned to face the artist, whose spine stiffened and whose eyes glared at Carr with an inexorable shame. "Whilst I did not know it at the time, the second point of interest in this cottage also connected with Mr Fisher. On the blotter of the bureau, Lorrimer had scrawled a curious phrase: *the snake isn't real*. Only later did I come to realise the importance and meaning of that phrase."

"What does it mean?" asked Dorothy Parrish, glancing strangely across to Fisher.

Carr lowered his gaze momentarily, and then, with a regretful darkening of his eyes, he looked at Elsa and Edgar Corrigan in turn. "What I am about to say will come as a shock to you, Mrs Corrigan, and to your son."

Arthur Corrigan grunted. "Just get it over with, Carr."

Carr looked across at him, his lips tightening in disdain. "Mr Corrigan and Mr Fisher will be taken into custody after this little meeting, I am sorry to say."

Elsa rose to her feet, her face contorted by flames of indignation. "Custody?"

Edgar looked over at Corrigan and Fisher. "Father?"

But it was Everett Carr who spoke. "*The snake isn't real.* I confess that for a time, my mind was distracted by Gerald Bowers and the scandal surrounding his relationship with Mary Jerrold, and I had reasoned that Lorrimer's misguided disgust at Bowers' apparent hypocrisy was the origin of this curious phrase. However, it was when I saw a rare reproduction of *The Trial Before Pilate* by Meryk Van Jansen that the truth hit me. This painting, you will recall, had been donated by Fisher and Corrigan to the church. When I compared the reproduction to the painting hanging above the altar at St Bartholomew's, I saw a subtle but distinct difference in the form of a serpent coiled around Pilate's leg. It could only mean one thing, of course."

Edgar's face had blanched and, when he spoke, he was almost unable to say the words, which came out in a hoarse whisper of disbelief and repugnance. "The painting is a fake?"

Carr gave only a small nod of his head. Harriet Delaney put her arms around her lover as he sank against her, deflated by disappointment and disdain. Elsa, for her part, was glaring at Corrigan as if seeing him for the first time, his wickedness and his deceit now seeming to have contorted his features as she saw them.

"You vile, sickening man," she hissed.

Carr looked across at Angela Ryman. She was staring at her feet, forcing herself not to look in the direction of her former lover, as if to do so would be both to betray her adultery with him, but also to suggest some complicity in his crimes. Carr found that he was pleased she had reacted in this fashion; it suggested, he thought, that her infatuation with him was finally at an end, and that could be nothing but for the best.

Fisher had reddened, and his eyes were wild with regret. "I'm sorry, for all of it. Sorry and ashamed."

But Corrigan, sneering at his confederate's penitence, was himself unaffected by his exposure. "You enjoyed the money though, didn't you, Elsa? You're not so morally superior that you couldn't live on the fruits of our little dodge."

"You disgust me, Arthur," she replied, summoning as much dignity as the situation and the eyes on her would permit. "God knows, you always have."

Edgar rose from his chair and went to his mother. He held her in a protective embrace for a moment, before releasing her when it was evident that she did not need the support. Her eyes were cold and hard, like the glaciers in the coldest oceans, and her lips were compressed in a pout of suppressed fury. She kissed her son's hand, but it was a mechanical gesture, an acknowledgement of her son's loyalty but distanced by her own consuming disgust.

Carr broke the tension with a gentle clearing of his throat. "The burnt paper in Fisher's grate showed that Lorrimer had written a note or letter to Fisher and that was an important point. I could conceive of no reason for Lorrimer to communicate with Fisher other than if he had discovered the forgery scheme. If he had, and if he threatened to expose the pair of them, it was a further insight into Lorrimer's character. It suggested that other people's secrets were of no consequence to him. I had learned already that he had threatened to write to Gerald Bowers' bishop about his relationship with Mrs Jerrold, and it seemed entirely in his character to suppose that he might be willing to expose a serious case of fraud in the village."

Philip Ryman shuffled nervously in his chair. "You're saying he was a blackmailer?"

Carr shook his head. "Not exactly, no, and certainly not for monetary gain. It was the power such knowledge gave him over a person which excited him. Think again of the comments about him pulling legs off spiders. In adulthood, the ability to ruin or to expose someone was that same urge being satisfied."

Ryman nodded. "I'll save you the trouble of explaining my part in all this, Mr Carr. Lorrimer was threatening to take his affairs away from my firm.

If he had done so, it would have ruined me."

Carr gestured for Ryman to resume his seat. "Mr Ryman has made some terrible professional mistakes. He lost his way and became financially desperate. The steps he took to save himself were reckless and dangerous. Lorrimer had discovered them. For Mr Ryman's part, he is on the road to redemption, but his story confirms the sort of man Lorrimer was and the power he enjoyed holding over others.

"All of which was of importance when I discovered the third point of interest in this cottage. Amid the mess of the burglary which I have mentioned, I discovered a newspaper clipping about a notorious orphanage, Linacre House. I need not go into the history of the place as I am sure you are aware of it. Let it be sufficient for me to say that its proprietors, Edwin and Marjorie Pryce, were deplorable sadists who should never have had children in their care. Linacre House was surrounded by rumours of abuse, cruelty, and neglect. I would go so far as to say that we may never know the true extent of the indignities inflicted on those children unfortunate enough to have been placed there, but it is safe to assume that the worst you can imagine is perhaps not the worst which occurred.

"And here was Lorrimer with a newspaper clipping about the place. What could he want with it? What connection could there be? Both Lorrimer and Laurence Fisher were orphans but my enquiries with Miss Delaney and Mr Fisher revealed that neither of them had been in Linacre House. What, then, was Lorrimer's interest in it?

"The answer to that question seemed rather obvious. Lorrimer had evidently discovered a connection with Linacre House in the village. Knowing what we do of his nature, this knowledge would have been a treasure trove to him but a serious danger to whoever was concerned. What was the connection? It seemed obvious to me that someone in the village had been at Linacre House in the past, and it was equally obvious that if it was not a child, then it must be one of the staff. The Pryces themselves had disappeared, believed to be dead, although some reports of them living abroad were received but never substantiated."

"And you think one or both of the Pryces are in Little Marsham?" asked

CHAPTER THIRTY-SEVEN

Angela Ryman.

Carr shook his head. "Not one of the Pryces, no. But I do think that someone else connected to Linacre House is living here, yes."

"Who?" asked Angela.

Carr stroked his moustache in silent but somehow melodramatic silence. "The Pryces employed a medical advisor at Linacre House. It was this man who attended to the broken bones caused by the beatings, to the welts and cuts caused by the birch and the cane, and to the other physical horrors inflicted on the children. When the scandal broke, this doctor was considered as evil as the Pryces themselves. Some even said that he was worse, because he must have known the extent of the abuse and yet had done nothing about it. The man's name was Dr Matthew Olson."

If the name meant anything, nobody was prepared to admit it. Carr watched each of them, looking for any sign of knowledge or recognition. There were blank or confused expressions looking back at him, but only one person had closed their eyes and lowered their head, as if in some silent confession of the truth. Carr approached this person and looked down at them.

"If the name Matthew Olson means nothing to any of you," he said, "you will all recognise the name Thomas Lewton."

The man concerned sat motionless, his eyes closed, so still that he might not have heard the accusation against himself and simply be drifting into slumber. Carr, undeterred, continued to look down at him, content for the silence to continue. Lewton, however, must have found it increasingly uncomfortable for, eventually, he slowly opened his eyes and looked up at his accuser. His words came out in a voice which was so quiet and weak that their denial was perfunctory rather than adamant.

"You're mistaken, Mr Carr," he said.

Carr simply smiled and looked across at Dorothy Parrish. "I think, dear lady, that you know that I am not in error. Your words in the church last night are sufficient proof that you had deduced Mr Lewton's true identity."

Dorothy looked into Carr's dark, persuasive eyes and, almost without control of the action, gave a small, defeated nod of her head. Lewton watched her silent confession and, in its wake, abandoned all of his previous, futile pretences. He lowered his head once more and sighed heavily.

"How did you know?" he asked.

"Your medical knowledge," said Carr. "When I first came to Miss Parrish's cottage and met you for the first time, I indicated that Lorrimer's death might not have been suicide. You were very eager, Mr Lewton, to convince me that the verdict had been correct. In those attempts to assure me of the fact, you may recall that you mentioned in passing that Lorrimer had shot himself through the sphenoid."

Lewton shook his head. "I don't remember."

Carr smiled kindly. "Very likely not, and the fact that you don't would seem to suggest that talking in such a fashion might be second nature to you."

"I must have heard it at the inquest," insisted Lewton. "It proves nothing."

Carr was politely insistent. "On its own, perhaps not, but the ease with which you administered a sedative to Miss Parrish last night might add significance to your casual use of such a biological term. And you did provide that sedative, did you not, and without hesitation. Any layman might not wish to take the responsibility, but you had no such qualms. If any doubt remains, it is surely dispelled with Miss Parrish's skill at crosswords."

Lewton was bewildered. "Crosswords?"

Car gave a nod of his head. "It was Mr Ryman who gave me the clue. He was talking about Lorrimer's threat to sell the cottage in which Miss Parrish was living. I had suggested that such a sale might be a possible motive to murder Lorrimer, but Mr Ryman said that I had it all mixed up if I thought that. Those were his words—*mixed up*. He was convinced that I was wrong."

"You are," declared Dorothy. "It's true that he had threatened to sell the cottage, but I didn't kill him."

Carr turned to her. "No, but you did break into this very cottage, did you not? The burglary I discovered when I first came here was your doing, the result of your frantic search to find any evidence of Lorrimer's plan to sell, which you could destroy at your leisure."

Dorothy's cheeks flushed with shame. "Yes, God forgive me."

"But you didn't find any such evidence," persisted Carr, "because Lorrimer had not yet instructed Mr Ryman to commence the sale of the property. Instead, you found various clippings and articles about Linacre House. One of them you dropped in your haste, and that was the clipping I found and which I have mentioned. But your crossword-influenced mind had shown you at once that Thomas Lewton was not who he pretended to be.

"You see," Carr continued, turning his back on his audience and resuming his place before the fire, "for some time now, crosswords have included what has become known as the cryptic clue, which very often employs the use of anagrams. Miss Parrish had a completed crossword of this type in her house, and I observed it when I was there. Later, when Mr Ryman talked about me being mixed up, I recalled that crossword, and I understood at last what had been so obvious from the start. What Miss Parrish had gleaned from the papers she stole from this house, and thanks to her continued solving of such puzzles, was that the name Thomas Lewton is an anagram of Matthew Olson."

There was a shocked intake of collective breath and the low rumblings of murmured words of surprise. Lewton felt the glares of the eyes which turned now to face him, and the fire of shame and regret of his past seemed to explode in the normally sallow, thin cheeks. He found that he was fighting for breath, and his mouth moved in a useless, soundless search for words to explain. He looked at Carr, who stood motionless before the mantelpiece, leaning on his cane and the lips pursed in expectation beneath the white of the moustache and Imperial. At last, Lewton sat back down slowly, as if afraid that his knees might buckle under him.

"I wish I could say that I am glad it is over," he said. "Telling the truth is supposed to lighten the burden of keeping a secret. Isn't that what they say? It doesn't feel much like that to me."

"Your secret was a shameful one, Mr Lewton," said Carr. "Releasing yourself from it will be a benefit to you in time. For now, it is your own shame and embarrassment which weighs you down rather than the deceit itself."

Lewton removed his spectacles and rubbed his eyes. "Shame. That is a constant companion to me. Not only the shame of what happened at Linacre House, but also the shame that I was too terrified to put an end to it. I could have acted, and I didn't. All the wounds I tended, all the tears I dried, and all the pleas for help which I ignored. They're what bring shame on me."

When Carr spoke, it was with a gentle, empathetic tone of voice, and, in the moment, it was as if only he and Lewton were in the room. "Why did you not help those children?"

Lewton was shaking, his eyes brimming with tears which he did not bother to wipe away. "To understand that, you'd have to know the Pryces. You'd have to understand how manipulative, how ruthless, and how detached from human emotions they were. For a doctor, they said, once struck off, always struck off. For them, the risk and the dishonour were all on my part. What happened to them was of no consequence. They told me that they had been investigated before, and nothing came of it. But, for me, it would have been disgrace and failure. Only later, after it was all over, did I come to realise that they had been lying. If they truly had recovered from a similar scandal, they wouldn't have disappeared as soon as questions began to be asked. Once I realised that, I knew that their blackmail was worthless. And that meant," he added, succumbing to the tears, "that my refusal to protect those children had been for nothing."

He began to sob silently but with violence. Dorothy Parrish ignored her instincts to put her arms around him, fearing that it would somehow lessen his admission of guilt or suggest that she was somehow forgiving him for it out of sympathy. Instead, she looked down at her feet and tried to distance her mind from the situation.

Carr waited for Lewton to regain something of his composure. "Lorrimer had discovered your secret. Perhaps he had overheard you using some medical terminology, as I did, and it is possible he had spotted the similarity in names and the anagram itself, just as Miss Parrish had done. In any event, he had deduced who you were. I don't need to repeat how the sort of man he was would have prompted him to react to the discovery."

"If he had betrayed me, I would have been ruined," said Lewton. "I had found happiness here, and I had begun to build something of a life I could be proud of once more. Lorrimer was a threat to that."

Carr nodded. "And the sale of the cottage, with Lorrimer's implied threat that Miss Parrish would be evicted, gave you a further motive for his murder."

Lewton's eyes now flashed with fear rather than shame. "I didn't do it. I swear, it wasn't me."

Carr bowed his head. "But Miss Parrish suspected you. When I met you for the first time in her cottage that day, I informed you that Isobel Croft had been murdered. I saw on Miss Parrish's face a strange expression which I could not explain. Now, I realise that the news of the murder had terrified her, because she thought you had committed it. Am I not right, dear lady?"

Dorothy lowered her head. "I'm afraid so."

If Lewton was appalled by her confession, he did not show it. He glanced at her momentarily, but his attention was fixed primarily on Carr. "But it wasn't me. You have to believe me."

Carr stared at him with a grave expression of judgement. "I do believe you. You may have had a strong motive to murder Lorrimer, but I know that you didn't do it."

"Do you know who did?" asked Dorothy.

There was a moment of tense silence, as people waited for clarification and confirmation of Lewton's guilt, either by way of his own confession or by further revelations from Everett Carr. And yet, for a long moment of suspense, neither came. At last, Carr raised his head and looked around the room. His voice was low, filled with regret, and his dark eyes seemed to have been consumed by sadness. "I know."

"Who was it?"

Nobody had noticed it, since they were sitting with their backs to him, but Dunn had risen from his chair and had crossed the room. Now, he stood behind the chair of the person upon whom Carr's mournful eyes had come to rest.

"The same person who murdered Isobel Croft and Gerald Bowers," Carr said. "The only person who, based on all the facts of this tragic case, could possibly have committed the murders and the only person whom Isobel Croft would have been able to identify. The person for whom I had great sympathy in the initial wake of the verdict of the inquest and the person who had been blamed for Lorrimer's death from the outset."

Edgar Corrigan was the first to give a voice to the conclusion. "But that was -"

Everett Carr was already nodding his head sadly. "Precisely, Mr Corrigan. The killer was none other than Lorrimer's former lover, *Miss Harriet Delaney.*"

Chapter Thirty-Eight

There was a brief moment of startled quiet which followed in the wake of Carr's announcement. Harriet was aware of the stares of the assembled group, but she was unable to focus on anything other than Everett Carr, who looked back at her with a disappointment which was almost paternal in its sadness. Somehow, it seemed to Harriet that this dapper little man's dejection weighed more heavily on her conscience than her guilt. It was as if she could forgive herself everything else, but that she would regret offending Everett Carr for the rest of her days.

"I am sorry, my child," said Everett Carr. "It is the truth, is it not?"

Edgar had gripped Harriet's hand, but he released it now and rose from his chair. His face was flushed, the amiability so often present in his eyes, now replaced by a frantic determination to disbelieve.

"It couldn't have been Harriet, Mr Carr," he asserted. "She had no reason to kill Lorrimer. She left *him*, remember. Even if you are right about him wanting revenge for it, surely it would have been he who would attack her. And if she didn't kill Lorrimer, she would have no reason to kill his sister."

Carr seemed not to have heard. His attention was still fixed on Harriet. "Tell us the truth, dear lady. I implore you."

But Edgar was not finished with his submissions in her defence. "Harriet had no opportunity to murder Isobel Croft. You know about the letter from the solicitors which Harriet received. I was with her when it was delivered. I told you that. She was with me all the rest of that day and into the evening. When she went home, she wrote her reply to that letter. She couldn't have done it."

Dunn felt obliged to speak. "It would have taken Miss Delaney a couple of hours to write that letter, Mr Carr, I can assure you. I saw the discarded drafts. She had no time to kill Mrs Croft."

Carr's attention remained fixed on Harriet Delaney. "Must it be done this way?"

She held his gaze but gave no reply. He closed his eyes and gave a deep sigh of resignation. Then, with a flourish, he made a dismissive gesture with his hand and began to pace the room once more, in his awkward, stilted gait. When he spoke, his voice seemed to lack any of his previous sadness and it had become the more assured, authoritative tone of a presiding judge.

"I confess that Miss Delaney's alibi was very well stage-managed," Carr said, "but, as with all magic tricks, the solution to it is really very simple. So much so, that it is baffling. Mr Corrigan did witness the delivery of the letter and he saw Miss Delaney open it. He heard her read its contents to him and she told him that she was to write a reply that evening. It is also true that Inspector Dunn saw the discarded drafts and, the reply itself. There is no way that Miss Delaney could have written a reply to a letter she had not yet received and there is no doubt that the letter was delivered on the day of the murder. Granted that no pre-existing letter in reply could have been written, it is certain that the reply Miss Delaney provided to the police was proof of her movements on the night of Isobel Croft's murder."

"There you are, then!" declared Edgar.

But Carr shook his head. "No, Mr Corrigan. What you say happened is not what actually took place."

Edgar bristled. "Are you calling me a liar?"

"No, no," smiled Carr. "You saw what you told us, but it is not what happened."

"I don't understand."

Carr's smile broadened. "That is because you are looking at the situation in the manner in which Miss Delaney wishes. Let us consider what you actually saw, Mr Corrigan. You witnessed an envelope being posted through the letterbox. You witnessed Miss Delaney open that envelope, and you saw the letter which she took from it."

"She showed it to me, yes."

Carr clicked his fingers. "But did she show you *the envelope?*"

Edgar frowned. "No."

"So how can you know, as a matter of undeniable fact, that the envelope which Miss Delaney opened was the envelope which had been sealed and stamped at the solicitors' office in London?"

"What are you saying?" Edgar's confusion was palpable, but some of the certainty in his eyes had faded.

"There is no proof, other than Miss Delaney's testimony, that the letter you witnessed being delivered had been sent from a solicitors' office in London. She was keen enough to show you the letter itself, but she was careful not to show you the envelope. And why? *Because, if you had seen it, you would have also seen that the postmark on it was from Lower Marsham itself.*

"Miss Delaney received that letter several days before. There was no great urgency to respond to it, in fact, as it was a simple but detailed letter explaining a minor legacy which had been bequeathed to her and inviting her to arrange an appointment at the offices. However, when Miss Delaney became aware that she would need an alibi, she saw at once the potential of that official summons. She placed the letter into a fresh envelope, addressed it to herself, and posted it back to herself at such a time as to be sure that it would be delivered on the morning of the day, she planned to murder Isobel Croft. Mr Corrigan, did you visit Miss Delaney on that morning by accident or on your own account?"

"No," murmured Edgar, "she invited me."

"Precisely. She needed a witness to the delivery of the letter, otherwise the challenge would be made that it could have been delivered on any day and the reply written in advance. If that happened, the alibi would be worthless. There had to be proof that the letter arrived on that specific day, so that the reply to it could only have been written on that evening and at no earlier time. *In fact, Miss Delaney had done exactly that and written the letter on that morning.*

"Ask yourselves, does it take a couple of hours and numerous drafts to write a response which, in actual fact, needed only to arrange a date for a meeting with the solicitors? Not at all. Miss Delaney's response was intentionally verbose, and the initial drafts purposefully discarded to give the impression that it had taken a significant period of time to draft. You see, the whole business of the letter was a carefully managed piece of theatre, designed to allow Miss Delaney to be in two places at one time."

She didn't say anything, but Harriet's hardened eyes told their own story. Her lips had tightened with that particular compression which only suppressed guilt can produce. Carr looked down at her, his own eyes now softened by regret, and he nodded his head at the sadness of the inevitability of it all.

"Isobel Croft had contacted you the day before she died, when she arrived in the village," Carr said. "You knew instantly that she had to die, and the sleight of hand with the morning post occurred to you at once. A small enquiry both with the solicitors and the post office will confirm the date the original letter was posted and delivered."

Harriet took her time to respond. "And my motive?"

Carr shook his head. "I think that is a matter best dealt with in privacy."

"But you know?" Harriet asked. When Carr bowed his head in response, she gave a small, humourless laugh of defeat. "How did you know it was me?"

Edgar took her hand and held it tightly, as if terrified that she would somehow blow away from him. "You didn't do it, Harriet. Why are you talking like this?"

When she looked into his flawed and contrasting eyes, she felt her own fill with tears. "You have to be strong, Edgar. We have to face the truth now." She placed her hand on his cheek. "I love you so very much and I am dreadfully, painfully sorry for it all."

Edgar looked up at Carr, his eyes helpless and his mouth moving uselessly, as if asking a thousand silent questions. Carr stepped over to him and placed a steadying but sympathetic hand on the young man's shoulder. Then, he looked across at Harriet and spoke gently to her.

"I was not certain it was you until Mr Bowers was killed," he said. "The fact that he was wearing his surplice and was on the altar steps suggested to me at once that he might have been kneeling there in prayer and the surplice suggested a formal session of prayer. The absence of any lights in the vicarage on that night seemed to me to show that Bowers had made some sort of previous arrangement to meet someone. If he had felt any sort of spontaneous need to pray, he might not have thought to turn out the lights and change into his robes. He did it for someone else's benefit.

"And then I recalled three things. Firstly, I remembered that Bowers said he had heard footsteps running away from the scene. He said he had seen nobody, but later, I remembered that he had said that he was sure that the murderer would come to the church to make peace with God. Now, not only did that suggest to me that perhaps he had seen the killer and knew who it was after all, but also that the killer was a religious person. Bowers would not have been certain that the killer would formally repent before God if he did not have some reason to think that the killer had faith. You told me yourself, Miss Delaney, of your strict, religious upbringing and of your father's profound, almost puritanical faith. You would have been able to say the words necessary to convince Bowers that you were there for God's forgiveness. You would have been able to inject those words with sufficient religious gravitas to make them convincing, simply because you had been brought up in a house where such words would have been commonplace.

"And Bowers believed you. He knelt down before God and began to pray for your salvation. Did he invite you to kneel beside him and join him in prayer? I am sure of it. But you had no intention of praying with him. All you wanted, Miss Delaney, was to silence him. And so, you took a candlestick and struck him down. You know," he added, his voice souring, "it is not the violence of the act, but the timing of it. Bowers was at his most vulnerable when you killed him. He was at prayer, and what sickens me most about it is that he was praying not for himself, but *for you*. I doubt he would have spoken to a soul of your guilt, if you had repented that night before God. It might not have held the sacrosanctity of the confessional, but I have no doubt that Bowers would have viewed your prayers as a contract with God. And if God forgave you, so would Gerald Bowers. That is the cruellest truth of all."

His speech, delivered with an undeniable but suppressed rage, served its purpose. Harriet's eyes now broke their banks, and the tears fell with shameful, guilty passion. A mournful groan of despair rumbled from somewhere deep inside her and out of her mouth. Her head sank, and she seemed to slump in her chair to such an extent that Edgar was compelled to hold her, fearing she might fall to the floor entirely.

There was a long silence, broken only by the sound of the sobbing of the guilty. Eventually, as it began to pass, Dorothy Parrish spoke. "The words which Mr Bowers said before he died. What did they mean?"

Carr turned to face her. "In answering that, dear lady, I shall explain also why I said earlier that only Miss Delaney could have been the murderer. Bowers had realised that he had remembered something incorrectly and so wrongly reported it. He told me that Isobel Croft had said that Lorrimer had been murdered, and she knew who the killer was. In actual fact, *she had not said that,* and it was this mistake that Bowers was trying to convey to you.

"You see, what Isobel Croft had said to Bowers, in fact, was that *she knew the killer.* Now, that may seem like the same thing, but there is a subtle difference. To say that you know who somebody's killer is might suggest only that you are aware of their identity. We know, for example, who assassinated Julius Caesar because history tells us, but we do not know the people concerned as individual people. But Isobel Croft said that she *knew* the killer. It suggested something more than simply being aware of a name. It implied a relationship. In short, it suggested that Isobel Croft *knew the killer personally.*

"And yet, Mrs Croft was a stranger in the village. Who amongst the people here could she possibly have known on a personal basis? Clearly, only Harriet Delaney could ever have been in the position of meeting Isobel Croft and being familiar with her, because it was natural that she should have met her before. As the lover and possible future wife of Isobel Croft's brother, Harriet would have been introduced to members of Lorrimer's family. The only family Lorrimer had left was his sister. When I told Edgar

Corrigan that Lorrimer had a sister, he was surprised, but Harriet knew enough about this unknown sister to be able to say that she had emigrated to America. That comment alone was enough to suggest a prior knowledge. If Isobel Croft knew Lorrimer's killer personally, the killer could only be Harriet Delaney."

Dunn looked down at Harriet. "And so, what happened on the night Mrs Croft was killed?"

"She had written a note to Harriet or else had called on her at her cottage," said Carr. "She said that she needed to speak to her urgently about William Lorrimer. The fact that the interview took place at the man's grave suggested to me at once that she wanted the killer to face what had happened to Lorrimer. A melodramatic gesture, perhaps, but an understandable one from a woman driven by retribution. The torn fragment of Lorrimer's stationery in her hand, as I have explained, suggested that he had written to her. The killer had removed that letter, which could only mean that it was incriminating. Whatever that letter said, the death of her brother almost immediately after writing it was sufficient proof for Isobel Croft."

"Do you know what it said?" asked Dunn.

Carr nodded. "Knowing what we do about Lorrimer's habit of discovering secrets and using them against people, we can all make educated guesses as to the nature of that communication. But the specifics are a matter of privacy."

"Why do you keep saying that?" asked Dunn.

Carr stared at Harriet Delaney. "Because the secret which this young lady was prepared to kill to keep hidden is a painful one. Moreover," he added, "it was not her secret to protect."

"Then whose was it?"

But Everett Carr merely shook his head. "Do your duty, Inspector. I have nothing further to say at this stage. This little audience of mine is over."

He stepped back to the mantelpiece and turned his back on the room, as if to emphasise the point. Dunn, although frustrated, saw little point in offering any further protest. He signalled to the uniformed officer, who duly escorted Arthur Corrigan and Laurence Fisher from the cottage. Their punishment lay ahead of them, just as Harriet Delaney's more terrible and permanent one lay ahead of her. At Carr's gentle insistence, however, she was allowed a final moment with Edgar Corrigan. She did not embrace him, but she kissed him lightly on the cheek. He looked down at her, as if seeing her for the first time as she truly was, and what he saw was not something he could properly understand.

"Please forgive me, Edgar," she said. "Don't think of me like this. Think of me when we were happy, before all this had to happen. Please, can you do that?"

He shook his head. "I don't understand. Why did you do it? How could you?"

"Because I love you." She nodded in confirmation, tears stinging her eyes once more. "Because I love you so much."

She waited for him to say more, but no words came. Instead, Edgar Corrigan shook his head once more and turned away from her. To Harriet Delaney, it was like the closing of a cold, impassive, damning cell door. Her eyes froze, and her tears seemed to stop in their tracks. She looked over once to Everett Carr, who offered no smile of assurance, and then she looked again at Edgar's back. He did not look back at her and his refusal showed her that at last she had lost him.

She allowed herself to be escorted out of the cottage by Dunn. The thought of dying at the end of a noose had frightened her once. Now, it seemed to be almost like a release, a relieving departure from a world which now had killed her hopes, her joy, and her love. And that, she thought without guilt, was the most wicked death of all.

Chapter Thirty-Nine

Once the guilty had been removed, the innocent did not know what to say. The shock and the confusion had rendered words almost meaningless, and anything which might have been said seemed to be either trite or offensive when balanced against the devastation and dejection which was so evident on Edgar Corrigan's face. It was undeniable that the young man had suffered two emotional calamities in the hour which had passed, although it was only evident to Carr that there was more unpleasantness to come.

Dunn stepped back into the room and walked over to Carr. "Barlow will deal with the preliminary interviews."

Carr nodded. "You will need to take formal statements from the solicitors in London about their letter to Miss Delaney."

"Already in hand."

Edgar looked at him. "It's all true, isn't it? She killed three people."

Carr walked over to him and placed a hand on Edgar's shoulder. "It is all true."

Dorothy Parrish rose from her seat. "Inspector, is there any need for us to stay here now? I am sure we would all like to get home, and I've no doubt Mr Corrigan needs some privacy."

Dunn looked at Thomas Lewton. "I will need a statement from you, sir, about your involvement with the Pryces and about Linacre House generally. There will need to be an investigation, and I'm afraid we may not be able to prevent your true identity from coming out."

Lewton nodded. "I've run for long enough, Inspector, and I've avoided

305

my responsibilities, both moral and professional, for too long, as well. I will do all I can to help you."

Dorothy took hold of his hand and smiled at him. For once, Lewton thought, he was able to look at her without the shadow of deceit looming over him, and he was able to see her look back at him without seeing the shimmer of suspicion in her eyes.

Dunn nodded and looked at Ryman. "The same applies to you, Mr Ryman. I'm aware of the arrangement Mr Carr has put in place with Scotland Yard, and I have agreed to act as a liaison for the Yard here in the village. If you pledge to co-operate with our investigations into the people to whom you're in debt, you may go home now, too."

It was Angela who replied. "We'll co-operate, Inspector, and we will return the money to the firm."

Carr smiled at her and gave a small bow. He watched as the Rymans followed Lewton and Dorothy out of the cottage. When Elsa Corrigan stated that she and her son would also be leaving, however, he held out a restraining hand.

"I would be most grateful if you would stay for a moment longer, Mrs Corrigan," he said in polite earnest. "As we agreed earlier today, there is more to be said."

Elsa shook her head. "It has been an awful night for Edgar, and I want him to rest."

She escorted the young man towards the door of the cottage, but she was not halfway across the room before Carr called her name. "Miss Delaney did say one thing of importance to your son, Mrs Corrigan. She said that the time had come to face the truth and that he had to be strong. She was right, and I think you know it."

Elsa shook her head. "What are you talking about?"

"A moment ago, Mrs Corrigan, you heard me say that the secret which Miss Delaney killed to protect was not her own."

Elsa turned to face him. "What of it?"

Carr fixed her with a compelling, dark stare. "It is time for that secret to come out, Mrs Corrigan, and the secret is yours to tell."

Edgar looked at his mother. "What does he mean?"

She found that she was unable to shift her attention from Carr. There was nothing accusatory in his expression. If anything, it was one of kindly encouragement, but it was no less persuasive for it. Elsa took a long breath and held it, as if to prohibit herself from having to say the words but, eventually, her natural instincts overcame her, and the breath exploded from her with a long, coarse sigh. Her eyes closed momentarily, and her shoulders rolled in a shrug of capitulation.

"Edgar, darling, you need to sit down," she said.

But Edgar was defiant. "I'm quite all right where I am. I want to know what's happening, mother."

Elsa went to take his hand in hers, but the young man took a step back from her. It was not a dismissive recoil, rather a cautionary distancing as if from something of which he was not sure and, perhaps, a little frightened. Elsa was struck by it, but she could not say that she was surprised by it, but the flickering of her eyes showed that she was saddened by it. She clasped her hands and turned away from Edgar, pacing slowly towards the centre of the room.

"I suppose there is no easy way to say it," she said. "Not long before you were born, Edgar, I met a friend of your father's." If Edgar noticed her falter over the word, he did not question it. "His name was Edmund Draper, and I fell instantly in love with him. For three months, we were together whenever we were able to be."

"You had an affair?" said Edgar. "You betrayed my father?"

"No, Edgar. That's just it; I didn't betray your father."

"I don't understand," Edgar said.

"I betrayed my husband with Edmund Draper," she said, the tears now falling down her cheeks, "but I didn't betray your father."

Now, Edgar moved. It was the lumbering, clumsy walk of a drunkard, and he fell onto the settee rather than sat into it. His eyes were staring, but they were vacant, as if focused on nothing in particular, and his mouth hung open in a dumbfounded expression of confused wonder. Anger, hurt, and outrage would come later; for now, there was only silent incomprehension.

Elsa looked at Carr. "How did you know?"

Carr spoke gently. "When you spoke to me of meeting Mr Draper after all these years, you said that his illness had aged him, but that his voice, his smile, and his eyes had remained the same. At least, that is what you would have said if tears had not cut short your sentence."

"I don't understand," Elsa said.

"You cried at the very mention of Draper's eyes. Evidently, there was something about them, which touched you very much or else the memory of them would not have induced such a reaction from you. When I first met her, Harriet Delaney said that she had felt a similarly instant attraction to Edgar's eyes. It was a simple connection to make, particularly when one bears in mind that neither you nor Arthur Corrigan suffer from the same defect. Such things are hereditary."

"It might have missed a generation," argued Elsa.

Carr inclined his head. "Possibly, but I fancied it was more common for such a flaw to pass from parent to child. There was no doubt that you were Edgar's mother. Corrigan's eyes precluded him from being Edgar's father. One only had to look at the nature of the two men to be sure. Edgar is polite, charming, amiable, and eager. Corrigan is almost the reverse of all those qualities. Your son, Mrs Corrigan, is a walking piece of evidence."

Elsa was nodding her understanding. "And what I had already told you about Edmund Draper convinced you of the truth?"

"You told me that the affair with Draper had been thirty years ago," Carr said, "and Edgar is of a similar age. The final proof, as you know, came earlier today in that photograph."

Dunn stepped forward. "What photograph?"

"I have kept a photograph of Edmund in my room all these years," confessed Elsa. "Mr Carr saw it this afternoon."

"It is a portrait of the man concerned," explained Carr, "and it is clear from it that Edmund Draper suffers from heterochromia. There can be no doubt."

"And Lorrimer had discovered the truth?" asked Dunn.

Carr nodded. "We know from his taking the medical textbook that he was not averse to snooping in the Corrigan household. He may have found the photograph, or he may simply have followed Mrs Corrigan on one of her trips to London to visit Draper. When he learned the truth, he wrote to his sister to explain the position to her. It would give him great satisfaction to tell Harriet Delaney the truth about her new lover's heritage. What more bitter revenge could he have?"

Elsa looked at him. "That's what you think he intended to do?"

"I am in no doubt," replied Carr. "He hated your son for taking Harriet away from him, and he hated their relationship even more. Destroying it would have given him immense satisfaction."

"And Harriet couldn't allow that," said Dunn.

Carr held up a finger. "You miss the point, Inspector. Harriet loved Edgar, I am sure of that, but she also loved his status. She told me that she had grown up poor. Her father had been devoutly religious and considered having money and possessions to be a sin. Marrying Edgar would have satisfied both her love for him and her love for his way of life."

Dunn nodded his understanding. "But then Lorrimer told her about Edmund Draper."

"Exactly. And she knew Arthur Corrigan well enough to know that if he discovered that his wife had betrayed him and that the son whom he had brought up as his own was a product of that betrayal, disinheritance would surely follow. That was what Miss Delaney couldn't allow to happen."

"So, she killed Lorrimer, found the letter he had written to her and left enough of it to appear to be a suicide note, and waited for the inquest to exonerate her."

Carr bowed in agreement. "She couldn't know that Lorrimer had told Isobel Croft what he had discovered. His letter to his sister might have been an insurance policy, but it might easily have been a product of spiteful gloating about what he was going to do. That, we shall never know for sure."

"And Bowers?"

Carr shrugged. "She had to murder him because he had put the various pieces together, far quicker than I did. If I had been more alert, perhaps we might have saved him. That, also, is something we may never know." It was clear from the sadness in those dark eyes that it would be something which Everett Carr would always believe and, as a consequence, it would be something which he would never forget.

Edgar had been silent throughout this exchange, but its meaning had not been lost on him. He rose from the settee and approached his mother. "This man, someone I don't know at all, is my father?"

She allowed the single syllable to do its painful but honest work. "Yes."

Edgar's tears might have been born of sadness or anger, but they were insistent. "And you met him again recently, after all this time?"

Elsa nodded, and her voice came in a strained, saddened gasp. "He's dying."

Edgar began to shake his head, as if to deny the truth or the happening of the situation. Carr stepped forward and placed his hand on Edgar's forearm.

"The truth can be difficult to hear, my boy," he said, "but it must be told. What you do with it is your own affair, but you cannot deal with the truth until it is known. Tonight, has been hardest on you of all of us, but you have survived it, and you will likewise survive its memory."

Edgar turned to face him. "Do you think so, Mr Carr? Forgive me, but I can't share your optimism. Not when I've just learned that my whole life is a lie."

Elsa reached out to him. "Edgar, please -"

But he only shook his head. "Leave me alone. Please, just leave me alone."

He took a few steps backwards before turning on his heel and racing out of the door. Elsa made a movement to follow him, but Carr held her back. He gave a shake of his head.

"Allow the boy some time to himself," he said. "Solitude can be an effective tonic for grief. Let him have his time of reflection overnight and you may be surprised what the daylight hours bring."

"He needs me," Elsa protested.

Carr nodded once more. "And when he realises that, as he will, you shall be there for him. Because you are his mother, Mrs Corrigan, and nothing about that has changed."

Elsa looked into his eyes, but their darkness was clouded by the distortion of vision caused by the returning tears. Carr handed her his handkerchief, and she dabbed her eyes with it. He gave a gesture that she could keep it, and then, with a shake of Dunn's hand, and with a word of farewell, he bowed elegantly to them both, before making his stiff and painful way to the door of the cottage. He pulled on his overcoat, placed his hat on his head, and stepped out into the refreshingly cool evening air.

Chapter Forty

Thomas Lewton and Dorothy Parrish had gone back to her cottage after Carr's gathering had dispersed. They had not spoken very much, and it was not until Lewton had poured them both some whisky that the silence between them was broken, and, out of a sense of duty, it was Lewton himself who spoke first.

"I'm so terribly sorry that I didn't tell you the truth about me," he said.

Dorothy shook her head. "You don't need to keep apologising. It wasn't so much your past as your present which frightened me."

"You mean Mr Carr was right? You did suspect me?" Lewton watched her head lower in affirmation. "I can't deny I wanted Lorrimer dead. Not just because of Linacre House, but because of you. Of this cottage."

She looked at him with concern in her eyes. "You wouldn't have killed Lorrimer for that. You mustn't say those things."

"Perhaps not exclusively for that. But I hated him for the way he was treating you. If I had killed him, part of my motivation would have been you. I am convinced of it."

She said nothing, but she could believe it. And she knew why she could believe he might have acted in that way. "I stole those papers about Linacre House to protect you."

"I know."

"When you go to see Inspector Dunn about your statement, I'm going to come with you."

He lowered his eyes. "You mustn't do that."

"I want to." She sipped the whisky. "Not just as support to you, but because I committed a crime. I burgled the cottage and stole Lorrimer's property."

Lewton gave a short laugh. "I doubt Dunn will have the time or the inclination to bring that to trial. His focus will be on Harriet Delaney and Corrigan's art fraud."

Dorothy shrugged. "Nevertheless. I want my conscience to be clear."

Lewton took her hand in his. "It's a shame more people aren't like you. I only wish I had shown an ounce of that type of courage all those years ago."

Her fingers began to stroke the back of his hand. "You were a frightened young man, who was manipulated by two very wicked people. Perhaps you should try to learn to forgive yourself, Thomas."

The use of the name startled him. "Should you call me that? After everything you know about me?"

"I never knew Matthew Olson. I've only ever known you." She was looking down at her glass and he could see that the whisky inside was moving and, only then, did Lewton notice the trembling of her hands. Slowly, she looked up into his face, her cheeks glowing with emotion as much as from the orange flare of the flames of the fire in the hearth. She seemed to him then more beautiful than he had ever known her to be, and the reflection of the flames in her hesitant eyes seemed to him to be enchanting.

"I didn't know Matthew Olson," Dorothy repeated, "so I couldn't have fallen in love with him, could I?"

He felt as if the breath had been crushed from his lungs. He gave a small gasp of what might have been relief or excitement. The laugh which followed it and the instinctive smile which formed on his lips were beyond his control.

"No," he said. "I don't suppose you could have."

"That's why I wanted to protect you and why I took those clippings."

He was laughing now, suddenly aware that this was the happiest he could ever remember being. "I know, God help me, I know."

He placed his glass at his feet, took her face in his hands, and kissed her. It was not a passionate kiss; rather, it was one of gratification that his dreams had been answered and her feelings now no longer the subject of his conjecture and fear.

"I love you too, Dorothy," he said, wondering whether it needed saying at all.

She was smiling now, her previous nervousness a feeling of the past. "I think I've always known it."

"I definitely have. From the moment we met."

"I'm sorry that tomorrow we shall have to go to the police station," she said. "Hardly a romantic start to our relationship."

Lewton was shaking his head. "I don't care where we have to go or what happens when we get there. Not anymore. For the first time, I don't feel afraid of anything."

"And the Pryces?"

He shrugged. "Wherever they are, they can't hurt me now. Not when I know that you love me. They can't do any more damage to my life while you're a part of it."

They remained on the settee, huddled together in an embrace of protective rather than passionate romance, and watched the flames of the fire flicker, dance, and eventually fade into embers. They said nothing more that evening, and, when the time for sleep came, they continued their embrace, and neither of them could remember any of the dreams which had come to them during their hours of slumber.

Epilogue: One Year Later

The village had changed little.

The small row of shops, the Corrigan mansion on the hill in the distance, and the church of St Bartholomew all looked as they had done when Everett Carr had first arrived. And yet, he knew that there was a difference to the place, one which could not be detected by any of the senses, but which he could feel keenly. Murder always left a trace of itself, one way or another. The village might look the same as it had been, but it wasn't. Confidences had been broken, secrets had been exposed, and unnatural death had invaded the tranquillity. The village might heal, but neither it nor the people who lived there would ever be the same.

It was thoughts such as these which ran through Carr's mind as he stood at the grave of Gerald Bowers. He had never spoken of the Little Marsham murders to anybody, preferring instead to keep his own counsel about them. Neither his friend, Jack Truscott, whom he had met for dinner several times over the past year, nor the members of the Icarus Club in London, whom Carr counted as his closest acquaintances, had known anything of the dark events of the previous year. It was not simply Carr's own reticence which prevented him from divulging the details, but also his overwhelming fear that any display of pride about his involvement would be inappropriate when set against his guilt over his failure. He had expressed it only once, to Inspector Dunn when the truth had been revealed, but Carr knew that he had been too slow in arriving at that truth. The breakdown of his instincts and deductive faculties had cost Gerald Bowers his life. Carr knew that he could not have prevented the deaths of William Lorrimer or Isobel Croft, but Bowers could have been saved. And now, on the anniversary of his death, Carr had come not only to pay his respects but also to offer his silent apologies to a man whom he had liked and respected. And perhaps, as the memory of the whip and its history returned to his mind, the man whom he had pitied.

"I hadn't expected to see you here, Mr Carr."

He recognised the voice, but when he turned to look at Edgar Corrigan, the face which confronted him was almost that of a stranger. The eyes were still fascinating in their juxtaposition, but they were dimmed now with the sadness of experience. His youthful enthusiasm and amiable eagerness were now somehow absent, soured by the cruel effects of the truth, so that his expression seemed harder than Carr had remembered it, aged with a sense of bitterness and regret.

"I came only to pay my respects," said Carr. "How have you been, my boy?"

Edgar smiled. "Do you ever fully recover from something like this?"

Carr raised his eyebrows. "I was having similar thoughts myself just now. I think, you know, that perhaps we don't. The best we can do is learn to live with our memories."

Edgar put his hands in his pockets. "Well, I think I've made peace with mine."

"I am pleased to hear it." Carr allowed a moment to pass. "How's your mother?"

Edgar began to walk slowly along the pathway of the churchyard, and Carr followed closely behind him.

"She's well, thank you," replied the young man. "I went to see Edmund Draper. I felt I needed to, before he died. He passed away two months ago, as a matter of fact. Mother is still grieving, but she will recover. She says she will, at least."

"Agreeing to go to see Draper was brave," said Carr.

Edgar smiled. "I'm not so sure about that. I felt nothing when I saw him. I don't think I will ever think of him as my father. Maybe I don't have to, I don't know."

"Have you heard anything from Mr Corrigan?"

Edgar shook his head. "Only to say that he was divorcing mother and disinheriting her bastard."

Carr frowned. It was painful to hear, even if it was predictable and inevitable. "I'm sorry."

"I don't think anyone expected anything less." Edgar stopped walking. "What hurts most about it is that all he's done is prove Harriet was right. If Lorrimer had exposed the truth, it would have had the very effect she feared." After a pause, Edgar added, "She wrote to me from prison, you know. To apologise again."

"Did you reply?"

Edgar nodded. "And then she wrote another letter and another. I didn't reply to one, and I burned the other unopened. I couldn't bring myself to engage with her anymore. I didn't leave the house on the day they..."

Carr knew why the sentence could not be finished. Edgar could not say now, and perhaps never would be able to say, that Harriet Delaney had been hanged. The young man's cheeks paled and began to quiver with emotion, and it was clear that he was fighting the urge either to scream or to sob.

Carr felt it prudent to steer the conversation away from the lady in question. "How will you manage? I presume you cannot stay at the hall."

Edgar looked at him with a curious glimmer in his eyes. "Edmund Draper was a wealthy man, Mr Carr, and he left everything to my mother."

"I see."

Edgar understood the hesitancy in Carr's voice. "He didn't know about me. I was mother's secret only. But Draper had never stopped loving her, and, of course, he had no other family."

"So, what will you do?"

"A new start," sighed Edgar. "We're moving to the United States. Far away from here." He said it as if it were a relief rather than a regret. "I thought I would feel uncomfortable living on Draper's money, but I don't. Perhaps that's because it's mother's money and not mine. I still find it all very complicated, too much to understand," he added with a short, embarrassed laugh.

Carr smiled. "Live your life, my boy, rather than dissecting it."

Edgar nodded. "Perhaps putting an ocean between this place and us will help Mother and I to do just that."

They walked for some time in silence. It was not an amiable quiet, nor did Carr find it a particularly awkward one. They had reached the end of the lane and stepped out onto the main street of the village before Edgar spoke again.

"The Rymans have had a similar thought," he said. "Ryman did his bit with Scotland Yard, as you suggested, and they let him go. He paid off the debts, sold the business, and they moved away. Somewhere in the North."

Carr was relieved to hear it. "And Mr Lewton?"

"He and Dorothy married about six months ago. They're still here."

"And what of Linacre House?"

Edgar shrugged. "Lewton gave his statement, and that seemed to be that. No charges or anything. After all this time, I suppose it would do no good. Dorothy insisted on making a statement about burgling Lorrimer's cottage, but I don't think Dunn was interested."

Carr smiled. "The inspector is a wise man. He will go far."

"I'm meeting Mother for lunch very soon. Would you care to join us?"

Carr considered it for a moment but gently shook his head. "A gracious offer, my boy, but I will decline if I may. I must make my way back to London. But," he added, as an afterthought, "the wine at *The Marsham Tuns* was surprisingly good. If you have time, I would be honoured if you would join me for a glass."

Edgar laughed. "I'd like that very much, Mr Carr."

And so, they made their way to the inn, as if they were two friends meeting up after a long time apart. Their conversation was engaging, but they did not touch again on the topic of the violent deaths which had brought them together, nor did they discuss its effects. It was time now, Carr thought, for the past to be laid to rest, buried for good, and for the future to have its time in the sun. The aftermath of murder might never be forgotten, but, as Edgar Corrigan had said, it could be possible to live with it. For Carr, that possibility was an important belief to hold. Its alternative seemed to him to be too desolate to contemplate.

The time passed, and the drinks were finished. Edgar walked some of the way back to the railway station with Carr, but the appointment with his mother prevented him from completing the journey.

"Don't worry, my boy," said Carr, "I am perfectly capable of finding my way, and you must go to your mother. Please, pass on my regards and best wishes to her."

"I shall," said Edgar. "There's something else I need to say to you, Mr Carr."

"What is that?"

Edgar took some time in replying, and, when he did, it was with a sincerity which Carr found both uplifting and touching. "Thank you for all you did."

In reply, Carr tipped his hat and gave a small bow. "Go now, and live."

He watched the young man walk back towards the village, and, for a moment, he stood in silent contemplation. At last, with a final breath of the village air filling his lungs, he made his way slowly back to the railway station. As he waited patiently on the platform, Carr considered that he had come back to pay his respects to the dead, and the news he had received from Edgar Corrigan, in the main, had both pleased him and justified his intentions. Nevertheless, there was a definite sense in Carr's mind that this was the end of the matter. There would be no reason for him to visit the place again and to do so, he thought, would serve only to remind the village of the dark and tragic events, which had played out here. It could only do more harm than good.

And so, even before the train had pulled into the station, Everett Carr had decided that he would never return to the scarred, mournful village of Little Marsham.

About the Author

As a lifelong aficionado and expert on Sherlock Holmes, Matthew Booth is the author of several books and short stories about the famous detective. He wrote a number of scripts for a Holmes radio series produced by Jim French Productions in Seattle, as well as creating his own series, featuring Anthony Rathe, about a disgraced former barrister investigating crimes, for the same production company.

He is the creator of Everett Carr, an amateur sleuth in the traditional mould, who appears in a series of novels which offer a contemporary twist to the classic Golden Age-style murder mystery.

An expert in crime and supernatural fiction, Matthew has provided a number of academic talks on such subjects as Sherlock Holmes, the works of Agatha Christie, crime fiction, Count Dracula, and the facts and theories concerning the crimes of Jack the Ripper.

He is a member of the Crime Writers' Association and is the editor of its monthly magazine, *Red Herrings*. He lives with his wife in Manchester, England.

SOCIAL MEDIA HANDLES:
  Twitter: @HolmesBooth
  Instagram: matthewboothauthor
  Threads: matthewboothauthor

Also by Matthew Booth

A Talent for Murder (Level Best Books)

The Dangers of this Night (Level Best Books)

The House of Skulls (Pegasus Elliot Mackenzie)

When Anthony Rathe Investigates (Sparkling Books)

The Further Exploits of Sherlock Holmes (Sparkling Books)

Sherlock Holmes & the Giant's Hand (Breese Books)

Milton Keynes UK
Ingram Content Group UK Ltd.
UKHW022229050424
440549UK00004B/265